BOUND BY TIDE

AARON MCLEAN

Copyright © 2025 by Aaron McLean

All rights reserved.

No part of this book may be reproduced in any form or by any electronic or mechanical means, including information storage and retrieval systems, without written permission from the author, except for the use of brief quotations in a book review.

This book is a work of fiction. Names, characters, places, and incidents are product of the author's imagination or are used fictitiously. Any resemblance to actual events, locales, or persons, living or dead, is coincidental.

authoraaronmclean.com

ALSO BY AARON MCLEAN

Where the Tide Meets the Sand

—

Echoes of Us

TRIGGER WARNINGS

EMOTIONAL & PSYCHOLOGICAL THEMES

- Survival, self-worth, trust, and rebuilding identity after abuse
- Honest, unflinching dialogue about scars, jagged edges, and the fear of being unlovable
- Heavy emotional intensity around healing, vulnerability, and choosing to love again
- Grief and loss woven into identity, purpose, and the aftermath of heartbreak
- Mental health struggles including guilt, emotional distress, and self-isolation
- Abandonment wounds and the quiet devastation they leave behind
- Emotional manipulation (push-pull tension, jealousy, possessiveness, power imbalances)
- Toxic family dynamics involving betrayal and manipulation
- Gaslighting and emotional abuse by secondary characters

ROMANTIC & SEXUAL CONTENT

- Explicit sexual content (detailed open-door scenes, dominance/submission dynamics)
- Sexual tension and power dynamics (consensual but intense control, teasing, edging, light breath-play references)
- Casual sex and one-night stands (referenced as coping)
- Infidelity (referenced/remembered)
- Unplanned pregnancy (secondary plot)

- Pregnancy and parenthood themes

SUBSTANCE USE & CONDUCT

- Frequent alcohol use as a coping mechanism
- Verbal confrontation and heated conflict
- Mild, non-graphic violence

ATMOSPHERIC & SYMBOLIC CONTENT

- Ocean/tide imagery tied to drowning, suffocation, and survival
- A dark, unromanticized portrayal of love that heals slowly and destroys quickly

NOTE FROM AUTHOR-

This story is *Real. Raw. Reckless.*

Not the pretty version of love you whisper about in daylight—but the kind that's drags its nails down your back and asks what you're willing to bleed for.

These pages don't soften the blow or dim the shadows.
They dive straight into the deep end. Into the places you don't talk about, the wounds you pretend aren't still throbbing, the heartache you swore you'd never let anyone touch again.

I will break you on purpose.
Not because I'm an ass, but because some stories aren't meant to be read with clean hands.

I'll twist your heart,
Steal your breath,
Fuck with your head,
and pull you under until you forget which way is up.

You'll feel the current grip your ribs and the ache settle into your bones.

You'll learn how to drown…
and then how to surface.

This is dangerous intimacy.
The kind that ruins your composure.
The kind that tastes like confession.
Reader discretion isn't just advised…
It's a warning.

Because once you step into this tide,
you don't come out the same.

BOUND BY TIDE

FOREWORD

WHY ROMANCE?

People ask me why I write romance like it's a genre—like it's some soft thing wrapped in lace and longing. And I used to try and explain it cleanly. Make it simple. Like maybe if I dressed it up in enough pretty words, they'd get it.

But love? Real love? It doesn't play gently.
It's a storm surge ripping through everything safe.
It's salt in your wounds, wind in your lungs, and waves that don't stop just because you beg.
It's a fucking hurricane with a heartbeat.

I write it because I've felt it—the kind of love that crashes into your chest like high tide, uninvited and merciless. It's the gasp between "don't stop" and "I shouldn't want this." It's the salted burn in your throat when you say goodbye but don't move. It's hands that tremble like tide-ripped anchors, touching them like it might drown you—but letting go would be worse. It's longing that lingers like ocean mist, settling in your skin and staying long after they're gone.

Love is thunder in your ribs.
Lightning behind your eyes.
Sand stuck to your body like a memory.
It's standing in the shallows, arms wide, daring the next wave to hit harder
—because the ache is the only proof that you felt something real.

It's obsession.

FOREWORD

It's surrender.
It's praying for calm and then missing the chaos when it finally settles.

Love is reckless.
It's raw.
It's the kind of wreckage you crawl toward, not from.

I write romance because nothing else digs that deep. Nothing else shatters you and calls it holy. Love carves you open like the tide carving the shoreline, again and again, until you're shaped by it. It doesn't knock. It crashes through like a rogue wave, destroying everything you swore you needed. It's lips on yours like they're drinking from your wreckage. Hands gripping like they'll never make it back to shore. A glance across the dock that cuts deeper than any goodbye.

I write the kind of love that scorches—like sun on salt-stung skin. Not measured in sweet nothings, but in how tight your fists clench when they brush past. In how loud your heart pounds when every instinct says swim away, but your soul says dive in. Because part of you wants to drown in it. Because real love doesn't whisper. It doesn't ask.
It roars.
It floods.
It owns you. It's the full moon dragging the tide, and you? You rise to meet it. Even if it means losing yourself in the pull.

I believe in the kind of romance that isn't found—it's survived.
And yeah, it hurts.
It has to.

Because love that doesn't leave a mark? That's not love. That's shallow water pretending to be deep. I want the kind that wrecks the shoreline. That strips you bare in a crowded dockside bar. That says you're mine with a single glance. I want the smirk that ruins your plans. The kiss that pulls you under. The fight that ends with tears in the sand and a slammed truck door—only for them to come back, pin you to the wall, and kiss you like they're trying to erase the storm off your skin.

FOREWORD

I want love that feels like war and worship in the same fucking breath.

So no—this isn't about fairy tales. This is about truth. The kind that tastes like sweat and salt and surrender. The kind that keeps you up at night, staring at the ceiling like stars over the inlet, chest cracked open and grateful for it.

That's why I write.
That's why I bleed on these pages. Because someone out there needs to remember what it feels like to ache like the tide pulling from the shore. To burn. To crave. To want so badly it wrecks every calm part of you.

And if you're reading this with your heart skipping, your body already leaning in, wondering what it's like to fall without a lifeline—

Then Bound by Tide was written for you.

This isn't a book that plays it safe.
It's not soft. It won't hold your hand. It'll rip your heart out, toss it into the surf, and ask if you still want to keep breathing. It'll give you the slow burn. The filthy tension. The heartbreak you never saw coming—and the redemption you'll beg for by the end.

It's possession.
It's ruin.
It's every don't fall answered with, *watch me.*
If you finish this breathless, broken, or touched in places no one sees?
Good.
That means I gave you exactly what you didn't know you needed.

Now fall—
hard.
wet.
wrecked.
And let the tide take you.

—Aaron

BOUND BY TIDE

AARON MCLEAN

PROLOGUE

LET ME TELL YOU A STORY.

Not the kind with picture-perfect timing. Not the kind with a perfect journey or tied-up timelines. This one? It's chaos. It's heartbreak. It's fucked-up and unforgiving. Love in its most brutal, beautiful, soul-shattering form. The kind of story that drags you under before you even know you're drowning.

Because the kind of love that burns straight through bone, doesn't ask for permission. It doesn't give a damn about what makes sense. Doesn't wait until you're ready. It just… wrecks you. And if you're lucky? It will rebuild you in the process.
But most of us? We're not that fucking lucky.
I used to think I was smarter than love. Thought I could outwork it, outrun it, outfuck it. That if I stayed in control, kept things surface-level, one night, no promises, I could dodge the hit. No strings. No vulnerability. Just bodies, sweat, and silence.

Love? Real love? It doesn't just break the rules. It levels them. It finds the cracks, hairline or hollow, and drives straight through 'em. And when it hits? It's not just a wrecking ball. It's demolition. Full force. No Permits. No warning. No blueprint. It doesn't stop at the walls. It takes the foundation too, leaving you in the rubble of everything you built to feel safe.

That's when she showed up.
And every wall I built, every line in the sand I drew, every fucking lie I told myself—collapsed the second she looked at me like I was something more than the ruin I'd become. Like maybe—just maybe—I was still worth saving.

She was never supposed to be mine. Hell, she was off-limits. But the walls I spent so many years building never stood a fucking chance against the way she made me feel. How she completely undid me with a single glance. With that mouth that knew exactly how to ruin me. With a laugh.

I tried to keep it casual. Told myself I could handle it. Keep her at a distance, play it safe, stay numb. But the truth? Some women aren't made to be loved in pieces. She's not built for surface-level. She's built to wreck you—in the most unforgiving way.
And I was so fucking tired of running.
So I fell. Hard. No warning. No backup plan. Just her—tearing through every beam, every brace, until the foundation cracked and everything I'd spent years guarding came crashing down.
She wasn't mine to want. But I did.
She wasn't mine to keep. But God, I tried.
And when I lost her…
It wasn't just heartbreak. It was drowning.
No air. No anchor. No one coming to save me. Because when she left… she didn't just take my heart.
She took the version of me that still believed in second chances.

I used to sit out on this dock—drink in hand, pretending the tide could carry the weight of her memory out to sea. Thinking that if I stared long enough into the water, maybe it'd give me something back. Peace. Clarity. A way to let go.
But the thing about a love like that? It doesn't let go. It lingers. Claws. It becomes a scar that never quite fades, no matter how many new foundations you lay.
She's in the silence between my sentences. In the ache that outlasts every fucking distraction. In the version of me that I fake for everyone else.

I've spent so long pretending I let go. Faking peace. Playing the part. But the truth? Some loves don't fade. Some ghosts never stop haunting you. And some stories—ours—aren't written in ink. They're carried with the tide.
But maybe that's the thing. Maybe that's the kind of love that pulls you under.

That steals your breath and never lets you surface…
Is the only kind that ever really mattered.

So if you're here looking for something easy,
Something simple, painless, forgettable.
Turn the fuck back. Now.
Because this story doesn't float. It sinks. It wraps around your ribs like the current. Drags you out past the breakers—and doesn't let go.
It's the kind of love that crashes through your chest, leaving you desperate to stay afloat, gasping for a version of yourself you'll never be again.

But if you want to know what it feels like to love someone so deeply, so violently, that they become the storm inside you. The air in your lungs. If you want the truth, even when it claws at you like saltwater in an open wound… then keep going.

Because this?
This is the part of me still thrashing beneath the surface.
The ache I never swam free from.
The tide that keeps pulling me back.
To her.
And no matter how far I drift, no matter how hard I fight,
I am still hers.
Still drowning.
Still reaching.
Still bound.

This is the wreckage.
This is the surrender.
This is Bound by Tide.

—Griffin Hayes

BOUND BY TIDE

1

THE LOCAL

TOPSAIL ISLAND—WHAT can I say? It's a 26-mile stretch of paradise. A thin, sun-soaked ribbon of sand where the Atlantic kisses the shore, and every single wave carries a secret. Especially if you're Griffin Hayes, the man who knew exactly how to use Topsail to its full potential. For a few months out of the year, when peak season hit and the tourists flooded in, the island wasn't just a getaway; it was Griffin's personal fucking playground. A matchmaking service without even trying.

They came in droves, fresh off the highway with their car windows down to let the salt air mix with the scent of coconut sunscreen and cheap gas station energy drinks.

The women? Fuck, so many women.

They arrived looking for an escape, their responsibilities abandoned miles behind them, inhibitions melting under the Carolina sun. Some came with girlfriends, dressed in barely-there bikinis, and intentions just as thin. Some came with boyfriends, but let's be honest—those men were nothing more than placeholders, temporary obstacles before they found something better.

And Griffin? He was better.

Topsail had a way of loosening them up, turning the prim and proper into the reckless and ravenous. It wasn't like Myrtle. Where the chaos never stopped—where the beaches were packed shoulder-to-shoulder and the neon lights bled into the night. No, Topsail was intimate, raw, just wild enough. The kind of place where sins felt lighter in the salt air, and regrets could be washed away with the tide.

And that's why Griffin fucking loved it.

Because every week?

Every single fucking week?

It brought in fresh prey.

Griffin wasn't just a local. He was *the* local. The kind of man whose name rolled off every tongue, whether it was spoken in admiration, jealousy, or breathless fucking moans. There wasn't a shop, bar, or stretch of beach where he wasn't known. Women whispered about him in seafood shacks over baskets of shrimp and grits. Their voices dropped to hushed tones when their boyfriends turned their heads. Men sighted him down the barrel of their beers, fingers tightening around the neck whenever their women leaned in too much when he spoke.

They knew what kind of man he was.

They knew exactly what he could do.

And it wasn't just his looks. Though, let's be honest, those fucking helped.

Tall. Built. Tattooed. A body made for sin, sculpted by hard work and bad intentions. Broad shoulders, tight waist, a chest that begged for claw marks. Just enough scruff to make you wonder how it would feel scraping down your thighs. He was the perfect mix of effortless charm and barely restrained hunger, the kind of man who could make you blush with a look, make you squirm with a smirk, and make you soaking wet with just his fucking voice.

The voice? Oh, that Southern drawl, slow and syrup-thick, curling around every word like a lazy promise.

He was every woman's favorite mistake.

And husbands?

They fucking hated him.

He was the reason they locked their wives' phones at night. The reason they pulled them closer when he walked by. The reason they suddenly felt the urge to be more affectionate, to hold hands in public, to act like they actually gave a shit about the woman they had long since stopped trying to impress.

But Griffin?

He didn't give a damn.

He didn't need to chase women. They came to him.

It wasn't just confidence—it was the ease of it. The way he made them laugh, blush, and shift in their seats, all in the span of a single conversation. He knew how to look at a woman and make her feel like she was the only thing in the damn world worth paying attention to.

And if their men were stupid enough to bring them around him?

Well, that wasn't his fucking problem.

By day, he ran Hayes Development, a project management firm that had its hands in every damn build on the island. If something was being constructed, expanded, or repaired, he was involved.

The funny part?

Everyone knew it.

And yet, somehow, whenever he did a site visit, at least one of the owners would be there.

But not just any owner.

The wife.

Fuck—it was always the wife.

They'd show up in their sundresses, pretending to care about zoning regulations and permit approvals. But Griffin knew what they were really looking at.

His hands.

Rough and calloused from the work, veins thick, pumping along his forearms.

The way his safety vest clung to his broad chest, how the sweat dripped down his neck as he worked in the Carolina heat.

They knew what they were doing.

And so did he.

But Griffin had rules. He wasn't the kind of man who got tangled up in town drama.

He didn't touch married women—not unless they asked.

Because, see, that was the thing about him.

He had two sides.

The first? The one everyone saw. The easygoing, well-respected businessman with a cocky grin. The man who could make a room laugh before he even said a word. A level of flirt that could make a nun rethink her vows. A man who can charm bartenders out of full-price tabs. And would have the local fishermen slipping him the freshest catch before it ever leaves the boat.

He was the life of every damn party.

But there was the other side.

The primal side.

Not everyone got to see it. Only the ones who asked.

Because that side of him wasn't just playful winks and teasing touches. That side of him was raw, demanding, and unrelenting.

He didn't make love. He didn't fuck.

He claimed.

And the ones who let him?

They never forgot.

Griffin didn't need ropes, chains, or elaborate setups. No help or assistance has ever been needed. He knew how to break you down with nothing but a flick of his wrist and his slightly curled fingers, the right amount of pressure from his tongue. The slow and devastating thrust of his hips.

He would have you screaming, squirming, and shaking before he even showed you the ten inches of destruction he carried beneath his belt.

And when he did?

It would wreck you.

And you would thank him for it.

Because Griffin wasn't just a summer fling.

He was the one you'd never forget, no matter how hard you tried. The one you swore you were done with—but never really wanted to be.

And Marshside Bar & Grill?

That was his hunting ground.

A dimly lit dive with good drinks and better opportunities. Where the music was just loud enough to drown out inhibitions. The tequila flowed, and the decisions got worse with every shot. Where a woman could pretend. Just for one night, she wasn't someone's wife, someone's mother, someone's responsibility.

Griffin could take his fucking pick.

And tonight?

Tonight, the hunt was on.

2

HUNTING GROUND

TUCKED along the Intracoastal Waterway in Surf City, Marshside Bar & Grill isn't just a place to eat—it's a rite of passage. Locals claim it as their own, a hidden gem where the beer is ice-cold, the seafood is fresh off the docks, and the view of the salt marsh at sunset is enough to make you forget the rest of the world exists.

But at 8:00 PM, something shifts.

The tourists arrive like the evening tide, drawn in by the hum of conversation and the clink of glasses. The kind of atmosphere that buzzes with possibility. Patio doors roll up, letting in the warm ocean breeze, with the music pulsing just a little louder. The dock becomes a place of lingering boaters, tying off for *just one more*. While new arrivals scan the bar for a familiar face or maybe someone they've never met before.

Here, stories are written in the condensation on whiskey glasses, and the night always holds the promise of something unforgettable.

Marshside Bar & Grill isn't just a stop on the map. It's where nights begin, where they sometimes end, and where, if you're lucky, you'll find yourself somewhere in between.

The bar smelled like bad decisions.

Tequila, sweat, and something dangerously sweet—coconut sunscreen, maybe, or the scent of a woman who'd come here looking for trouble. The kind of trouble Griffin had a habit of finding.

He leaned back against the bar, whiskey glass in hand, taking in the scene. The air inside Marshside was thick with something electric, something primal. The hum of conversation, the clink of ice against glass, the slow throb of bass that vibrated through the floorboards. It all came together in a heady mix, which set the tone for the night.

And Griffin fucking thrived in it.

Across from him, Aiden leaned against the bar, sipping a beer. Eyes scanning the room the same way Griffin's were. Aiden Sinclair. His closest friend, his wingman, and the only person who knew exactly how deep Griffin's game ran.

They were the best fucking duo the island had ever seen. Or the worst. Depending on who you asked. Aiden had spent years watching Griffin work his magic, soaking in every move, every smirk, every well-timed pause. And now? He was almost as good at the game. Almost. But still so far away.

Aiden tilted his beer toward Griffin, nodding toward the other side of the bar. A blonde. A brunette. A redhead. The holy trinity of bad decisions.

"You're gonna have to pick one eventually," Aiden mused, smirking over the rim of his bottle.

Griffin smirked back. "What's the rush?"

Aiden chuckled. "You love this part too much."

He wasn't wrong. The chase. The game. The slow, simmering burn before the inevitable.

But Griffin wasn't the only one who played it well.

Aiden was already on the move, his gaze locking onto the blonde across the bar. She was watching him.

He didn't need to approach her. Didn't need to say a word. Just a slow tilt of his head, a lazy smirk, the briefest flick of his gaze over her body.

She shifted in her seat, subtly straightening her posture. Hooked.

Griffin chuckled. "Damn. You're getting good."

Aiden shot him a knowing look. "Learned from the best."

Griffin didn't argue. He just lifted his glass in silent acknowledgment.

But he wasn't paying attention to Aiden anymore.

Because across the room… she was watching him.

THE DANCE BEGINS

The brunette. Legs crossed, fingers tracing the rim of her glass.

Normally, he would've gone for the redhead. But she wasn't throwing out bait like the other women in the bar. She wasn't desperate for attention.

She was waiting.

Waiting for him.

Her name, he'd find out later.

He dragged his gaze over her, slow and deliberate, making sure she felt it. Making sure she knew exactly what this was.

She did.

Her lips curled, just slightly. A dare.

Griffin exhaled, whiskey burning its way down his throat, as he took his time deciding.

Let her wait.

Let her wonder.

Aiden followed his gaze, smirking. "The brunette?"

Griffin rolled his shoulders. "Maybe."

Aiden chuckled. "She's different."

Yeah. She was.

Griffin had seen every type of woman in this bar. But this one? She carried herself like she wasn't looking for a distraction.

She was looking for trouble.

And Griffin? He was more than happy to give it to her.

She stood, slow and deliberate, making her way toward the bar. Each step measured, calculated—the kind of confidence that only made him more interested.

Aiden let out a low whistle. "Damn."

Yeah. Damn was right.

Griffin turned just as she reached him, letting their bodies brush as she settled in beside him at the bar. Close, but not too close. Enough to feel the heat radiating between them.

The air between them crackled.

"Waiting for someone?" she asked, her voice smooth, practiced. But there was something in her eyes—something uncertain, something hungry.

With a slight grin, he said, "Maybe."

She inhaled sharply. He could feel it—the way her body responded, the way the tension coiled beneath her skin.

Griffin set his glass down with a soft clink, turning toward her fully, crowding her space just enough to make her breath catch. "But—I hope she's late."

Her lips curled at the edges, a ghost of a smile. She tilted her head just so, exposing the curve of her throat.

Her pupils blew wide.

Hook. Line. Sinker.

"Then let's make sure she is," she murmured, dragging her fingertip along the rim of his glass before lifting those dark, knowing eyes to his.

He sat there for a moment, his eyes dancing between hers. "If you're going to take my time. What do you want me to call you?"

"Adrianna," she said, while holding out her hand.

Griffin's eyes dance a little longer before looking down at her hand floating in the air. His pause is just long enough to make her flutter at the awkwardness. He turns to Aiden with a shit-eating grin before taking her hand and pulling her closer to him. Letting her name settle between them, savoring the way it tasted on his tongue before he spoke. "Adrianna," he repeated, voice low, rough.

Aiden chuckled under his breath, finishing off his beer before clapping Griffin on the back. "I'll leave you to it."

Griffin didn't even acknowledge him. His attention locked on Adrianna now.

She tilted her head, studying him. "You do this often?"

His lips quirked. "Do what?"

Her gaze flicked to his lips, then back to his eyes. "Stand in a bar looking like temptation itself, waiting for women to fall at your feet."

He smirked. "Sometimes, but only for the good ones."

Adrianna exhaled, shaking her head, but he caught the way her breath hitched just slightly.

"So," he mused, leaning in just a little closer. "Are you a good one, Adrianna?" He said, trying to get a reaction.

She didn't react to the tease or the way that he said her name. She just smiled.

"I have a feeling you get exactly what you want," she mused, ignoring the question.

His eyes narrowed. "Sometimes."

Adrianna tilted her head, eyes flicking over him with slow, unhurried appraisal. "And what do you want?"

Griffin let his gaze drop, trailing over her body with deliberate ease, before meeting her eyes again. "Tonight?"

She raised an eyebrow. "Tonight."

"I don't know," he murmured. "I have a few things in mind."

Adrianna's lips curled, playful but intrigued. "Is that so?"

He nodded, letting the weight of his stare settle on her. "Depends. What is it that you're wanting?"

Her fingers toyed with the stem of her glass. "Whatever you want to do."

Griffin leaned in slightly, voice lower now, silk-wrapped danger. "Be careful what you wish for, sweetie. That will get you in trouble."

She exhaled, her body tilting just a fraction closer to him, an instinctive reaction. "Maybe I like trouble."

His grin deepened. "You don't even know what kind of trouble I can be."

She held his gaze, eyes dark, waiting. "Then why don't you show me?"

His fingers brushed against her thigh, a barely-there touch, a test. And her body responded before her mind had the chance to catch up. Her eyes rolled as his fingers ghosted across her skin, sending chills over every inch of her perfectly sculpted frame.

"You're playing with fire," he warned, voice rough against her ear.

Her breath came out in a shaky whisper. "Good. I hope it burns."

His grip tightened around her thigh, teasing, testing. The tension on her lips wavered, her eyes rattling between his, her body betraying just how much she wanted this.

The tension was unbearable, thick enough to drown in.

He finished the last sip of his whiskey, then stood, offering her his hand.

By the time he had her outside, the air was thick with humidity, heat wrapping around them like a second skin.

By the time he had her against his truck, her body was already his.

By the time they made it inside, she was begging.

And when the night was over—when her body was spent and her voice was hoarse from screaming his name—she would leave like they always did.

Because Griffin Hayes wasn't meant to be kept.

He was meant to be remembered.

3

OFF LIMITS

THE SUN STREAMED through the cracks in Griffin's blinds. Slicing across the room like it had a personal vendetta against anyone trying to sleep off a night they barely survived. The kind of light that didn't just wake you—it announced itself, bold and unapologetic.

Griffin groaned, dragging a hand across his face as if he could wipe the morning away. His body protested every movement. Muscles stiff and sore, in all the ways that told the story of the night before, without needing a single word. He rolled onto his stomach, burying his face in the pillow, like it might grant him a few stolen moments of darkness. It didn't. All it did was remind him that his sheets still smelled like her.

Coconut and sin.

Adrianna.

That faint, lingering scent was a ghost, a tease taunting him. The kind that seeped into your skin and made you wonder if you were really alone. But Griffin didn't wonder. He knew better. She was gone. Like they always were. Like he wanted them to be.

That was the rule—no attachments, no exceptions. No waking up tangled in limbs and lies. Just a night, a memory, and a door closing quietly behind them before dawn.

With a heavy sigh, he flipped onto his back, staring at the ceiling as if it might offer him answers he wasn't asking for. His joints popped as he stretched. Every ache served as a reminder that even a man like him—disciplined. Controlled—wasn't immune to the aftermath of whiskey and a woman who knew exactly how to leave a mark without leaving a trace.

His stomach growled, sharp and insistent, pulling him back to reality. Bad decisions and charm didn't fill you up. Food did. Groaning, he swung his legs over the side of the bed, feet meeting the cold floor like a punishment.

"Jesus," he muttered, cracking his neck as he stood. His reflection in the bathroom mirror greeted him like an old rival. Hair a mess, scruff thick along his jaw. Eyes shadowed with exhaustion that went deeper than just a lack of sleep. He braced his hands on the sink, leaning in, studying himself. Like a man trying to remember who the hell he was, beneath all the layers of bravado.

A grin tugged at his lips—crooked, unapologetic.

"Still pretty, though," he muttered, shaking his head before grabbing his toothbrush.

A quick shower washed away the remnants of Adrianna's touch, but not the memory. That would fade on its own, like they always did. By the time he laced up his running shoes, the scent of soap and aftershave replaced the coconut. And Griffin Hayes was back to his usual self—put together, sharp, untouchable.

Coffee first. Jog later.

Grounds & Grit was already buzzing when he pushed through the door. The familiar chime of the bell overhead greeted him like an old friend. The scent of espresso, fresh pastries, and worn wood wrapped around him, grounding him in a way little else could. This was his town. His routine. The place where everyone knew his name. And his reputation.

"Morning, Griff. The usual?"

Molly's voice cut through the hum of conversation, her grin already waiting for him behind the counter. She was young, sharp-tongued, and immune to his charm—or at least, she liked to pretend she was.

He winked without thinking, a reflex as natural as breathing. Molly rolled her eyes but reached for his coffee anyway.

"You don't even look hungover," she said, shaking her head as she worked. "I swear, you're part machine."

"Good genes, sweetheart." Griffin slid a bill across the counter before she could argue, smirking when she gave him that 'you're impossible' look.

"You could at least pretend to be human," she muttered, tucking the money away.

"What fun would that be?" He took a slow sip, letting the caffeine work its magic.

Molly leaned on the counter, eyes narrowing. "One of these days, some woman's gonna break you."

Griffin chuckled, savoring the heat of his coffee. "Sweetheart, they try."

She shook her head, lips twitching despite herself. "One day, someone's gonna make you forget all your damn rules."

He pushed off the counter, that signature grin firmly in place. "When that day comes, I'll be sure to send you a postcard."

Molly laughed, waving him off as he headed for the door. The weight of her words trailing behind him, like a shadow he refused to acknowledge.

The crisp morning air hit his lungs as he started his jog, the rhythmic slap of his shoes against the pavement syncing with the crash of distant waves. The beach was nearly deserted. Just a few early risers, the kind of people who weren't running from anything but enjoyed pretending they were.

This was Griffin's favorite time of day. No noise. No distractions. Just the steady pace of his breath and illusion of control.

By the time he circled back to his truck, sweat clung to his skin and his muscles burned with satisfaction. He felt clearer. Sharper.

Until his phone buzzed.

> Aiden: Wake up, asshole. We're doing something today.

The fucker smirked while his thumbs flew across the screen.

> Griffin: I've been up. Try again.

> Aiden: Overachiever. You free or nah?

> Griffin: Depends. What are we doing?

> Aiden: Drinking. Something reckless. Maybe both.

He huffed out a laugh, shaking his head.

> Griffin: You do realize it's barely noon, right?

> Aiden: Weak.

Griffin didn't bother arguing. Aiden had a way of pulling him into chaos, and truth be told, he welcomed it.

> Griffin: I'll meet you in thirty.

Tossing his phone onto the passenger seat, he fired up the engine, already bracing himself for whatever stupidity Aiden had lined up.

Because if there was one certainty in Griffin Hayes' life, it was this—Saturdays with Aiden were never boring.

THE DAY UNFOLDS

The go-kart track.

Of course, Aiden picked the go-kart track.

Griffin stared at the neon sign flashing above the entrance like it was mocking him. "This is your grand plan?"

Aiden, already halfway through signing the waiver, flashed that cocky grin that usually meant trouble. "Tell me it's not gonna be fun."

Griffin sighed, grabbing a pen. "Fine. But if I win, you're buying the first round."

"If you win," Aiden shot back, eyes squinted and teeth flashing.

They raced like two grown men with no regard for dignity—or safety. Griffin's competitive streak flared, sharp and relentless, while Aiden thrived on pushing every button he could find.

Laughter echoed through the track, curses flying as they took corners too fast, tires screeching in protest. For a while, it felt good—reckless, free, like they were kids again. Before life got complicated.

By the time they stumbled out, breathless, and grinning like idiots. Griffin's adrenaline was still humming.

"Admit it," he said, clapping Aiden on the back. "I smoked your ass."

"Barely," Aiden muttered, but the grin on his face said otherwise.

They made their way to The Sandbar, settling into their usual spot overlooking the ocean. The first beer went down easy. The second even easier.

Then, as always, Aiden shifted the mood.

"So," he drawled, eyeing Griffin over his bottle, "ever think about stopping?"

Griffin raised a brow, already wary. "Stopping what?"

"The game. The women. The no-strings-attached bullshit."

Griffin raised a brow, leaning back. "Why would I?"

Aiden didn't answer right away. He just studied him, like he could see beneath the surface. See the cracks Griffin kept hidden from everyone else.

"Maybe it gets old," Aiden finally said. "Maybe you wake up one day and realize none of it means shit."

Griffin scoffed, masking the way those words hit a little too close. "Sounds like a problem for future me."

Aiden's gaze sharpened. "Or maybe it already is."

Silence settled between them, tense and heavy—until Aiden shifted gears.

"My sister's coming to town next week."

Griffin blinked. "You have a sister?"

Aiden shook his head. "Exactly why I never mention her."

Details unfolded—slow, guarded, like Aiden was testing just how much to reveal. Griffin's curiosity flared, but so did Aiden's warnings.

"No games," Aiden said, his voice edged with something serious.

Griffin held up his hands, grin tugging at his lips. "Scout's honor."

But beneath the playful banter, something darker simmered. Aiden's accusations weren't wrong. And Griffin knew it. When the conversation circled back to why he lived by his rules, the humor drained away, replaced by something raw. Something real.

"There is more to me than you know; I haven't always been like this," Griffin admitted, his voice rougher than before. "I've fucking loved. And I've been broken for it."

Aiden didn't press. Didn't need to.

Griffin's stare dropped to his beer, watching condensation pool around the base. Like it could distract him from the weight pressing against his ribs.

Griffin let out a humorless laugh, shaking his head as he nursed what was left of his beer. "So don't worry. I won't mess with your sister. Whoever the fuck she is."

Aiden's lips twitched, but there was no humor in it. More like... hesitation, leading into what was coming next.

"Yeah," Aiden muttered, tipping his bottle back before setting it down a little too carefully. "Let's just hope she doesn't mess with you."

That made Griffin pause.

He glanced over, eyebrow raised. "What's that supposed to mean?"

Aiden didn't answer right away. He just stared out at the ocean, watching the waves roll in like they held a secret he wasn't ready to share.

Griffin studied him, the shift in his friend's demeanor impossible to ignore now. Aiden wasn't usually cagey—not unless there was a reason.

"What's her deal?" Griffin pressed, his tone more serious now. "You've known me for years, and you've never once mentioned her. Now she's moving here, and you're acting like I'm the least of your worries."

Aiden's jaw tightened, his fingers tapping a restless rhythm against his bottle. When he finally spoke, his voice was quieter—measured.

"She's been through a lot, Griff. More than I'm gonna lay out over a couple beers."

Griffin frowned, leaning forward. "Bad breakup?"

Aiden huffed a laugh, but there was no amusement behind it. "If only it were that simple."

That answer sat heavy between them.

Griffin didn't push, but his curiosity sharpened, instincts kicking in like they always did when something—or someone—felt like a puzzle worth solving.

"She trouble?" Griffin asked, a slow grin tugging at his lips, though it didn't quite reach his eyes.

Aiden shot him a look that could've cracked stone. "Not the kind you're used to."

That... intrigued him more than it should've.

There was a warning laced in Aiden's words—don't look at her like you do the others. But it only made Griffin wonder what made her different. What kind of woman had Aiden this on edge? This, protective?

And why the hell did that make Griffin want to meet her even more?

He leaned back in his chair, stretching his legs out. Gaze drifting back toward the ocean as his mind worked through the possibilities. He didn't chase women—never had to. And he sure as hell didn't get curious about ones he hadn't even seen yet.

But this?

This felt... inevitable.

Aiden must've caught the shift in his expression because he groaned, dragging a hand down his face. "Don't even start, man. I know that look."

Griffin smirked, but it was softer this time. Thoughtful. Dangerous.

"Relax," he drawled, grabbing his beer again. "I told you. I won't mess with her."

But they both knew better.

Griffin might've meant it when he said it. Might've even believed it in that moment. But fate had a way of laughing at men like him—men who thought they could control every game they played.

And something told him Aiden's sister wasn't the kind of woman you planned for.

She was the kind that happened to you.

Aiden sighed, sensing the battle he'd just signed up for. "Just... Don't say I didn't warn you."

Griffin tipped his bottle toward him, a glint in his eye that even he couldn't fully explain. "Noted."

But as the conversation drifted back to safer topics, Griffin couldn't shake the feeling that something was already shifting beneath his feet. Like a tide pulling out before the storm rolled in.

He didn't know her name. Didn't know her story.

But he knew one thing for sure.

Whatever lines he thought he wouldn't cross—

He'd be standing at the edge soon enough.

4

FALSE ESCAPE

THE WEEK DIDN'T PASS—IT dragged. Pulling Griffin through each day like an anchor tied to his chest. There was no comfort in the rhythm he kept, no satisfaction in the repetition. It wasn't routine. It was survival.

Barely.

His mornings started the way they always did—before the sun had a chance to rise. Before the world could demand anything from him. The house was silent, empty in a way that felt louder than noise. He filled the quiet with the scrape of a chipped *World's Hottest Boss* mug across the counter. The mug was a joke from his operations manager.

After pouring the morning jolt, the bitter scent of black coffee hit his senses like a warning.

Scalding. Harsh. Unforgiving.

Exactly how he liked it.

The first sip burned down his throat, but he welcomed the sting. It was the only thing sharp enough to remind him that he was still here. That despite the restless sleep, the ache in his bones, and the ghosts crowding his head, he could still stand.

Then came the run.

Bare feet hit wet sand with practiced force, the cold bite of the tide snapping at his heels like it wanted to drag him under. The ocean air was thick with salt, sharp enough to carve its way into his lungs and leave a mark on the way out. Every mile wasn't about fitness. It was punishment. Penance for sins he never confessed but carried all the same.

Some mornings, he wondered if he'd just keep running. Let the horizon swallow him whole.

But he always turned back.

Because no matter how fast or far he pushed himself, there was always something waiting—the weight he could never outrun.

After the run, he didn't stop. He couldn't. Stillness was dangerous. Stillness meant thinking.

So he shifted.

Straight to the site.

The house rose like a challenge against the skyline, each beam and nail a middle finger to everything temporary in his life. This wasn't just a project—it was his. Set back from the chaos of tourists and neon lights. Tucked along the quiet of the sound, it stood as the only thing he could point to and say…

This won't leave me.

It wasn't just lumber and blueprints.

It was proof.

Proof that he could build something that lasted—even if he didn't believe people could.

MONDAY

The skeletal frame of the house stretched toward the sky, raw and unfinished. Like it was daring him to complete it. The wind whistled through the open beams, carrying the scent of sawdust, salt, and something else. Something that smelled like possibility but tasted like pressure.

Griffin arrived before sunrise. Pale light spilled across the dirt lot, casting long shadows in its wake. His body ached—a dull, constant throb that had become as familiar as his own heartbeat. But pain was welcome. Pain meant progress.

Rick was already there, leaning against a stack of lumber. Cigarette hanging from the corner of his mouth, like it permanently belonged there. His clothes wore yesterday's sweat and years of labor, his face carved by time and hard living.

"You look like shit," Rick greeted, his voice rough from smoke and truth.

Griffin didn't bother with a comeback. He tossed his tool bag into the truck bed, stretching his neck until it popped. "Feel like it too."

Rick chuckled. The sound low and knowing. "Maybe by the time this place is done, you'll stop running from whatever the hell's chasing you."

Griffin's jaw tightened, but he didn't rise to the bait. Rick wasn't wrong—not entirely. The work wasn't just about building a house. It was about silencing the parts of him that screamed when the noise of the world faded.

He climbed the unfinished steps, boots heavy against raw wood, and stood in the hollow frame of what would soon be a home. His home. Open beams stretched around him, empty spaces waiting to be filled. He could already see it—the way the light would pour through the windows, the porch where he'd sit and pretend peace was something you could pour into a glass.

But daydreams didn't lay foundations. So when Rick called out about roofing schedules, Griffin answered without hesitation.

"Metal," he said, dragging a hand through his hair. "I'm not interested in things that don't last."

Rick nodded, cigarette ash falling to the dirt. "Didn't think you were."

And with that, they got to work... because making permanent decisions was one job Griffin refused to clock in for.

TUESDAY – THURSDAY

The days bled together, indistinct and relentless. Time didn't pass in hours or minutes—it passed in muscle strain, in the sting of sweat dripping into his eyes, in the weight of a hammer swinging until his arms went numb.

Wake. Run. Build. Collapse.

Repeat.

The house grew taller, sturdier. Framing turned into walls. Gaps filled with glass. A roofline carved against the sky like a promise he wasn't sure he believed in. Every board he nailed down felt like he was anchoring himself to something real—something permanent in a life full of temporary fixes.

But the quiet?

That was harder.

At night, his phone lit up like it always did. Names he didn't care to remember. Invitations he used to chase. The promise of distractions wrapped in short skirts and shorter attention spans.

He let them all fade into the dark.

The old Griffin would've answered. Would've smiled, charmed, and disappeared before dawn left a mark. But that version of him? The one who lived for the game?

He was buried somewhere beneath the floorboards he was laying.

By Thursday, the weight in his chest had settled into something heavier than exhaustion. As he stood staring at the house, Rick's voice cut through the haze.

"You're thinking again."

Griffin wiped the sweat from his brow, smirking without humor. "Trying not to."

Rick's eyes narrowed, reading more than Griffin wanted to give. "That's what scares me."

Griffin let out a rough chuckle, but deep down, he knew Rick was right to be worried. The more he let himself feel, the closer he got to remembering why he built walls around his heart in the first place.

And lately?

Those walls didn't feel as sturdy as they used to.

FRIDAY NIGHT

Griffin stood in front of the mirror, towel slung low on his hips, steam curling around him like a ghost he couldn't shake. His reflection stared back—same smirk, same sharp jawline, same eyes that knew exactly how to play the part.

It was muscle memory at this point.

Shower. Shave. Button-down. Dark jeans. Just enough scruff to make it look like he didn't try—when in reality, every detail was deliberate.

This was who they expected.

Who he needed to be.

Because if he wasn't this—the confident, untouchable Griffin Hayes—then he'd have to face the man underneath. And tonight wasn't the night for that.

Neon lights from Marshside pulsed in the distance as he eased into the lot, voices floating like ghosts through thick summer air. Saltwater curled in the breeze, tangled with smoke and perfume sweet as regret, heavy with choices that never end well.

Inside, the bass thrummed low, vibrating through the soles of his boots. Bodies moved in a slow, drunken rhythm—laughing too loud, leaning too close. It was familiar. Comfortable in its chaos.

He made his way to the bar, nodding at the bartender, who already had his drink poured before he even sat down. That was the thing about Griffin—he didn't have to ask. People just...knew.

Leaning back, glass in hand, his eyes scanned the room. Not with desperation, never with desperation, but with precision.

This wasn't searching.

This was hunting.

A blonde at the corner table, pretending to be lost in conversation but stealing glances when she thought he wasn't looking.

A brunette swaying to the music, her hips making promises her eyes hadn't caught up to yet.

They'd come to him. They always did.

Because Griffin Hayes didn't chase.

He waited.

And when they finally crossed the room—drawn in by the danger they didn't understand—he'd smirk, close the distance, and remind himself that this was just another night.

Another distraction.

Another game.

Because as long as he kept playing, he didn't have to think about why the silence at home felt heavier. Or why the house he was building felt more like a question than an answer.

No—tonight wasn't about reflection.

Tonight was about forgetting.

And Griffin Hayes was a master at both.

5

CRIMSON TIDE

TONIGHT, Marshside wasn't just crowded; it was alive. Buzzing with that dangerous energy that made people forget consequences existed. The kind of night where inhibitions slipped off faster than dresses. Where every touch lingered a little longer. Where bad ideas tasted sweeter under neon lights.

The bass throbbed beneath the floorboards, vibrating through barstools and cheap whiskey glasses, syncing with the reckless heartbeat of everyone inside. Laughter spilled out from dark corners, pool cues cracked against billiard balls, and somewhere near the jukebox, a drunken chorus of too-loud singing joined the chaos.

The air was thick—spilled beer, sweat, salt, smoke—and Griffin inhaled it like oxygen. This wasn't just a bar. It was a haven for the damned. A playground for people looking to forget who they were for a night.

And Griffin?

He was the king of that game.

Griffin sat in his usual spot—the corner barstool that wasn't just a seat anymore. It was a throne. A worn-down piece of wood and steel that had seen more confessions, bad decisions, and unspoken regrets than a damn priest. If this stool could talk, it'd call him by name, pour itself a drink, and remind him of every woman he didn't bother remembering.

He leaned back, the picture of effortless control—one hand wrapped around a glass of whiskey, the other draped over his thigh like he owned not just the seat but the air surrounding it. His gaze swept across Marshside, sharp and calculated. Not hunting. Just waiting. Like a predator too confident to chase because he knew—they always came to him.

And why wouldn't they?

His phone buzzed against the sticky wood of the bar.

> Aiden: Getting off later than expected. If I come, it'll be late. Have fun and good luck.

Luck? Please. In Marshside, luck had nothing to do with it. He could pull without trying. Hell, half the women in here already knew what it felt like to be pressed against his truck at midnight, moaning promises they'd forget by sunrise.

His eyes flicked across the room, more out of habit than interest.

The brunette near the jukebox?

Already picturing him between her thighs.

The blonde at the bar?

Giggling at some poor bastard's joke while giving Griffin that look. The kind that screamed, *I'll leave with you the second you crook your finger.*

It was clockwork. Predictable.

And tonight?

It felt… dull.

He swirled the whiskey in his glass, debating if he'd even bother. Or if he'd just finish his drink, head home, and let the silence of his half-built house swallow him whole.

And then—she walked in.

The redhead.

Griffin didn't believe in clichés—not really—but damn if time didn't slow the second she stepped through that door. She didn't stumble in like a tipsy tourist, didn't cling to a group of friends for validation. No, she moved like gravity bent around her. Like she didn't just own the room—she was the reason it existed.

No hesitation. No scanning for approval. Straight to the bar, ordering her drink with a look that dared anyone to speak to her. Claiming a booth in the corner like a queen surveying her kingdom.

Fire-lit hair that looked like it'd burn you if you touched it. Green eyes sharp enough to cut through bullshit before it was even spoken. Confidence wrapped around her curves like sin tailored just for her.

Griffin's smile was slow. Dangerous. The kind that usually came right before a very bad decision.

There was something about her—something that didn't scream for attention like the others. No, this one… Dared you to come closer. Dared you to try your luck and see how fast she'd ruin you.

And then she looked at him.
Not a glance. Not curiosity.
A summons.
One flick of her fingers—elegant, effortless—as if to say, *Come here, boy*.
Griffin arched a brow, a laugh threatening at the corner of his mouth. No woman had ever called him over like that. Not without a hint of nerves. Not without at least pretending they weren't already undressing him in their head.
But her?
She didn't flinch.
For once, he was the one moving first. Not because he wanted to chase, but because he had to.
Sliding into the booth across from her, he sprawled back like he owned the seat, but they both knew—this was her game now.
"Didn't think that would work," he said, voice dripping with amusement, eyes locked on hers like a challenge.
Her lips curved, slow and sinful, as she toyed with the rim of her glass. "Neither did I. But here you are."
Cocky. Unapologetic.
Griffin's pulse kicked up—not with lust, but with something rarer. Interest.
"Wrenley Raine," she offered, leaning back like she had all night to destroy him. "But you can call me Wren."
"Hayes," he returned, letting the name hang between them like a loaded gun.
Her brow lifted, playful but sharp. "First name or last?"
Griffin leaned in as his eyes flicked to hers. "Whichever one gets me invited to sit here a little longer."
That earned a soft laugh—low and warm—the kind of sound that promised nothing but trouble.
They went back and forth like seasoned fighters, each jab smoother than the last, each lip twitch hiding sharper teeth. It wasn't flirting. It was combat in heels and whiskey.
"You always this easy to summon?" she teased, sipping her drink, eyes gleaming with wicked delight.
"Only when I'm intrigued," he shot back, gaze dropping to her lips, then lower—just enough to make her breath catch before she masked it.

"You must get bored easily."

"Lately? Yeah." The shape of his lips became something more sinister. "But you're making tonight more interesting."

She leaned in, elbows on the table, chin resting on her hand, like she was studying him under a microscope. "Careful, Hayes. Interest can turn into obsession real quick."

He laughed—a deep, genuine sound. "Sweetheart, you'd be lucky to have me obsessed."

It wasn't just her hair that blazed; it was the ruthless fire in her confidence. She leaned back, her jade eyes smoldering with a dangerous glow. "Oh honey, I plan to control. I don't do lucky."

Fuck.

That wasn't just a line. Griffin felt it settle in his chest like a slow-burning fuse, igniting something he hadn't dared touch in years. His pulse quickened, sharp and reckless, threatening to expose the cracks he kept hidden beneath layers of control. Because she didn't just say the words. She owned them. And that kind of fire didn't just burn; it consumed.

By the time she asked him to "tell her something real," he wasn't sure who was playing who anymore.

But when he mentioned the house—when her teasing flickered for just a heartbeat—he knew she wasn't here for surface-level games. She was peeling back layers, seeing how far she could push before he snapped.

And he liked it.

Hours passed, but it felt like minutes. The bar emptied around them, but neither moved—locked in a battle neither of them planned to lose.

At her car, she didn't flirt. She didn't promise.

She just handed him her phone like she was giving him a weapon he didn't know how to use.

When she leaned in, her breath warm against his ear, she whispered, "We'll see."

And just like that, Wrenley Raine walked away. Leaving Griffin standing in a parking lot with his game shattered at his feet.

Griffin stood in the parking lot longer than he'd ever admit—hands shoved deep in his pockets, head tilted back like staring at the stars might give him a damn answer. But all he saw was the faint glow of streetlights and the fading memory of taillights disappearing into the night.

Wren.

That name already tasted dangerous in his mouth.

Women didn't do this.

Not to him.

They didn't flip the script.

They didn't call him over like he was the entertainment.

They didn't sit across from him with that knowing look, peel back his layers without even touching him. And then walk away like they'd won a game he didn't remember agreeing to play.

But here he was—standing still, watching the empty road like a man who'd just been hit by a storm he didn't see coming.

"Son of a bitch…" he muttered, dragging a hand through his hair, his fingers tightening at the roots as a sharp, surprised laugh escaped. It wasn't bitter. It wasn't annoyed.

It was pure, unfiltered admiration.

Because damn… She was good.

Wren hadn't just walked into his world; she'd set fire to it, handed him the match, and told him to thank her for the burn. She didn't flirt. She didn't chase. She didn't fall into step like every other woman who crossed his path.

No—she'd flipped the entire fucking board, smiled at the wreckage, and left him standing in the ashes wondering when the hell he lost control.

Griffin exhaled, pulling out his phone like it weighed more than it should. His thumb hovered over the screen, eyes locked on her contact.

Wren.

No emojis. No playful nickname. No bullshit.

Just her name. Simple. Clean.

But somehow, it felt like a loaded gun in his hand.

He stared at it, jaw tightening. A smirk ghosting across his lips as the haunting of her brake lights fading replayed in his mind, the dust of the gravel still kicked up. As if it too was changed by her. All he could do was cling to the illusion that this was still his game.

But deep down, he knew better.

This wasn't the kind of woman you forgot by morning.

She wasn't a name you deleted after a night of fun.

She was the kind that etched herself into your thoughts—showing up when you least wanted her there, daring you to call, knowing you'd cave eventually.

Wren didn't just bend rules.

She didn't even acknowledge they existed.

She dared him to break every single one—and smiled like she already knew he would.

Pushing off his truck, Griffin let out another laugh—low, dark, and a little bit wrecked. He could feel it already. The shift. The crack in his armor he hadn't felt in years.

"Alright, *Red...*" he muttered, sliding his phone back into his pocket like that would somehow lessen its weight. "You wanna play? Let's see who taps out first."

The smirk stayed on his lips as he climbed into the driver's seat, but it wasn't the cocky grin everyone else knew. No, this one was different.

This wasn't confidence.

This was anticipation.

That slow, simmering awareness that he wasn't walking away from this clean.

Because women like Wrenley Raine?

They weren't a one-night story.

They were the kind you survived—or didn't.

And Griffin Hayes?

Yeah, he'd survived a lot.

But something told him this was a different kind of storm.

He let the engine rumble beneath him, rolling down the windows as the salty night air filled his lungs, but it didn't clear his head. It just carried the ghost of her—her voice, the curve of her lips, how she leaned in like she already owned him, and whispered promises disguised as threats.

She wasn't going to be a chapter.

She was the whole damn book he never meant to write.

As he pulled onto the main road, headlights cutting through the dark, Griffin shook his head—half amused, half already addicted.

Because he knew himself.

Knew exactly how this would go.

He didn't chase.
Didn't fall.
Didn't lose.
But for her?
He just might do all three.
And that?
That was the most reckless thing he'd done in years.

The smirk lingered, half-dangerous, half-desperate, as Griffin drove toward home. If you could call a half-built house mingled with the bitter ghosts of whiskey and bodies whose faces blurred into shadows by morning, home.

Tonight was different.

It wasn't about numbing himself with strangers' skin or drowning memories in cheap drinks. Every damn thought sharpened, every nerve rippling like waves beneath his skin, raw and relentless, refusing to fade. Tonight was about remembering—and hell, if it wasn't the sweetest torture he'd ever known.

Every look. Every word. Every spark she lit just by existing.

The wild tumble of her hair, catching the light like embers. Those jade eyes—slow, assessing, hungry. Never just seeing, but undressing and daring him in the same breath. Full lips curled in a smirk that promised trouble, the kind you taste for days. And her body, fuck. All curved lines wrapped in dangerous confidence, every shift of her hips a silent invitation and a warning. She moved like sin, knowing exactly the kind of chaos she could wreck, every motion daring him to cross a line she drew, just to watch him try.

Griffin drummed his fingers against the steering wheel, the road blurring beneath his tires as one thought repeated like a dare in his head.

You don't play women like Wren.
You survive them.
If you're lucky.
And Griffin?
He wasn't sure if luck had anything to do with it anymore.

6

UNFINISHED

THE NEXT MORNING, Griffin did what he always did.

Coffee. Black. Bitter enough to match his mood.

A run. Fast enough to outrun the thoughts clawing at the edges of his mind.

A stop by the job site, pretending like blueprints and lumber could distract him.

Routine.

But it didn't work.

Not even close.

Because between every sip, every pounding step against the sand, every glance at a half-built house—she crept in.

Green eyes that didn't just look at him. They saw him.

That smirk that promised sin without needing to say a damn word.

The way Wren spoke to him, like she wasn't impressed but interested.

It wasn't just her confidence. It was how she didn't wait.

Didn't hesitate.

Didn't play by the rules he'd perfected.

Griffin told himself it was nothing. Just a night. A good conversation wrapped in whiskey and ego.

But that was bullshit.

And he fucking knew it.

Because no woman had ever left him feeling like this. Like he was the one being toyed with. Like he was the one wondering when he'd get more.

Then, at exactly 2:00 PM, his phone buzzed.

> Wren: Hayes, it's Wren. I'll be at Marshside tonight.

That was it.

No question.

No invite.

Just a statement. Like she was letting him know where to find her if he had the balls to show up.

Griffin stared at the screen, jaw tight. The ball was in his court. But she wasn't waiting to see if he'd swing.

If he didn't show, she'd move on.

If he did... Would that make him look desperate?

Fuck.

He tossed his phone onto the passenger seat, scrubbing a hand over his jaw, annoyed at how backwards this felt.

Women chased him.

They sent the first text. They waited for his reply. They begged for a second round.

And sure—technically, she texted first.

But now?

He's the one doing the chasing.

Because Wren didn't flirt. She dared.

She didn't follow. She led—and made it look effortless.

By 3:00 PM, he was still replaying the way her fingers traced the rim of her glass like she was toying with him, not the drink.

By 4:00 PM, he'd read her message five times and told himself it didn't matter.

By 5:00 PM, he was pacing—restless, irritable, hard as hell just thinking about the way her body leaned into his without ever touching.

By 6:00 PM, he swore he wasn't going.

She could wait.

She could fucking wait.

By 7:30 PM, he was under scalding water, telling himself it was just a habit. Just cleaning up.

Not for her.

By 7:45 PM, he was standing in front of the mirror, towel slung low, running a hand through his damp hair, asking himself why the hell his heart was beating like he was new to this game.

By 8:00 PM, he was pulling into Marshside.

And there she was.

Same booth. Same whiskey. Same damn smirk that told him she'd known he'd show up before he did.

Griffin took his time walking over, his pulse steady but his blood running hot. When he reached her, Wren didn't look up immediately—didn't give him that satisfaction.

When she finally glanced at him, she grinned like a woman who already knew the ending to a story he hadn't even started.

"Took you long enough," she murmured, swirling her drink like she wasn't seconds from wrecking him.

Griffin leaned against the booth, arms crossed, letting his eyes drag over her—slow, unapologetic. "You didn't ask a question," he shot back, a brow raised. "Figured I'd let you sweat."

Low, sultry, and dangerous, Wren laughed. "Cute. Did it work?"

He slid into the seat across from her, leaning forward just enough to let the tension coil between them. "You tell me."

Her gaze raked over him, slow and deliberate, like she was deciding whether he was worth devouring or dismissing.

"Figured you'd chicken out," she teased, fingers trailing along the condensation on her glass. "Thought I might've scared you off."

Griffin flashed that lazy, panty-melting smile. "Sweetheart, you're good… but you're not that good."

Her lips curved into something wicked. "Mm. Keep telling yourself that."

Every word was a game of tug-of-war. Neither of them willing to let go, both pulling harder with every glance, every smirk.

They talked.

Flirted.

Fought with words so sharp they should've come with warnings.

"You always this cocky?" she asked, sipping her whiskey, watching him like a predator sizing up competition.

Griffin's tongue swept across his bottom lip, his gaze locked on hers. "Only when I know I've already won."

Wren's laugh was sinful, her eyes glinting with challenge. "Honey, if you think you've won, you're playing the wrong game."

The tension was suffocating—thick enough to drown in.

Every time her knee brushed his under the table, his jaw clenched.

Every time his fingers ghosted over hers reaching for his drink, her breath hitched just enough for him to notice.

By last call, neither had made a move.

But both were starving for it.

Outside, the humid night wrapped around them like a second skin.

They didn't speak at first—just walked, side by side, the weight of everything unsaid pressing between them.

Wren stopped beside her car, leaning back against it, her head tilted like she was waiting to see if he'd finally snap.

"So?" she asked, voice soft but laced with heat.

"So…" Griffin echoed, stepping closer, his hands sliding into his pockets to keep from grabbing her too soon.

Her gaze dropped to his lips, then back to his eyes—dark, dangerous, and daring.

"You gonna kiss me, Hayes, or just stand there looking pretty?"

Griffin chuckled, low and rough. "I don't kiss women who don't beg."

Wren pushed off the car, closing the space between them until her chest brushed his.

"Guess you'll never know what it's like then."

But before he could fire back, her fingers fisted in his shirt and dragged him down.

The kiss wasn't sweet.

It wasn't soft.

It was a battle. All teeth, tongue, and a fight for dominance neither was willing to surrender.

Griffin's hands gripped her waist, pulling her flush against him. Feeling every curve, every breathless gasp, as her nails scraped down his neck.

When she whispered, "Which one's yours?" against his lips, he barely managed to nod toward his truck before she was dragging him with her—owning him without saying a word.

The back seat door swung open, and then it was just heat, hands, and hunger.

She straddled him, thighs tight around his hips, pressing down just enough to make him grit his teeth, control shredding at the edges.

"Tease," he muttered, voice low and wrecked, hands dragging up the inside of her thighs like he owned every inch. His fingers slipped beneath her shorts, feeling the heat of her skin, the soft, slick confirmation that she was already fucking drenched for him.

She tilted her head and rolled her hips, grinding against him slow and deep—like breaking him was foreplay.

Her nails scraped against the back of his neck as she leaned in, dragging her teeth along his jaw, her breath hot, teasing.

"Maybe I just like watching you lose your patience," she whispered, voice thick with amusement. But the way she gasped when he squeezed her hips, pulling her down harder, deeper—she was just as wrecked as he was.

"That's fine, I can do the same," he murmured, his lips tracing over her throat, sucking, biting, branding her with heat.

"You're welcome to try," she moaned, her voice like sin, like a promise meant to be broken.

His hands slid lower, pushing past lace, two fingers slipping inside her with a slow, agonizing precision, curling just right.

She gasped, her whole body jerking, tightening.

His thumb dragged slow, deliberate circles over her clit, coaxing out sounds that sent fire straight through him.

Her nails dug into his shoulders as she rocked against him. Breathy moans mixing with the heat of his own ragged exhale.

"You feel that?" he whispered, dragging his fingers deeper, drawing out another broken moan. "How fucking wet you are for me?"

Her response was nothing but a choked, needy sound, her hips rolling, chasing the friction, chasing his hand like she couldn't get enough. She was riding his fingers now, a slow, desperate rhythm that had him seconds from losing every ounce of restraint. She reached between them, fingers fumbling with his belt, her urgency a goddamn aphrodisiac.

His cock throbbed beneath her touch, aching, straining against the fabric, desperate to be buried inside her.

Her lips traced his jaw, her voice nothing more than a whisper of air. "I want—"

Then the shrill sound of her phone sliced through the haze.

Wren froze, her entire body tensing, the high they'd been riding crashing down in an instant.

"Fuck," she breathed, pulling back, her chest heaving, eyes wide and haunted.

Griffin, still wrecked, still hard enough to hurt, caught her wrist before she could escape.

"Are you married?" His voice was rough. Part demand, part desperation.

Her head snapped up, fury flashing in those green eyes. "No."

She yanked her hand free, running shaky fingers through her tangled hair, her lips swollen from his kiss, her body still trembling from how close she'd been to falling apart.

"I just—I have to go," she muttered, her voice tight, panic bleeding through the bravado.

Before he could stop her, before he could figure out what the hell had just ripped her away, she was out of the truck, slamming the door behind her.

And then...

She was gone.

Griffin sat there—chest heaving, fists clenched, every nerve in his body screaming for release that never came.

Unfinished.

Unsatisfied.

And completely hooked.

The scent of her still lingered. On his skin, on his fingers, in the air thick with sweat and frustration.

He let his head fall back against the seat, a bitter, breathless laugh slipping out.

"What the fuck are you doing to me, Red..."

But he already knew the answer.

She wasn't just playing hard to get.

She was playing for keeps.

And Griffin Hayes?

Yeah...

He was already losing.

7

UNRAVELED

GRIFFIN WOKE up like he'd been in a fight he didn't remember starting—and sure as hell didn't win.

His body was wired, every muscle pulled tight like a coil seconds from snapping. His jaw ached from clenching it in his sleep. His chest felt too damn tight, like his ribs were caging something in that didn't want to stay there anymore.

He scrubbed a hand down his face, exhaling sharp and bitter as he pushed up on his elbows. Staring at the ceiling like maybe, just maybe, the cracks in the paint would offer an answer.

They didn't.

Of course they didn't.

Because nothing about this made sense.

He could still feel her.

On his hands.

In his head.

In the places no woman had ever fucking stayed.

Wren had been soaked, panting his name, her nails digging into his shoulders like she couldn't stand the idea of space between them. She'd come apart on his fingers—hard—her body trembling, breath hitching against his skin like he was the only thing holding her together.

And then—

She ran.

Like she hadn't just begged for more.

Like she hadn't been seconds away from letting him ruin her completely.

Griffin let out a growl, slamming his fist against the mattress, as if that would shake her ghost off him.

This didn't happen to him.

Ever.

He didn't wake up with women still under his skin.

He didn't replay every fucking second like a man obsessed.

But here he was. Restless, pissed off, and clawing at answers he didn't have.

His pulse ticked in his jaw as his mind spun—uncontrollable, relentless.

The way her body arched into him.

The way she gasped his name like a prayer and a curse all in one.

The heat of her breath, the slick of her thighs, the desperate roll of her hips…

And then that shift.

The second her phone rang, it was like a switch flipped.

Gone was the woman who couldn't get enough of him.

In her place?

Panic. Ice-cold. Distant.

Griffin's stomach twisted, a sick, sharp ache settling low in his gut.

Who the fuck had called her?

And why did she react like she'd been caught committing a sin?

He shoved out of bed, the tension in his body too much to sit with. His bare feet hit the floor hard, like the impact might jar the thoughts loose. But they stuck. Clung to him like sweat on a humid day.

Is she married?

No. She'd said no. Swore it.

Engaged?

Boyfriend?

Some asshole waiting at home while she gets off in strangers' trucks?

The thought tasted like acid.

Bitter. Burning.

Something ugly he didn't want to name twisted beneath his ribs—a mix of jealousy, frustration, and a sting he refused to call hurt.

Griffin dragged himself through the motions—brushing his teeth, like he wasn't seconds from grinding them down. Stepping under a scalding shower that did nothing to cool the heat simmering beneath his skin.

By the time he threw on shorts and a T-shirt, grabbed his coffee, and hit the pavement, he felt like a grenade with the pin half-pulled.

Run it off.

That was the plan.

Pound the frustration into the sand, let the tide take whatever the hell this was, and drag it out to sea.

But fate wasn't done fucking with him yet.

Because as he rounded the corner past Grounds & Grit, coffee in hand, sweat dripping down his spine—

He saw her.

Casually strolling out of the shop, sunglasses perched on her nose, hair pulled back in a messy knot, holding her coffee like she hadn't just wrecked him twelve hours ago.

Like she hadn't left him aching, unsatisfied, and questioning every rule he lived by.

Too calm.

Too fucking normal.

That was what snapped the last thread of his control.

Griffin slowed, his breath heavy, not from the run, but from the wildfire igniting in his chest.

And when her eyes met his?

She didn't flinch.

Didn't hesitate.

She just smirked. Like this was nothing. Like he was nothing more than a good time, a memory already fading.

No fucking way.

He closed the distance in three strides, his shadow swallowing hers as he crowded her space.

"You gonna tell me what the fuck that was last night?" he demanded, his voice low, sharp. Dangerous.

Wren tilted her head, lips curling into that infuriating, intoxicating smile. "A good time?" she teased, taking a sip of her coffee. "You seemed to be enjoying yourself."

Griffin's jaw flexed so hard it hurt.

Cute. She wanted to play coy? Not today.

He stepped in, so close he could feel the heat radiating off her skin, the same heat he'd had beneath his hands, between his fingers.

His voice dropped, rough and laced with something darker than anger.

"Don't fuckin' play with me, Wren. You don't get to run. Not from me."

For a split second—just one—he saw it.

The crack.

The way her throat bobbed as she swallowed, her breath catching before she masked it with that same damn smirk.

But Griffin wasn't stupid. He felt the shift.

His heart hammered against his ribs, not just with rage but with something worse.

Something that felt dangerously close to giving a damn.

"If that's how this is gonna be…" His voice sharpened, cutting through the charged air between them. "If you've got some guy waiting in the wings—if this is your twisted idea of fun—then I'm out. I don't do secrets. I don't do messy. I don't fuck women who are already claimed."

He could hear his pulse in his ears, the taste of regret already building on his tongue. But pride wouldn't let him stop.

Before she could say a word, before he gave her a chance to spin more games, he turned on his heel.

Didn't step foot in the coffee shop.

Didn't look back.

He was done.

Or at least, that's what he told himself.

Behind him, he heard it.

The hesitation.

The first sign that Wren Raine wasn't as untouchable as she pretended to be.

"Hayes… please, don't—"

Her voice cracked, soft, almost pleading. But Griffin forced his legs to keep moving.

Because if he stopped—if he looked back—he wasn't sure he'd walk away again.

And that scared him more than anything she could've said.

Every time his feet pounded against the pavement, her voice echoed through his skull—taunting him.

"*Hayes... please, don't—*"

The words clawed at him, over and over, like they meant something more than just a last-ditch effort to stop him from walking away.

What the fuck did that even mean?

The wind was warm against his face, the salt air thick and heavy in his lungs. But it didn't matter. He ran harder, like speed alone could outrun the mess she left behind. Sweat dripped down his spine, his muscles burned, his heart jackhammered against his ribs.

But no matter how fast he moved, he couldn't outrun her.

Couldn't outrun the memory of her body pressed against his—hot, desperate, grinding like she needed him more than air.

Couldn't shake the sound of her moaning his name, breathless and wrecked, like he was the only thing keeping her tethered to this world.

Couldn't stop replaying the way she started to shatter against his hand. Only to vanish like it never happened.

Fuck.

Griffin pushed until his legs screamed in protest, until his lungs burned, until the edges of his vision blurred. But the knot in his chest? That fucker stayed tight.

The tension didn't ease.

The frustration didn't fade.

It only grew, festering beneath his skin like a wound he couldn't reach.

By the time he stumbled back into his condo, drenched in sweat and running on fumes. His body was wrecked. But his mind was still a live wire, sparking with every image of her.

He stripped off his clothes like they were suffocating him and stepped into the shower. Cranking the water until it was scalding—until his skin turned red and the steam filled the room, like a fog meant to drown him.

His hands braced against the tile. Head bowed under the pounding stream as the heat beat down on his shoulders.

But no amount of water could wash her away.

In my fucking truck...?

That thought hit him harder than it should've. The realization that she didn't even hesitate.

She didn't ask to go somewhere private.

Didn't slow down.

Didn't care about comfort or space or time.

She wanted it rough. Fast.

Like she didn't have a choice.

Like she needed to forget something—and he was her escape route.

The more he thought about it, the more it twisted inside him.

Yeah, she'd been desperate.

But not just for him.

For distraction. For release.

For something to pull her out of whatever the fuck she was running from.

And Griffin hated how much that bothered him.

This wasn't supposed to be his problem.

He didn't care why women wanted him—he just let them.

But with Wren, it wasn't just about sex.

It was the way she made him feel out of control. The way she crawled into his head and refused to leave.

His fists slammed against the tile, jaw clenched so tight it ached.

He wasn't this guy.

Wasn't the type to get caught up.

But here he was—burning for a woman who might've only touched him to forget someone else.

Who kissed like she meant it…

Then vanished like she didn't.

By the time he stepped out of the shower, his skin was raw and his patience was gone. He yanked on a fresh shirt, grabbed his keys, and headed out before he talked himself into doing something stupid—like calling her.

He needed a distraction.

Something solid.

Something that didn't come with green eyes and secrets.

With nothing but his thoughts riding shotgun, the drive to the job site was quiet, too quiet.

The sun was brutal, beating down from a cloudless sky, but the heat outside had nothing on the fire still smoldering in his chest.

When he stepped out of his truck, the familiar scent of sawdust hit him, grounding him for half a second. The marsh birds called in the distance. The soft hum of wind through the unfinished beams filled the air.

This place was supposed to be where shit made sense.

Here, things followed plans. Measurements. Deadlines.

No surprises.

No games.

But as he walked through the skeletal frame of his future home, boots echoing against the subfloor, all he could think about was her.

His fingers dragged along the raw wood, tracing lines that weren't finished yet. Just like every thought he had about Wren.

This house was supposed to be his fresh start.

His clean slate.

Proof that he could build something that lasted.

But right now?

All he felt was the hollow ache of something unfinished—not in the walls, but in his fucking chest.

He gripped a railing post, knuckles white as frustration bled into something else—something dangerously close to hurt.

Not my fucking problem, he told himself.

But even his inner voice sounded like a liar.

His phone buzzed in his pocket, pulling him out of the spiral.

> Aiden: Can I get your help?

> Griffin: Yeah, what's up?

> Aiden: Looking at houses today. Could use your expertise.

> Griffin: Just let me know when and where.

Stuffing his phone away, Griffin exhaled hard, his gaze flicking back to the framework around him.

This was supposed to be the thing that kept him grounded.

Kept him focused.

But standing there, surrounded by beams and promises he wasn't sure he believed in, it didn't feel like a beginning.

It felt like he was still stuck at the starting line, watching something he couldn't control spiral further out of reach.

So yeah, helping Aiden sounded good.

Anything to get out of his own head.

Anything to stop thinking about the woman who'd left him aching for answers.

And for her.

Because as much as he tried to bury it, Griffin knew the truth:

It wasn't just lust twisting him up inside.

It was the fact that—for the first time—he cared why she ran.

8

WHIPLASH

GRIFFIN'S DIESEL rumbled through the pristine neighborhood, the low whistle of the engine slicing through the kind of quiet that only existed in places built to look perfect.

He hated neighborhoods like this.

Every house stood tall and polished, lined up like soldiers in a war against individuality—fresh siding, manicured lawns. Identical mailboxes standing at attention. Winding streets designed to look charming, but really? It was the kind of place that looked perfect from the outside—neatly trimmed lawns, friendly nods at mailboxes. The illusion of charm.

But underneath?

It was a maze of sameness and monotony.

Where people smiled at their neighbors but kept their curtains drawn. Where secrets sat behind every door, polished and polite. Just like the last one and the one before that.

Griffin knew this development better than anyone—Hayes Development had overseen every square inch of it. He could tell you which houses had faulty plumbing before the drywall went up. Which driveways would crack first. Which buyers thought they were getting something special when, really, they were just another number in a long line of "custom" builds.

It was ironic as hell.

He could build this world, but he'd never live in it.

As he pulled into the drive, his phone lit up with a name that stopped him cold.

> Wren: I didn't like how you brushed me off this morning. I want to explain last night. Can I call you later?

Griffin's fingers tightened around the steering wheel, knuckles turning white. He stared at the message like it might change if he glared hard enough.

Explain?

What the hell was there to explain?

Last night wasn't a misunderstanding.

It wasn't some drunken mistake.

It was intentional.

Every kiss. Every moan. Every desperate grind of her hips.

She'd wanted him—needed him.

And then she ran.

Now she wanted to talk?

Now she wanted to make it neat. Put words around something that was never supposed to be clean in the first place?

"Fuck," Griffin muttered, shoving his phone into his pocket like it burned.

His gaze snapped to Aiden, already standing on the front steps, arms crossed, watching him with that knowing smirk, the same one he always wore when Griffin's truck rolled up.

If only Aiden knew the storm brewing just beneath his best friend's skin.

Griffin slammed the truck door shut, forcing the weight of Wren's text out of his head—or at least trying to.

"So," he called out, plastering on a grin he didn't feel, "you came to your senses and finally decided to introduce me to this mystery sister of yours?"

Aiden snorted, shaking his head. "Knew you'd start this shit the second you showed up."

Griffin smirked, pulling his sunglasses off and hooking them onto his collar, playing it cool even as his pulse hammered beneath his skin. "What? Can't a guy be curious? Is she pretty? Trouble? Or did she inherit your charming personality?"

"Fuck you, Griff," Aiden shot back, but there was no heat behind it, just the usual banter.

Griffin laughed, but it was hollow. His mind wasn't here. It was still stuck on that damn message. Still stuck on her.

"She drove in late last night," Aiden added, stretching out his back. "Technically early this morning. Around two."

Griffin's breath caught, but he masked it with a shrug.

Two AM.

Right after she left him wrecked in his truck.

Ironic, wasn't it?

He'd spent the night memorizing every curve of a woman he should never see again—and now he was supposed to play house-hunting wingman like nothing happened.

"Relax, man," Griffin muttered, needing to steer himself away from the edge. "Told you, you've got nothing to worry about."

Aiden studied him for a second too long, then nodded, satisfied. "Good. Anyway, how'd Friday night go? You meet anyone, or did you cry yourself to sleep because I bailed?"

Griffin let out a breath, raking a hand through his hair. "Yeah… about that."

Aiden raised a brow. "That bad?"

A dry laugh escaped before Griffin could stop it. "Met a woman. Gorgeous. Sharp as hell."

Aiden grinned, already assuming the ending. "And I'm guessing you didn't sleep alone."

Griffin shook his head, smiling, but it didn't reach his eyes. "Didn't take her home."

Aiden froze, his grin dropping like Griffin had just confessed to murder. "You what?"

"Nope."

"Jesus Christ." Aiden gawked at him. "You sick? Should I call someone?"

Griffin chuckled, but there was no real humor in it. "She wasn't like the others, man. She played the game better than me. Every move I made… she matched it. Hell, she owned it."

Aiden let out a low whistle, clearly impressed. "Damn. She must be something if she dodged the Griffin Hayes charm."

Griffin drifted off for a beat, eyes distant. "I'll tell you one thing, she was like nothing I've ever seen." A slow, wicked grin crept across his face. "Hell, I'd drink her fucking bathwater."

Aiden choked on his coffee, sputtering. "That's fucking disgusting, man." He shook his head, laughing despite himself. "But damn, if that ain't a visual, I don't know what is."

Before Griffin could respond, before he could even process how to explain the mess in his head, a voice rang out.

"Aiden, is your buddy here? I'm ready to go in the—"

She rounded the corner.

And everything stopped.

Griffin's stomach hit the floor. His pulse detonated in his ears. His entire body locked up like he'd been punched in the gut.

Wren.

Standing there, frozen mid-step, looking at him like she'd just seen a ghost—and judging by the way his heart was trying to claw out of his chest, maybe she had.

His mind scrambled to make sense of it, but there was only one brutal, undeniable truth:

Wren is Aiden's sister.

Mother. Fucking. Hell.

If it hadn't felt like the universe had just ripped the ground out from under him, the irony would almost be laughable. Almost.

Aiden, oblivious, waved her over. "Wren, come meet Griffin."

Griffin forced his face into something resembling composure, biting back every curse threatening to spill out.

As she walked toward them—too calm, too composed—her eyes betrayed her.

Wide. Dark. Wrecked.

Mirroring exactly how he felt.

When Aiden made the introduction, Griffin barely heard the words. His focus was locked on Wren, on the silent war waging behind her steady gaze.

"My friends call me Raine," she said smoothly. Extending her hand like they hadn't been tangled up in heat and desperation less than 24 hours ago. "You're Griffin? The smooth one?"

That damn smirk tugged at her lips, but he saw the tremor beneath it.

Felt it in the way her hand hesitated before touching his.

The second his skin met hers, it was like a match to gasoline—every memory igniting at once.

Her body grinding against his.

The taste of her moans.

The way she'd melted under his touch… before running like hell.

He should've let go.

But neither of them moved.

"Yes," he rasped, his voice rougher than it should've been. "Griffin Hayes."

Her lips curled, eyes flashing with something unreadable. "Of Hayes Development?"

"That's the one."

Aiden's voice cut through, still blissfully unaware. "Alright, enough of that. Griff, don't even think about trying your shit with my sister."

Griffin forced a laugh, letting go of her hand even though it felt like peeling off a brand. "Relax, man. No worries there."

But Wren's eyes told a different story.

They both knew. This wasn't over.

It couldn't be.

Even if it had to be.

As they moved toward the house, Griffin's mind was a mess of rules, desire, and the crushing weight of knowing he'd crossed a line he couldn't uncross.

Inside, the tension was suffocating—every glance between them sparking like a wire about to snap. Aiden chatted about square footage and upgrades. But Griffin couldn't hear a damn word.

When Aiden finally wandered off, Griffin knew what was coming before Wren even opened her mouth.

"Can we talk?"

His arms crossed over his chest, every muscle in his body coiled tight. "There's nothing to talk about."

But Wren?

She wasn't backing down.

"Last night—Griffin, that wasn't nothing."

He exhaled sharply, shaking his head. "It has to be."

Her jaw tightened, defiance flickering behind the hurt in her eyes. "You don't believe that."

His voice dropped, raw and rough, barely above a whisper. "Aiden is your brother."

The words hung there, heavy and brutal.

Wren swallowed hard but stood her ground. "You don't know everything."

"I don't need to," he snapped, but it sounded more like a plea than conviction.

Before she could fire back, Aiden's voice echoed through the empty house—rescue or curse, Griffin wasn't sure.

"Griff! Come check this out."

Griffin didn't hesitate.

Didn't give her another second to twist him up even more.

He walked away, every step heavier than the last. Leaving Wren standing alone, her pride holding her up while the weight of what they'd started threatened to pull them both under.

And as he followed Aiden onto the deck, Griffin knew one thing for certain:

This wasn't over.

Not even close.

No matter how much he wanted it to be.

No matter how much he told himself it needed to be.

9

WAR GAMES

BY THE TIME they reached the second house, Griffin was pure ice. Cold, composed, and maddeningly silent. He moved through the rooms like she didn't exist. Rattling off specs to Aiden. Pointing out fixtures and floor plans with the ease of a man who hadn't had his hands buried between her thighs less than forty-eight hours ago.

Wren trailed behind him, her gaze locked on his broad shoulders, every step fueling the fire in her chest. This wasn't about lust anymore. This was about principle. About proving that Griffin Hayes didn't get to act like she was forgettable. Like the way he touched her hadn't left fingerprints on her skin, and somewhere deeper she didn't want to name.

Last night still burned in every corner of her memory. The rough drag of his fingers, the guttural way he growled her name, the feel of his breath hot against her neck as he made her come, before the phone rang. Like he was built to ruin women exactly like her.

And now?

Now he wanted to pretend none of it happened. That she was just Aiden's sister. That she wasn't still soaked from the memory of whispered moments, touches that lingered, and the ghost of his lips as they—

No.

Fuck that.

If Griffin thought he could shut her out, he didn't know who the hell he was dealing with.

She thought about every teasing word. Every glance. Every time his eyes darkened when she leaned in too close. He wasn't going to pretend this didn't exist. She wouldn't let him.

So, she played dirty.

Every time they passed, she touched him—light, barely there. A brush of her fingers against his arm. A graze along his knuckles. Skin to skin, like a whisper he couldn't ignore.

But he did.

Fucking nothing. No reaction.

So, she pushed further. Trailing her fingers along the waistband of his jeans in the hallway, letting one slip just beneath his belt. Still nothing. His shoulders tightened, his jaw ticked—but he kept walking.

Oh, he was good. Too good.

But Wren wasn't here to lose.

The next time he stepped into a room, she cut in front of him, no hesitation. His chest collided with her back, heat rolling off him in waves. His breath hit her neck, sharp and uneven.

Her hand slid back, slow and deliberate. Fingers dragging down the hard lines of his stomach, skimming every flexed ridge beneath his shirt. She didn't rush. She owned every inch.

Lower.

Then lower. Right to the waistband of his jeans.

She grabbed his zipper.

Not tentative. Not sweet. Firm. Unapologetic. Bold as fuck.

The sound of it—that slow, metallic rasp—ripped through the silence like a promise.

His breath stuttered.

His entire body snapped taut, muscles pulled so tight she could feel the restraint vibrating beneath his skin.

He didn't move. Didn't speak.

Just stood there, fucking wrecked, while she undid him with nothing but her touch and a little fucking nerve.

Still—she didn't stop.

Didn't pull away. Didn't even fucking blink.

She held him there. Zipper half-down.

Her ass pressed flush against the thick, undeniable proof that he was just as affected as she was.

And then, just to push him one step further—

Her fingers dipped lower.

A whisper of contact. Just enough to make him feel it.

A barely-there graze, featherlight, teasing. The smallest of touches that could unravel a fucking monster.

His breath left him hard and fast. His fingers twitched at his sides, like he was fighting every instinct to grab her, flip her around, and finish what she'd just fucking started.

Then, just when she knew she had him—

She let go.

Stepped away.

She walked ahead, throwing him a glance over her shoulder.

Smirking.

And that did it.

His control snapped.

Before she could take another step, his hand wrapped around her wrist, yanking her back so hard it stole her breath. He spun her, slammed her into the wall—fast, rough, every inch of him pressing into her like he was trying to fuse them together.

His palm tensed around her throat. Not quite squeezing, not yet, just holding her there, letting her feel the weight of what she'd just unleashed.

Her pulse pounded against his palm, chest rising harder with every second he didn't speak.

When he did, it was lethal. Low. Dark. Dangerous. "The fuck do you think you're doing, Wren?"

Her lips parted, breath shaky, but she didn't answer.

Didn't need to.

He knew exactly what she was doing. His eyes dragged over her, slow and devouring, like he was memorizing the way she looked when she was caught, cornered. Craving.

His fingers flexed around her throat. "This what the fuck you want?" His voice was a growl now, lips so close she could taste the warning in every syllable. "You wanna fucking play?"

For a second, she thought he'd lose it, thought he'd forget about Aiden, about the house, about everything except wrecking her right there.

Even as her body betrayed her, arching into him, heat pooling between her thighs, there was defiance flickering in her eyes.

With just a twitch of her lips, she whispered, "Try me."

Instead, he leaned in, lips brushing her ear, voice dropping to something darker than sin. "Keep it up, sweetheart. I'll make you beg. I'll ruin your fucking world."

And just like that—he let go. Stepped back and walked the fuck away. Leaving her standing there. Heart pounding. Pulse slamming. And wet.

So fucking wet.

Fucking aching. Because this?

This wasn't over. Not even fucking close.

He didn't talk to her for the rest of the walk-through. Not one glance. Not one sharp remark. Just stone-cold, ruthless fucking silence. And it was driving her insane. Because she knew exactly what he was doing. Punishment.

Griffin wasn't ignoring her because he didn't care. He was ignoring her because he fucking did. Because if he looked at her—really looked at her—he'd lose it. And she wanted that. Needed that. Needed to see him snap. To watch him come apart. To make him forget every goddamn reason why he was trying so hard to hold back. So, she pushed him.

Brushing against him in the hallway. Letting her fingers drag along his hip again. Just a tease, barely pressing into the thick muscle beneath his jeans.

Nothing. No reaction. But his jaw ticked. His hands curled into fists at his sides. And still…

He didn't break.

Fine. She'd take it further.

She could wait.

Waited until Aiden was on the other side of the house. Then she stepped in front of Griffin.

Blocked his path. Didn't touch him. Didn't say a word. Just stood there. Looking up at him and holding his stare.

Then—slow as fucking hell—she bit her lip, dipping her tongue out to wet it. Her eyes held his, then she lingered them on his lips. A challenge. An invitation. A fucking test.

And Griffin? He failed spectacularly. Because he grabbed her. Hard. Fast. His fingers wrapped around her wrist like a vise, yanking her into him so quickly she barely had time to gasp. Before he slammed her against the nearest wall again. Her breath tore from her lungs. But she didn't have time to catch it. Because suddenly, with one hand holding her wrist above her head and the other gripping her throat, his body was everywhere.

Heat. Muscle. Hunger. And fuck—she felt it.

Felt how fucking hard he was, pressing into her stomach, thick and fucking ready. Felt the way his chest rose and fell in deep, barely contained breaths. Felt the way his fingers dug into her hip, rough, dominant, controlling.

He leaned in. His breath seared across her lips. "You really wanna push me?" A guttural growl so dark, she swore she could feel it between her thighs.

Her pulse pounded, slamming against her ribs, but she refused to back down. Refused to look away. Not that she wanted to. Not when his eyes were locked on her like that.

Dark. Hungry.

Like he wasn't just looking at her; he was stripping her. Tearing through every layer like he already knew what she looked like coming apart.

She was drowning in him.

Not waves—a riptide.

Unforgiving.

Dragging her under and daring her to fight it. But she didn't want to fight.

She wanted to fall. To sink so deep she forgot what the surface ever felt like.

Her answer came soft but sure.

A whisper.

A dare.

A fucking promise.

"Yes."

And that was it. That was the fucking breaking point.

His grip on her throat stayed firm, possessive, claiming as he released her wrist. His fingers dragging slowly down the length of her arm, the rough scrape of his skin leaving fire in its wake.

His hand found her jaw, tilting her chin up, forcing her to meet his gaze.

And fuck—the way he looked at her.

Like he was memorizing her.

Like he was already imagining her wrecked beneath him.

His thumb dragged across her bottom lip, like he was seconds from shoving it into her mouth just to see how pretty she looked sucking on it.

But then—he moved. That same hand slid lower. Down her throat. Over her chest.

The tips of his fingers skimming just above the neckline of her shirt. That subtle tease taunting her. He knew exactly what the fuck he was doing.

Her back arched as she sucked in a sharp breath.

Her own hands flew up, fingers wrapping around his wrist like she could stop him. Like she even fucking wanted to.

His lips curled. "You gonna try and stop me, sweetheart?" His voice was mocking, low, and devastatingly fucking smug.

His palm covered her breast, rough fingers pressing into the soft flesh, dragging his thumb over the stiff peak until she whimpered. Then he squeezed, stealing what little breath she had left.

Her nails dug into his wrist, but not to push him away. To hold him there. To keep him right fucking where she needed him.

His mouth was on her throat then, teeth grazing, tongue soothing, sucking just enough.

He kept going. His hand moved lower. Lower. Fucking lower. Sliding down her stomach, over her waistband—he gripped her pussy. Hard. His entire hand cupping her like he owned it, like he was seconds from proving just how much of a fucking mess she already was for him.

A ragged sound tore from her throat as her body jerked, head tipped back against the wall. A desperate gasp catching in her lungs as his fingers pressed deeper. Controlling. Making her feel exactly how fucking soaked she already was.

Then, he pulled her against him. Flush. Tight. Nothing but heat and dominance. A warning in his eyes that told her she wasn't ready for what the fuck was coming next.

His lips hovered against her ear. "Is this what you want?" he whispered.

She went to respond, but his voice came out as a growl. The kind that makes your whole body vibrate. Thick, dark, and absolutely fucking filthy.

"Then don't fucking run next time."

His teeth scraped along her jaw. Fingers flexed against her hip, like he was seconds from bending her over right there against the wall. Like he was seconds from forgetting about Aiden, forgetting where they were, forgetting every last reason he wasn't supposed to fucking want her.

And that's when—He just let go.

Leaving her wrecked. Leaving her soaking all over again. Leaving her so fucking desperate she almost ran after him.

Almost begged.

And for the first time, Wren realized—

This wasn't about teasing anymore.

This was about who was going to break first.

10

SILENT WAR

THE TOURS WERE OVER.

But the real game?

Yeah, that was just getting started.

Griffin stood there—arms crossed, that wicked smirk curving his lips like he already knew exactly how this night would end. His eyes never left Wren. Watching her come undone without even having to fuck her. And God, she looked wrecked.

Not the kind of wrecked anyone else would notice. Wren was too stubborn, too proud for that. But Griffin? He saw it all. The way her gaze was unfocused, locked on nothing. Her chest rising a little too fast, like every breath was a battle she was losing. The way her fingers twitched at her sides, like she didn't trust herself to move—because she could still feel him. Still trapped in the echo of his hands on her body. His mouth at her ear, whispering all the filthy promises he'd cash in if Aiden wasn't five feet away.

Perfect.

He let the silence stretch, watching her drown in it. Watching her squirm beneath the weight of everything they weren't saying. Then, when he could see the panic flicker in her eyes, when she was so far gone she didn't even realize, he struck.

"So, Wren..." His voice dropped, all smooth. Laced with sin and satisfaction. "Which house did you like best?"

Her head snapped up, lips parting like she'd just been yanked out of a dream she wasn't ready to leave. Confusion. Panic. Desire—all flashing across her face in a split second.

She had no fucking clue what he'd just asked.

Griffin nearly laughed. But held back just to savor this moment—the way her body shifted like she was searching for balance, like her legs were barely holding her up.

Aiden's voice cut through the tension, oblivious as ever. "Wren, what the fuck is wrong with you?"

Griffin kept his smirk lazy, casual, like he wasn't already inside her head. Like he hadn't just reduced her to a shaking breath and a racing pulse with only the slightest of touches.

"I'm sorry, what?" Her voice cracked, breathless. "I was…lost in a thought."

Griffin's gaze raked over her, slow and possessive, his voice a low scrape of memory and intent as he murmured, "Yeah… I bet you were."

The flush that crawled up her neck was everything. Proof she was still feeling him. Still burning from every ghost of his touch.

But he wasn't done. Not even close.

"I said…" he stepped in, voice dropping to something low and intimate, edged with heat and warning, "which house did you like best?"

She hesitated. Too long. Because they both knew damn well she hadn't seen a single fucking house today. Her mind had been wrapped around him —the way his fingers brushed her back when no one was looking, the way his breath hit her ear when he reminded her exactly who she was playing with.

Finally, she straightened her shoulders, clinging to whatever pride she had left.

"This one had the best feeling," she said, pointing somewhere behind her, voice shaky and weak in all the ways she couldn't hide.

Griffin arched a brow, the corner of his mouth twitching into something far from innocent. "The best feeling," he repeated, slow and deliberate, like he was savoring the taste of her words. Like he was savoring her.

"Don't start," her brother warned, shooting Griffin a look, oblivious to the wildfire already lit between them.

Griffin just shrugged, eyes never leaving her.

"I'm just agreeing with her."

Then, lower, just for her, but not low enough to miss—

"Yeah?" he murmured, tone dipping into something darker, playful but edged in warning.

"I can see that."

She swallowed hard, her pulse stuttering.

Griffin saw it. He saw everything and loved every second of watching her try—and fail—to hold it together.

He let the silence settle again, thick and suffocating. Let her squirm beneath it, knowing she was seconds away from falling apart. Not being able to resist, he leaned in for the kill.

"Thing is…" Another step closer, close enough that his cologne wrapped around her, invaded her lungs, made her dizzy with want. "It's gorgeous, sure. But I'd make a few changes."

Her brows pulled together, confused. "And what would that be?" she snapped, trying to reclaim footing she'd never really had.

Griffin let a beat pass, watching her squirm, then delivered the blow.

"Well, it's got good bones. Firm. Solid." His gaze dropped to her mouth, catching the way her breath hitched, the way her chest rose too sharply.

"But if I were buying…" Full of intent, his voice dropped. "I'd open the interior up."

Her fingers twitched. Her pulse pounded at her throat.

"Rearrange a few things." His eyes gleamed as they dragged over her body like a promise.

"Make room for me to move in."

That was it. The sharp inhale. The way her thighs pressed together like she could hold in the ache he'd carved into her. The way her tongue flicked out to wet lips gone dry from wanting. But it was her eyes that gave her away. Glowing with something hot and reckless.

Desperate. Exposed. Lit from within, like the truth was burning through her ribcage.

And Griffin?

He just stood there, watching her drown in everything she didn't want to admit. Fully aware that Aiden was still right there.

Still weighing every word.

Still standing between them.

But not stopping a damn thing.

She wanted to fight back; he saw it in her eyes. Wanted to tell him to stop. But before she could even form the words, Aiden spoke.

"We're heading back to my place. Might look up a few more homes before dinner. Oh—Wren, if you're serious about a condo, you should check out Griffin's place."

Griffin caught the way her head snapped up, like she was struggling to remember where the fuck she was. "You live in a condo?" she asked, voice still breathy.

"I do," he answered, that smirk never leaving his face.

She tried to deflect, tried to throw some snark, but Griffin could see it. She was already too far gone.

"That's the thing," he said, voice low and knowing. "People don't really know me. They just know the image."

And in that moment, Wren realized exactly how dangerous he was. How easily he could twist words, twist her, and make her fall without even trying.

She opened her mouth—whether to challenge him or surrender, even she didn't know. But Aiden cut in with a warning she was far too late to heed.

"Wren, don't fall for his charm."

Too late.

She already had.

When Aiden suggested dinner at Driftwoods, Griffin didn't answer right away. He let his gaze slide to Wren, watching her squirm under the weight of anticipation. Watching her wait for him.

Then, with that lazy, devastating smile, he nodded. "Yeah. I'll go shower and change."

The way her lips parted, flushed and trembling, said more than words ever could. There was a wild and molten glow in her eyes, like the hunger had taken root somewhere deeper than breath. Fingers twitched at her sides. A swallow caught in her throat. Skin flushed, kissed pink like he'd already touched her without even having to lay a hand on her.

And Griffin couldn't fucking wait.

GRIFFIN STEPPED OUT OF THE SHOWER, STEAM CURLING AROUND HIS BODY, thick and heavy; it clung to his skin like a memory that refused to fade. Water dripped from his hair and slid down the curve of his neck, tracing the hard lines of his chest before gliding over the ridges of his abs—slow, deliberate, like it wanted to be watched. He dragged a towel over his face, down his arms, but it didn't do shit to cool him off. Because he was still fucking burning. Not from the heat of the water. Not from the steam in the air.

From her.

From the way she touched him today. The way she pushed, teased, fucking tested him. Like he didn't feel every brush of her fingers like a match dragged over gasoline, like he was made of stone. As if she thought he wouldn't break. Wouldn't snap, but she had no fucking idea what she was playing with.

Slowly, trying to regain control, he exhaled, his jaw ticking as he dropped the towel and moved toward his dresser.

Tonight, he was going to end this game.

She thought she was the one playing? She thought she had control?

No.

Not fucking tonight. Tonight, he was going to own her. Make her so fucking flustered she'd barely be able to sit still. Make her squirm in her fucking seat, thighs clenched together, knowing damn well she wouldn't be able to do a damn thing about it. And it would start the second she saw him. He knew.

So, he dressed accordingly. Tactical. Strategic. Every single choice designed to make her fucking suffer. He pulled a fitted black Henley from the drawer. The soft cotton stretched just right across his chest, tight against his biceps, hugging his torso like a second fucking skin. The top three buttons? Undone. Just enough to show a tease of his sun-kissed caramel skin. A glimpse of collarbones. A whisper of muscle. A reminder of exactly what she had been pressed up against the night before.

He gave a slow, no-teeth smile—cool, dangerous, knowing. She was already so fucked.

Dark jeans came next. Low on his hips. Fitted. The kind that made women stare when he walked by, made their fingers twitch like they wanted to reach out and touch. The kind that would have Wren losing her damn mind.

And to finish it off? The cologne. The one that had women leaning in a little closer, their breathing slowing when they caught the scent. The one that stayed on their skin long after he'd left.

She was going to fucking drown in it.

He grinned at his reflection, all cocky and unbothered, rolling his shoulders just to watch the fabric stretch tight across his arms. Knowing exactly what he was doing and liking the view just as much as she would.

Perfect.

His phone buzzed. Aiden.

> Aiden: Will be at Driftwoods in 20.

Griffin exhaled through his nose, responding.

> Griffin: Okay, see you there.

Then, without hesitation, he sent another text. This time to Wren. He grinned because this meant…

Game-Fucking-On.

This wasn't just about teasing her anymore. This was about making her fall apart. In the middle of a restaurant. In front of her brother.

While she couldn't do a damn thing but sit there and fucking take it.

11

POWER PLAY

THE RESTAURANT HUMMED with quiet conversation, the clink of glasses, and the soft pulse of jazz weaving through the air like a lazy heartbeat. But Wren didn't hear any of it.

All she could hear was the rush of blood in her ears. Feel the way her pulse pounded, hot and frantic, as her eyes locked onto the glowing screen in her hand.

> Griffin: I bet you're still wet for me, aren't you?

Like the words had wrapped around her throat and squeezed, her breath caught. Sharp. Ragged.

Because fuck...

She was.

One text. That's all it took for him to completely unravel her. One cocky, filthy sentence, and suddenly she was squirming in her seat. A slow throbbing ache bloomed between her legs—slick, insistent, impossible to ignore.

Her fingers trembled around her phone, knuckles white from how tight she gripped it. Like letting go would mean surrender. Like the screen wasn't already winning.

He knew exactly what he was doing. He knew she'd read that message and immediately feel every inch of him all over again. Knew her body would betray her—just like it always did with him.

Her lungs felt too small, the air too thick. The lace of her panties already ruined.

Her pride screamed at her to ignore it, to rise above, to not give him the satisfaction. But her body? Her body didn't give a damn about pride.

So before she could think twice, before logic could catch up to lust, she fired back.

> Wren: Maybe... But I am sure you're still hard for me. Aren't you?

A challenge. A dare.

She hit send, her pulse still racing when she set the phone down. She tried to steady her breathing, tried to remember how to function like a normal human being.

And then—

She felt him.

Before she even looked up, before the door had fully shut behind him, she felt Griffin Hayes enter the room like a stormfront rolling in. The air shifted, thickened, bending around him as if gravity itself knew who the fuck just walked in.

Slow and hesitant, her eyes dragged up, already knowing she was fucked.

And there he was.

Griffin.

Every inch of him weaponized.

THAT BLACK HENLEY CLUNG TO HIS CHEST LIKE IT WAS PAINTED ON. Stretched across muscles that flexed with every step he took—deliberate, powerful, predatory. The top buttons undone, revealing just enough golden skin to remind her how it tasted. His sleeves pushed up, forearms on full display with veins like ropes beneath sun-kissed skin. Hands she could still feel bruising her hips in the best possible way.

And those jeans...

God, those fucking jeans.

Low on his hips, hugging his thighs, framing the kind of body that didn't just belong in bedrooms—it belonged in sins whispered against church pews.

Her mouth went dry.

Her core pulsed, needy and desperate. Angry at how easily he owned her without saying a single word.

His ocean blue eyes locked onto hers, and it wasn't a glance.

It was a goddamn claim. A silent reminder of everything he'd done to her... And everything he still planned to do.

He threw that crooked grin that had her clenching her thighs.

Lazy. Lethal. Laced with intent.

He stalked toward their table, each step radiating confidence that bordered on cruel. Like he was already playing with his food, savoring how easy it was to ruin her.

Wren's thighs clenched so tight it hurt. Her nails dug into the menu, heartbeat thundering in her ears.

Griffin slid into the seat across from her, lazily stretching out, his fingers drumming against the wood like he had all the time in the world.

Then his phone buzzed.

She watched—helpless—as he pulled it from his pocket, his eyes flicking down to read her message.

For a split second, she saw it. The dilation of his pupils, the subtle drag of his tongue across his bottom lip.

Victory.

Except... It didn't feel like a win.

Not when his gaze lifted.

His baby blues turned smoldering, heavy... full of filthy promises.

"Something wrong, sweetheart?" His voice was velvet-wrapped sin, soft enough that Aiden couldn't catch it, sharp enough to slice straight through her composure.

Her throat closed. She couldn't swallow, couldn't breathe.

Aiden sat beside them, oblivious, rattling off something about appetizers. But Wren? She was drowning in Griffin. In the weight of his stare. In the heat curling low in her belly, spreading like wildfire.

She reached for the wine list, fingers unsteady, gripping it like it could anchor her, but nothing could ground her now. Not when Griffin's knee brushed against hers beneath the table—casual, deliberate, devastating.

Her breath hitched, pulse spiking.

He didn't look at her.

Didn't need to.

He kept talking to Aiden, the image of cool and calm. Asking about whiskey brands like he wasn't currently setting her body on fire with nothing but a touch.

Fine.

Two could play this game.

Wren shifted in her seat, sliding her foot forward until it found his calf beneath the table. She dragged her toes up, slow and deliberate, the contact light but full of intent. Then, without breaking her gaze, she slipped off her shoe—wanting more. Needing skin. Her bare foot pressed against him, the heat of his skin searing against hers.

Griffin didn't flinch. He simply sipped his drink, his eyes half-lidded, watching her like a man amused by how deep she was willing to dig her own grave.

But when her foot crept higher, up the inside of his thigh, her toes brushing dangerously close to where she really wanted to touch him. That's when she felt it.

The flex of his thigh.

Saw the sharp clench of his jaw.

Her lips twitched. Not enough to be noticed by Aiden, just small and smug.

Until she felt him.

Thick. Heavy. Not fully hard—but aware. Awake. Waiting.

Her breath faltered, heat crashing over her in waves.

She risked a glance up, and that's when she realized her mistake.

Griffin wasn't flustered.

No, he was fucking thrilled.

His molten gaze pinned her in place, daring her to keep going. Daring her to see what would happen if she pushed him too far.

The tension between them snapped tight, strung so high it was a miracle Aiden couldn't feel it suffocating the entire damn table.

Just as Wren had decided to see how much further she could push him—

Griffin's phone buzzed again.

Another message.

Except... she hadn't sent one.

Confused, her brows knit together for half a second until she watched him glance down at the screen and smirk. Like he wanted her to ask. Like he wanted her to wonder.

Jealousy burned through her chest, hotter than the desire pooling between her thighs.

Who the fuck was texting him now?

But she didn't ask. She wouldn't give him that satisfaction.

Instead, she dragged her foot back—slow, retreating—not because she wanted to stop, but because suddenly, she realized something far more dangerous than lust was creeping in.

This wasn't just about teasing anymore.

This was about control.

And Griffin Hayes?

He was holding the leash.

Her heart pounded as she forced herself to focus on Aiden's words, nodding along to a conversation she couldn't hear.

All she could think about was the man across from her.

The man who could make her body ache with a glance.

The man who could turn her into a mess without laying a single hand on her.

The man who, with one text, reminded her exactly who the fuck was in charge.

And the worst part?

She didn't want to take that control back.

Not yet.

Because part of her wanted to see just how far Griffin would go.

How much he could wreck her.

How completely he could ruin every rule she thought she lived by.

So when his foot slid forward, brushing against her ankle, a silent promise that this wasn't over—Wren didn't pull away.

The tension coiled so tight between them it was suffocating.

Her phone buzzed. Another message. From him.

> Griffin: By now it's dripping down your thighs.

The words hit her like a fucking wrecking ball, legs twitching against the unforgiving cushion beneath her. She barely glanced down before his expression shifted, like he already knew exactly what it was doing to her and wasn't in any kind of rush to stop. He brought his eyes up to her slowly, with the kind of arrogance that had Wren holding her breath.

He decided to finish her off; right then and there, he sent one more message.

> Griffin: I should have made you scream my name, right there against the wall. Made you beg. Made you fucking drip down my cock before I was done with you.

She read it.

He saw it hit her. The subtle bite of her lip. The shift in her seat. The quick glance to see if Aiden was watching. Griffin knew she was trying to keep from falling apart right there at the table.

She was wet.

Her pussy, soaked for him—he was sure. Throbbing. Aching. Desperate. And now? Now she knew she wasn't going to get away with teasing him under the table like that.

His cock throbbed, a heavy, pulsing need straining against his jeans. A demand to be inside her, to stretch her, to drag out those pretty little sounds she'd made last night. He thought back to when he had her pinned against the fucking wall earlier, one hand locking her wrist above her head, the other holding her still while she squirmed beneath him, her breath hitched and his name spilled from her lips like a goddamn prayer.

Fuck. The sound of his name coming from her pouty lips alone was almost enough to bring him to his knees.

But they weren't alone.

Aiden was right fucking there, oblivious, scrolling through his phone. Probably thinking about appetizers. While Griffin was sitting across from his little sister, rock fucking hard. Fighting the urge to drag her out of her seat, bend her over the table, and make her pay for every inch of teasing she thought she could get away with.

So he leaned back, spreading his legs wider under the table, making sure she felt the heat of him pressing against her thigh, thick and rigid. Right. Fucking. There.. He took another slow sip of whiskey, letting the burn slide down his throat, and smirked.

"So, Wren," he drawled, voice deep and thick with implication. The kind of tone that had her pupils blown wide, just a hint of those glowing jade eyes still visible.

She looked up at him, her lips parting just slightly. And fuck. All he could think about was shoving his fingers past them. Making her suck them down. Making her taste herself before bending her over and fucking her so hard she wouldn't be able to sit still tomorrow.

"Tell me—" he tapped his fingers against his glass, rhythmically, like he was already planning out exactly how he was going to make her come, "did you get everything you wanted tonight?"

Aiden didn't notice the sharp breath she pulled through her nose or the subtle shift of her hips as her thighs pressed in just a little tighter—like she was trying to trap the heat, to keep it from spilling over. The way her nails dug into the tablecloth, like she needed something to ground her, to keep her from coming undone right then and there.

But Griffin did.

Because she knew.

She fucking knew.

This wasn't over.

This was just the beginning.

He licked his lips, letting her watch. Letting her imagine that tongue sliding between her thighs, dragging over that soaked little pussy. Until she was crying for him, begging, trembling.

And when her breath hitched? When her teeth dug into her bottom lip and her fingers flexed on the table?

Griffin smirked. *Game fucking on, Red.* But he wasn't done with her yet. Under the table, he shifted slightly, his knee pressing more firmly against hers. His fingers drifting up to toy with the rim of his glass, movements slow, measured. He wanted her to feel it. Wanted her to squirm. Wanted her to *need*.

And fuck, she was unraveling.

He could practically smell her arousal, thick and heady. Drowning out the scent of whiskey and grilled steak.

He reached for his phone again, typing out another message without looking away from her.

> Griffin: Lace thong or nothing? You're dripping for me, aren't you? Maybe you should excuse yourself. Go to the bathroom. Slide your fingers between those slick little petals and pretend it's me.

He hit send.

The second her phone vibrated, she jolted, thighs clamping tight beneath the table. Just the sight of it made his cock twitch.

But the room didn't stop for them.

Silverware clinked softly from a nearby table, someone laughed too loud at the bar, and the faint hum of music pulsed through the air, just enough to make every second stretch. A waiter passed behind her, carrying a tray of drinks. The scent of roasted garlic and something citrusy drifted past. Life moved on.

But he only watched her.

The way she reacted. How her pupils dilated, swallowing up the color of her eyes like she was seconds from forgetting where she was.

Still, she didn't break.

She picked up her phone with fingers that trembled—but not out of fear. No, it was restraint. Precision. She read the message, lips parting just enough to catch the edge of her bottom lip between her teeth. Her cheeks flushed, thighs shifting once beneath the table.

But this time, when her gaze lifted to his, she didn't look ashamed.

She looked aware.

Daring.

Like she knew exactly what she was doing to him. And liked having him on the edge of fucking groaning in a crowded restaurant.

A second later, his phone vibrated in his pocket.

> Wren: I don't need to pretend. My fingers are already soaked. If you were smart, you'd meet me in the bathroom to find out what I'm wearing.

Griffin's cock throbbed, hard and unrelenting, his entire body locking up with white-hot arousal.

Fuck.

He clenched his jaw, his grip tightening around his glass. His gaze locked onto hers, and she smirked—fucking smirked—before sucking her bottom lip between her teeth like she knew exactly what she was doing to him.

Oh, she was going to fucking pay for that.

Griffin leaned forward, his voice a low growl meant only for her. "You better finish your drink fast, sweetheart. Because when I get my hands on you, you won't be able to stand."

Wren's breath hitched, but she held her ground. Calm on the surface, fire just beneath. Her legs shifted beneath the table, a subtle squeeze, slow and deliberate, like she was chasing the friction on purpose. Her pulse fluttered in the hollow of her throat, but her eyes? Those jade greens didn't waver. Her eyes stayed steady, smoldering, drinking him in. Daring him to react.

This wasn't just a game anymore.

It was war.

And Griffin had every intention of winning.

But Wren wasn't about to let him have all the control.

She shifted under the table, her foot dragging back up his calf, slower this time, more purposeful. Griffin barely reacted, his expression unreadable, but she knew better. She could feel the tension in him, the way his body locked up, the way his fingers gripped the glass just a little tighter.

She raised a brow as her red lips stretched across her face.

She traced the inside of his thigh, pushing higher, pressing the arch of her foot against the thick bulge straining beneath his jeans. His jaw flexed, his nostrils flaring slightly, but he didn't move. Didn't react.

So she pressed harder.

Griffin exhaled through his nose, taking another sip of whiskey like she wasn't deliberately trying to break him in front of her brother. Like she wasn't rolling her foot just enough to make his cock twitch, just enough to make it impossible for him to ignore.

Aiden cleared his throat, looking up from his menu. "So, what are we thinking? Starters?"

Griffin didn't take his eyes off Wren, placing his elbows on the table. "Whatever Wren wants," he murmured, voice thick with heat. "She seems… hungry."

Her breath came shallow, tight in her chest.

He was playing along, but he wasn't cracking. Not yet.

Fine.

She slid her foot up just a little more, rubbing deliberately, feeling how painfully hard he was for her. "I think I'll start with something light," she said, deceptively sweet. "Something I can… savor."

Griffin's fingers twitched around his glass, his gaze darkening, but still —he didn't budge.

The bastard.

Aiden nodded, completely unaware. "Sounds good. Maybe some bread too."

Wren barely heard him. She was too focused on Griffin.

She leaned forward, resting her chin in her hand. "You're awfully quiet, Griffin," she murmured, tilting her head. "Not enjoying yourself?"

His lips curled, slow and lazy, his fingers dragging along the rim of his glass. "Oh, I'm enjoying myself just fine, sweetheart."

She smirked, pressing her foot harder, rubbing slow circles. "Good," she whispered. "Because I'm just getting started."

Griffin's throat bobbed, a flicker of something dangerous crossing his face before he schooled his features again. But Wren knew—*knew*—he was barely holding on.

The waiter arrived, breaking the moment, and she reluctantly pulled her foot away. But the damage was done. He was wrecked. And he was going to do something about it.

As dinner wound down, the air between them only got heavier and thicker. *Needier.*

They couldn't do anything here. Not with Aiden right fucking there. But they had to get out of here. Had to be alone.

Griffin shot her a look, something dark, something knowing, and she felt her pulse spike.

They needed to figure out a way to slip away.

And soon.

12

RUINS

IT WAS JUST past eight when they stepped outside the restaurant, the ocean breeze curling through the warm night air. Salty wind danced along Wren's skin, but it did nothing to cool the heat still simmering beneath the surface.

Griffin leaned against his truck, arms crossed, his gaze flicking between Aiden and Wren as they talked beside him—pretending like the last two hours hadn't been a silent war waged beneath the table. His posture was relaxed, but every muscle in his body was coiled tight, wired from the way she'd pushed him… teased him… made him ache with only her eyes and the slightest of touches.

Aiden shifted, glancing between them, oblivious to the tension crackling in the air. "So, what's next? Calling it a night?"

Wren didn't miss a beat. This was the moment she'd been waiting for. She slipped on that sweet smile, the one that always meant trouble. "Well, since we're out and you brought it up earlier…" Her eyes slid to Griffin, full of challenge. "We should go see Griffin's condo. You know, so I have more housing options to consider."

Aiden frowned, already shaking his head. "I'm sure Griffin doesn't want company this late. It's Sunday—man has to work in the morning."

Wren's smile was laced with both mischief and innocence. "Aiden, he owns the fucking company. Do you want to ask him, or do I need to?"

The hesitation in Aiden's eyes was brief but telling. "If you don't want to go, I can get my car and check it out myself."

"That's not happening." Aiden's response was instant, protective.

With a heavy sigh, he finally turned to Griffin. "You cool with this?"

Griffin let the silence stretch, watching Wren through hooded eyes. He could see the way she stood a little taller, defiant, waiting to see if he'd fold. Or if he'd remind her exactly who held the reins.

He exhaled through his nose, dragging out the moment before giving a slow nod. "Yeah, fine. Let's go."

Aiden headed to his car, but Wren lingered, her gaze locking onto Griffin's. No words were exchanged—just that look. The one that said this isn't over. The one that dared him to make good on every filthy promise he'd whispered without speaking.

Griffin's lips twitched as he climbed into his truck, the weight of anticipation settling low in his stomach.

The drive north was filled with hollow conversation. Aiden rambled about house specs and property values, while Wren and Griffin stayed locked in a silent battle of glances through rearview mirrors and reflections in windows. Every mile stretched tighter, every breath heavier.

By the time they reached his private lot, Griffin could feel the restraint fraying at the edges.

Inside the condo, Aiden's curiosity took over—asking about square footage, market value, and how long Griffin had lived there. Wren played along, nodding and smiling, but her focus wasn't on the view or the design.

It was on the counters. The shower. The bedroom.

Her voice dropped when she asked, "The bathroom must be nice. A walk-in shower? I bet it's spacious, right?" Her fingers trailed along the marble countertop like she was already picturing being bent over it.

Griffin's lips twitched, fighting the urge to drag her onto it right then. "Plenty of space," he answered smoothly. "And the counters? They can handle… a lot."

Aiden, oblivious as ever, chimed in with a nod. "Good craftsmanship."

But Wren wasn't done. Eyes locked on Griffin as she asked, "And the bedroom? I bet that's something worth seeing."

Griffin cocked a brow, the heat in his gaze darkening. "Do I show her or tell her?"

Aiden waved a hand dismissively. "You can tell her."

Griffin pointed down the hall. "End of the hall, to the left."

Wren didn't hesitate. She disappeared down the hallway, her hips swaying with every step—a silent taunt Griffin felt in his cock.

In his bedroom, her fingers glided over the sheets, the furniture. She took her time taking in Griffin's sanctuary. And then, with a wicked grin, she slipped out of her lace thong and laid it on the corner of his bed like a calling card.

By the time she returned, Aiden was wrapping up his questions. Griffin stood at the kitchen counter, arms crossed, his gaze razor-sharp as it followed her every move.

"Well," Aiden stretched, glancing at his watch, "we should head out."

Wren forced a casual nod. "Yeah, it's late."

Griffin's smirk was lethal. "I was about to take a shower and call it a night anyway."

Her stomach flipped, heat pooling low as she caught the double meaning.

As they walked out, Wren's fingers danced over her phone, typing a message before she even reached the car.

> Wren: You in the shower yet? I keep thinking about how much space you have in there... plenty of room for company.

It didn't even take a full minute for her phone to vibrate.

> Griffin: And yet, you're not here. Guess you'll have to keep imagining.

She bit her lip, slipping into Aiden's car, her mind already racing with images she couldn't shake.

GRIFFIN STRETCHED OUT IN BED, TV FLICKERING IN THE BACKGROUND, BUT his focus wasn't on the screen. It had been two hours since Wren and Aiden had left, and his body was still tense, still burning from every look, every word, every silent promise Wren had made with her eyes.

Then he saw it.

Resting on the corner of his bed like a declaration of war—the lace thong. Delicate, black, and sinful.

His fingers curled around it, the soft fabric almost mocking him. He brought it to his nose, inhaling deeply, his jaw ticking as her sweet and intoxicating scent wrapped around him. Fucking. Dangerous.

The clock read 11:15 when a knock echoed through his condo.

Griffin exhaled sharply, already knowing.

When he opened the door, there she was—leaning against the frame, that same infuriating shit-eating grin playing on her lips.

"I think I left something behind earlier," she purred, her voice like silk wrapped around a dare.

His grip tightened on the doorframe. "That so?"

Her brow arched, playful and bold. "Are you going to let me in? Or are we having this conversation in the hallway?"

He should've told her to leave. Should've slammed the door and walked away.

But he didn't.

"Come in." His voice came out rough as he stepped aside.

She brushed past him, her body grazing his, every movement calculated to push him closer to the edge.

The door clicked shut behind her, the sound final, like the start of something neither of them could stop.

Griffin stood there, arms crossed over his chest, muscles flexed beneath the dim light. His voice was a low growl. "What the fuck are you doing here?"

Wren's gaze dropped, lingering over every inch of his bare torso, down to the clear outline of his cock pressing against his sweatpants.

"I told you," she whispered, stepping closer, "I think I left something behind."

His smirk was dark. "You mean the lace thong sitting on my bed?"

Her lips curled. "No idea how it got there."

He caught her wrist when she reached for him, his grip firm. "You're playing a dangerous game, ma'am."

"And what happens when I win?" she shot back, her chin tilting defiantly.

"You won't."

The air thickened, tension snapping like a live wire between them. She placed her hand on his chest, nails scraping down, her breath ghosting over his lips. "Maybe you need to relax."

His fingers wrapped around her wrist tighter. "You need to stop."

"Make me," she challenged, her voice barely a whisper.

His restraint shattered for half a second—just enough for his hand to find her throat, his thumb brushing over her pulse as it pounded beneath his touch.

"I'm serious, Wren," he warned, his voice lethal. "You don't want this side of me."

Her smirk only deepened. "I do."

When she guided his hand to her throat, offering herself up like a sacrifice, his control frayed at the edges.

"You don't know what you're asking for," he rasped, his other hand skimming down her waist.

"Then show me."

For a heartbeat, he nearly did. But then—he shoved her back, stepping away like she'd scorched him. "No."

She blinked, breathless. "No?"

His hands balled into fists, he said through clenched teeth, "I respect your brother too much."

Frustration flashed in her eyes. "Since when do you care about rules?"

"Since it's you."

She stepped forward again, refusing to back down. "What if I don't care?"

His hands shot out, gripping her hips, yanking her flush against him before pushing her away, his voice a growl. "That's the problem. I do."

She dragged her nails down his chest one last time, voice low and edged in heat. "This isn't over."

She turned to leave. But didn't make it far.

His hand caught her throat, not gentle, not asking. Fingers curling with intent, thumb pressing just enough to make her pause, to make her feel it.

Daring her to move.

Daring her to stay.

Her breath sharpened, spine snapping straight, but her eyes burned when they met his.

His voice was molten, slow, and savage against her skin. "Wren... I wouldn't fuck you. I'd claim you. Possess you. Ruin you."

Her pulse thundered in her ears, heat flooding every inch of her body as he finished, "Make you mine in ways you don't even understand."

Then he opened the door, casting one last look over his shoulder, voice low and lethal. "Think real hard before you come back in here, Wren—because next time, I won't let you leave."

As she drove back to Aiden's house, her grip on the steering wheel was unsteady, her mind a hurricane of tangled thoughts and raw, aching need. His words clawed at her, burrowing deep, making her pulse throb between her thighs. *Claim. Possess. Ruin.*

Was that what he meant? Was that the side of him no one ever saw? The part he hid behind that sharp control, the part that could break her? And why—why did she want to be broken by him?

Her breath came shallow, her body still tingling, her core still drenched in the heat he'd left behind. Did he care? Or was this just about power? About marking her, making her his?

Because if Griffin Hayes decided to claim someone... She knew with absolute certainty that he wouldn't just take.

He would *own.*

And Wren was already halfway his.

13

EDGE OF US

GRIFFIN WOKE to the sharp blare of his alarm slicing through the quiet; the harsh buzz rattled against the wood of his nightstand like a warning shot. His eyes cracked open, the early morning light bleeding through half-closed blinds, casting long, golden streaks across the room. Dust floated in the beams like tiny ghosts, swirling above the tangled mess of sheets twisted around his legs.

His body felt heavy. Every muscle weighed down, tense, and aching. Not from lack of sleep, but from something far worse.

Her.

Wren fucking Sinclair.

Even with the cool morning air brushing over his skin, his body still burned, still wired from the night before. His jaw clenched as flashes of her filled his head—the way she stood in his doorway, daring him with every look, every breath. The way her pulse had pounded beneath his palm when he wrapped his hand around her throat, watching her unravel without him even needing to undress her.

And those words...

"I wouldn't fuck you. I'd claim you. Possess you. Ruin you."

His own voice haunted him—low, dark, final. A promise disguised as a threat. And then, like a fucking idiot, he let her walk away.

Griffin exhaled sharply, scrubbing a hand down his face, dragging his palm across the stubble lining his jaw. He never let women get in his head. Never let lust turn into something that clawed beneath his skin and stayed there gnawing at his control. But Wren? She wasn't just under his skin. She was in his veins. Pulsing with every heartbeat. Every breath. Like she'd carved herself into his bloodstream and didn't plan on leaving.

His fingers threaded through his hair, tugging at the roots as he sat up on the edge of the bed, muscles coiled tight, chest heavy. The ache between his legs was impossible to ignore—morning wood, yeah, but this wasn't just biology.

He glanced down, jaw ticking when he saw the thick outline pressing against his boxers. Pulsing. Deprived—still aching for the release he'd denied himself last night. His cock throbbed at just the thought of her. How she would've sounded with his name breaking past her lips, muffled against his mouth as he fucked her against the sink in that restaurant bathroom. Her dress bunched around her waist, one hand gripping her throat, the other dragging her hips back to meet every brutal thrust. Until she was dripping down his cock, legs shaking, voice gone.

But no. He hadn't done it.

Instead, he made her leave. Let her walk out with that pout tugging at her lips, all attitude and temptation, knowing damn well she had him wrapped around her finger—without even taking what they were both starving for.

"Fuck," he muttered under his breath, shoving himself off the bed.

The cold bite of the hardwood floor did nothing to ground him as he stalked into the bathroom, flipping the shower on and stepping beneath the scalding spray. The water hit him like needles, burning down his back, but it couldn't wash her away. He couldn't shake the phantom feel of her. How close she'd gotten, how far she'd pushed him without crossing the line. Her scent still lingered in his sheets somehow, like temptation had soaked into the fabric.

And the only thing she left behind?

A pair of panties he hadn't even earned. A reminder that she could wreck him without ever letting him have her.

His hands braced against the tile, head bowed as the water cascaded over him, muscles tense, every nerve ending still wired with frustration. His cock didn't soften. Not even under the punishing heat. If anything, the memory of her only made it worse—made him harder—needier. Angry at himself for letting her leave, for pretending like walking away made him noble.

Soap. Shampoo. Rinse. He forced himself through the routine, clinging to the structure like it could drag him out of the mess she'd left him in. He needed to clear his head. He had work. Meetings. Shit that actually mattered.

Work didn't tease him under the table until he was ready to snap.

Work didn't leave lace panties on his bed like a trophy. Work didn't make him wake up so hard it hurt.

By the time he stepped out of the shower and toweled off, Griffin had almost convinced himself he could compartmentalize it. That he could shove Wren Sinclair into the same box he put every other reckless decision he didn't have time for.

He yanked on a pair of fitted khakis, a crisp polo, and his boots—defaulting to professionalism like it was armor. Like fabric and routine could fix what was unraveling inside him.

But the second he grabbed his keys and stepped into his truck, reality punched him square in the chest.

He didn't start the engine.

Didn't move.

His hands gripped the steering wheel, knuckles white, muscles in his forearms flexing with the effort it took just to breathe. His jaw locked tight, his pulse thudding in his ears as the silence closed in around him.

And then... His eyes dropped to his phone.

It sat in his lap. Silent. No messages. No missed calls.

She hadn't texted.

Of course she hadn't.

Wren knew exactly what she was doing. Leaving him mindfucked. Letting him stew in it. Letting him wonder if she was thinking about him the way he couldn't stop thinking about her.

His fingers twitched, the urge to grab the phone overwhelming. To type out something—anything—just to hear her voice, to know if she was as fucked up over this as he was.

But he didn't.

Griffin Hayes didn't chase.

At least, that's what he kept telling himself.

With a growl low in his throat, he tossed the phone onto the passenger seat like it was the problem, not the fact that his mind was still replaying every second of last night. The way her breath hitched when he pressed her against the door. The way her eyes darkened when he told her exactly what he'd do if he lost control.

He dragged a hand down his face, exhaling through his nose before finally throwing the truck into drive.

Work.

Focus on work.

It was a lie, and he fucking knew it.

Because no matter how fast he drove, no matter how many spreadsheets or contracts waited on his desk, he couldn't outrun the truth.

Wren Sinclair wasn't just in his head.

She was everywhere.

And Griffin had a sinking feeling that no amount of control was going to save him from what came next.

THE DAY DRAGGED LIKE HELL.

Meetings blurred into emails, emails bled into phone calls. And through it all, Griffin Hayes sat there. Pretending to give a damn. Every spreadsheet he stared at. Every voice that tried to pull him into logistics and numbers was nothing but static. White noise in a headspace that had been hijacked by one person.

Wren.

No matter how hard he tried to focus, she was there. Etched into every thought. Branded beneath his skin like a scar he didn't want to heal.

The image of her across the table last night was burned into his memory. The way she toyed with him, those legs sliding up his thigh like she owned him. The wicked gleam in her eyes when she licked her lips, fully aware of the war she was waging under the table. And when he whispered filth in her ear—when he promised to ruin her—she didn't flinch. She fucking squirmed.

Now? Now he was the one squirming.

Ruined by Wren Raine Sinclair, without her even laying a hand on him today.

Voices droning and figures flashing across the projector screen, the boardroom buzzed around him, but Griffin wasn't there. Not really. He sat at the head of the table, fingers tapping against the polished wood, his mind miles away, tangled in red hair, green eyes, and the memory of a smile that could bring any man to his knees.

"Griffin?"

His name snapped him back. His gaze flicked to Justice, his operations manager. Who was eyeing him like he'd grown two heads. Griffin cleared his throat, straightening in his seat, forcing himself to look the part of the man in charge.

"Run it by me again."

Justice hesitated, brows pinched and concern flickering across her face, but launched back into supply chain numbers. Griffin nodded along, but it was useless. His head wasn't in freight costs or delivery schedules.

It was still in that fucking condo with his hand wrapped around Wren's throat and the sound she made. Sharp and shallow, like the gasp of a match right before it ignites.

Why did he stop?

That question gnawed at him. Griffin Hayes didn't hesitate. He didn't pause when he wanted something. He took it. That was how he built his business, how he lived his life. No apologies. No second guesses.

So why hadn't he taken her?

Because she was Aiden's sister? That should've been enough. That should've been the red line he never crossed. But deep down, he knew that wasn't the reason—not really.

His desk was a mess of contracts and supplier agreements. Pending deals stacked high like they could distract him if he just buried himself deep enough. He tried—God, he tried. Signed papers without reading them. Took calls he couldn't remember five minutes later. Sat through a luncheon where he barely touched his food.

But all day, it was her.

Her voice in his ear. That *"make me"* whisper she teased. The way she challenged him. Not just with her words, but with every look, every breath, like she knew he was fighting himself.

His grip tightened around his pen until it nearly snapped in half. This wasn't about a quick fuck. It wasn't about the thrill of chasing his best friend's off-limits sister.

It was Wren.

And that was the most dangerous part.

By the time the office lights dimmed and the last meeting ended, Griffin should've been exhausted. Instead, he was wired, strung out on adrenaline, frustration, and the kind of tension that didn't fade when the sun went down.

He sat in his office, the glass of whiskey sweating beside him, untouched. His head tipped back against the chair, eyes staring at the ceiling like it held answers he already knew.

She was under his skin.

That was the truth—the ugly, undeniable truth.

He hadn't walked away last night because of Aiden. He hadn't walked away because he was playing by some bullshit code of honor. He walked away because Wren Sinclair wasn't temporary. She wasn't a quick fix. She was the type of woman who'd rip through his life like a goddamn hurricane and leave him begging for the wreckage.

And that scared the hell out of him.

Griffin Hayes was always in control. Always the one holding the leash. But with Wren?

For the first time, he didn't know if he was the one doing the claiming. Or if he was already the one being claimed.

He pushed out of his chair, unable to sit still any longer. The walls of his office felt too tight, too suffocating, like if he stayed there another second, he'd combust.

So he drove.

No destination. No thought. Just asphalt under his tires and the growl of his engine drowning out the chaos in his head.

It wasn't until he pulled up to his job site that he realized where he'd gone.

The skeleton of his future stood before him—wooden beams stretching toward the darkening sky, bare bones framed against the horizon. This was supposed to be his escape. His reset button. The place where things finally slowed down.

But as he stepped out, boots crunching against gravel, all he felt was the same damn storm swirling inside him.

The house was quiet. Unfinished. A reflection of everything Griffin couldn't admit: that even when he built something solid, something meant to last, there was always a part of him waiting for it to fall apart.

His fingers dragged along the raw beams as he walked through the frame, picturing the porch, the wraparound views, the mornings spent watching the tide roll in. Something permanent in a life filled with temporary fixes.

But even here, even in the middle of what was supposed to be his sanctuary, all he could think about was her.

Twenty-four hours. That's all it had been. And she'd already fucking branded herself into every corner of his mind.

His phone buzzed in his pocket, cutting through the heavy silence.

He didn't look right away. Didn't have to.

Somehow, he knew.

When he finally pulled it out, her name lit up the screen.

> Wren: I meant what I said, Griffin. And I need to talk to you.

His stomach tightened, jaw clenching as he leaned against the wooden frame. Talk? Since when did Wren Sinclair ever want to talk?

Conflicted, his fingers hovered over the screen, expression tense and sharp, like he was seconds from unraveling and pretending not to care.

> Griffin: Talk? That's all you want? Didn't seem like that last night.

Her reply came fast. Too fast.

> Wren: Would you rather I say I miss you? That I haven't stopped thinking about your hands on me?

A low curse rumbled in his chest, his grip tightening around the phone like he could squeeze the tension out of himself. That word—*miss*—it shouldn't have hit as hard as it did.

But it did. It hit everywhere. He dragged his tongue across his bottom lip, staring at her message like it might explode.

> Griffin: Miss me? That's a dangerous thing to admit, sweetheart.

Her response was a dagger straight to his already fragile control.

> Wren: Why? Afraid you might miss me back?

His pulse pounded in his throat. Fuck, she knew exactly how to pull him apart piece by piece.

> Griffin: You think I haven't?

This time, she made him wait—and it only made things worse. His chest was tight, every second stretching longer than it should've. When her message finally appeared, it wasn't playful. It wasn't coy.

It was lethal.

> Wren: Then why did you let me walk away?

Griffin's breath left him in a harsh exhale. He didn't have an easy answer. At least not one he was willing to give. But he wasn't going to lie either.

> Griffin: Because I don't do things halfway. And if I'd kept you there last night, you wouldn't have left at all.

Let her sit with that.
But Wren? She didn't sit still.

> Wren: Then maybe you should keep me.

> Wren: I mean... should have kept me. There.

That slip, that almost, had Griffin's lips curling into something possessive.

> Griffin: That almost sounded like a want and need.

> Wren: Maybe it was. Maybe it wasn't.

He chuckled low, shaking his head.

> Griffin: You don't get to play coy now, sweetheart. You typed it. Thought about it. And still hit send.

Her answer was sharp. Honest.

> Wren: Maybe I was hoping you'd notice.

His chest tightened, fingers flexing against the railing.

> Griffin: Trust me, I notice everything about you.

The pause that followed was heavy, like they both knew they were toeing a line neither of them could uncross.

What she sent next had him pausing, trying to find any semblance of control.

> Wren: I want to see you.

That was it. No games. No teasing. Griffin glanced out over the empty lot, the unfinished walls casting long shadows in the fading light.

> Griffin: I'm at my house—the job site.

> Wren: Where's that?

He smirked, feeling the shift, the power tilting back in his favor.

> Griffin: Figure it out and come find me.

He tossed his phone onto the sawhorse beside him, arms crossing over his chest as the breeze picked up off the marsh.

But before she could fire back, before she could challenge him again, he dropped a pin location.

A tease. A test.

A fucking invitation.

And now?

Now, he waited.

14

BLUEPRINTS

IT HAD BEEN twenty minutes since he sent that text.

Griffin leaned against his truck, arms crossed, fingers drumming lightly against the metal. Every tap a reminder of the storm brewing beneath his skin. The air was thick with humidity, the scent of saltwater drifting in from the marsh, but it wasn't the weather making him sweat.

It was her.

He heard it before he saw it. The slow crunch of gravel beneath tires rolling over the drive. That sound alone pulled a smirk to his lips, but in the back of his mind, her last message played on repeat.

Maybe you should keep me.

That wasn't a line. That wasn't a tease. That was dangerous. That was a sentence loaded with implications Griffin Hayes didn't entertain. Women didn't say shit like that to him, and if they did, he shut it down before it could sink in.

But Wren? Wren let it fester. Let it claw at places inside him he didn't even realize were vulnerable.

Her car came to a stop. The engine cut off and the door creaked open like the calm before a storm. And then she stepped out.

Wren.

All long legs and effortless confidence, her sharp green eyes locked onto him like she was sizing up a fight she had every intention of winning. There was something different in her gaze this time—not just heat, not just challenge, but curiosity. Like she was trying to figure him out… and maybe herself, too.

Her lips curved into that infuriating grin as she let her eyes drag over him, slow and deliberate. "Well, look at you," she drawled, amusement coating every word. "Mr. Halfway-Dressed-for-Business."

Griffin tipped his chin, a smirk playing on his lips, welcoming the game. "This is how we dress. Can you imagine wearing a suit and shit to a job site?"

She stepped closer, her gaze lingering on the way his polo clung to every inch of muscle, her fingers twitching at her sides like they were itching to touch. "Just figured it was to show off those arms."

His eyes darkened, that spark flaring to life between them. "If I wanted to show off, sweetheart, you'd know it."

Her soft laugh was more breath than sound, but Griffin caught the way her throat worked when she swallowed, the way her gaze flickered too long over his chest. She was holding back, and not well.

He let the silence stretch between them, waiting her out, before finally exhaling. "So, what did you want—"

But she cut him off, her voice shifting. Softer. Real.

"Griffin... This house is going to be beautiful."

His words caught in his throat. He wasn't expecting that—not from her. Not after the way they'd spent the last forty-eight hours wrapped in tension and teasing. But now? Now she was looking at the frame of his future like she could see more than just wood and nails. Like she saw him.

She turned toward the skeleton of the house, her fingers trailing along the raw beams. Silently and guarded, Griffin watched as something unspoken passed over her face.

"Can I see it?" she asked, glancing back at him, her voice quieter this time.

He hesitated. This was his sanctuary. The only thing in his life that wasn't temporary. But as she stood there, waiting, not pushing, not teasing, he realized she wasn't here to play games.

Finally, he nodded. "Sure. Come on."

WREN STEPPED INSIDE LIKE SHE BELONGED THERE, HER FINGERTIPS GLIDING over the exposed wood with a reverence that made Griffin's chest ache. She wasn't just looking, she was feeling it. Understanding it in a way no one else ever had.

"It looks familiar," she murmured, her voice almost wistful. "It's beautiful."

Griffin leaned against a support beam, arms across his chest as he studied her. "Looks familiar?"

She nodded, a soft smile curving her lips, and for once, it wasn't laced with sarcasm or challenge. It was… honest. "It's similar to my dream house."

That caught him off guard. His head tilted, genuine curiosity creeping in. "Yeah? Tell me about it."

She hesitated, and for a moment, he thought she'd deflect. That she'd turn it into another flirtatious quip. But then she breathed out, slow and steady, her walls dropping just enough to let him in.

Her hands lifted, like she was painting the image in the air. "The siding will be gray, board and batten," she said softly, her voice carrying that faraway tone of someone who had pictured this a thousand times before. "The color of stormy skies… or driftwood after the tide's dried it in the sun."

Griffin's chest tightened as he followed her words, seeing the vision take shape through her eyes.

"Roof?" he asked, his voice lower now, gentler.

"Black," she replied without missing a beat. "Clean contrast. But the accents—those will be golden weathered oak. Imperfect. Real."

She turned to him then, and for the first time since he met her, there was no armor in her gaze. No sharp edges. Just… Wren. Unfiltered and raw.

"The porch columns," she continued, stepping closer to the heart of the frame, "stone base, then oak. The kind that tells a story just by standing there. The porch will wrap around, grounding it, making it feel like it's always belonged."

Griffin swallowed hard, the weight of her words settling in places he didn't know were exposed. She wasn't describing a house.

She was describing a home.

Her voice dropped to a whisper as she glanced toward the marsh. "And a dock. Stained to match. Lanterns on every post, lighting the way even when it's dark."

She smiled—soft, sad, and full of longing. "At the end of it? A fire pit. A place to sit. To just… be."

Griffin's throat felt tight, his usual smirk nowhere to be found. Because in that moment, he didn't see the bold, reckless woman who pushed every one of his buttons.

He saw her.

The version no one else got to see.

And fuck… It did something to him.

Without thinking, he reached out his hand.

"Like this?"

Wren blinked down at his hand, something fluttering in her chest she wasn't ready to name. Slowly, she placed her hand in his, letting herself be led, for once.

Griffin grabbed the cooler off his tailgate and guided her around the corner of the house.

When they turned the bend, Wren froze.

Her breath caught, eyes wide as they landed on the dock stretching out over the water—unfinished, rough. Bathed in golden light from a few scattered lanterns the crew must've left behind. Two fold-out chairs sat at the edge, perfectly framing the horizon where the sky kissed the marsh.

Emotion slammed into her chest before she could stop it.

Her throat tightened. Her vision blurred. A tear slid down her cheek, uninvited and unstoppable.

Griffin saw it, but he didn't say a word. He didn't tease. Didn't smirk. He just stood there, letting her feel whatever the hell this place had stirred up inside her.

She wiped at her cheek, laughing softly through the lump in her throat. "I'm sorry."

Griffin shook his head, his voice a steady whisper, "There's nothing to apologize for, Wren."

She looked at him, really looked at him, and realized this was the side of Griffin Hayes no one got to see. The side buried beneath sharp words and cocky grins. The man who understood moments like this. Who respected them.

"I didn't expect that from you," she whispered.

He smirked, but it wasn't arrogant, it was something softer. "Told you… most people only know Hayes. They don't know Griffin."

Her heart stuttered at that. At how simple he made it sound—and how fucking important it felt.

She took a shaky breath, stepping closer, her voice barely more than a murmur. "Well, Mr. Hayes… I'd like to know Griffin."

For the first time in a long time, Griffin felt something dangerous stir in his chest.

Because letting her in? Letting her see him?

That wasn't a game.

That was everything he'd spent his life avoiding.

And yet, standing here with her hand still in his, he realized…

He wanted to.

15

WALLS CAVING

AT FIRST, Griffin answered her questions like it was second nature. With the same kind of ease and confidence that came from building something with his bare hands. He talked about Hayes Development the way most people talked about a lifelong friend—steady, reliable, always there when nothing else was. The late nights grinding through plans, the early mornings on job sites before the sun even thought about rising. The risks he shouldn't have taken. The failures that nearly gutted him. The moments he stared at the ceiling wondering if it was all about to collapse.

His voice carried the weight of survival, the pride of a man who had poured everything he had into something that couldn't just walk away.

Wren listened, drawn in by the rawness beneath his words. There was no bravado here. No cocky smirk or flirtatious glint. Just a man who had fought tooth and nail to carve out a life that couldn't be taken from him.

But then—she asked the last two questions.

And everything shifted.

Griffin's words died on his tongue, his posture stiffened, and that easy confidence, the armor he wore so damn well, cracked.

It wasn't obvious at first. Just a slight narrowing of his eyes. The way his jaw ticked once…twice… Before he looked away.

But Wren felt it.

The air between them thickened, no longer charged with playful tension, but something heavier. Darker. The kind of weight that settles deep in your bones. The kind that only comes from a scar you stopped talking about years ago.

She watched him carefully, her heart tightening as his gaze drifted toward the horizon. But she knew he wasn't looking at the sunset. No—he was staring at something far beyond it.

A memory. A ghost. A wound that never really closed.

Wren's throat bobbed. She knew that look. Knew what it meant when someone's past reached out and wrapped its hand around their throat, squeezing just enough to remind them that pain doesn't forget.

Her fingers twitched before she finally reached out and settled her hand on his forearm, soft and tentative. A grounding touch. A silent *I'm here if you need it.*

"If you don't want to answer…" she whispered, her voice careful, "it's fine."

For a moment, she thought he'd shut down completely. That Griffin Hayes would retreat behind that wall of sarcasm and indifference, toss out a cocky remark, and leave her question to die in the space between them.

But instead, he inhaled, like he was dragging something out of himself he'd sworn never to touch again.

"No," he rasped, his voice rough around the edges. "It's been long enough. I just… I don't talk about it."

Wren opened her mouth to tell him again—he didn't have to.

But then his hand covered hers, right where it rested on the arm of the fold-out chair.

Warm. Firm. Steady.

And just like that, she felt it.

This wasn't for her curiosity. This wasn't a story he told to anyone.

This was trust.

"I want to tell you," he murmured, his thumb brushing against her knuckles. "I want you to know."

Her chest ached, tightening in a way she wasn't prepared for.

Because this wasn't the man her brother always talked about. This wasn't the legend of Griffin Hayes—the smooth talker, the heartbreaker, the man who could make any woman fall into bed with a single look.

This was something raw. Unfiltered. A man cracking open a door he'd welded shut long ago and letting her see the wreckage inside.

So she stayed quiet. Let him lead. Let him bleed.

"I haven't always been this guy," he began, his voice steady but hollow, like he was reciting an obituary for the version of himself he'd buried. "The guy that doesn't call. The guy that leaves before the sheets even cool. The one everyone expects to disappear before dawn."

Wren's breath hitched, her heart pulling tight in her chest.

"There was a time I believed in all that fairytale shit," he continued, his gaze locked on the horizon like it was the only thing holding him together. "In love. Forever. The whole 'better or worse' bullshit they sell you when you're too young to know better."

His throat bobbed hard.

"I wanted that," he confessed, voice dropping lower. "I wanted it more than anything."

A heavy and suffocating silence stretched between them. Until he spoke again.

"Until her."

The word landed like a punch.

Not a name. Not at first.

Just... *her*.

Wren's hand tightened around his forearm, offering him something. She didn't even know what, but needed him to know she was still there.

"What happened?" she asked gently, even though she already knew where this story was headed.

THE WATER LAPPED BENEATH THE DOCK IN LAZY, UNEVEN STROKES, SOFT and constant, like it had been whispering there long before they arrived and would keep whispering long after they were gone. A breeze drifted in off the sound, cool against their skin, but laced with intermittent waves of heavy, lingering heat—thick and pressing, much like the emotions they were trying to unpack with every quiet breath and half-finished sentence.

The breeze also carried the smell of the fresh cut lumber still in the air from the dock being half complete, the sharp tang of sawdust clinging to the air like memory.

Two fold-out chairs sat close, fabric faded, metal frames creaking every time they shifted. Their elbows nearly touched, close enough to feel the heat coming off each other yet not close enough to lean on it.

At their feet sat a battered tent-top cooler, the white of the Igloo logo nearly worn smooth. Sweating under the weight of the heat, a ring of damp settled into the wood beneath it as condensation slid down the sides in lazy streams. Somewhere inside, bottles clinked faintly over slowly melting ice.

Everything was still.

Waiting.

Holding its breath right along with them.

Jaw flexing, he swallowed hard and turned without a word, reaching into the cooler and pulling out a beer like he needed something solid to hold onto.

The bottle hissed as he twisted the cap off, condensation sliding over his knuckles, grounding him in the present even as his mind drifted backward.

As if preparing to go into battle, Griffin let out a deep exhale before he finally spoke.

"Her name was Lia."

The way he said it—it wasn't bitter. It wasn't angry.

It was hollow. Like her name was a ghost that still haunted the edges of his mind.

"We met in college," he continued, his voice distant. "She was… everything. Smart. Driven. Beautiful in that effortless kind of way that made you think you were the luckiest bastard alive just to be in her orbit."

Wren stayed silent, her chest aching as she watched him unravel slowly, piece by piece.

A soft breeze rolled in off the sound, brushing salt and memory across their skin. Crickets sang from the tall grass lining the shore. Filling the silence neither of them dared to break.

Griffin held the bottle loosely in one hand, watching the condensation glide down the glass. It moved slowly, like it was a piece of him unraveling. Like it mirrored the part of him finally letting go—letting Wren see the rubble behind the wall. His fingers tapped against it in an uneven rhythm, quiet but steady, as if the sound was the only thing keeping him tethered.

"We built a life," he said at last, voice frayed at the edges. "Plans. Dreams. The kind of future you don't question… because you're too blind to see the cracks forming underneath."

He didn't look at her. His eyes strayed out to the water, dark and rippling beneath the Carolina sky. Through the reflection in his eyes, she could see the soft seagrass swaying in the wind, unbothered by the weight settling between them.

The bottle tipped in his hand, resting against his thigh as he exhaled a humorless breath and shook his head. "I thought I was doing everything right. I worked my ass off to give us the life we said we wanted. Late nights, early mornings; I kept telling myself it was for us."

His next words were sharp. Bitter.

"But it turns out," he said, clearing his throat, voice tight like the words cost him something. "While I was building our future… she was finding comfort in someone else's present."

Wren's heart sank.

"I came home early from a job site one day," he said, his voice flat now—numb from repeating the memory in his head too many times. "Found her in our bed. With someone else."

Her breath caught. "Griffin…"

He shrugged, but it wasn't casual. It was survival. "After that, I learned my lesson. Don't get attached. Don't believe in forever. Build things that don't fucking leave when they get bored."

His gaze swept across the house frame, the dock, the empty stretch of land.

"This?" he said, motioning around them. The still water, open sky, the quiet that didn't ask for anything. His voice cracked, raw around the edges. "This doesn't lie to you. Doesn't pretend. It doesn't smile in your face while it's falling apart behind your back."

He paused, jaw clenched, swallowing hard. "It doesn't promise you forever and then rip it out from under you." For a moment, the only sound was the wind rustling through the seagrass, the world holding its breath with him.

"Now?" he said, softer. "I'm just a guy who gets good news…" He swallowed. "And have no one to tell it to."

WREN'S THROAT BURNED, TEARS THREATENING TO SURFACE; NOT JUST FOR him, but because every word he said echoed something inside her own broken past.

"That story sounds familiar," she whispered, her voice cracking despite herself.

Griffin finally looked at her—really looked—and for the first time, there was no teasing, no mask. Just two people sitting in the middle of unfinished wood and open wounds.

When she told him her story—the college sweetheart, the engagement, the betrayal—it wasn't rehearsed. It wasn't polished. It spilled out raw and jagged, like she'd been holding it in for far too long.

And Griffin? He didn't interrupt. He didn't offer empty words or sympathy.

He just listened.

When she finished, her chest felt lighter and heavier, all at once.

Griffin emptied the remainder of his bottle. He reached into the cooler, pulled out two beers, and handed her one, their fingers brushing in a silent acknowledgment of everything that had just been laid bare.

He twisted off the cap, lifted his bottle, and the curve of his mouth tugged into something faint. Wry, but real.

"Here's to getting fucked," he said, voice low, a flicker of humor beneath the wreckage. "Getting lost…"

His gaze met hers; something soft curled around the edges of something dangerous. Steady yet unreadable.

"…and maybe getting found."

Wren's lips curved, not quite steady but honest, and she clinked her bottle gently against his.

She didn't think. She just moved.

Resting her head on his shoulder, letting herself breathe him in, letting the weight of the moment settle.

And Griffin?

He didn't flinch. Didn't shift away.

For once, neither of them ran.

No teasing. No games.

Just silence. Just breath. Just this.

Two broken people sitting on a dock in front of the skeleton of a house, wondering if maybe, just maybe, there was still something worth building.

Not from blueprints or beams. But from what remained.

From what had survived the wreckage.

And maybe, from what hadn't.

THEY SAT IN SILENCE. THE KIND THAT WRAPPED AROUND YOU AND SETTLED deep in your bones, the kind that didn't beg to be filled. It just existed. Heavy. Beautiful. Real.

Wren let herself breathe in it, her head still resting lightly on Griffin's shoulder, feeling the steady rise and fall of his chest. For a moment, it was easy to pretend this was normal. That this wasn't complicated. That it wasn't dangerous.

But the universe had a cruel sense of humor.

Just as her body finally relaxed, just as that rare gut-pouring peace began to settle, her phone rang.

The sharp buzz sliced through the calm like a damn buzzsaw.

Wren groaned like it physically hurt, already pulling the phone from her pocket, not needing to check the screen.

Of course.

Aiden.

Because of course. Why wouldn't it be him?

She glanced up, and Griffin was already watching her. Not with that usual cocky grin, though. This one was softer, laced with something quieter. Something she didn't have the nerve to name.

It was a reminder.

A reality check.

That no matter how easy this felt, no matter how natural it was to sit beside him, peeling back layers they didn't show anyone else—this wasn't supposed to be happening.

She swiped to answer, tossing a casual tone into her voice even though her pulse had just shot straight through her throat.

"Nothin'," she said, leaning back in her chair like she wasn't sitting in dangerous territory.

Griffin's beer rested loose in his hand, but his eyes didn't leave her. He didn't need to hear the other side of the call to fill in the blanks:

Where are you? Who are you with? Have you seen Griffin?

Wren rolled her eyes, her lips twitching with that special mix of affection and deep, bone-deep irritation reserved solely for siblings. "I'm in town," she answered coolly, her voice sharp enough to slice through Aiden's next question before he even asked it.

There was a pause, long enough for her posture to shift, for her jaw to tighten.

"I'm not twelve, Aiden. I can go where I want to."

Griffin took a slow sip of his beer, his gaze narrowing; not at her, but at the situation. At the lines they were toeing. The ones they were seconds away from crossing, if they hadn't already.

Wren's voice softened slightly, and Griffin caught the flicker in her expression before she spoke again.

"No, but if you talk to him…" She hesitated, her eyes darting toward Griffin, something unspoken lingering in that glance. "Tell him I wouldn't mind a dinner with him again."

Griffin arched a brow, the corner of his mouth tugging upward despite the weight sitting square in his chest.

She was reckless and playing with fire.

And fuck if it didn't make him want to hand her the match.

"I'll be back when I get back," she finished, all bite again, then hung up and set her phone in the cup holder of the chair, like it hadn't just reminded them how fragile their little bubble actually was.

. . .

Griffin let out a low chuckle, shaking his head. "You really like poking the bear, huh?"

Wren stretched out her legs, her curved lips sliding back into place like armor. "Sorry," she said, zero percent sorry. "I just like fucking with him."

He couldn't help the grin that pulled at his lips. "Yeah, I caught that."

She glanced at him, the playful glint in her eye dimming just a little. "He asked if I ran into you," she admitted, watching him carefully now. "Said he tried to get up with you earlier."

Griffin's tongue swept across his teeth, eyes drifting toward the water. He didn't answer right away. Didn't need to.

"Yeah," he finally muttered. "He's protective over you."

Wren sighed, grabbing her beer, her fingers tracing the condensation on the bottle. "He knows how hard it was for me after... everything. I get it. I do. I appreciate him looking out for me." She paused, her voice firming up. "But I'm capable of making my own decisions."

Griffin nodded.

That wasn't the issue.

She wasn't the issue.

It was the choice they were both making in slow, inching steps. One look, one touch, one lingering second at a time.

He tipped his bottle toward her, his voice quieter now. "True. But Wren..." His eyes locked with hers, serious in a way that made her pulse skip. "This is dangerous. Me and you."

She didn't flinch.

Didn't blink.

Didn't back down.

Instead, she arched a brow, that defiant smirk tugging at her lips. "Mr. Hayes... Are you afraid of a little danger? Or is it my brother you're scared of?"

Half laugh, half frustration, he let out a breath, shaking his head. "Neither," he said, his voice rough around the edges and low. "But both."

That made her pause.

Because for the first time, the teasing dropped away. And what remained? It was heavier than flirtation. It was truth.

"Your brother isn't just a friend to me, Wren," Griffin continued, his voice steady but filled with something she couldn't quite place—regret, maybe. Or warning. "He's my closest friend. The only person I've trusted since… since everything went to shit."

Wren's chest tightened at the way he said it. Like the words hurt just to admit.

He took a slow breath, like he was choosing his next words carefully, like they mattered more than he wanted them to.

"He asked me to steer clear of you. Told me not to try anything. And I might be a lot of things…" His gaze sharpened, pinning her in place. "But a liar? That's not one of them."

Her throat bobbed as she shifted toward him, her voice softer now. "Griffin… Since you found out Aiden's my brother, you haven't tried anything."

He held her stare, his jaw tight.

"It's been me," she said lightly.

The muscle in his jaw flexed, his fingers curling tighter around his bottle like it was the only thing keeping him grounded.

She leaned in, her breath brushing against him, a spark of mischief lighting her eyes. But beneath it, there was something deeper. Something that scared them both.

"If he finds out about this…" he murmured, his voice a warning.

"Then let's make sure he doesn't," she whispered back, smirking like the devil and his favorite sin all wrapped into one.

Griffin exhaled slowly, his smile crawling back, but this time it wasn't amused.

It was dark. Inevitable.

Damned.

"This is going to end so badly," he muttered.

Wren's grin widened, reckless delight shining through. "So… you're admitting something's started?"

He rolled his tongue across his lips, looking at her like she was gasoline and he was already on fire.

"What was it you texted me earlier?" he teased. "Maybe. Maybe not."

She groaned, laughing despite herself, and nudged his arm like she couldn't decide whether to slap him or straddle him.

"You're such a dick."

Griffin grinned, full of sin and little restraint. "You have no idea, sweetheart."

THEY SAT THERE FOR A WHILE, WRAPPED IN THAT DANGEROUS KIND OF silence again. The kind that felt too easy. Too comfortable. Like they'd somehow skipped the hard part and fast-forwarded to whatever comes after the storm.

But comfort was dangerous.

And Wren?

Wren didn't do still.

"I was serious about what I told Aiden," she said suddenly, slicing through the quiet like she hadn't just obliterated his peace of mind. She stretched, her shirt riding up just enough to snag his attention—and of course she caught him looking. Her grin said so. "Treat me to dinner tonight."

Griffin froze mid-sip, fingers tightening around his beer like it could protect him from the chaos that was Wren Sinclair.

Dinner. Public. Alone. No Aiden.

FUCK…

A thousand warning sirens went off in his head. And every single one of them sounded like devilish decisions and heavenly nights. "What are you in the mood for?" he asked, cautious but curious, like a man poking a bear with a stick just to see what happens.

Her gaze dropped—directly to his lap—slow, deliberate, unapologetic. She tilted her head, lips curling into something wicked as her brows raised. "Hmm…" she hummed, dragging the sound out like a sin. "Well, that's not food…"

Griffin coughed on his beer. Legitimately choked.

She didn't even blink.

Her eyes met his again, full of fire and absolutely no remorse.

"So if I have to settle…" She sighed, like this was such a sacrifice. "I guess seafood."

He blinked. Opened his mouth. Closed it again. Then laughed. Deep, wrecked, helpless.

This woman.

This absolute fucking menace of a woman.

She was going to ruin him.

And worse?

She knew it. She was planning it.

He set the bottle down like it had personally betrayed him and pushed to his feet with a groan and a grin that promised vengeance.

"Come on," he muttered, grabbing his keys. "I know a spot."

Wren stood, brushing past him with the smug strut of someone who had definitely won something.

And Griffin?

He was already in way too fucking deep.

16

UNDERCOVER

GRIFFIN KNEW damn well there wasn't a single place on Topsail Island where he and Wren could disappear—not really. Too many familiar faces. Too many whispers waiting to happen. If Aiden didn't catch them, someone else would. And Griffin wasn't about to let his best friend find out like that.

So, he did the only thing a reckless, half-possessed man could do when temptation looked like Wren Sinclair.

Wren walked beside him, her steps unhurried, like she wasn't in a rush to leave the moment behind. Griffin reached for the passenger door, pulling it open with a teasing smile and a wink that landed just shy of cocky.

"After you," he said.

She climbed in, the leather seat sighing beneath her. He shut the door with a quiet push, like a secret was being kept inside.

Rounding the front, boots crunching the gravel, Griffin hopped up and slid behind the wheel. He looked over with his hand already on the shifter, like he'd been waiting to ask her this for a while.

"You ready?"

No explanation. No hint. Just him, her, and the road.

Then he drove.

An hour south, past the comfort of routine and reputation, straight to Wrightsville Beach. To a place where no one gave a damn about who he was or who he was with.

The Low-Tide Tavern.

Neutral ground. A safe haven for dangerous choices...

And, maybe, something more.

Wren didn't ask where they were going.

Didn't need to.

She just sat there, legs crossed, stealing glances at him like she was committing him to memory. The way his hands gripped the wheel—strong, steady, veins dancing beneath sun-kissed skin. The same hands that had once held her like she was the only thing tethering him to earth.

The cab of his truck felt smaller with every mile.

Not just charged, but intimate.

Silent confessions passing between them without a single word.

Her gaze lingered on him, catching how his jaw flexed every time her knee brushed his.

She wanted him to pull over.

Wanted him to look at her with that dark, dangerous glint—the one that promised sin without apology.

But she didn't move.

Didn't speak.

Because somewhere along that stretch of highway, they both realized—

This wasn't just lust anymore.

It wasn't even just a game.

It was something that felt a hell of a lot like belonging. And that... scared them more than anything.

By the time they pulled into the gravel lot of The Low-Tide Tavern, Wren finally dragged her eyes away from him, her pulse still thudding in places she wasn't ready to name.

String lights hung from the awning, swaying lazily in the coastal breeze, casting golden halos over worn wood. The neon sign above the door flickered like a quiet promise—no questions, no judgment, just be.

"Is it good?" she asked, her voice playful but edged with something softer. Like she knew this wasn't just about the food or the distance.

Griffin cut the engine, turning toward her with a smirk that didn't quite hide the way his eyes softened when they landed on her.

"Damn, Wren... You think I'd bring you here if it wasn't?"

She smiled, unbuckling her seatbelt, but there was something different in that smile now. Less teasing, more... tender. Like she was starting to understand what this night really was—a place where they didn't have to hide. Where they could finally exhale.

Inside, the tavern was warm, dim, and familiar, wrapping around them like an old friend. Blues music hummed low through the speakers.

The kind that sank into your bones and made everything slow down. A few regulars sat scattered at the bar, lost in their drinks and stories. No one looked their way. No one cared.

Griffin led her to a booth in the back, his hand hovering at the small of her back, not possessive, not teasing… just there. Like instinct.

For the first time in days, they weren't pretending.

They weren't the secret glances across crowded rooms.

They weren't the near-misses and brushed fingertips when no one was looking.

They were just two people trying to figure out what the hell this thing between them really was.

Wren leaned into the corner of the booth, her fingers lazily tracing the condensation on her glass. The sharp wit she usually wore like armor was gone, replaced by quiet curiosity. She asked him about Hayes Development, not the numbers or the success, but the why. Why he pushed so hard. Why he needed to build something permanent in a world that felt temporary.

Griffin found himself answering before he could even think to guard himself. Told her about the nights he'd driven out here just to clear his head, about sitting at this exact table when he signed his first real deal, about how this place reminded him of the man he was before expectations buried him.

And when the conversation shifted, when she started sharing pieces of herself no one else got to see, Griffin felt it.

That pull.

The way her eyes lit up when she talked about music. The way her voice softened when she admitted she never felt at home in any city she'd lived in. The way she twirled her straw when she got nervous talking about dreams she thought were too far gone.

He watched her like she was the first sunrise after a storm—something fragile, something worth slowing down for.

At some point, Wren slid her hand across the table, her fingers brushing his.

Not to tease.

Not to provoke.

Just to feel him.

To remind herself that this was real.

Griffin didn't pull away.

Instead, he turned his palm up, lacing his fingers through hers like it was the most natural thing in the world.

Neither of them spoke. They didn't need to.

As if the universe couldn't resist, an old country song spilled through the speakers. Slow, haunting, the kind of melody that wrapped around your ribs and squeezed.

Wren's lips curved as she stood, tugging at his hand.

"Dance with me."

Griffin chuckled, shaking his head.

"You know I don't dance."

Her gaze held his, unwavering. "You don't... Or you won't?"

That challenge—that quiet dare—was his undoing.

With a sigh that was more smile than surrender, he stood, letting her lead him to the open space near the jukebox. His hands found her waist, tentative at first, like he was afraid if he held her too tightly, she'd vanish.

But when she pressed closer, resting her head against his chest, Griffin closed his eyes for half a second—and let go.

One hand slid to the small of her back, the other curling around her hand; their fingers intertwined against his heart. He swayed with her, slow and steady. Feeling every breath she took. Every beat that synced with his.

"You're full of surprises, Hayes," she whispered, her lips brushing the fabric of his shirt.

He smiled—soft, real. The kind that no one else ever got to see.

"Only for you, Sinclair."

They didn't talk after that. They didn't need to.

The song played on, but neither of them noticed when it ended, too lost in the quiet rhythm they'd found together. Too wrapped up in the warmth of something that felt dangerously close to peace.

When they finally made their way back to the booth, Wren didn't sit across from him.

She slid in beside him, curling into his side like it was where she belonged.

Griffin draped his arm around her shoulders, pulling her close, pressing a soft kiss to the top of her head without thinking.

And that was the moment, the exact second, he realized this wasn't just a fling.

This wasn't just sneaking around or testing limits.
This was her.
Wren.
And for once, Griffin didn't feel the urge to run.
Didn't feel the weight of what-ifs or consequences.
All he felt was her, soft and steady against him.
That night didn't end when they left the bar.
It followed them home.
In the way her hand found his on the drive back.
In the way he walked her to her car, but neither of them moved to leave.
In the way he brushed a strand of hair from her face, letting his thumb linger against her cheek like he wasn't ready to let her go.

"Goodnight, Griffin," she whispered, her voice full of something that made his chest ache.

"Night, Wren," he murmured, his lips ghosting over her forehead.

But as he watched her drive away, his heart thudded harder than it should have—he knew.

THAT WAS HOW IT STARTED.

Not with a plan.

Not with a line crossed in the dark.

But with something simple. Something easy. Something that felt like breathing after holding it in for far too long.

One night turned into two.

Then three.

Then four.

Days were for distance—separate lives, separate routines.

Griffin buried himself in job sites and contracts. Wren fielded calls, answered emails, pretended like her world wasn't slowly tilting toward his.

But every evening? Every sunset belonged to them.

It became effortless, their unspoken ritual.

No texts. No calls.

Just the quiet understanding. When the sky began to bleed orange and pink over the horizon. She'd be on his balcony, barefoot, glass in hand, waiting.

Some nights, it was whiskey.

Some nights, it was beer.

But every night, it was him and her—shoulders brushing, hearts syncing to a rhythm neither of them dared to name.

They talked. About everything. About nothing.

About childhood memories that still made them laugh. About the kind of dreams you don't admit out loud because they feel too big—or too fragile.

About fears. Regrets. The ghosts that still lingered in the quiet spaces between words.

Griffin found himself telling her things no one knew.

Like how he'd drive to the job site at midnight just to feel like he was building something that couldn't leave him.

Like how the ocean didn't calm him. It reminded him how easy it was to drown.

And Wren?

She stopped hiding behind sarcasm.

She let him see the woman beneath the mask, the one who craved more than late nights and empty promises. The one who wasn't afraid of him… but was terrified of how much she wanted this.

Some nights, they didn't speak at all.

They'd just sit there—her head resting on his shoulder. His arm draped around her, fingers tracing lazy patterns against her skin, watching the stars claim the sky.

It was reckless.

It was inevitable.

But God, it was easy.

Griffin stopped thinking about why this was a bad idea.

Wren stopped caring about the risk.

Because nothing had ever felt so damn right.

Until Friday.

Until the world reminded them that moments like this don't stay untouched forever.

The steam from his shower clung to Griffin's skin as he stepped out, towel slung low on his hips, water dripping down his spine. His muscles ached, not from labor but from the weight of wanting her. From nights spent tangled in conversation instead of sheets, from holding her hand like it was a secret he wasn't ready to share with the world.

He rubbed a hand over his face, trying to shake off the exhaustion—the kind that didn't come from work but from feeling too much.

His phone buzzed against the counter, pulling him back to reality.

> Aiden: You down for Marshside tonight? Few drinks, maybe a game of pool?

Griffin exhaled through his nose, dragging his fingers through damp hair.

Of course.

A Friday night at Marshside was tradition.

But tradition didn't come with green eyes and a shimmering smile that tasted like temptation.

Before he could type a response, another buzz.

> Wren: What are we doing tonight?

Griffin grinned, shaking his head.

Bold as ever. His thumbs moved across the screen.

> Griffin: Damn, do you not communicate with your brother? He just sent me a text about Marshside. This is the messy part.

The three dots appeared, taunting him.

> ...

Then—

> Wren: I'll handle it.

Griffin frowned, his stomach tightening. That could mean a thousand things—and with Wren, it usually meant chaos wrapped in confidence. He tugged a black T-shirt over his head, still staring at his phone like it might give him a hint of what the hell she was planning.

Minutes later—

> Aiden: If you're cool with it, Wren is coming with me.

Griffin groaned, dragging a hand down his face.
Fuck.
This wasn't just messy; it was a ticking time bomb.
Before he could curse her name properly, another message lit up his screen.

> Wren: See you there 😉

Griffin stared at the damn emoji like it was a loaded weapon pointed at his sanity.

What the hell had he gotten himself into?

Keys in hand, he headed for the door, every step heavier than the last. The whole drive to Marshside, his mind raced—not with exit strategies, but with memories. The way her laugh sounded softer when it was just for him. The way she'd curl into his side like she belonged there. The way her fingers would find his without thinking.

Could he sit across from her tonight and pretend none of that existed?

Could he listen to Aiden talk about women like they were disposable, knowing damn well the only woman Griffin wanted was the one sitting a little too close?

As the lights of Marshside came into view, Griffin's grip tightened around the wheel.

The choice had already been made.

The lines were already blurred.

He just prayed they didn't snap tonight.

Because if they did?

There wouldn't be any pretending after this.

No more hiding behind smirks and sarcasm.

No going back to who they were before belonging started to feel like home.

And deep down, Griffin knew—

He didn't want to go back.

Not if it meant letting her go.

17

IN PLAIN SIGHT

GRIFFIN PULLED into the gravel lot at Marshside, headlights sweeping over the place that had seen too many nights like this—nights filled with bad decisions, good whiskey, and the kind of stories that didn't survive the morning after. The neon lights buzzed against the dark, casting familiar shadows over the worn-down wood exterior. Music and laughter spilled into the salty air, mixing with the quiet hum of tension already coiling in his chest.

His eyes landed on two vehicles parked near the entrance.

Aiden's truck.

Wren's car.

Separate rides.

Griffin's grip tightened on the steering wheel, a slow smirk pulling at his lips. She wasn't waiting on anyone tonight. No curfew. No brother hovering over her shoulder. Wren Sinclair was free to make any reckless decision she wanted.

And every instinct told him—

That decision was already made.

And it sure as hell wasn't her car she'd be leaving in.

He killed the engine, stepping out into the night, gravel crunching under his boots, a warning he was too far gone to hear. This wasn't smart. Hell, it was borderline suicidal. But when it came to Wren? He'd already thrown logic out the window.

Inside, Marshside was alive in that easy, familiar way. Low lights, old country twanging through the speakers, and the scent of fried food clinging to the air like a second skin. A couple of regulars were hunched over the bar, pool balls cracked in the corner, but Griffin didn't see any of it.

Because his eyes had already found her.

Wren.

Sitting in that same damn booth where this chaos began, like she owned the place. And maybe she did. One arm draped casually along the backrest, legs crossed, that signature upside-down frown tugging at her lips, like she'd been waiting for him to walk through the door.

Dangerous.

Effortless.

Fucking perfect.

Griffin let out a breath he didn't realize he'd been holding, shaking his head as he made his way toward her. Every step felt heavier, like he was walking straight into a storm he had no intention of surviving.

Leaning down, he dropped his voice low and whispered words meant just for her.

"Really? This fucking booth?"

Wren's green eyes sparkled with mischief, her smile deepening as she glanced up at him.

"I figured you'd appreciate the nostalgia."

He huffed a laugh, sliding in beside her—close, too close—because sitting across from her wasn't an option anymore. Not when every inch of space between them begged to be crossed.

"Oh yeah," he muttered, stretching his arm along the back of the booth, his fingers brushing her shoulder. "I'm feeling real sentimental."

Before Wren could fire back, Aiden appeared, two beers in hand, sliding into the seat across from them with a skeptical glance.

"Well, isn't this cozy," Aiden remarked, eyes narrowing as he looked between them. "You couldn't find your own side of the booth, Hayes?"

Griffin didn't miss a beat, flashing that cocky grin that had gotten him out of too many situations to count.

"Just following orders, man. Your sister's running this show."

Wren lifted her glass, unbothered.

"I told him to use me."

Aiden nearly choked on his beer.

"What the actual fuck, Wren?"

Griffin bit back a laugh, watching the color rise in Aiden's face, confusion twisting into suspicion.

"She means we're giving a little performance. Make it look like I'm taken, get her curious, then I make my move." Griffin clarified smoothly, nodding toward the blonde at the bar, who kept sneaking glances their way.

Aiden stared at them for a beat, processing, before a grin slowly spread across his face.

"Damn... That's cold. I like it."

Wren shrugged, sipping her drink like this wasn't the most dangerous game they'd ever played.

"Figured I'd be useful for once."

"Shit," Aiden laughed, shaking his head. "You're more devious than I thought."

Griffin felt Wren shift beside him, her thigh pressing against his, fingers ghosting over his knee beneath the table. No one could see it—but he felt everything.

"Alright then," Aiden continued, clearly enjoying himself now. "You gotta sell it. Put your arm around her, lean in—make it look real."

Griffin hesitated—just for a second.

But Wren didn't.

She glanced up at him, those green eyes daring him, her fingers creeping higher, nails grazing the inseam of his jeans.

Griffin swallowed hard, masking the way his pulse spiked with a lazy smirk.

"Anything to help a friend," he muttered, slinging his arm around her shoulders, pulling her in like it was nothing.

But it wasn't nothing.

Not when Wren melted into his side like she belonged there. Like this wasn't pretend at all.

Leaning in, his lips brushed her hair, his voice a low warning only she could hear.

"You're playing a dangerous game, sweetheart."

Wren tilted her head, her breath teasing his jaw.

"And you're loving every second of it."

Aiden, oblivious, flagged down the waitress for another round, rambling about how Griffin better seal the deal with the blonde or risk tarnishing his reputation.

Griffin barely heard him.

Because all he could focus on was the way Wren's fingers were still tracing slow, torturous patterns on his thigh. The way her body fit against his, like they'd done this a thousand times before.

Like they weren't pretending at all.

"So," Aiden said, leaning back with a grin, "you think she's buying it?" He nodded toward the blonde, who was now blatantly staring.

Wren smirked, resting her hand on Griffin's chest—too high to be scandalous, too low to be innocent.

"Oh, she's buying it," Wren purred. "But don't worry, big brother. Griffin knows where home is tonight."

Griffin's heart damn near stopped.

Aiden laughed, clueless.

"Good. I'd hate to see you get too attached, Hayes."

Wren's fingers curled into his shirt, her nails dragging lightly against his chest—out of Aiden's sight but not out of Griffin's mind.

Griffin forced a grin, lifting his beer in mock salute.

"Yeah... wouldn't want that."

But the truth sat heavy between them.

Because as much as they joked, as much as they played this off, Griffin could feel it.

The shift.

The weight.

The quiet, creeping realization that this wasn't just a fling wrapped in bad timing.

This was her.

And as Wren leaned into him, laughing at something Aiden said, her fingers still anchored to his chest like a silent claim, Griffin knew.

They could pretend all night.

Hell, they could fool the whole damn island.

But they weren't fooling themselves.

Not anymore.

And when this blew up—and it would—there'd be no walking away unscathed.

Because somewhere between the smirks and the secrets, they'd stopped playing with fire.

They'd stepped right into the flames.

18

SHIFTING TIDE

AIDEN LAUNCHED into a story about work, completely oblivious to the tension filling the space between Griffin and Wren. The air was electric, a humming sound that drowned out his entire damn monologue.

He was rambling about a supplier screw-up, something about delayed lumber shipments, and subcontractors dropping the ball. But Griffin wasn't hearing a damn word. Not really.

Because Wren was winning.

Her fingers kept tracing those slow, torturous circles on his thigh. Each pass a little bolder, a little closer to wrecking the last shred of control he had. Every time she shifted, her body brushed against his—soft curves pressing into hard muscle—and it was driving him insane. The scent of her shampoo mixed with the whiskey on her breath, wrapping around him like a noose he didn't want to escape.

Meanwhile, Aiden kept talking. Drinking. Laughing at his own misery.

"Man, I needed this tonight," Aiden muttered, dragging a hand through his hair. "Work's been a goddamn shitshow."

Griffin nodded absently, lifting his glass to his lips—because if he didn't, he was going to fucking growl. Wren's nails scraped along the inseam of his jeans again, dangerously close to the throbbing ache she'd been fueling all night.

Fuck.

This wasn't flirting anymore. This wasn't playful touches under the table.

This was her owning him. In public. Right in front of her brother.

And Griffin? He was letting her.

The worst part? He didn't know if he'd stop her, even if Aiden did notice.

Another drink disappeared down Aiden's throat, his words slurring just enough to signal the shift. Griffin knew this version of him too well. The sentimental drunk. The one who stopped bullshitting and started talking like life was some fragile thing he was terrified of wasting.

Aiden leaned back in the booth, glass dangling from his fingertips, eyes glassy but sharp enough to cut when they wanted to. He stared at nothing for a beat, then let out a breath that sounded too heavy for the room.

"I don't wanna do this forever," he muttered, his voice gravelly, like the confession cost him something.

Griffin's attention finally snapped to his friend, his brows pulling together, even as Wren's hand kept up its slow, maddening path along his thigh.

Aiden swirled the last sip of whiskey in his glass, eyes distant. "The bars... the women," he let out a slow breath with a slight muse. "All this temporary shit. I want something real, you know?"

Griffin felt that knot tighten in his chest, but before he could process it, Aiden's gaze flicked toward him, and that's when he said it.

"I don't wanna live like Griff—one night, a different bed at a time."

The words dropped like a grenade between them.

Griffin froze.

His jaw clenched so hard it ached, his teeth grinding together as heat flooded his veins. Not in embarrassment. Not guilt.

Rage.

Because Aiden didn't know a damn thing about what Griffin wanted. About why he lived the way he did. About what it cost to never let anyone close.

His grip on Wren's shoulder tightened, fingers digging in just enough to make her inhale sharply, but not from pain.

From warning.

He was seconds away from snapping, words already forming and sharp enough to cut through years of friendship. Ready to remind Aiden that some people didn't get the luxury of believing in forever anymore.

But Wren's hand slid higher, her fingers wrapping around his thigh, firm and steady this time.

Breathe, that touch said.

Not like this.

Griffin's gaze dropped to her hand, his chest heaving once, before he forced himself to lean back against the booth like he wasn't seconds away from losing it.

Wren turned to her brother, her voice calm, too calm. "Aiden," she said, her tone sharp enough to sober anyone with half a brain. "What the fuck?"

Aiden blinked, like he was only just realizing what he'd said out loud. His brows furrowed, confusion bleeding into regret, but he was too drunk to backpedal properly.

"I'm just saying," Aiden muttered, rubbing a hand over his face. "Griff's my boy, but he's not exactly the poster child for settling down."

Wren's eyes flicked to Griffin—who was staring at the table like it had personally offended him. His knuckles were white against his glass, his entire body tense, coiled like a predator deciding whether or not to pounce.

She could see it. The storm brewing beneath that calm facade. The weight of a thousand unsaid things pressing down on him.

Her heart tightened. Because this wasn't about Aiden's careless words. It was about Griffin, the man sitting beside her, who carried scars no one else could see. The man who built walls so high even he forgot what was on the other side.

Wren shifted closer, her hand moving from his thigh to his forearm, her fingers tracing along the vein that pulsed beneath his skin.

Grounding him.

Choosing him.

Aiden kept rambling, oblivious to the silent war happening beside him. "I just mean... Some people aren't built for that kind of thing. And that's fine. But me? I want more."

Wren didn't answer. Neither did Griffin. Because in that moment, words would only make it worse.

Instead, she let her touch speak for her—anchoring Griffin to the booth, to her, to the fact that he wasn't who Aiden thought he was.

Not anymore.

Minutes passed—Aiden draining the last of his drink, mumbling something about hitting the restroom.

The second he was gone, Griffin slowly exhaled like he was releasing the fury one breath at a time.

Wren didn't move her hand.

"Griff..." she started, her voice softer now, layered with something he hadn't expected.

But he shook his head, cutting her off before she could try to fix what didn't need fixing.

"I'm fine," he muttered, but the grit in his voice betrayed the lie.

She studied him, her thumb brushing over his pulse point.

"You're not," she whispered, leaning in, her forehead almost touching his. "But you don't have to be."

His eyes closed for half a second, just long enough to let her words sink in.

When he opened them, that guarded smirk was gone. All that was left was Griffin—the real one. The man who was dangerously close to letting someone see him for the first time in years.

Aiden's footsteps echoed as he made his way back to the table, breaking whatever fragile truth had settled between them.

Griffin straightened, the mask sliding back into place, but Wren felt it. The shift.

The crack in the armor.

HER VOICE SOFTENED, BUT ONLY JUST. A CALM BEFORE THE STORM. "I think Griffin is a good guy."

Aiden scoffed, rubbing a hand over his face, the flush of whiskey making him bolder than he had any right to be. "He is, Wren. The best. But not when it comes to women." He shook his head, like he'd seen this play out too many times before. "If he wants them, he goes after them. Uses them."

Griffin's grip on Wren's shoulder hardened, his fingers pressing deep, as if he held on tightly enough that he could tether himself to her instead of the storm rising inside him.

Wren's grip on his thigh answered right back—firm, steady, like a heartbeat against his muscle.

I'm here.

But fuck, this was dangerous. So fucking dangerous.

Aiden was too far gone to realize the weight of what he was saying.

Too drunk. Too blind to see the storm unraveling right in front of him, how close Griffin was to snapping. How close Wren was to shattering every rule Aiden thought he could enforce.

Wren's tone sharpened, a quiet storm brewing beneath each word. Controlled, but only just. "Is that so, brother?" she asked, tilting her head, her voice laced with something lethal. "Is that what you truly think of him?"

Aiden didn't even blink. "I know so. I've seen it," he said, his words slurring at the edges but sharp enough to cut. His eyes locked on Griffin, a pointed glare. "That's why I said he can't go after you."

And there it was.

The line.

Drawn in permanent ink, like Aiden thought he could control the tide by telling it where to break.

Wren inhaled slowly, like she was breathing in the very moment everything was about to change. She turned toward Griffin, fully this time, and for the first time that night, he looked at her.

Really looked at her.

And what he saw? It nearly knocked the wind out of him. That fire in her eyes—it wasn't rage. It wasn't defiance.

It was pride.

Pride in him. In them. In the fact that she knew exactly what she was about to do, and she didn't give a damn about the consequences.

Her hand pressed against his thigh, slow and deliberate. A pulse. A tether. A silent, *Don't you fucking move.*

Her voice sliced through the thick air, calm, but sharp enough to leave a scar. "Aiden, have you ever thought that there might be more to someone than just what they allow you to see?"

Aiden frowned, confused and annoyed. "What are you talking about?"

But Griffin wasn't watching Aiden. He was watching her.

The way she held her chin high. The way her eyes never wavered, like she was steadying herself on the edge of something dangerous and ready to jump anyway.

Then, her voice softened—just for him. "Griffin. Look at me."

His chest constricted. His pulse hammered against his ribs. He hesitated for a breath. Just one. But when he turned his head and met her gaze—fuck.

That wasn't a look you survived.

That was a look you drowned in.

"Be honest with me right now," she whispered, but there was nothing soft about it. It was a demand dressed as a request. A line wrapped in silk and steel.

Aiden shifted, sensing something but too slow to stop it. "Wren, what the hell are—"

"Shut up and listen." Her finger lifted without looking at him, silencing him like it was second nature.

Her eyes stayed locked on Griffin.

Griffin, who felt like the floor had disappeared beneath him.

"Griff?" she pressed.

His voice was rough when it finally came. "Yeah?"

Her lips parted, her stare unrelenting. "Remember, you have to be honest."

His throat bobbed. He nodded. "Okay."

And then she asked it. The question that ripped the air from the room.

"Do you want me?"

The bar noise faded into nothing.

Griffin's lungs burned, but he couldn't breathe. Not with her looking at him like that. Not with Aiden sitting across from them, oblivious to the earthquake about to split his world in two.

Wren lifted a finger toward Aiden again, daring him to interrupt.

But Griffin? He didn't run. He didn't hide. He let the truth fall from his lips, like it had been waiting there all along.

"I do."

Her lashes fluttered, but she didn't break. Didn't let emotion crack through.

"How long?" she asked, voice steady. "How long have you wanted me?"

Griffin exhaled sharply, like the confession hurt more coming out. "Since the day I met you."

Wren's lips twitched, but she wasn't finished.

"Have you tried to get with me?"

"No."

"Why?"

His answer came fast. Too fast. "Because I told your brother I wouldn't."

The weight of that truth slammed into the table like a tidal wave—silent but impossible to ignore.

Aiden shifted uncomfortably, finally realizing this wasn't some sibling joke. But Wren didn't flinch. Didn't give him a single glance.

Her gaze stayed on Griffin.

"And is that all it is?" she whispered, her voice a little more fragile now. "Do you just want to fuck me?"

Griffin's chest rose and fell, slow and deliberate. His hand trembled against his glass.

"No," he rasped, the word almost a vow.

Wren swallowed, her throat tight, but she had to finish this.

"Why, Griffin?"

Her fingers squeezed his thigh again, not playful this time. Reassuring. Anchoring.

Griffin leaned in, his voice raw, stripped down to the bone. "Truthfully?"

Wren nodded, eyes glistening.

He stared at her, letting every wall fall, letting every part of him—every scar, every fear—bleed out into the space between them.

Griffin could read it in her eyes. The hesitation, the silent question, the way she was desperately waiting for an answer. They both knew what she was doing. She was proving a point—to Aiden, to him, and maybe even to herself.

But Griffin knew. This wasn't just a game anymore. This was her asking him for the truth. Really asking. And Griffin—he didn't lie; he couldn't. Not about this. Not about her.

He paused, swallowing hard, because he knew that the second the words left his mouth. Everything would change. Everything would come crashing down in an instant. The walls they had both spent years building, perfecting, hiding behind would crumble. And yet, looking at her, with that plea in her eyes, with that silent hope clinging to every fiber of her being, he couldn't hold back. He couldn't hide behind his perfectly constructed walls any longer.

A warmth bloomed in his chest. It was unfamiliar, yet felt like home. Like something he had felt once before but buried so deep it was almost unrecognizable. His lips parted, the words rolling off his tongue like they had always belonged there.

"Because from what I know about you…" His voice cracked, but he pushed through. "You deserve more than a good lay."

Her breath hitched, but Griffin wasn't done.

He leaned closer, his lips barely a whisper away. His voice dipping into something so soft, so *wrecking*, it felt like a prayer meant only for her.

"You deserve the ocean. The sand. You deserve the air that wraps around you, clinging to your skin like a promise." His gaze softened, but his words carried weight, carried meaning.

"You deserve someone who can't wait to come home to you."

Her eyes filled, a tear slipping free as his words carved straight through her.

"Someone who wakes up grateful every morning just to feel your breath on their skin. Someone who knows—without a single fucking doubt—that you are the best thing that's ever happened to them."

His voice dropped lower, breaking entirely as he finished, "You deserve love. The kind that's *bound by tide*."

A soft gasp slipped from Wren's lips. Barely a sound. But it cracked something wide open in the space between them. Her fingers curled tighter into the seat, her chest rising and falling. Like she was drowning on dry land.

Aiden let out a scoff, cutting through the moment like a blade. "Jesus Christ, man. The tide? Really?"

Griffin didn't flinch. Didn't blink. He couldn't look away from her.

"Yes," he said, his voice like stone in a storm. "The tide."

Wren's lip trembled. A tear slipped down her cheek, slow and quiet, like it didn't want to be seen. But he saw it.

And Griffin wasn't done.

"The tide doesn't ask," he said, voice intimate now. "It doesn't knock. It crashes. It consumes. It drags you out and pulls you under. Daring you to breathe through it. And no matter how far you run, how far inland you try to escape, it always finds a way to return to you."

Her tears hit the table—soft echoes of a heart breaking open.

"The tide pulls what belongs to it," he finished, his voice barely holding together, "Always."

Silence swallowed them whole.

He didn't have to say the words, *I love you*.

Because he'd already told her.

In every word.

In every metaphor carved from the sea and the sky.

Drunk and blind, Aiden laughed again, *clueless*.

"That sounds like bullshit," Aiden scoffed, shaking his head. "I've heard way better lines from you."

Wren's gaze snapped to her brother, fire burning in her chest, but she didn't say a word. Because she knew the truth. She felt it. In her heart. In her soul. In her fucking bones. Griffin Hayes was everything. Everything she had ever wanted.

Aiden rolled his eyes. "Might wanna try something else, man." He let out another laugh. One that was too loud, too careless.

Griffin just stared at him. No expression. No reaction.

Then, without breaking eye contact, he exhaled, his voice eerily calm. "I guess it's true."

Aiden frowned. "What?"

Griffin's jaw ticked. "A drunk man's words are a sober man's thoughts."

And then, before Wren could say a damn word, before she could even breathe—

Griffin turned to her. His voice was quiet but final. "I'm sorry, Wren."

Her heart cracked.

"This has been fun."

His arm slid off the back of the booth. He slid out of the seat. Wren's head snapped up, watching him move. Watching him walk through the bar, like he hadn't just ripped her world apart.

She wanted to stop him. Fuck, she wanted to grab his hand, make him stay, make him see.

But she didn't.

Because he was looking at her.

One last time.

And in his eyes, she saw it. A question.

He had just poured his fucking heart out to her. And he needed to know if she felt the same.

AARON MCLEAN

But she couldn't answer.
She couldn't say a damn thing.
And just like that—he was gone.

19

DEPTH BETWEEN US

FADING INTO THE NIGHT.

That's exactly what he did.

Griffin fucking Hayes walked out of her life, and Wren didn't even have the chance to breathe before Aiden's voice shattered the fragile pieces left behind.

"He's good. I'll give him that. But that was the stupidest fucking thing I've ever heard."

The cruel and careless words sliced through her like a sharp blade.

Her hands clenched into fists beneath the table, nails digging into her palms so hard it hurt. Good. She wanted it to hurt. Because anything was better than listening to her brother mock the man who just laid himself bare in front of them.

Aiden kept going—because of course he did. Oblivious. Drunk. Digging his own grave with every fucking word.

"Love like the tide. Can you believe that shit?" He let out a laugh, bitter and hollow, like he hadn't just burned down everything that mattered.

Wren's vision blurred, not from tears, but from rage. A slow, simmering fury that curled beneath her skin, begging to be unleashed.

"Yes," she snapped, her tone laced with ice. "I can believe it," her voice now trembling, not with weakness, but restraint.

Aiden frowned, blinking like her words didn't compute. "What?"

"I do believe it," she repeated, louder this time. Sharper. Deadly.

The confusion on his face was almost laughable—if she wasn't seconds away from throttling him.

"Wren—"

"No." She shot to her feet, the legs of the booth scraping against the worn floorboards. "If you knew what was best for you, you would've shut the fuck up long before you opened your mouth tonight."

The weight of her glare pinned him to his seat, but Aiden, drunk and dense, just shrugged like this was nothing.

"He'll get over it," he muttered, waving a hand. "Griff'll call me tomorrow."

Wren let out a bitter laugh. "No, Aiden. He won't."

Because Griffin Hayes didn't run from problems.

He ran from pain.

And tonight? Aiden had given him enough pain to last a lifetime.

"Get up," she ordered, her voice like ice. "Get in the fucking car."

Aiden sighed, muttering under his breath, but he followed her out of the bar, still rambling, still blind to the storm he'd unleashed.

The cool night air hit her like a slap. Thick with salt and regret. Every step across the gravel felt like walking further away from the only thing that mattered.

Griffin.

Aiden was still talking. About Griffin. About his past. About the women. Like listing off every mistake Griffin had ever made would somehow erase what just happened. Like it would convince her that Griffin was nothing more than a polished version of every man who'd ever let her down.

But it was too late.

She was already his.

Mind. Body. Fucking soul.

THE DRIVE TO AIDEN'S HOUSE WAS A BLUR. TWENTY MINUTES OF SILENCE on her end, while Aiden kept digging that knife deeper—not realizing he wasn't cutting into Griffin.

He was cutting into her.

When they finally pulled into the driveway, Wren moved on autopilot. She guided Aiden inside, ignoring his slurred protests, his half-assed attempts to justify himself. He collapsed onto his bed, mumbling nonsense.

"Wren," he slurred, eyes already closing, "Griffin's no different than—"

But he never finished.

Because even Aiden's subconscious knew when to shut the hell up.

She stood there for a second, staring at him—her brother, her protector. The man who thought he was saving her.

But tonight? He hadn't saved her.

He'd destroyed her.

Turning off the light, Wren walked out, her chest tight, her pulse thudding in her ears. The house felt suffocating. The walls too close. The air too thin.

She needed to breathe.

She needed... *Him.*

The shower scalded her skin, but it didn't burn away the weight pressing down on her. She tilted her head back, letting the water cascade over her, wishing it could wash away the ache in her chest. Her fingers ghosted over her collarbone—right where Griffin's hand had been. She could still feel it. The warmth. The unspoken promise. The way his touch said more than words ever could.

Her lips parted in a shaky breath as her mind replayed it all, over and over like a cruel highlight reel.

The way his voice cracked when he told her she deserved more.

The way his eyes begged her to see him—not the man Aiden described, but the man he was when no one else was watching.

And the way she silently sat there when he needed her to speak.

When she finally stepped out, the steam clinging to her skin, Wren felt raw. Stripped bare in a way she hadn't felt since... Josh.

Her ex's name flickered through her mind like a ghost. But that wasn't what this was. Griffin wasn't Josh. Not even close.

Josh had promised her the world and handed her lies.

Griffin hadn't promised her anything.

He'd given her the truth—and walked away when she couldn't handle it.

She collapsed onto the guest bed, her heart pounding, her mind spiraling. Her phone was already in her hand before she realized it, her thumb hovering over Griffin's name.

The empty screen mocked her.

Because what could she say? Sorry I let my brother rip you apart? Sorry I didn't tell you that I felt it too? That I'm already drowning in you and I don't want to come up for air?

Her fingers trembled as she typed.

> Wren: Griff?

Pathetic. But it was all she had.

...

Hope flared in her chest—too bright, too desperate.

And then... gone.

Her stomach twisted, the sting of rejection sharper than she expected. But what did she expect? He'd bared his soul, and she left him standing alone in the wake.

A tear slipped down her cheek, but she didn't bother wiping it away.

She could still hear Aiden's voice echoing in her head. *Griffin's no different...*

But he was. God, he was.

Griffin wasn't pretending with her.

He never had.

And that's when the hard and unforgiving truth hit her.

If she didn't fight for this now, she'd lose him.

Not just tonight.

Forever.

Her pulse kicked into overdrive. She threw the covers back, adrenaline surging through her veins. She grabbed her purse, her keys, her phone—her heart.

Because Griffin Hayes had given her everything.

And she was done being afraid to give it back.

She didn't care that it was late.

She didn't care that Aiden would lose his shit.

All she cared about was getting to him. Before that tide pulled them too far apart.

Before the man who said he was done drifting decided to let go of the only thing anchoring him.

She bolted out the door, the cool night air hitting her like freedom.

Because love, like the tide, doesn't wait.

It crashes.

And Wren Raine Sinclair was about to fucking crash into Griffin Hayes.

Whether he was ready for it or not.

20

THE RECKONING

IT WAS 11:30 when Griffin heard the knock.

One sharp rap.

Then nothing.

Not a second one. Not a shuffle of feet. Just silence pressing against the door, like a weight he wasn't sure he was ready to carry.

But he already knew.

Before he crossed the room, before his bare feet hit the hardwood. Before his pulse started pounding like a fucking war drum in his chest, he knew.

It was her.

It could only ever be her.

His hand hovered over the handle, fingers flexing as he dragged in a breath that did nothing to steady him. He told himself to play it cool. To hold the line. But the second he opened that door and saw Wren standing there, everything inside him fucking shattered.

She looked wrecked.

Not in the way that begged for pity but in the way that stripped every ounce of pretense away. Gym shorts hanging low on her hips, a thin cami clinging to damp skin, no bra, no makeup—just Wren. Bare. Breathless. Her hair still wet from the shower, tendrils sticking to her neck, tears clinging stubbornly to lashes that refused to fall.

God, she was beautiful.

Not because she was put together—but because she wasn't.

Because for the first time, she wasn't wearing confidence like armor.

She was standing in front of him like a wave that had been crashing for too long and was finally ready to let the tide pull her under.

She didn't speak.

Didn't ask if she could come in.

She just stepped past him, and Griffin let her, because where the fuck else would he want her to be?

The door clicked shut behind them, but the silence screamed. Louder than anything either of them could've said.

He watched her as she moved, slow and heavy, like every step cost her something. She sank into his couch like her legs couldn't hold her up anymore, her hands clenched in her lap so tightly her knuckles turned white.

Crossing the room, Griffin swallowed hard and lowered himself beside her. But not too close. Not yet.

Because whatever this was? It wasn't about heat or lust or the magnetic pull that usually existed between them.

This was something deeper.

Something dangerous.

His hand hovered for a second before resting on her back, a silent *I'm here*, warm and steady. When words felt too damn fragile to hold.

Her skin was hot beneath his palm, but she was shaking, standing in a storm only she could feel.

He traced slow circles between her shoulder blades, grounding her the way he wished someone had done for him when his world fell apart.

"Wren..." His voice was barely a whisper, careful not to spook whatever fragile thread was holding her together. "Talk to me."

Her breath hitched, sharp and uneven, like she'd been holding it in for miles.

Seconds passed. Maybe minutes.

Finally, she spoke, so soft he almost missed it.

"Griff..."

His name on her lips felt like a prayer and a plea all at once.

His chest ached. "I'm right here."

She leaned into his touch, and for the first time, he felt it—her walls collapsing. One by one. Every defense she'd ever built crumbling beneath the weight of something she couldn't outrun anymore.

Her voice cracked, but her words were steady.

"The tide pulls what belongs to it."

Griffin's heart stopped.

Those were his words.

But hearing them from her lips? It was like being dragged under all over again, but this time, he wasn't fighting it.

She kept going, each word a slow unraveling of everything they'd been too scared to face.

"It doesn't ask... it crashes." Her voice trembled, but she didn't look away. *"It consumes you. Pulls you under. Makes you decide if you're strong enough to survive it."*

Griffin's throat burned, his hand sliding to her jaw, tilting her face toward him. He needed to see her. Needed to read every emotion bleeding from those green eyes that had haunted him since the moment they met.

"And no matter how far you run..." she whispered, a tear slipping free, *"it always finds its way back."*

Goddamn her.

Goddamn this.

Because he was already drowning, and she was the only thing keeping him breathing.

His thumb caught the tear on her cheek, but it was useless. More followed. Not broken tears. Not weak.

These were the kind of tears that came when you stopped lying to yourself.

She leaned into his palm, her hand covering his like she was terrified he'd pull away.

But he wouldn't.

Not now.

Not ever.

Her lashes fluttered shut for a second, gathering the last bit of courage she had left before her gaze locked onto his. And he saw it.

All of it.

The fear.

The hope.

The reckless fucking love she didn't know how to name yet. But he felt it. God, he felt it.

"Griffin..." Her voice cracked, her lip trembling as she forced the words out. "I'm ready."

His heart slammed against his ribs.

She wasn't finished.

Her next words came out in a breathless whisper, but they hit harder than anything he'd ever been told in his life.

"I'm ready to be yours."

Silence.

But not the empty kind.

The kind that held every unspoken word they'd never dared to say.

Griffin searched her face, looking for hesitation, for any sign that this was fear talking. That this was a moment of weakness.

But no—this wasn't weakness.

This was Wren Sinclair, standing in the eye of the storm, daring him to claim what they both knew had always been inevitable.

His hand slid into her hair, fingers threading through the damp strands, slowly pulling her closer—slow and deliberate, giving her every chance to back out.

She didn't.

Their lips met, and it wasn't fireworks.

It was gravity.

It was the kind of kiss that didn't burn.

It bound.

Her fingers fisted in his shirt, dragging him closer like she couldn't get deep enough, couldn't get full enough of him. But this wasn't about sex.

It was about surrender.

About letting go of every fear, every doubt. Every wall they'd built between themselves and the rest of the world.

He kissed her like a man who had been starved for something real—and finally found it.

When they finally pulled apart, foreheads resting together, breath mingling in the charged air, neither of them spoke.

Because there was nothing left to say.

They weren't pretending.

Not anymore.

Wrapped up in a moment that felt too big for either of them, Griffin held her as he realized something terrifying.

For the first time in his life, he wasn't afraid of being pulled under.

He was afraid of what would happen if she let go.

Because Wren Sinclair wasn't just the tide.

She was his anchor.

And he'd gladly drown—if it meant she was the one holding him down.

21

UNMASKED

THE WORLD OUTSIDE didn't exist. Not at this moment. Not when it was just them—two people who had spent so fucking long pretending they didn't want this, that it wasn't real, that it wasn't something worth risking everything for.

The air between them was thick with unspoken desire, with the weight of everything that had happened between them. They wanted more. God, they wanted so much more. The pull between them was suffocating, pressing into their skin, demanding more, demanding now. Every brush of Griffin's fingers against Wren's. Every glance, every shift in their seats sent waves of electricity between them. They could've gone to the bedroom. Could've given in to the heat, to the undeniable ache that had been burning between them for days, weeks, maybe even years without them realizing it. Could've stripped each other bare, flesh against flesh, hands gripping, mouths devouring, tangled in sheets and desperation.

Fuck, they wanted to.

But this? This was deeper.

Griffin saw it in her eyes: the need, the want, but more than that, the trust. The fucking trust. It was raw, unfiltered, something he didn't know he was starving for until she looked at him like that. Like he wasn't just the sum of his past, his choices… his mistakes. Like he wasn't the broken, guarded version of himself that he had become.

Like he was worth this.

They sat there on the couch, neither rushing to fill the silence, because the silence wasn't empty. It was full. Full of everything unspoken, everything they had been too afraid to say.

Then, the dam broke.

They talked, really talked. Not surface-level shit. Not polite small talk. The kind of talking that only happens when guarded walls have crumbled to the ground and when there's nothing left to hide behind. They told the stories that shaped them. The memories that still lingered. The moments that haunted them.

Wren curled into the corner of the couch, her knees tucked up, one arm draped over the back, fingers occasionally trailing through Griffin's hair like it was the most natural thing in the world. Like she had done it a thousand times before.

"You want to hear something stupid?" she asked, a lazy smirk pulling at her lips.

Griffin tilted his head back against the couch, his fingers skimming the inside of her wrist, tracing slow, absentminded circles against her skin. "Always."

She rolled her eyes. "When Aiden and I were kids, we used to think we were untouchable. He was so cocky about it. He thought he could get away with anything. And I? I just followed his lead."

Griffin smirked. "Sounds about right."

Wren laughed, shaking her head. "So one summer, when I was fourteen and he was sixteen, he convinced me we could sneak out. Make it to the beach and back before our parents even noticed. We thought we had the perfect plan."

Griffin grinned. "Let me guess. You got caught?"

She snorted. "No, he got caught. I got away with it."

Griffin's brows lifted. "Of course, you did."

"Our parents didn't even think to blame me. I was the baby, after all," she said, smirking. "Aiden got his ass handed to him. And I? I just sat there, looking all innocent and wide-eyed. While he tried to explain how he ended up in the backyard at two in the morning, covered in sand."

Griffin let out a low chuckle, shaking his head. "Damn, Sinclair. Ruthless."

She grinned. "Survival of the fittest."

Griffin loved this. The way she told stories, the way she got lost in them, like she was right back in the memory, feeling it all over again.

Realizing what was happening, his chest tightened.

Because this? This wasn't just a moment. This was her letting him in.

And for a man who had spent so fucking long keeping people out, he wasn't sure how to process it.

He exhaled slowly, shifting slightly, rubbing the back of his neck. "Wren."

Her expression softened at the change in his voice. "Yeah?"

His jaw tensed as he hesitated for a second, "Can't believe I am telling you this," then said it anyway. "Aiden's words at Marshside…" He swallowed, rolling his shoulders. "They got to me."

Her lips parted, but he held up a hand before she could speak.

"Not because he said it," he clarified. "But because it was true."

She stilled.

"I hate who I've become, Wren," he admitted, his voice raw, unfiltered. "Beneath the image, beneath the Hayes reputation, I'm just Griffin. Just a man who's afraid."

Her breath caught.

"I don't let people in. I don't let them get close. Because I know what comes from that." His fingers flexed against his knee, his voice tightening. "No one truly knows me. I don't give them the chance. Probably never will."

A pause.

"But somehow, for some reason… I let you."

Her chest ached.

"I let you truly see me," he murmured, his voice barely above a whisper. "And that scares the hell out of me."

Griffin's breath stilled in his chest, his entire world narrowing to the woman in front of him. The way she looked at him—not with pity, not with judgment, but with something so unshakable, so fierce, it threatened to undo him entirely.

She saw him. Not the version of himself he presented to the world. Not the reputation. Not the mask.

She saw *him*. And somehow, she stayed.

His throat burned, the kind of ache that started somewhere beneath his ribs and clawed its way up. She lay curled beside him on the couch, her knees tucked between them. One of his arms was draped across her waist, the other wrapped between her back and the cushion. His head rested on her chest like a fucking lifeline. Her fingers moved through his hair. Slow, steady, and grounding. Tracing patterns that calmed the chaos roaring inside him.

His grip tightened around her, needing the anchor, needing her. Like she was the only solid thing in a world that had always felt like shifting ground beneath his feet. His heart pounded so damn hard it was a miracle it didn't shatter straight through his ribs and into her hands.

Wren's fingers trailed up his jaw, her touch gentle, but her gaze was anything but. It was steady, filled with the kind of quiet certainty that wrecked him. "You don't have to be afraid of me," she whispered, her voice so soft, so certain, it made something in his chest ache. "I'm not going anywhere, Griffin."

His entire body tensed at that. Not because he didn't want to believe her. But because he did. And fuck, that was even scarier.

"I am," he admitted hoarsely. "I am fucking terrified, Wren." His voice cracked slightly, the weight of it all crashing into him. He swallowed hard, his grip on her tightening, afraid she'd slip through his fingers if he didn't hold on.

"I built every wall, every piece of armor, convinced myself I was protecting something worth keeping," he murmured. "But the truth is, I wasn't protecting anything. I was just… alone." His voice dropped lower, rough and raw. "And then you walked in, and fuck, you didn't just get inside. You tore it all down before I even knew what was happening."

Her breath hitched, her eyes shining. "I didn't mean to—"

"I know," he interrupted, fingers tangling in her hair, holding her close. Needing to feel her warmth to believe this was real. "That's the fucking thing. You weren't trying. You were just you. And for the first time in my life, I didn't want to keep someone out. I didn't want to run."

Her eyes shimmered with unshed tears. She lifted a hand, pressing her palm over his heart, feeling the erratic rhythm beneath her fingertips. "Then don't run," she whispered. "Don't hide. Don't keep waiting for me to change my mind, because I won't."

Griffin squeezed his eyes shut for a moment, swallowing past the lump in his throat. When he opened them again, fuck, he was gone.

Because she meant it.

He could see it in the way she held him, anchoring him. In the way she touched him like he was something precious, not something to be used or left behind.

She wasn't just saying she was staying.

She was choosing him.

Griffin sucked in a shaky breath, tilting his forehead against hers. "You make me want to believe in something, Wren," he admitted, his voice wrecked, barely more than a whisper.

Her lips trembled. "Then believe in me. Believe in us."

His chest ached, everything in him breaking apart and putting itself back together all at once. "I do," he whispered. "I do."

The tears finally spilled over, sliding down Wren's cheeks, but she didn't break. She just curled her arms around his neck, pulling him close, her breath warm against his skin. "I don't want to be your exception, Griffin," she murmured. "I want to be your reason."

His breath hitched, a sharp exhale against her hair.

"You already are."

Leaning forward, he kissed her.

Slow and deep, with every ounce of feeling neither of them had ever spoken aloud. His lips memorized her, his hands mapping every curve of her body, learning her like she was something sacred.

Not rushed. Not reckless. Just right.

Because for the first time in forever, Griffin Hayes wasn't just taking a risk.

He was falling.

And for the first time in her life, Wren knew, without a doubt—

She wasn't just falling too.

She was home.

22

LAST WALL

THE AIR between them was no longer heavy with uncertainty; it was instead weighted with certainty. A quiet, unshakable truth that neither of them had the strength or desire to deny anymore. There was no fear. No hesitation. Just them. In a space where walls had crumbled and hearts had been laid bare.

Griffin had spent his life constructing barriers, convincing himself that love was a battlefield he never wanted to step onto again. But here, in the stillness of this moment, in the depth of her, he realized something.

Love wasn't supposed to be a war.

It was supposed to be this.

The way Wren looked at him, not as if he were a risk or a gamble, but as if he were hers. As if she saw every part of him—the broken, the jagged, the unpolished edges—and loved him anyway.

She wasn't just staying.

She was choosing him.

His forehead pressed against hers, his breath shallow, hands cradling her like she was something rare, something precious—because she was.

"You do something to me, Wren," he said quietly, the words scraped out like they'd been dragged out of the darkest corners of him. "I don't know what the hell this is, but it feels like… breathing after years of holding it in."

Her hand flattened over his chest, right where the tension was. "Then let yourself breathe with me; let me breathe for you."

A shaky exhale left him, the kind a man gives when he's spent too long pretending he can carry the world alone. "I want to," he admitted. "I just don't know how."

"You don't have to know, Griff," she whispered while sliding closer, allowing her eyes to undo him. "Just stop running and you'll catch your breath."

His jaw clenched, fighting the instinct to close off, to put on his armor, to return to the version of himself that never let anyone see his cracks. But her thumb brushed against his skin, gentle and sure, like she saw every fracture and didn't give a damn.

And in that moment, Griffin Hayes did something he never thought he would again.

Something inside him faltered.

Not fear, not regret... but surrender.

With Wren's arms wrapping around him, breath warm against his skin, Griffin let go.

Of the past. Of the weight of regret. Of the fear that love would only ever end in loss.

And for the first time in forever—he fell.

And Wren?

She became the place he landed.

Their kiss was slow, unhurried, a memorization of this moment. Of every whispered truth, every barrier that had been shattered between them. There was no urgency, no desperate need to claim or possess.

Because this—whatever it was, whatever it had become—was already theirs.

Even with Wren wrapped in his arms, her warmth sinking into him like a balm over wounds he didn't know were bleeding, Griffin couldn't stop the weight pressing against his chest.

No matter how tightly he held her, one truth wouldn't let go.

Aiden.

His name wasn't just a thought. It was a fucking noose. Tightening. Closing in. Every second that passed felt like they were borrowing time they hadn't earned. Like this impossible, terrifying happiness was something fragile. Something that could shatter the second reality caught up to them.

And Griffin hated that.

Hated that for the first time in his life, something felt right, but all he could think about was how fast it could be ripped away.

He swallowed hard, his hand trailing absentmindedly down Wren's spine. Memorizing the way she felt in his arms, because deep down, he was terrified this might be the last night he'd ever get to hold her without regret clawing its way in.

He didn't want secrets. Not with her.

Not when this felt bigger than anything he'd ever let himself believe in.

He shifted slightly, pulling back just enough to see her face. To really see her. The way her lashes brushed against flushed cheeks, the way her lips were still parted like she'd been on the verge of saying something but didn't. Like even she was afraid that words might break the spell they'd wrapped themselves in.

Griffin's fingers traced along her jaw, slow and deliberate. Grounding himself in the curve of her skin before his voice finally broke through the silence.

"Wren…" Her name came out cracked, like it hurt to speak.

Her eyes flickered open, glassy and soft, but beneath that softness, he saw it.

She knew.

Before he even said it, she fucking knew.

He let out a shaky breath, his forehead pressing gently to hers, like maybe if they stayed this close, they wouldn't have to face it. But that wasn't who he was. Not anymore.

"Everything I've told you," he murmured, "it's all *real*. Every goddamn word."

Her fingers tightened around his shirt, holding him like she could keep him from unraveling.

"I've had the fall before," he continued, his throat burning with every word. "The kind where you think you've landed somewhere safe… Until you realize you were just crashing the whole fucking time."

Wren's breath hitched, her thumb brushing against his chest, right over where his heart was breaking itself open for her.

"If we're gonna do this…" His voice cracked, but he pushed through it. "If we're going to be more than just two people hiding in the dark... then we can't keep pretending Aiden isn't standing between us."

Her body tensed against his, barely, but enough for him to feel it. Enough to know that she wasn't just afraid for herself.

She was afraid for him.

For what this would cost him.

Griffin cupped her face, forcing her to meet his eyes. "I'll tell him," he said, steady now. "If that's what it takes, I'll fucking tell him myself."

She swallowed hard, her voice so quiet he almost didn't hear it. "You'll lose him."

The words hung in the air like ash after a fire—proof that something was already burning.

Griffin let out a bitter breath, a hollow smile tugging at his lips. "Yeah," he admitted. "I probably will."

His hand slid to the back of her neck, pulling her closer, not because he was trying to make her feel better, but because he needed to feel her. Needed to remind himself why this was worth it.

"But I can live with that," he whispered, his voice breaking against her skin. "I can live with losing him..."

He pulled back just enough to lock eyes with her, his gaze so raw, so exposed, it felt like it could bring the strongest person to their knees.

"...what I can't live with is losing you."

Her heart shattered.

Not because it was tragic. But because it was true.

Because Griffin Hayes wasn't the kind of man who needed anyone. He wasn't the guy who said things just to say them. If he let you in, if he gave you even a piece of himself, it was because you were already holding parts of him he could never get back.

And right now? He wasn't holding anything back.

Tears welled in her eyes, but she didn't dare look away. She wanted to memorize this, the man behind the reputation, behind the fear. Him. Behind the carefully constructed walls that everyone else thought were impenetrable.

Because she was the only one who knew the truth.

Griffin wasn't made of steel.

He was made of scars.

And she loved every single one of them.

Her voice trembled when it finally came, but it didn't waver. "We tell him," she whispered, her hand finding his, threading their fingers together, a promise carved in bone.

Griffin searched her face—desperate for doubt, for hesitation, for any excuse to say no and keep her safe. But all he saw was fire.

All he saw was them.

"Together," she added, her voice stronger now, steady and certain.

That word. Together.

It undid him.

Because for so long, Griffin had been alone, even when he was surrounded by people. Even when he was in a room full of friends, full of women, full of noise. He had always been alone.

But not anymore.

Not with her.

He let out a breath he didn't realize he'd been holding, pressing his forehead to hers, his hand clutching the back of her neck like she was the only thing keeping him tethered to the earth.

And in that moment, he realized something so fucking terrifying it made his chest ache.

He wasn't afraid of Aiden.

He wasn't afraid of fallout.

He was afraid of how much he needed her. Of how much of himself he'd already handed over without a second thought.

Because Wren wasn't just a risk.

She was the thing that made him believe that some risks were worth losing everything for.

They didn't sleep right away.

They stayed up talking, holding, existing in that fragile space between fear and hope.

And when exhaustion finally pulled them under, it wasn't the kind of restless sleep Griffin was used to, the kind where his mind wouldn't shut off. Where the ghosts of his past kept him wired, waiting for the next hit.

No—this was different.

This was peace.

Because for the first time in his life, he wasn't waiting for the other shoe to drop.

He already knew it would.
But he also knew that when it did?
He'd still have her hand in his.
And that was enough.
That was everything.

23

CROSSING LINES

THE SOUND of the knock cut through the quiet like a gunshot. A sharp intrusion into the soft, slow world they had built overnight. Griffin's eyes opened instantly, his body tensing before his mind even caught up. The warmth of Wren still wrapped around him, legs tangled with his, breath steady against his chest. Her fingers were still loosely curled against his side, like she hadn't wanted to let go. Like some part of her had been afraid he wouldn't still be there when she woke up.

She stirred slightly, a soft inhale against his skin, and then she felt it. The tension rippling through him, his entire body had gone rigid beneath her., She lifted her head, pushing up slightly on her elbows, brows drawn in sleepy confusion. She didn't have to ask, she already knew.

Another knock, harder this time, heavier, like the person on the other side wasn't going to wait much longer. Griffin exhaled sharply, jaw tightening as he shifted, untangling himself from her warmth. It was the last thing he fucking wanted to do. Dragging a hand through his already-messy hair, his voice was quiet, certain… resigned.

"It's Aiden."

Wren froze.

For a moment, she didn't breathe. Didn't move. Reality slammed into her like a wrecking ball, shattering the illusion of safety that had wrapped around them in the dark. What felt untouchable beneath the hush of night now felt exposed and fragile, too fucking real. And she wasn't ready. Not for this. Not for him to see. To know. To react—because she knew he would. There was no version of this that didn't end in a storm, and her first instinct, the one buried deep in muscle memory, was to run.

She sat up quickly, the blanket clutched against her chest like it could shield her from what came next. Her mind was already racing, already scanning for exits. The bedroom, the hallway, anywhere but here. If she could just slip away, vanish for a little while, let Griffin process it alone… just maybe it wouldn't spiral into the wreckage she felt creeping toward them.

But when she saw his face.

She stopped.

There was no fear in his eyes. No hesitation. No panic. Just this quiet, unwavering certainty that hit her harder than anything else could've. He wasn't hiding or running. Wasn't reaching for excuses or scrambling to protect himself behind silence. There was no attempt to bury the truth. He wasn't trying to bury her.

And the second she saw that, her heart slammed against her ribs so hard, it hurt. In this moment, she knew…

He was choosing her.

He was choosing them.

Another knock.

He stood, stretching slightly, before rolling his shoulders. Griffin was prepared for this battle, no hesitation in his movements. This wasn't the time for second-guessing. He crossed the room, fingers flexing at his sides. Steeling his features, he pulled the door open—

And there was Aiden.

Still in the same clothes from last night, shirt wrinkled, hair a mess, face pale. Drawn with the kind of exhaustion that only comes after a night of drinking too much and thinking too hard. And Griffin already fucking knew, before his best friend even opened his mouth, why he was here.

Glancing down for a split second before rubbing the back of his neck, Aiden exhaled. Shifting on his feet, his voice was hoarse. Rough. Genuine in a way Griffin hadn't heard in a long time.

"Man, I wanted to come and—"

That's when Aiden saw her.

Standing there, at the edge of the living room.

Hair in a messy bun, face flushed. Still in the same damn cami and shorts she had fallen asleep in. Looking so fucking soft in the morning light. Aiden's entire body went rigid. His face morphing from exhaustion to realization to betrayal in a matter of seconds. Eyes locking onto Griffin's like he didn't even know the man standing in front of him anymore. Like whatever he had been about to say had just fucking died in his throat.

No one moved. No one breathed for a long, tense, stretched-out moment between them.

Then, suddenly, Aiden snapped.

"You motherfucker," he spat, his voice sharp, laced with a fury Griffin had never seen. Utter disbelief marring his features. Hurt plain as day, and before Griffin could even blink, Aiden swung.

The impact was solid. Sharp. A clean right hook that caught Griffin just below his left eye, snapping his head to the side slightly. The force of it vibrating through his bones, into his chest, slicing the air between them.

The moment Aiden's fist connected with Griffin's face, Wren felt her heart drop straight to the fucking floor. The sound of the impact was solid, brutal, and unforgiving. It echoed in her chest, vibrating through every nerve in her body.

"Aiden!" she screamed. Her feet moved forward on instinct.

Griffin barely reacted. He took the hit. Absorbed it like he'd been expecting it. He knew this was how it had to go. Jaw clenching, he curled his fists at his sides, but didn't strike back. Straightening, he exhaled slowly, shaking off the sting, expression unreadable.

Aiden wasn't finished.

"You fucked my sister?" he shouted, voice breaking, rage pouring through every syllable.

The words cracked through the air like a whip.

Wren flinched. Her breath caught like she'd been hit. Like those five words had reduced her to something dirty. Something disposable.

"Aiden—" she started, her voice barely a whisper.

But he was already moving.

He swung.

Griffin stepped back, smooth and measured. Dodged it.

Another swing. Missed.

Then another. Wild. Reckless. Controlled fury meeting calm precision. Griffin didn't flinch. Didn't even blink.

But when Aiden reared back for one more, fist cocked, eyes wild, breath heaving, Griffin's voice cut through the air, low and final.

"That's enough."

Quick. Effortless. A lifetime of instinct snapping into place.

Before Aiden even knew what was happening, Griffin had him hooked under the arm, flipped with his own momentum, and slammed onto the hardwood. One clean, brutal movement.

Griffin pinned him down, forearm pressed across his chest, firm enough to hold, not enough to crush. His breath was steady. Controlled. Like he'd been here before. Too many times.

His voice came low. Calm. Dangerous.

Wren gasped, the sound sharp in the silence. Her hands trembled at her sides, torn… Run to Aiden, pull Griffin off, do something. But she didn't move.

Because that voice, with that quiet, lethal edge, told her everything.

Griffin wasn't out of control.

He was choosing not to be.

"Relax, Wren," he said, without looking at her, his focus solely on Aiden, on the side of his face that wasn't pressed into the floor. "I'm not fighting him."

He let the words settle, let them sink in, before his voice dipped lower, firmer.

"But he is going to listen to what I have to say."

Wren swallowed hard. Watching Aiden's chest heave, nostrils flare, hands twitching. He wanted to swing again. But Griffin's hold would make it fucking useless. He wasn't getting out of this. Not until he let him.

"Ask the question again," Griffin said, his voice like steel.

Aiden's jaw ticked. "What?"

"You asked me if I fucked your sister." Griffin's grip tightened, just slightly. Just enough to make it clear who was in control here. "So ask me again."

Aiden glared up at him, chest rising and falling in sharp, furious bursts. "Did. You. Fuck. Her?"

Wren felt her entire body seize, shame rising in her like a tidal surge—hot, unrelenting, suffocating. Not because she'd done anything wrong. Not because she regretted a single moment with Griffin. But because standing here, under the weight of Aiden's judgment, it was like everything real was being twisted into something filthy. Like falling for Griffin, truly falling, had somehow made her the villain in her own story.

She wanted to scream. To claw through the tension and drag them both back to who they were before this moment. She wanted to tell Aiden to shut the fuck up and stop acting like her body, her heart, her choices were his to control. And she wanted to tell Griffin to stop handling this like some carefully worded negotiation. Like Aiden's approval was more important than the love that had wrecked and rebuilt them both.

But Griffin wasn't done.

Quiet and certain, "No," he said. His voice cut through the thick, electric air like the fucking fist that hit him.

And for just a second, she didn't feel ashamed.

She felt seen.

Aiden stilled.

Wren barely had time to exhale before Griffin kept going.

"I haven't," he admitted, his expression unreadable. "God, I've wanted to."

Her stomach clenched. Her pulse drummed. The room seemed to close in around her.

Aiden growled, his entire body surging beneath Griffin's hold, but Griffin didn't flinch.

He didn't waver.

He didn't let go.

"But I haven't," he continued, voice dipping lower. Rougher. Like he needed Aiden to hear every damn word. "Because she's not some fucking mistake. Not some one-night thing I'd get bored of and move the fuck on from."

His grip loosened slightly—not in surrender, but in a way that forced Aiden to really listen.

"She's Wren, man," Griffin said, his voice was raw now, like it had been scraped from the inside of his chest. "Wren."

His eyes didn't leave hers, not for a second. And in that look was everything.

Every stolen moment.

Every brush of skin.

Every breathless laugh and every broken silence that had passed between them like a goddamn lifeline. He wasn't just saying it to Aiden. He was telling her. Showing her.

"If you think for one fucking second," he went on, each word sharper than the last, "that I'd treat her like she's anything less than everything to me, then you never fucking knew me at all."

Wren didn't blink.

She couldn't.

Her throat tightened, a sob caught somewhere between heartbreak and wonder. Because Griffin wasn't defending her like she was a mistake.

He was claiming her like she was the only thing that had ever made him whole.

And goddamn it, she felt it. In her chest. In her bones. In the way he looked at her. Like she was the only thing in the fucking universe that mattered.

Aiden's breaths were ragged beneath Griffin's weight. Jaw clenched so tight it looked painful, hands balled into fists. His entire body vibrating with fury.

But Wren could see it. Beneath the anger, beneath the betrayal, beneath the fight…

The hurt. The disbelief. The way his best friend, the one person he trusted most, had done the one thing Aiden never saw coming.

Wren stepped forward, hesitating for only a second, before lowering herself beside them. Her voice was soft, tentative. "Aiden," she whispered.

He didn't look at her.

She swallowed hard. "This isn't—this isn't just some thing. It's not something we did to hurt you."

His breath came in short, sharp bursts, but he still wouldn't look at her.

"We didn't plan this," she continued. "I didn't mean to fall for him. But I did." She exhaled, shaking her head. "And I won't apologize for that."

Aiden's eyes snapped to hers, a mixture of disbelief and betrayal swirling in his stormy depths.

Griffin's jaw tensed. "I'll let you up," he said, voice controlled and even. "But if you swing at me again, your face will catch more than the floor."

Aiden's eyes flicked back to him, an edge of sharpness there. But after a beat, his body slackened.

Griffin exhaled slowly, easing back, giving Aiden space to push himself up.

Wren held her breath.

Aiden wiped his mouth with the back of his hand, his chest still rising and falling too fast, his fists still tight at his sides. But he didn't lunge again.

He just stared at them. "You really think you can do this?" he snapped. "You really think you get to just—" He let out a bitter laugh, shaking his head. "You're a fucking joke, Hayes."

"Aiden," she started.

He was already turning toward the door.

Griffin didn't stop him.

Because there was nothing left to say.

The door slammed.

And then there was nothing but silence.

Wren's breath shuddered.

Griffin stood there, still staring at the door.

Wren's hands were shaking. Her heart was still pounding, her skin still burning from the adrenaline. She sucked in a breath, turning to look at Griffin, expecting… something.

But he just ran a hand down his face, exhaling sharply, shoulders still tense.

Then, after a long, heavy beat, he muttered, "Well. That went about how I fucking expected."

Wren let out a choked laugh, equal parts disbelief and exhaustion.

Then she stepped toward him. Pressing her forehead against his chest, her body curling into him like it was the only place she could breathe.

He hesitated for only a second before wrapping his arms around her, pulling her in tight.

They stood there like that, tangled in the wreckage of what had just happened.

Griffin just stood there, holding her; his mind was elsewhere.

And for the first time since all of this started, he doubted himself.

Maybe Aiden was right.

Maybe he didn't deserve this.

Maybe he had just lost everything.

And maybe Wren would wake up tomorrow and realize it, too.

Wren felt the tremor in Griffin's chest before she heard his breath shake. His arms were strong around her, unyielding, but his body had stiffened. Like he was bracing for a hit that hadn't come yet.

She lifted her head, just enough to see his face, and the sight of him nearly split her in two.

His expression was unreadable, locked down, but she knew better. She could see it in the way his jaw was set too tight. In the way his fingers flexed once against her back before stilling completely. He wasn't just standing there, holding her. He was retreating. The walls were creeping back up, that familiar doubt clawing its way into his chest.

And she fucking hated it.

"Stop," she whispered, pressing her palm against his heart.

Griffin didn't answer. Didn't move. Just kept staring at the door like he was waiting for Aiden to come storming back through it. Waiting for more blows to land—maybe not with fists this time, but with words. Words that would tear him open in a way he wasn't sure he could recover from.

She knew exactly what was happening in his head. Knew exactly where his thoughts had gone.

"You don't get to do that," she said, firmer now.

"Do what?" His voice was hoarse, empty.

She tilted her chin up, forcing him to look at her. "Doubt yourself."

His throat worked, Adam's apple bobbing once, but he still didn't say anything.

Wren exhaled sharply, stepping back just enough to make sure he saw her—really saw her. "Aiden is pissed, Griffin. Of course, he is. But he'll get over it."

Griffin's jaw twitched. "You don't know that."

"I do," she countered. "He's my brother. I know him better than anyone." She paused, voice softer. "I know you, too."

A bitter laugh scraped from Griffin's throat as he ran a hand down his face. "You think Aiden's just gonna let this slide? He's never gonna look at me the same way again."

"Maybe not," she admitted. "But does that mean I'm supposed to just pretend like none of this ever happened? That I'm supposed to just walk away from you to make him feel better?" She shook her head. "Because I can't do that, Griff. I won't."

His shoulders hunched slightly, his body betraying just how deep Aiden's words had gotten under his skin. The weight of them sat heavy on him, pressing down, suffocating.

And she wasn't going to let him sit in it. Not alone.

She reached for him again, this time gripping his face between her hands, forcing his eyes back to hers. "You fought for me, Griffin. And now it's my turn to fight for you."

Something cracked in his gaze. "Wren—"

"I need to talk to him."

His entire body locked up. "Wren—"

"I have to," she insisted. "Because you were right. We can't do this in the dark. And Aiden needs to hear this from me."

His grip on her waist tightened, like he was already preparing for her to walk out the door. Like this was the part where she left.

Her fingers slid up, threading into his hair, grounding him. "I'm not going anywhere," she whispered. "But he's my brother. I have to at least try."

Griffin exhaled sharply, his hands flexing once against her hips before he nodded. "Okay."

Wren pressed one last lingering kiss against his lips, her heart thundering as she whispered, "I'll come back."

Before she could change her mind, before she could let the sight of him, the feel of him, tether her here for good—she turned, grabbed her keys, and left.

Wren wasn't stupid.

She knew Aiden wouldn't be ready to hear her out. Knew she was probably walking into a wall of stubbornness, rage, and betrayal. But she had to do this. Not just for Griffin. Not just for Aiden.

For herself.

Her brother had always been her protector, the person who took care of her when she needed it. But she wasn't a kid anymore. And for the first time in her life, this wasn't something she needed him to fix.

24

TRUTHS OUT

SHE PULLED into Aiden's driveway, her grip so tight on the steering wheel that her knuckles ached. Every mile that led her here had been spent stewing in frustration. Rehearsing what she would say, mapping out exactly how she would make him understand. But now that she was sitting there, staring at the house she knew as well as her own, it wasn't anger that sat heavy in her chest.

It was heartbreak.

Not for herself. Not even for Griffin.

For Aiden.

For the fact that he couldn't see what was right in front of him. For the fact that he had spent years taking for granted the very people who would have walked through fire for him. And now, when faced with the truth, he wasn't just rejecting it.

He was rejecting her.

She climbed out of the car and slammed the door, not giving herself a chance to hesitate. The house was dark, but his truck was in the driveway. He was home. And he was ignoring her.

Coward.

She stormed up the porch steps, knocked—once, twice. Nothing.

"Aiden," she called, knocking harder. "I know you're in there."

Still nothing.

Fine.

Her jaw tightened as she crouched down, grabbing the spare key from under the welcome mat. Stupid. Predictable. Just like the man inside. She shoved it into the lock, turned the handle, and let herself in.

The moment she stepped inside, the smell of stale beer and regret hit her in the face.

The house was a wreck with bottles scattered across the counter, an untouched pizza box sagging on the coffee table. Cushions were tossed haphazardly like he'd been pacing, restless, maybe even throwing shit. It had only been a few hours, but it looked like he had spent days drowning in his own misery.

And then, there was Aiden.

Slumped on the couch, beer in hand. Face unreadable in the dim glow from the streetlight filtering through the blinds. He was staring at the blank TV screen like it had personally offended him, his jaw clenched so tight she could see the muscle ticking from across the room.

His eyes flicked to hers.

Hard. Unforgiving.

"What the fuck do you want?" His voice was edged in exhaustion but still laced with that same resentment that had simmered between them when he walked out earlier.

Wren shut the door behind her, locking it. "You already know."

Aiden scoffed, shaking his head, exhaling a humorless laugh as he set his beer down with a dull thud. "Nah. You got what you wanted, Wren. You don't need to explain it to me."

Her throat burned, her pulse roaring in her ears. "I do."

Aiden sat up, rubbing a hand down his face before leveling her with a glare. "What do you want me to say, huh? That I'm happy for you? That I'm totally fucking cool with the fact that my best friend—the guy I trusted—went behind my back with my little sister?"

She flinched at the words. Not because they weren't expected.

But because they weren't true.

"I'm not a fucking kid, Aiden."

"You're my kid sister," he snapped. "You always will be."

"Then maybe it's time you started treating me like the grown-ass woman I am."

His nostrils flared, his hands curling into fists on his knees. But Wren didn't back down. Not this time.

She took a breath, steadying herself.

And then she said it.

"I love him."

Aiden's entire body went rigid.

Wren felt her chest squeeze, the weight of the admission settling into the space between them. "I didn't plan on it. I didn't expect it. But I do."

She saw it. The way his throat worked, the way his breathing changed. But he said nothing.

"And we haven't even slept together." Her voice wavered, but her conviction didn't. "So whatever fucked-up narrative you've built in your head about him using me, about this being some kind of game, it's bullshit."

Aiden flinched, his face twisting with something raw, something wounded. But Wren didn't stop.

"I know this pisses you off," she continued, pushing through the lump forming in her throat. "I know it feels like some kind of betrayal, but I need you to hear me when I say this. I'm not asking for your approval. I'm not asking for your blessing."

Her voice softened, but it didn't break.

"But I am asking for you."

Aiden exhaled sharply, his face an unreadable mask of tension, his hands white-knuckled as they pressed against his knees. He looked at her like she had just ripped something from him.

"You don't have to like it," she murmured. "But you're not taking him from me."

The words hit the air like a gunshot.

Wren clenched her fists, bracing for his reaction. She had expected anger. Fury. Another cruel jab to push her away.

Instead, Aiden just sat there.

Silent.

Like he had nothing to say. Like he was actually listening.

"He didn't betray you," she said, voice edged with frustration. "Griffin didn't try anything with me, Aiden. He never crossed that line."

Aiden's head snapped up, his eyes burning with barely contained rage. "You expect me to believe that?"

"Yes," she shot back, her voice cracking. "Because it's the fucking truth."

Aiden scoffed, looking away, shaking his head.

"I was the one who pushed it," she continued, stepping closer, refusing to let him dismiss this like it was some meaningless fling. "I was the one who wanted more than the surface-level bullshit conversations around you. I was the one who started this."

Aiden's jaw locked, his fists tightening, but she didn't stop.

"We lost time, Aiden," she said, voice softer now, but still laced with steel. "Because you never got to know Griffin. You never saw him for who he really is."

He frowned, brows knitting together. "What the hell is that supposed to mean?"

She exhaled sharply, pressing her fingers to her temple, the weight of everything pressing against her ribs. "You just used Hayes. You used the name, the reputation, the business connections he could get you. You used him to make yourself look good, to get women, to build your fucking career."

Aiden's expression darkened. "That's bullshit."

"Is it?" she challenged, voice thick with emotion. "Tell me one thing about Griffin that doesn't have to do with business. Tell me something real about him. Something that has nothing to do with the deals he's gotten you or the reputation you love to use when it benefits you."

Aiden opened his mouth.

Nothing came out.

And that told her everything.

"Exactly," she whispered. "You never saw him, Aiden. You saw what he could do for you."

A muscle ticked in his jaw, his fists clenching at his sides. "That's not fair."

"Neither is what you're doing to him," she shot back, voice breaking. "Neither is acting like this is some massive betrayal when you never even fucking noticed the man beneath the name."

Silence.

Wren swallowed hard. Then, her voice lowered. Deadly. Final.

"And he's not an idiot, Aiden. He knows."

Aiden's brows furrowed, but she kept going.

"He knows your friendship is a front. That it's surface-level. That you've only ever taken from him without ever giving a damn about the man behind it. And do you know what's worse?" She tilted her head, letting the words sting. "He sees through your bullshit. And still, for some damn reason, he respects you."

Aiden recoiled like she had slapped him.

"You wanted the truth?" she continued, voice thick. "I came into town two days before you saw me. My first night here, I met Griffin at Marshside. And do you know what happened?" She stepped forward. Closer. "We sat and talked. For hours."

Aiden's face twisted, a mess of anger, confusion, and something else—something she couldn't quite place.

"You weren't a factor," she said, her voice raw. "You weren't on my mind, and you weren't on his."

Aiden's breath hitched.

"But you sure as hell are now."

Wren didn't waver. Didn't blink. Didn't let him slip out of this.

She had Aiden exactly where she needed him, trapped in the weight of his own guilt, staring at the truth like it was a loaded gun pressed against his ribs. And she wasn't going to let him run from it.

Not this time.

"You weren't a factor, Aiden," she repeated, her voice steady despite the fire in her chest. "You weren't on my mind, and you weren't on his. We were just two people in the same place at the same time. And for once you weren't the center of it."

Aiden sucked in a sharp breath, nostrils flaring, fists trembling where they rested on his knees. But he said nothing. Because what the hell could he say?

Wren took another step closer, closing the space between them, her presence a slow, suffocating burn against his anger.

"And then," she continued, voice laced with something razor-sharp, something lethal, "your dumbass had him come look at houses for you."

Aiden's jaw locked.

"Neither of us knew," she pressed. "Not until that day. That first house. And do you want to know what he did?" She didn't wait for an answer. Didn't let him interrupt. She wanted him to fucking hear it. "He stopped. He looked me in the eyes, and he said, *'You're Aiden's fucking sister. I'm not doing that.'*"

Stunned, Aiden blinked, like the words knocked the wind from his chest.

Wren let it sink in. Let the words dig in deep, into the marrow of his fucking bones.

"So yeah," she whispered, eyes burning into his. "The truth? I am the fucking woman you asked him about that day."

Aiden swallowed hard, his Adam's apple bobbing as his gaze flicked to the floor, like he couldn't bear to look at her. Like he didn't want to acknowledge that he was wrong.

But she wasn't finished. Not yet.

"You think he doesn't fucking know what he's risking by being with me?" she asked, her voice breaking now, the weight of it all pressing hard against her ribs. "You think he doesn't know that he could lose you? That he could lose everything?" She shook her head, stepping back just slightly, giving herself space to breathe, because if she didn't, she might fucking break. "And he still chose me."

Aiden's head snapped up then, his eyes wild, his chest rising and falling in sharp, uneven bursts. "Wren—"

"No," she cut him off, shaking her head. "You don't get to talk your way out of this. Not this time."

He clenched his jaw so tight she could see the tension rolling through his body, his hands twitching, his entire frame rigid. But she didn't let up.

"You used him, Aiden," she said, her voice like a dagger, slicing straight through him. "But I see him."

Aiden sucked in a sharp and jagged breath, but he still didn't speak.

Silence stretched between them, thick and suffocating, the weight of everything pressing down on both of them. The years of friendship. The trust. The unspoken expectations. The way Aiden had never once thought this could happen, that Griffin could ever want something—someone— that wasn't tied to the life Aiden had built around him.

And now, it was crumbling.

Wren exhaled shakily, her voice softer now, but no less resolute. "Three days."

Aiden blinked, his brows furrowing. "What?"

"Three days," she repeated, folding her arms across her chest, grounding herself, holding her fucking line. "That's all I'm giving you. I won't push you, I won't call, I won't bring this up. But after that?" She lifted her chin, her throat tight, her heart pounding. "You don't get to ice me out. You don't get to decide who I love."

Aiden didn't move. Didn't breathe.

Didn't speak.

For the first time in her life, Wren saw something in her brother's eyes that she had never seen before.

Doubt.

And for the first time, she didn't feel guilty for putting it there.

She turned for the door, pausing only long enough to look back at him, her voice quiet and final.

"I hope you use those three days to really think about the kind of friend you've been."

Then she left.

And Aiden?

For the first time since this whole thing started, he had nothing left to say.

25

ALTAR CONFESSION

WREN DIDN'T FEEL relief when she walked out of Aiden's house.

She felt like she'd left pieces of herself behind, scattered across the battlefield of blood ties and broken expectations. Her lungs burned, her throat raw from words that tasted like betrayal but felt like freedom. Every step she took away from that house wasn't just distance.

It was a fucking declaration.

She wasn't looking back.

Her hands trembled against the steering wheel as headlights blurred past in streaks of white and gold. The world kept spinning, oblivious to the war she'd just waged and to the brother she'd stood in front of and said no to. No to his control. No to his ignorance. No to the idea that love —real fucking love—had to fit inside the lines he drew.

Her heart was still pounding, but not from fear.

Her heart was pounding from certainty.

Because she'd chosen Griffin Hayes.

And she'd do it again.

Every reckless, beautiful, devastating time.

By the time she pulled into his complex, the weight of it all finally settled. She wasn't exhausted from regret. She was exhausted from fighting. For him, for them, for something that mattered more than keeping the peace. That weight and exhaustion didn't feel like a burden, though; it was more like armor.

But beneath that steel resolve, under every layer of defiance and pride, there was something softer.

Something fragile.

Because she knew exactly where he'd be.

Where Griffin always went when the storm inside him got too loud, when the demons whispered lies that sounded too much like truth.

The balcony.

The fucking altar where he sacrificed every piece of himself the world told him he wasn't allowed to feel.

And when she pushed open his door and stepped into that darkened room, her chest tightened like a vise.

There he was.

Back turned, shoulders tense, whiskey glass dangling from his fingers like a lifeline he didn't believe in. The wind tangled through his hair, the ocean roaring beneath him like it could swallow him whole if he let it.

God, he looked like a man drowning on dry land.

And it wrecked her.

Because she didn't just see him.

She felt him.

EVERY FRACTURED PIECE. EVERY UNSPOKEN FEAR. EVERY WALL HE WAS rebuilding in real time, convinced she was about to walk through that door and tear him apart. But he didn't get to decide that. Not tonight. She crossed the room, her bare feet silent against the floor, but the weight of her presence hit him long before she spoke.

"You're quiet," she said, her voice softer than she wanted because no matter how strong she felt, seeing him like this knocked the breath from her lungs.

"So are you," he muttered, raising the glass to his lips, his eyes never leaving the endless horizon.

Her stomach twisted into knots. Because she knew exactly what he was thinking.

"You think I regret it."

He didn't answer. Didn't have to.

The way his shoulders tensed, the way his grip tightened around that glass—it was all the confirmation she needed.

Wren's throat burned as anger surged beneath the heartbreak. "You think I'm going to wake up tomorrow and wish I hadn't chosen you."

That made him pause. A single, fleeting hesitation. But it was enough to light the fuse.

Her nails bit into her palms as fury and pain tangled in her chest. "You think Aiden was right."

His knuckles turned white around the glass.

That was it. That was the fucking last straw.

"Look at me," she snapped, closing the distance between them, her heart slamming against her ribs.

Nothing.

"Griffin."

Silence.

So she did what any woman in love with a stubborn, broken man would do.

She ripped the glass from his hand and slammed it onto the railing, the sharp crack slicing through the night like a warning shot.

His head snapped toward her, eyes blazing with something between shock and surrender. But before he could open his damn mouth, she was on him.

"No," she seethed, her chest heaving with every ragged breath. "You don't get to fucking stand here and doubt me."

His jaw clenched, muscles twitching beneath his skin like he was holding back a thousand words he didn't know how to say.

"Wren—"

"No," she cut him off, stepping so close her body pressed against his, her pulse roaring in her ears. "You think I don't *see* you?"

His breath hitched, his eyes dark and wild like a man on the edge of losing everything and too afraid to believe he could actually keep it.

"You think I don't know why you're out here?" she whispered, her voice breaking as her hands fisted in his shirt. "You're waiting. Waiting for me to regret this. Waiting for me to leave, because that's easier than believing someone could actually stay."

His entire body went rigid, his walls slamming up too late—because she was already inside.

"*I see you, Griffin Hayes,*" she breathed, her tears falling freely now. "I see every fucking piece of you. The man who's convinced himself that love is just a countdown to pain. The man who would rather drown in whiskey than risk being wanted."

Her fingers curled around his jaw, forcing his gaze to hers.

"But you're wrong."

His throat worked, something shattering behind his eyes.

"You're fucking wrong," she repeated, her voice cracking under the weight of it all.

He tried to look away.

She didn't let him.

"You don't get to doubt me. Not when I fought for you. Not when I walked away from my brother and every ounce of comfort I've ever known. Because… I. Chose. You."

His breathing turned ragged, his hands twitching at his sides like he didn't trust himself to touch her, to feel this.

"You think you're dangerous?" she whispered, a broken laugh slipping past her lips. "You think you're the storm?"

Her forehead pressed to his, her tears wet against his skin.

"*I am the danger,* Griffin. Because I know you. I know every reason you think I should run, and I'm still fucking here."

His control snapped like a live wire sparking in the rain.

She felt it, the shift, the exact moment he realized he couldn't outrun this anymore.

"I know why you walked out," she whispered, her breath trembling. "I know why you kept pulling back. Why you didn't sleep with me."

His hands shot to her hips, bruising, desperate.

"Not because you didn't want to…" Her lips hovered over his, teasing, taunting, owning him. "But because you already fucking loved me."

That guttural sound tore from his chest—raw, wrecked, real.

"Say it," she begged, her voice nothing but a breath. "Say you love me."

His body trembled, his grip tightening like she was the only thing keeping him tethered to this world.

Right then, she dropped the final blow.

"Because *I love you, Griffin Hayes,*" she whispered, her voice cracking wide open. "*I love you so much it fucking hurts.*"

Those words detonated inside him.

He snapped.

His mouth crashed onto hers, wild and unrestrained. Like he'd been starving for this—for her—since the second they met. His hands roamed her body like he was afraid she'd disappear if he didn't memorize every inch.

"Fuck," he growled into her mouth, his voice breaking apart as he backed her against the wall, lips never leaving hers. "I love you. I fucking love you."

He said it again.

And again.

Like every repetition was a piece of his soul being handed over. No take-backs, no regrets.

Her legs wrapped around his waist, her nails raking down his back, pulling him closer, deeper, home.

"Griffin…" she gasped, her head falling back as his mouth found her neck, teeth grazing over her pulse like he needed to brand her from the inside out.

"I'm yours," he rasped against her skin, his voice wrecked and reverent all at once. "I've always been yours."

Equal parts relief and devastation, a sob tore from her throat because she knew. She felt it.

This wasn't just love.

This was survival.

Wren's fingers tangled in his hair, yanking his head back. Her eyes were dark and dangerous as they met his.

Her lips curved into a wicked, breathless smile.

"That's good," she whispered, her voice dripping with sin. "Because now, I want you to fuck me like you hate me."

Griffin's entire body shuddered, a curse falling from his lips as his control obliterated.

"Now, put me down. I want you to remind me why I walked through fire for you," she breathed, her mouth teasing his jaw, nails leaving trails of possession down his chest. "Why I chose the storm."

He didn't answer. Just let her drag down his chest like she owned him. Then eased her down his body, one hand locked on her hip like he wasn't ready to let her go, not even for gravity.

Because the second she pulled him inside, slamming the door behind them, Griffin Hayes made her a silent promise. One she'd never forget. Not who he was. Not who they were.

And as his mouth claimed hers again—ruthless and worshipping all at once—they both knew:

This wasn't just a confession. It was a vow.
And tonight?
They weren't surviving the storm.
They were the storm.

26

EDGE OF WORSHIP

THE SECOND she led him through the sliding door, Griffin's hands locked around her thighs like he'd been waiting to claim her. There was no hesitation. No finesse. Just pure, brutal possession. He lifted her effortlessly, her legs wrapping tight around his waist, heels digging into his back. His grip on her ass wasn't just firm, it was punishing; his fingers digging deep enough to bruise, like he wanted her sore tomorrow. Like he wanted to leave fingerprints as a reminder that she was his to grab, to hold, to fuck.

Wren didn't want soft. Not tonight.

Her mouth slammed into his, messy and wild—teeth clashing, lips bruising; tongues locked in a battle neither of them planned on losing. She devoured him like she was starving, breath frantic, body already grinding against his. And Griffin? He let her. Let her take. Let her steal. But fuck... He was about to take it all back.

She bit down on his lip, then dragged her mouth to his ear. Her voice was a weapon soaked in sin.

"I want your cock down my throat until I can't breathe."

His breath punched out of him like thunder, his arms tightening around her until her spine arched with the pressure.

"I want you to bend me over and make my knees fucking shake."

He was unraveling by the second, every ounce of control slipping through his fingers like sand soaked in gasoline.

She licked the edge of his ear, then bit it—hard. "I want to feel you ruin me."

And just like that, he broke.

He set her down, her feet barely catching the floor, like it killed him to let go, even for a breath.

She didn't have time to exhale before he pinned her to the wall with a growl so low it vibrated through her chest. His mouth crashed into hers, tongue fucking past her lips, demanding, claiming, owning. Her moan poured into his mouth like fuel to the fire already tearing through his veins. And when he pulled back, panting and wild-eyed, she stared up at him with lips swollen and eyes alight with something dark and delicious.

Trouble. She was nothing but fucking trouble. Her hands slid up his chest, slow and taunting, until they wrapped around his wrists and shoved them above her head. She pinned herself to the wall, caging herself beneath him like she wanted to play helpless. "What's wrong, Hayes?" she purred, voice seductive. "Afraid I can't handle it? Or are you afraid I can?"

Like a switch was flipping inside him, his entire body snapped tight. His eyes rolled shut, just for a second.

When he opened them again? He wasn't the same man. The darkness in his stare was lethal. His smile? Gone.

She reached for his hand and pulled it to her throat, pressing his fingers down, pushing him into the dominance she craved.

"I told you to be careful what you ask for," he muttered, voice like gravel. "There's no coming back from this."

She smiled, lips curling with defiance. "I don't need to come back." She paused as his grip loosened. "Just make me come." His hand slid away from her as she turned toward the bed, smug, victorious—like she'd won.

But she barely made it one step.

His hand flew back to her throat, and he slammed her into the wall. Hard.

The force knocked the breath from her lungs and her hands flew to his wrist. Not to pull him away, but to hold him there. Her body jolted with pleasure as his grip tightened, cutting off just enough air to make her head spin. His mouth brushed against her ear, his voice dark and unrelenting. "Is this what you fucking wanted?" He pulled back, just enough to look at her. Enough to let her burn beneath the weight of his stare.

Those warnings he'd given her before? They weren't words. They were oaths.

And she believed every one of them now.

He leaned in again, his grip flexing against her throat. "Before you answer, you better be sure. Because once I start—" he paused, dragging his thumb along the curve of her jaw, "—you're not getting out. You're going to beg me to stop. And I won't."

His teeth grazed her ear. Pulling a whimper from her.

She ignited, panties drenched. Her thighs had trails dripping down them. Her whole body pulsed with the need to be taken. And when her eyes dropped down… Fuck. The outline pressing beneath his jeans looked dangerous. Massive. Ready to fucking wreck her. She didn't wait. Her hand dropped between them. Bold. Needy. Desperate. She grabbed him. Tight. Thick. Hard. Throbbing.

The breath ripped out of him. His jaw clenched so hard his teeth ached. His fingers tightened around her throat, sending another wave of heat shooting between her thighs. His free hand snapped around her wrist, holding her right there, right on his cock, making sure she felt what she'd done.

"Okay," he growled. "Just remember, you fucking asked for this."

Her voice was a purr. Wrecked. Wicked. "I didn't ask." She dragged her nails along the thick ridge of him. "I begged."

He made a dark and primal sound. She had *him* fucking feral.

Then his mouth was back on hers—biting, devouring, filthy. His hands tore down her sides like he was trying to rip her open. He shoved her into the wall, hips grinding, his cock rubbing against the soaked fabric between her thighs in one slow, brutal roll.

Then he pulled back. Smirking. "I'm going to get a towel."

Her brows pulled together, breathless. "Why?"

His eyes flashed. "Because I don't want the bed to look like a fucking swimming pool."

Her entire body seized. Her clit pulsed. She thought she was already wet… until that.

"You keep talking like that and I'm gonna come before you even touch me," she teased.

And then he leaned in, lips brushing hers like a sin-stained promise. "Then be a good fucking girl and be on the bed. Naked. Waiting." It wasn't a request. It was a command.

Her body moved before her mind could catch up. Clothes ripped away. Skin flushed. Pulse thundering.

Griffin reentered the room, the towel slung over his shoulder, his jaw tight. Muscles coiled like a predator who just spotted his prey. His eyes locked on the bed—and fuck.

There she was.

Laid out like a fucking offering.

Naked. Glowing. Legs parted just slightly. Her fingers were back between her thighs, gliding across her clit in slow, lazy circles like she couldn't wait. Like she was edging herself for him. Keeping it warm. Wet. Ready. Her body already his to command.

His cock twitched. Hard. But that wasn't what broke him. It was her eyes. That wicked little fucking smirk. That look that said, *You thought you were in control.*

Griffin exhaled slowly, his body tight as a fucking vise, his control nothing more than splinters at this point. "I didn't say you could do that, Raine."

Oh. My. Fucking. God. Wren's breath caught in her throat, nipples instantly tightening. That voice—low, rough, pure goddamn ownership. He wasn't asking. He wasn't teasing. He was staking a claim.

He stood at the foot of the bed, eyes locked on hers, unmoving.

But her gaze dropped right to the heavy, pulsing bulge behind his jeans. Thick. Angry. Desperate to be freed. Her fingers stilled, but she didn't pull away.

"Show me," he growled.

Her pussy clenched, tight and aching, slick already coating her petals like her body knew exactly who it belonged to. Every throb pulsed between her legs, raw and demanding, a heat that wouldn't wait. She didn't think. Couldn't. Her legs parted wider, shameless and hungry, instinct stripping away every layer of hesitation.

Her fingers moved slowly, trembling with the weight of the moment. Then she found her slick and swollen clit throbbing beneath her touch, like it had been waiting for him to give the order. She circled it once, just to feel the way her body jolted, thighs twitching open even wider.

She was dripping. Desperate.

The soaked pink of her pussy glistened under the low light, glossy and obscene, a fucking masterpiece painted in lust. Wet clung to her thighs, smeared proof of what he'd done to her with nothing but his voice. She was already wrecked.

And he hadn't even laid a hand on her.

Griffin's breath caught. Ragged. Shallow. Then he fucking moved. His hands clamped around her thighs, dragging her down the bed so fast she cried out, her back arching as the sheets twisted beneath her.

She didn't fall. Only because he was between her legs, holding her there like he owned her. Like she was something he paid for with blood, and now it was time to collect.

Her breath came in shaky, shallow pants as he slowly peeled off his shirt. And when it dropped to the floor, her mouth dried. She knew he was built, but nothing could've prepared her for the raw, cut muscle. The wide chest. The deep grooves of his abs. The sharp V slicing down his hips like a fucking arrow pointing to exactly what she needed.

Her thighs trembled. Her pussy ached.

And he smirked as he saw every reaction.

Dark.

Knowing.

Dangerous.

He leaned in as his mouth claimed hers. Tongue deep. Possessive. It wasn't a kiss. It was a fucking warning.

She moaned into it, hips lifting off the bed, grinding against the thick press of his cock still trapped behind denim. Her hand flew down, desperate for him.

But he caught it—slamming it above her head, pinning it like it belonged there. Like she belonged there. His grip was steel. His presence? Suffocating. "Not yet, baby."

The sound of his voice alone made her clit throb.

His lips slowly traced a soft and cruel path down her neck. But his stubble burned. Each graze a promise of pain wrapped in pleasure. Then his mouth was on her breast.

Hot. Wet. Open.

He devoured her. Tongue flicking. Teeth grazing. Sucking until she gasped. His other hand pinched the other nipple—rolling it, tugging it, making her writhe.

Her back arched. Her hips searched. But he didn't give her what she wanted. He kept going.

Lower. Slower.

Dragging his tongue down her stomach, dipping into the sensitive spot just above her core. And then he stopped. Right at her waistband.

She could feel it. His stare. The way he looked at her. Like she was a meal, and he was about to feast.

The smirk that curled his lips when he saw the wetness soaked through the towel beneath her? Fucking filthy. He leaned down, brushing his lips against her inner thigh, and spit. Hot and heavy, right on her clit.

She jolted, body snapping. And then... two fingers. Thick. Deep. One brutal thrust and he was knuckle-deep inside her.

Her entire body bowed off the mattress. Her gasp? Shattered.

Just as she was getting used to his finger, he used his tongue.

Holy. Fucking. Hell.

It was slow at first. Wide licks. Up and down. Gathering every drop she had. Then his lips latched onto her clit and sucked.

Her hands shot down, yanking his hair, grinding her pussy against his mouth like she was possessed.

He groaned into her, the vibration turning her inside out. His fingers curled. His tongue flicked. His hand gripped her thigh so tight she'd bruise.

And she didn't give a single fuck. She was close. So fucking close. Then he stopped.

Just like that.

Gone.

She let out a scream, her body twitching, her pussy pulsing on nothing.

Then he was above her again. Fingers still inside, still working her. But his mouth? On hers.

Fuck—she tasted it.

Herself.

On his tongue. On his lips. On the scruff as it dripped down his beard.

He fucked her mouth with his kiss while his fingers fucked her open, harder now—curling, pulsing, grinding against her G-spot like he needed her to break.

And then his voice. Right at her ear. Rough. Low. Feral. "I thought you wanted to come." And just like that, he slammed his fingers harder, faster, deeper.

Her back arched, a cry tearing from her throat. Her entire body seized.

Until she exploded.

Her orgasm ripped through her like a fucking storm; thighs trembling, hips jerking, her pussy squirting so violently it soaked the sheets beneath her.

But he didn't stop. He went harder.

She thrashed beneath him. Her moans turned to cries. Her whole body was trembling like it couldn't take it. And still, he didn't let up.

She came again. Fast. Relentless. Wet. A puddle beneath her. Her chest heaving. Body burning.

Griffin looked down at her like he'd won a war.

He had. His voice was pure fucking filth. "Now you're ready for me."

She was still shaking. Still breathless.

Her thighs were a mess. Her core was ruined. Her body was trembling.

Without pausing and eyes locked on hers, "Turn over and get on your knees."

She obeyed. Fast. No thought. No hesitation. She was already moving before the words had settled. Her knees hit the mattress. Her ass lifted. Soaked petals on full display, begging for him. She heard the sound of his belt—metal clinking, leather sliding. It sent lightning through her spine. Her fingers clenched the sheets. Her body braced. Then she felt his hands.

Rough. Big. Owning.

He dragged her back until her ass pressed against his cock. His chest hovered above her, his breath hot at her ear. "Stay right fucking there, Raine."

She froze. His words were raw steel wrapped in velvet and made her throb. She heard the rustle of his jeans hitting the floor.

Then silence. Then heat. His cock—hot, thick, already wet with her gloss—dragged through her lips.

Slow. Taunting.

He coated himself in her gloss, again and again, teasing her ruined pussy with the head of his cock.

She gasped. Whimpered. Begged.

"Do you want it?" he asked, voice rougher now.

She nodded, breathless.

But that wasn't enough.

"Use your fucking words."

"Please," she choked out, her voice barely there. "Please, Griffin, I need it."

He let out a dark chuckle.

"Good girl."

That praise, those words, wrecked her.

Her pussy clenched so hard she moaned.

Only then did he push in. Thick. Deep. Fucking endless. And she lost it.

HE DIDN'T EASE IN. HE DIDN'T GIVE HER A SECOND TO ADJUST. HE FED her every brutal inch, dragging his cock through her slick, ruined cunt until the resistance turned into submission. Walls stretching wide around him. Her back bowed, and a broken moan spilled from her lips like it'd been ripped from her soul.

Griffin hissed between his teeth. "Fuck, you're tight. You didn't know that you missed this cock, did you?"

She nodded, breath stuttering. Her cheek pressed into the sheets, thighs trembling as she tried to take it all.

He gripped her hips tighter, his fingers digging into soft flesh—owning every part of her body like he'd paid in blood to claim it. "Say it."

Her voice cracked. "I never knew. I never had it. I missed it. I missed you."

Slowly, he pulled out just to the tip, then slammed back in, hard enough to jolt her entire body up the mattress. "Say it right."

"I missed your cock—fuck—Griffin, I missed your cock so bad."

"Good girl," he said, voice low. Deadly.

She whimpered.

He started to move then. Slow. Cruel. Deep, punishing strokes that forced her to feel every inch. His hips slammed into her ass with each thrust, the sound echoing like a fucking rhythm—wet, raw, obscene.

Her hands clawed at the sheets, nails dragging fabric as her body took everything he gave her.

He leaned forward, chest pressing into her back, voice pure gravel at her ear. "You feel that, baby? That stretch? That ache? That's me. That's what happens when I own you."

She choked out a moan, her back arching, ass lifting higher to take him deeper.

And he gave it to her.

He fucking gave her all of him. He reached around, hand slipping between her thighs, fingers finding her clit and rubbing tight, relentless circles that had her seeing stars. "Come on," he snarled. "Cream on my cock. Soak it. Show me what that ruined little pussy was made for."

And again, she shattered. Her cry ripped through the room. Her entire body locking up as her orgasm detonated through her.

And still, he didn't stop. He fucked her through it. Fucked her harder. Faster. "Yeah, that's it," he growled. "Make a mess. Drip down my cock. Soak the fucking sheets."

She came again. Less than a minute later. Her thighs convulsing. Her moans breaking into sobs. Her voice was gone.

Her body was wrecked.

But Griffin wasn't done.

He yanked her up by the hair, forcing her back into his chest. One hand wrapped around her throat. The other gripped her breast like it was his. He fucked up into her, toes barely grazing the mattress now. Her body completely suspended—helpless. Owned.

She let out a strangled sound, her head falling back against his shoulder, tears brimming from how good it felt. From how deep he was.

"How does it feel?" he snarled. "Being used like this? Being nothing but a toy for me to fuck?"

She tried to answer, but he squeezed her throat, cutting off the words and replacing them with a shuddering moan.

His mouth pressed to her temple. "That's right. You don't need to talk. You just need to take it." *Thrust* "Like the good." *Thrust* "Fucking." *Thrust* "Girl." *Thrust* "You are."

With one final thrust, he spun her around and threw her onto the mattress.

She bounced. Gasped. Her legs still spread, dripping.

He grabbed her ankles and dragged her to the edge.

Then he knelt. And spit on her pussy. Twice.

Grazing it with his hand, he spread the gloss and spit with his fingers before licking up the mess like it was fucking nectar. He devoured her— lips locked to her clit, tongue ruthless, fucking her with it as she screamed his name over and over again.

Her thighs clamped around his head. But it didn't matter.

He kept going until she squirted. Again. Until her body gave out, twitching and spent.

And then?

Then he stood. Grabbing her hand, guiding her to a seated position. Fisting his cock in his hand. Slick with her glaze. Veins bulging. Tip flushed and leaking.

He dragged it across her lips. "Open," he ordered.

She obeyed.

He shoved the head into her mouth and groaned as her tongue wrapped around it. "Yeah. See what you taste like."

She moaned, spit dribbling from the corners of her lips.

He pulled out.

Too soon.

She whimpered, eyes pleading.

He just smirked and pushed her onto her back. Then he lined himself back up between her legs and slammed in. No buildup. Just brutal, ruthless, desperate fucking.

The bed shook. The walls thudded. The only sounds were skin, gasps, growls, and slick.

"Where do you want it?" he growled, panting, sweat dripping down his chest. "Where do you want me to fucking release, baby?"

She was gone. But she still managed to say it: "Inside." Her legs wrapped around his waist, locking him in.

"You made me soak you," she panted, voice wrecked. "Now I want you to fill me."

His response was that of an animal.

One more thrust.

Another.

Then another.

He snapped.

His body seized, cock pulsing deep inside her as he came. Thick, hot ropes of it. Filling her. Coating her walls. So much it spilled back out. And her pussy milked it from him.

Her body clamped down, taking every fucking drop.

But he didn't pull out. Didn't soften.

He stayed there, buried, hands gripping her thighs like handles. Forehead pressed to hers, breathing hard. Their bodies locked, the aftershocks pulsing through them both. Neither one willing to move first or let go.

Finally catching his breath, his lips curled.

"Satisfied?" he rasped, his voice rough, wrecked, taunting.

Her fingers tightened in his hair, eyes still half-lidded, body still thrumming, completely fucking used. Dark and wicked, she smirked. "For now."

Griffin exhaled, a breath between a laugh and a groan, shaking his head. His grip on her tightened, fingers digging into her thighs, still holding her exactly where he wanted her.

He wasn't done. Not even fucking close.

And then he whispered:

"You're mine now."

27

WORSHIP ME

THE ROOM still smelled like sin.

Like sweat-slicked skin, tangled sheets, and every filthy promise Griffin Hayes delivered between gritted teeth and gasping breaths. The air was heavy, thick with the ghosts of moans. The echoes of last night's wreckage clung to Wren's body like a second skin.

Beep, beep, beep—the shrill buzz of Griffin's alarm cut through the haze.

It was almost offensive. Like the universe had the audacity to think time mattered when she was still drunk on him.

Griffin let out a low, gravelly groan that rumbled from deep in his chest and vibrated straight through her core. His arm shot out, blindly fumbling for his phone on the nightstand, muscles flexing as he silenced the world.

Silence reclaimed the room, but it wasn't peaceful.

It was charged.

Barely awake, Wren's eyes flicked to him, her hair a mess, lips swollen from hours of kissing and biting. Owning.

God, he was beautiful like this.

Raw. Unpolished. Hers.

And something in her snapped.

Without a word, she reached out, her fingers curling around his wrist and yanking him flat onto his back. His confused grunt barely had time to escape before she was straddling him—thighs framing his hips, black lace pressing down against the hard length already straining beneath his boxers.

Griffin's eyes cracked open, lazy and dark, a slow smirk tugging at the corner of his mouth like he knew exactly what game she was playing and he was more than ready to let her lose.

His hands slid down her thighs before gripping her ass, fingers digging into the soft flesh through the lace he clearly appreciated far too much.

"That's my favorite thing you could wear," he murmured, voice thick with sleep and desire. His thumbs stroked slow circles over her hips, eyes dragging over her like he was memorizing every inch. "Aside from nothing."

Wren's lips curved, heat sparking in her veins. "Fuck—he even wakes up smooth as silk," she breathed, gawking at him.

"Good morning, Hayes," she teased, her voice dripping with satisfaction, her body already aching for more of him.

His grin deepened, eyes glinting with mischief. "Damn. Back to Hayes already?"

She leaned down, her lips brushing his ear, her words soft but lethal. "When you make me look like I spilled a bottle of water on the floor and then fuck me like I begged for it?" Her teeth grazed his earlobe, making his whole body come alive. "You're definitely Hayes."

A low growl rumbled in his chest, but he didn't argue. Instead, he let his hands roam slowly and possessively, like he was reminding her exactly who she was dealing with.

And God, she loved it.

They stayed like that for a beat, letting the weight of last night settle between them. The bruises, the bite marks, the soreness in all the right places. Wren could still feel him—every place he'd touched, claimed, ruined.

Her heart stuttered when he reached up, brushing a strand of hair from her face with a tenderness that didn't match the wickedness in his eyes. "How do you wake up looking like an angel that crawled out of my dirtiest dream?"

Her breath caught. No teasing comeback. No snarky remark.

Just feelings. Real. Raw. Reckless.

And fuck, wasn't that exactly what he did to her?

Her fingers traced along his collarbone, nails dragging lightly over his skin, feeling the heat beneath. "I want to kiss you so bad right now."

His grin was pure cocky satisfaction. "I appreciate you waiting. Neither of us have brushed our teeth yet."

Her laugh was genuine and soft, but it died when she shifted her hips just enough to feel him press against her, hard and ready beneath thin fabric.

Her pulse spiked, smile turning dangerous.

"Careful," she whispered, glancing down between them. Voice dropping into something filthy, something that made his grip on her tighten. "Or I'll make you my mouthwash."

His jaw ticked. That muscle, the one she now knew drove her insane, pulsed with restraint. His fingers flexed against her hips. Like he was one second away from flipping her over and reminding her exactly who was in charge.

A low, primal sound escaped him. "That would be a great start to my morning."

Her head tilted, feigning innocence. "I was thinking spectacular."

But before she could so much as grind down on him, the world spun.

In a blur of sheets and a sharp gasp, Wren found herself pinned beneath him; his hand wrapped around her throat, weight pressing her chest into the mattress. His cock a thick, teasing promise against her ass.

Her heart pounded, heat flooding through her, but before she could open her mouth—

"I'm going to shower," he muttered, lips brushing her ear.

And then he was gone.

"The bastard!" she mumbled as she rolled to her back.

She lay there, breathless, staring at the ceiling like it had all the answers to why Griffin Hayes could ruin her so completely before 6:05 AM. Without even fucking trying.

The sound of the shower turning on snapped her out of her haze, but it only made things worse. Memories of last night rushed back—how he'd had her gasping his name, clawing at his back, begging for more when she didn't even know she had anything left to give.

She heard his toothbrush scraping, followed by the gurgle of mouthwash, and rolled her eyes.

That was one thing she hadn't tasted yet.

Yet.

Kicking off the sheets, Wren padded into the living room, grabbing her toothbrush from her bag before heading toward the bathroom. Her body still ached but in the best way. Her thighs were sore. Her lips swollen.

She couldn't remember the last time she felt so thoroughly ruined and so damn alive.

Standing at the sink, she started brushing, but her eyes?

Her eyes found him.

Through the fogged-up glass, Griffin's silhouette was pure fucking art. Broad shoulders. Lean muscle. Water cascading down his back like it was worshipping him the way she wanted to. His hands slicked through his hair, head tilted back, letting the spray beat against his chest, oblivious to the way she stood there, mesmerized.

Her pulse quickened. Her thighs pressed together instinctively.

She rinsed her mouth. Stepping closer to the glass, her breath fogged up the already misted surface as her eyes devoured every inch of him.

And that's when her lips curled.

Slow. Sinister. Decided.

Because Wren Sinclair didn't believe in waiting.

Not when that was standing right in front of her.

Not when every nerve in her body screamed for more.

Her fingers trailed across the cool glass, a silent promise to herself.

He thought he was in control?

Not a fucking chance.

The second Wren's eyes connected with his through the glass. She knew exactly how this was going to play out.

"So," she mused, voice echoing off the tile, "you said my black lace hipsters are your second favorite thing I could wear?"

Griffin's lips quirk. He loves how she thinks about this shit long after the moment has passed. "That's right." His voice is muffled by the hiss of the water.

She takes a slow step forward. "So what is your favorite thing I could wear?"

The shower door swung open just enough for her to slip inside.

He drinks her in, steam curling around them. "Perfection." His gaze sweeps over her, slow and worshiping. "And that's exactly how you are."

Fuck. She hates how he can say one thing and mean it ten different ways.

Her eyes flickered down, trailing over his collarbone, how his chest moved with each deep breath, the sharp ridges of his abs, then to his thick, chip-can sized cock that hung heavy between his legs.

He reached for her, slow and deliberate, the heat in his gaze making her dizzy.

When he pulls her in, his breath is hot, his body burning. "Now you can kiss me."

Their lips crashed together, tongues tangling, fingers digging into skin. She reached down, brushing against the thick length of him, a touch so light it made his breath stutter.

"Wren," he warned, his voice tight, strained.

She pulls back just enough to meet his gaze. "I didn't bring my mouthwash. Do you have anything that I can use?"

Fuck. His eyes widened, his body locked.

She fucking had him.

She felt the way his cock jumped in her hand, how his breath hitched, how his fingers twitched at his sides.

"Wren—"

She shoved him against the cold tile. His breath left him in a sharp exhale, the shock flashing through his gaze.

Then, he stepped forward.

She stopped him. One hand to his chest, pushing him back.

Her eyes flickered—dark, dangerous. He'd never seen that before. He'd never had someone even try to take control.

She pressed up on her toes, her lips hovering by his ear, breath warm, wicked, and filthy. "Now be a good boy and stand there," she said, voice low like she was whispering a dangerous secret.

Pulling back slightly, slow and deliberate, her fingers dragged up his chest like she was memorizing every inch. Her gaze locked on his, wicked and unflinching.

"Wait for me. Wait for me to slide your cock into my mouth. Down my throat. Wait until I gag and choke."

She licked her lips like she already tasted him, then trailed her hand down his stomach, stopping just above his waist.

"Wait for me to drain your cock," she whispered, her breath brushing his skin. "Wait for me to milk every drop out of you."

Her eyes flicked up, burning with hunger.

"Then watch me swallow everything you give me."

That wasn't a tease.

It was a damn promise. And what the fuck?

No one had ever even tried to control him before, much less succeeded.

But Wren? She owned him at that moment. His entire fucking body was locked in place, muscles wound tight as he watched her mouth slide down his neck, tongue flicking across his chest. Her lips puckering against every other ab muscle like she was worshiping him.

His breathing was uneven and shallow, thighs flexing so hard they ached.

She was taking her time, watching him unravel. She reached his hip bones, fingers tracing the dips and sharp angles before she kissed the edge of his hip.

He wanted to grab her hair, shove her down, take what was his—but she was in charge now. And fuck, she knew it.

She looked up, her emerald eyes alight with something wicked. He barely had time to admire the dimples on her cheeks before her lips wrapped around him.

FUCK.

She knew exactly how to break him.

One hand cupped his balls, and the other gripped the base of his shaft, keeping him steady as her tongue flicked over his tip. It was the lightest, teasing touch, but it was just enough to drive him insane.

Then, she flattened her tongue against the underside and pressed— like she was trying to blow bubbles. His thighs twitched, his hands clenched into fists.

She looked up, her eyes asking the silent question: Do you want more?

His breath hitched. His answer was in the way his body reacted.

That's when she took him.

Hand working in time with her mouth, one racing the other, her grip tightening around his balls.

His head fell back against the tile, vision hazing at the edges. A low, guttural growl tore from his throat.

She could feel it—how good it was for him. That deep, throbbing ache that wrapped in his core. She wanted more. She wanted to feel more. She pushed him deeper, her hand twisting, grip tightening.

Wren looked up, watching his head roll back, mouth parted, and abs flexing. His back was against the tile, but the rest of him? Nowhere fucking near.

And then, she hollowed her cheeks, taking all of him.

Griffin looked down. Watched as her throat flexed and saw the bulge. His eyes locked on hers, on the tears welling at the corners. But what ruined him was the sound. That sloppy, wet, messy gagging sound.

She pulled back, her lips slick, eyes locked onto his. "Do you want more? Do you want me to choke on your cock? Do you want me to swallow when you release in my mouth?"

He barely nodded before she taunted.

"Use your words, sweetheart."

FUCK.

His body burned, his mind blanked. His chest heaved as he swallowed hard. "Please."

A slow, wicked smile curled her lips. "Good boy."

Then she ravaged him. Fast. Deep. Hard.

Her head bobbed while her tongue swirled. Her fingers dug into his thighs. Her mouth was relentless.

Every time he thought she'd slow down, she went harder.

Every minute that passed, she got wetter, the sounds got filthier. His fingers twitched, aching to grab her, to pull her closer.

She pulled back, stroking him fast and ruthlessly, her grip tighter than before. "When my lips wrap around your cock again, I want you to fuck my mouth."

His stomach tightened. His eyes widened, shaft jumping under her touch.

Her tug became faster.

"I want you to grab my head and make me take it. Make me choke on it."

Her grip got tighter. Faster. Meaner.

"Just before you release, I want you to shove it down my throat. I want you to hold me there until you have nothing left."

His entire body jolted. His muscles locked.

Then, the final fucking blow—

"Can you be a good boy and come down my throat?"

His groan was wrecked, hoarse, feral. And the second her lips wrapped around him again, he snapped.

His fingers tangled in her hair, pulling tight as he thrust forward. He fucked her mouth like his life depended on it.

No hesitation. No restraint. Just a raw, carnal need. His body tensed, abs flexing so tight it almost hurt.

Then he felt it. That first telltale pulse.

She knew it too.

She moaned around him, the vibration sending shockwaves through his body. She reached out and gripped his waist, pulling him deeper, taking him to the fucking hilt.

And fuck. That's when it happened.

Every muscle in his body locked up as his vision went white-hot. Each pulse of his release sent a wave of satisfaction crashing through her. She took it all. Swallowed it all.

As soon as he stopped pulsing, as soon as he stopped releasing, his body collapsed against the tile. He had never been this... Wrecked.

Never been this destroyed.

She pulled his cock from her throat, slow, deliberate, letting her teeth graze the sensitive skin on the way out.

A full-body shiver raked over him.

She released him with a slick, teasing pop.

Then, she stood. Met his ruined, dazed stare.

And wiped her mouth with the back of her hand.

"Good boy."

With a wink, she turned and stepped out of the shower, disappearing into the steam like a fucking phantom.

Leaving him standing there.

Soul-snatched.

Drained.

Ruined.

Loved.

28

DEVINE POSSESSION

THE NEXT FEW days were a different kind of war.

No guns. No casualties.

Just sweat-slicked skin. Bruises blooming beneath wandering hands. Sharp nails. Bitten lips. Filthy whispers. And guttural moans echoing off the walls.

A battle of wills neither of them declared—

But both were hellbent on winning.

Sometimes, Griffin owned her.

Manhandling her like she was his to mold, bend, and break. Holding her down, fucking her so hard and deep she forgot how to breathe and left nothing but a trembling, wrecked mess who could only feel where he'd claimed her.

Other times?

Wren flipped him onto his back and rode him like a sin she refused to repent for; she'd grind down until he was cursing her name, hands bruising her hips, begging for mercy she had no intention of giving.

And then there were moments when neither of them fought.

No games. No control.

Just raw, reckless need.

Like when she crawled into his lap, panties soaked, hips rolling until he was hard beneath her; no words spoken before she sank down on him, like they were made for this kind of ruin.

Or when he bent her over the balcony railing, growling in her ear about how anyone could look up and see just how filthy she was for him, ocean waves crashing below, and his cock buried so deep she saw stars.

. . .

By the time the sun rose on the fourth day, her body was bruised, aching, and thoroughly claimed.

But Wren?

She was never the type to learn her lesson.

She took a step toward the door, hips swaying like she wasn't tempting fate.

Like she didn't know exactly what she was doing.

She pushed him.

That subtle curl of her bruised pink lips—one that dared him to do something about it.

The sway of her hips, like she wasn't already drenched just from testing him.

That glance over her shoulder? Pure evil.

Catch me. Break me. Claim me.

And Griffin?

Griffin didn't need a second invitation.

His hand shot out, wrapping around her throat with brutal precision, dragging her back until her body slammed into his. His cock pressed hard against her ass, and his growl rumbled through her spine.

"Where the fuck do you think you're going?" he rasped, tightening his grip just enough to steal her next breath. "You tease me like that and expect mercy?"

Her laugh was breathless—wicked.

"If you're gonna act like you own me..." she whispered, grinding back against him, "prove it, Hayes."

That was it.

He spun her, slamming her into the wall so hard the air whooshed from her lungs. His knee shoved between her thighs, grinding into her soaked panties.

"Dripping already," he cooed, ripping open her shorts, his fingers sliding straight to her bare petals. She slick and swollen, practically begging for him. "All that attitude, but this pussy's honest."

Wren whimpered, rocking against his hand, but that defiant gleam in her eyes never faded.

"Well, keep me honest," she taunted, licking her lips. "Unless you're scared you'll break me."

With his patience gone, "On your knees," he demands.

She dropped instantly, like gravity had been waiting for his command.

But before she touched him, she looked up, her eyes dark, lips parted, tongue teasing the air.

"Spit in my mouth first," she breathed. "Mark me before you make me choke on it."

His cock twitched, already thick and throbbing as he stroked it slowly, watching her with that predatory stare.

"Open wide, baby."

Tongue out, she obeyed, eyes locked on his like she lived for this.

Griffin let a thick string of spit fall onto her tongue. She moaned as it hit, swallowing it down with a devilish grin.

Then she wrapped her hand around his length, leaning in to drag her tongue along the underside.

"Let me make you forget how to fucking breathe," she whispered before her mouth latched onto him—hot, wet, starving.

She didn't tease. She devoured, taking him deep, her tongue swirling around the head before swallowing inch after inch. Her throat was molded just for him.

Griffin groaned, his hand fisting in her hair, guiding her pace, forcing her to choke on him until spit dripped down her chin and onto her chest.

It was wet. Messy. Desperate.

"Fuck, Wren…" Griffin groaned, thrusting into her mouth without restraint. "You're fucking starving for it, aren't you?"

She pulled off with a gasp, panting and lips swollen, but dropped lower, licking and sucking his balls until his knees nearly buckled.

"I want all of you," she whispered, licking back up his shaft before sucking the head back into her mouth.

Griffin yanked her to her feet, his control hanging by a thread.

He dragged her to the bed, but before tossing her down, he lined up at her entrance, pressing the head of his cock between her soaked lips and thighs.

"You wanted to be fucked like you're nothing but mine?" he rasped, his voice pure gravel.

Her grin didn't fade.

"You haven't even seen filthy yet," she whispered while lowering herself, licking a slow stripe up his shaft before he could react. She was taunting him, knowing exactly how to set him off.

That was the last push.

He threw her onto the bed, grabbing her ankles and yanking her down until her ass was on the edge. He didn't bother removing her panties. He ripped them clean off, tossing the shredded fabric aside.

Her swollen entrance glistened—dripping, flushed, inviting.

"Look at this fucking mess," he muttered. Slapping the head of his cock against her clit, watching her jolt. "All because you needed to be put in your place."

"Then stop talking and fuck me," she snapped, grabbing his wrist and dragging him closer. "I want to feel it tomorrow."

Griffin's smirk to that was a dark and dangerous thing.

"Oh, you will."

He slammed into her, forcing a scream from her lips as her fingers clawed at the sheets.

"Yeah… take it," he growled, snapping his hips against her ass, his grip bruising her hips as he pounded into her without restraint. "You're not going anywhere until I've ruined this pussy."

Her moans turned to cries—high, desperate, wrecked.

Griffin reached forward, wrapping his hand around her throat again, pulling her back against his chest while still driving into her from behind.

"You feel that?" he hissed against her ear, squeezing tighter. "That's me owning every inch of you."

Her legs trembled violently, body on the edge of collapse.

But he wasn't letting her fall.

Not yet.

"Come on, Wren. Show me how bad you need it. Flood my cock."

And she did. Her orgasm crashed over her like a violent wave, her body convulsed as a gush of wet heat drenched them both.

"Fuck yes," he snarled, not slowing for a second. "You're so fucking messy for me."

Her voice was gone, just gasps and sobs of pleasure. But he wasn't finished.

He dragged her fully onto the bed, laid flat, cock thick and heavy against his stomach, and hauled her over him—chest to his, her ass flush against his thighs, legs spread wide.

But he didn't stop there.

He hooked his arms beneath her knees, bending her in half, locking her open. She was helpless, exposed, and dripping onto his cock.

"You wanted to know what it means to be owned?" he rasped against her ear. "Let me show you."

She barely had time to gasp before he slid inside, slow, but devastating. Inch by inch, until her body screamed, until she could feel him in places no man had ever touched.

Her scream tore through the room.

Griffin grinned.

"Fuck, listen to you. This pussy's soaked—made to be wrecked."

She sobbed out a moan, her body trembling in his grip.

"Say it."

"Y-Yes—fuck—yes—ruin me—"

He spit down, watching it land where they were joined, watching it mix with her arousal before driving into her hard.

Every thrust was savage. Deep. Designed to remind her exactly who she belonged to.

Her legs bounced uselessly in his hold, her hands clawing at his arms, but she wasn't going anywhere.

"Nowhere to run," he whispered darkly, thrusting up into her with savage precision. "All you can do is take it."

His grip wasn't soft. It was a fucking collar. Commanding. Controlling. And the way her thighs clenched told him exactly what he needed to know.

"Harder," she whimpered, dizzy and soaking. "Please..."

Griffin growled—deep, feral—and gave it to her. Tight. Brutal. Until her vision blurred and her pussy clenched around nothing, begging to be filled.

There was nothing but the sound of skin slapping against skin. The slick, wet noise of him pounding into her dripping cunt. Her breathless cries. His growls.

It was fucking filth.

Then her body snapped.

A white-hot wave ripped through her, her back arching, mouth falling open in a silent scream before—

She squirted.

A gush that soaked them both, her release pouring over his cock, down his thighs, drenching the sheets.

Griffin didn't stop.

"There it is," he snarled, fucking her harder. "Look at this messy little cunt. Squirting all over me like a toy that knows who fucking owns it."

She couldn't breathe. Couldn't think.

But he wasn't done.

His cock twitched deep inside her, thick and pulsing, stretching her to the brink.

"You've got one job left, Raine," he growled, voice dark and wrecked. "Tell me where you want it."

Her voice was a wrecked whisper, barely audible and broken wide open.

"Inside… please… claim me…"

That was all it took.

With a brutal thrust, Griffin buried himself as deep as he could go, his cock twitching, release pouring into her in thick, hot waves as his teeth sank into her shoulder.

And he stayed there.

Buried. Possessive. Marking her from the inside out.

His arms tightened around her, locking her in place.

"You're mine now," he whispered breathlessly, voice hoarse. "I fucking claimed you. And you begged for it."

Wren nodded weakly, her body trembling, soaked, and completely ruined.

And Griffin?

He wasn't close to finished.

Her body was limp, and her skin slick with sweat, thighs soaked with the mess he made of her.

Griffin stayed buried inside her, his breath ragged against her neck, arms locked tight like he wasn't ready to let her go. Like he couldn't.

But after a minute, Wren moved.

Slow. Deliberate.

She let out a shaky breath, rolling off of him. His cock slipped free with a filthy, wet sound, followed by the immediate, sinful drip of him spilling from her wrecked pussy onto the sheets.

Griffin watched through hooded eyes, fully expecting her to collapse.

But Wren didn't collapse.

She turned, straddled his thigh, and crashed her lips into his with a kiss that was more tongue and more claiming than soft gratitude.

And before he could process it, she grabbed his hand, dragging it down between her legs.

Her fingers laced with his, she guided two of his to slide through the sticky, dripping mess between her legs. Thick with both of them.

Griffin's cock throbbed at the sight. Watching her bite her lip as she coated his fingers in everything he'd left inside her.

Her dark, wrecked gaze lifted to his.

Without breaking eye contact, she brought his hand to her mouth.

Wrapped her lips around his cum-soaked fingers.

And sucked.

Slow. Purposeful.

Her tongue swirled around them, savoring the taste of being owned.

When she finally pulled back, a strand of spit connecting her lips to his fingers, she smirked. Her voice came out low and breathless, but dripping with sin.

"None of that's going to waste," she whispered, her voice a hoarse purr. "Not when it belongs to me."

Griffin's muscles locked, a vein ticking in his base as his cock—already spent—started to harden again at the sight of her devouring the proof of his claim, like it was a goddamn delicacy.

"You're fucking dangerous," he muttered, sitting up, grabbing her jaw with a firm grip, pulling her into another bruising kiss—tasting himself on her tongue.

When he pulled back, his eyes were dark. Wild. Like a predator locked onto his next meal.

"You think you can do shit like that and not expect me to flip you over and start again?"

Her smirk deepened, grinding her soaked pussy against his thigh, letting him feel how ready she still was.

"Maybe that's exactly what I'm hoping for," she whispered, nipping at his bottom lip. "You said you'd ruin me… but I'm still breathing, Hayes."

Griffin's hand shot to her throat again, squeezing just enough to make her gasp, his cock now fully hard against her ass.

"Oh, sweetheart…" he rasped, "You really don't know when to quit, do you?"

Her only response was a wicked glint in her eye as she rocked against him harder. Challenging him.

"Make me."

And just like that—

Griffin flipped her onto her stomach, grabbing her wrists and pinning them above her head.

"You asked for this," he growled, lining up behind her, pressing his cock—still slick from round one—against her overstimulated entrance.

She gasped, her body already trembling from the anticipation.

But she didn't beg him to stop.

She arched her back, offering herself up like the filthy little addiction she was.

"Do your worst," she dared, glancing back at him with a wrecked smile. "If you've got it in you…"

Griffin's laugh was wicked.

"Oh, I've got plenty left."

Raw and relentless, he slammed into her all over again.

29

CHECK, PLEASE

GRIFFIN HAD FINALLY TALKED her into leaving the condo. It had taken some convincing, though not in the way one might think. Wren didn't resist because she didn't want to be out with him.

It was because stepping into the world together felt like an admission, a declaration. Behind closed doors, wrapped up in the safety of his home, they existed in a bubble. Raw. Unfiltered. Safe.

But outside? That was different.

That meant letting people see them. It meant exposing what they were to the world and giving them something to talk about, to whisper about.

And Griffin wanted that.

Not because he needed validation, not because he wanted to parade her around like some trophy, but because he needed her to understand. To feel it. That *they*—*this*—was real.

He belonged to her just as much as she belonged to him. There was no halfway, no hesitations. He was all in, and he needed her to know it.

She picked Driftwoods.

Close by. Good food. Nothing fancy. Just them, together.

The moment they sat down, conversation flowed effortlessly. It always did. They didn't force anything. It just was. The laughter, the teasing, the way they unraveled and folded into one another like they'd done it for a lifetime.

They talked about the last time they were here—the first time they met.

Griffin leaned back against the booth, smirking as he ran a hand over his jaw. "You should've seen me that night," he said.

She raised a brow, mirroring his smirk. "Oh?"

"I was in hell," he said, shaking his head like he was still suffering.

Wren tilted her head, feigning curiosity. "How so?"

His eyes flicked to hers, a knowing glint behind the blue. "Blue balls from hell."

Wren snorted, nearly spitting out her wine. She was laughing so hard she had to set the glass down before she lost it completely.

It wasn't just what he said, it was how he said it. The absolute indignation in his tone, like she had committed some heinous crime against him.

She wiped at her mouth with a napkin, catching her breath. "Oh my god."

Griffin grinned. "I'm serious. You walked out, and I just sat there… fucking stunned."

She laughed harder, shaking her head. "You? Stunned?"

He nodded, dead serious. "I forgot how to function. I think I ordered another whiskey and just stared at the door like a dumbass for ten minutes hoping you'd walk back in."

Wren cackled, covering her face. "That's pathetic."

He shrugged. "Oh, I know."

An hour passed without them even realizing it. Their plates were nearly clean, though neither could eat another bite.

The world outside of them faded into nothing.

Sure, they were getting looks—because she was with Griffin Hayes.

The guy who never brought women out in public. The guy who never kept anyone around long enough to bring them out in public. And yet, here they were. Sitting together like they'd done it a hundred times before. Like it was the most natural thing in the world.

Neither of them cared.

They were lost in their own world.

Until Wren excused herself to the restroom.

SHE STOOD AT THE SINK, WASHING HER HANDS, UNABLE TO STOP THE SMILE that spread across her lips. It wasn't forced. It wasn't fleeting. It was real. Effortless.

Happiness.

She almost didn't recognize the feeling.

She thought about them. About Griffin. About the house on the sound. Even if it was still white—the color she swore she'd change the second they moved in—it could be theirs. Home.

She dried her hands, grabbed a paper towel to open the door, and tossed it in the trash as she stepped out.

Her smile held. Until she was halfway back to the table.

Then, it started to fade. Something was wrong.

Wren's steps slowed.

Griffin was still sitting there, but his body was different now.

Rigid. Stiff.

Not in the way she was *used to*. Not in the way his muscles tensed when he was holding back before *wrecking her*.

This was something else. This was discomfort.

A woman stood beside him. Close. *Too fucking close.*

Well-dressed. Composed. Definitely *not* a server.

The air around them was heavy. The kind of silence that wasn't really silent. That buzzed with something unspoken. And that's exactly what Wren *cut into* when she reached the table.

Griffin's face told her everything she needed to know before she even opened her mouth.

She knew him. She knew how he carried his chest when something was *off*. How his jaw locked when he was trying to control himself. How he *didn't* look at someone when he wanted to pretend they weren't there.

And right now? *He wasn't looking at her.*

It had to be.

That bitch Lia.

Wren stood still for only a second before Lia turned to her, barely sparing her a glance. "I'm sorry, but we don't need anything right now," she said dismissively, her *freshly manicured* hand resting on Griffin's shoulder.

Griffin's entire body went taut. His eyes widened. That *oh shit* look. His gaze flicked to Wren, *locking on.*

Exuding confidence, Wren smiled and slid into her seat. She looked at Lia. Then Griffin.

"Griff," she said lightly, tilting her head, her voice *sweet* but *deadly* underneath. "Are you about ready to go *home*?"

Lia flinched. That single word had weight. "*Home?*" she repeated, as if it were a foreign concept.

Griffin exhaled, his jaw tight. "Wren, this is Amelia."

Wren's lips curved into a razor-sharp smile. *Time to cut a bitch.*

"I know who she is," she said smoothly. She turned to Lia and extended a hand, her expression perfectly polite—*weaponized hospitality*. "I should have introduced myself earlier, when you thought I worked here." Her eyes sparkled with malice. "I'm Wren. *Griffin's wife.*"

Griffin smirked against his whiskey glass, eyes dancing with amusement. He knew this was about to go nuclear. Hell, he was just lucky to be holding the glass, because he was going to need every ounce of alcohol to survive this.

The man at the next table, who had been discreetly pretending not to listen, slowly set down his beer and leaned the fuck in.

Lia's brows lifted, and her eyes flicked down to Wren's left hand. "Wife?"

Wren wiggled her fingers in mock surprise. "Yeah. Hayes thought it'd be a great idea to fuck me in the shower the other day." She let out an exaggerated sigh, her tone dripping with fake disappointment. "Well, when I was stroking his cock—his third arm, girl, you know—my ring slipped right off. I've told him for a year to fix the damn drain flange, but you know how he is. So now, my ring's gone." She tilted her head, pressing a thoughtful finger to her lips. "Which means he gets to buy me a new one. Maybe one with a smaller diamond, so it doesn't catch on everything."

Griffin nearly spit his whiskey back into his glass, covering his mouth with a napkin, shoulders shaking.

The guy at the next table let out a wheezed "Oh, shit."

Lia's jaw clenched so tight it could've crushed diamonds. "Oh. You call him Hayes?" Her gaze flicked to Griffin. "Didn't know you were married, Griff."

Wren's smile widened, all sharp edges and unchecked menace. "Yeah. Griffin is sweet, kind, charming," she said, tilting her head. "Hayes is who he is when he fucks me. Claiming. Wild." She gave Griffin a wink, "And possessive."

Griffin made a strangled noise in his throat, gripping his glass like it was his damn lifeline.

Lia inhaled through her nose, nostrils flaring, but she wasn't done. She crossed her arms, shifting her weight onto one hip. "So this is what you went for?" she asked, voice laced with pure venom. "Interesting." She took a slow, deliberate step back, scanning Wren like she was sizing up a cheap handbag. "You might want to hold on tight," she added with a smirk. "We both know how long he stays interested."

Griffin mumbled under his breath, "Oh fuck," as he pulled his hand across his face.

The guy at the next table hissed through his teeth. "Damn, she went there."

Oh, hell the fuck no. Wren's entire demeanor shifted. The humor faded from her eyes, her jaw tightening just slightly before she inhaled through her nose, sitting up straighter.

Then she smiled.

A slow, cold, devastating smile.

"Oh, honey," she purred, resting her chin on her palm. "You really don't want to play this game with me."

Lia tilted her head in faux curiosity. "Why's that?"

Wren's expression didn't falter. "Because I fight dirty."

Lia scoffed. "Please. I had him first." She tossed her hair, grinning. "He used to say so many things to me. About how I was the best he'd ever had. How he'd never wanted anyone more." Her gaze flicked to Griffin. "Tell me, Griff, do you still—"

"OH BITCH, DON'T EVEN START," Wren cut her off, voice loud enough that the guy at the next table slapped his hand over his mouth to keep from cackling.

Lia's eyes widened slightly before narrowing again.

Wren's tone sharpened, her voice steady, controlled—deadly.

"You wanna talk about the past?" Wren continued, eyes gleaming. "Let's talk about it, Lia from Boone. Why are you in Topsail, exactly? Because last I checked, you hated the coast. Said it was, what was the word? Tacky?"

Griffin dragged his hand down his face, barely covering his grin.

Lia's face twisted, but Wren wasn't fucking done.

"See, I get it now," Wren continued, voice smoother than a fresh shave. "It wasn't that you didn't want the coast. It was that you didn't want Griffin. Not when he was working sixteen-hour days, busting his ass to build a company that you weren't patient enough to stand by."

The guy at the next table slapped the table. "Oh shit—"

Griffin's hand shot out, gripping his glass with white-knuckle force to stop himself from dying at the table.

Lia's jaw twitched. "I—"

"No, no, you wanted to play—let's keep going," Wren said brightly, waving her hand in a please-let-me-continue motion. "Because what's really funny about this whole 'I had him first' thing is that you also had someone else."

Lia's entire body stiffened.

Griffin suddenly wasn't laughing anymore.

Wren's smile turned downright dangerous. "Oh, you thought I wouldn't bring it up? Thought I didn't know that while Griffin was pulling sixteen-hour shifts trying to build a life for you, you were—what was it again? Entertaining company?" She let out a mocking gasp. "Or was it more than one? I lose track."

The guy at the next table nearly fell out of his chair. "HOLY SHIT."

Griffin froze, eyes locked on Lia.

Lia stammered, her face paling. "I—it's—"

Wren leaned in, voice dropping to a whisper. "You wanna talk about who had him first?" she murmured, tone slicing through the air like a knife. "You didn't even want him when you did."

Lia's face crumpled.

Griffin sat there, his entire brain blue-screening at the sheer brutality.

The guy at the next table? Hands on his knees, hunched over, losing his mind.

Lia took a step back, her lips trembling slightly before she snapped. "You're a fucking bitch," she spat, voice shaking.

Wren just smiled. "You're right," she said sweetly. "But you still lost."

Griffin choked.

Lia spun on her heel and stormed the fuck out, leaving behind a trail of humiliation.

The guy at the next table let out a slow, appreciative whistle, shaking his head. "Ma'am," he said, lifting his beer in a salute. "I ain't never seen someone get verbally curb-stomped like that in my life."

Wren flashed him a wink, then turned back to Griffin, who was still processing what the fuck just happened.

Griffin exhaled hard, running a hand down his face as they walked toward the truck. He was still processing everything that had just happened. The entire restaurant probably was. Hell, even the guy at the next table had been left stunned into silence after Wren verbally eviscerated Lia with the precision of a seasoned executioner.

He scrubbed his hands over his face, shaking his head. "Jesus Christ, Wren."

She arched a brow as he unlocked the truck. "What?"

He let out a dry laugh. "I didn't know she was in town."

Wren slid into the passenger seat, closing the door as he got in beside her. "I know you didn't," she murmured. "Your face told me everything before you even saw me."

Griffin clicked his seatbelt, leaning back against the headrest. "Still. I'm sorry you had to deal with that."

She exhaled, drumming her fingers against her thigh before turning to face him. "You're sorry?" she repeated, giving him a look. "Babe, I had the time of my life."

That startled a laugh out of him.

He shook his head, smirking as he started the truck. "I should've known you were gonna go scorched earth the second she opened her mouth."

"I mean," she said innocently, "I could've been the bigger person—"

"No, the fuck you couldn't," Griffin immediately cut in, shooting her a look.

She laughed. "Okay, yeah. I couldn't."

His grin widened as he backed out of the parking lot. "I'm sorry our first time in public ended like that."

Wren scoffed. "Ended like that?" She turned in her seat, tossing a hand in the air. "Griffin, that was the highlight of my week. Maybe my year."

He glanced at her, chuckling. "You enjoyed that?"

"Oh, thoroughly."

He groaned, dragging a hand down his face. "That line about the shower—Jesus Christ, Wren. I about lost it."

"So did I," she admitted, laughing. Then her expression sharpened, voice cooling just slightly. "But you don't fuck with me, and you damn sure don't fuck with what's mine."

Griffin let go of the wheel for a second to reach over, placing his large hand on her thigh, his fingers warm against her skin.

"Griffin," she said, her tone softening just slightly as she placed her hand over his. "That's what you are. Mine."

His fingers flexed slightly against her leg.

She turned toward him fully, eyes locked onto his. "We own each other," she murmured. "Don't ever fucking forget that."

Griffin smirked, squeezing her thigh before sliding his hand just slightly higher.

"Yes, ma'am," he muttered, his voice low and teasing.

Wren smirked, tilting her head. "Damn right."

Griffin laughed under his breath, shaking his head as he turned onto the road. "I love you."

She grinned, looking out the window, still riding the high of the night. "I know."

Griffin chuckled, shaking his head again.

Jesus Christ, he was so fucked.

30

STORM WARNING

BACK AT THE CONDO, the adrenaline high was gone. The dust had settled. But the silence that followed wasn't peace—it was war disguised in stillness. The air was thick with the kind of quiet that didn't soothe but suffocated—heavy and charged. It felt like the moments after a storm, when the sky hasn't decided if it's done breaking yet. It filled every inch of space like smoke seeping into the walls, into the floor, into her lungs, becoming something she'd never fully breathe out. Wren could still feel it crawling beneath her skin, deeper than the adrenaline. Deeper than the sting of bitter words and sharp glances. It wasn't just anger lingering, it was something far worse. It twisted low in her stomach. A sickness she couldn't shake, curling tight around her ribs, until she felt both too full and too hollow. A contradiction she knew too well. A wound she hadn't realized was still open.

Because this wasn't just a fight. This wasn't just a moment they'd move past.

This was Griffin. And his past.

Her eyes found him—like they always did—in the aftermath. Standing a few feet away, silent but watching her like she was the only thing anchoring him. Like he could already see the storm churning in her chest, even if she hadn't let a single word slip. His gaze was steady, unreadable to anyone else. But she wasn't anyone else. She could see the questions behind those dark eyes, the worry he'd never voice, the tension in his jaw that told her he knew. He always fucking knew.

Griffin was solid. Unshaken. The same immovable force he'd been from the start.

And that was the fucking problem.

Because for the first time—she wasn't.

For the first time, Wren felt like her foundation cracked beneath her feet, and she didn't know if it was from the argument... Or from the terrifying realization of what it all meant. Of what she had just proven to herself without even thinking.

She'd moved first.

No hesitation. No second-guessing. The second someone laid a hand on Griffin, her body reacted like it wasn't even hers to command; like every instinct, every ounce of blood in her veins screamed mine before her mind could catch up.

Mine.

The word slammed into her chest, knocking the breath from her lungs like a hit she hadn't braced for. It wasn't new. It had been there for weeks, lurking in the shadows of every glance, every touch, every whispered confession in the dark. But now? Now it wasn't lurking.

It was screaming.

It was in every shaky breath she took, in every frantic heartbeat, in the ache that bloomed at the thought of losing him. She hadn't just defended him. She had gone to fucking war for him—without question, without thought—like her soul already belonged to him and was willing to destroy anything that threatened what was hers.

And standing there in the wreckage, heart pounding, fists still unclenched, one thought gripped her harder than all the rest.

Would he have done the same for me?

Sharp, cruel, and uninvited, the question sliced through her. She didn't want to think it. She hated herself for even letting it form. Griffin had never, *never*, given her a reason to doubt him. But doubt didn't give a fuck about truth.

Doubt was born in the dark corners of fear. And Wren was drowning in it.

Because this wasn't just about trust. This wasn't about logic or reason.

This was about how she loved and how fucking dangerous that was.

Wren didn't love halfway. She never had. She loved like she lived—reckless, fierce, without brakes or safety nets. When she gave her heart, it wasn't in pieces or conditioned on promises. It was all or nothing. A hurricane that didn't ask permission before it tore through everything in its path.

And Griffin Hayes... He was the first man she had ever loved like that.

The first man she wanted to destroy her. The first man she wanted to crash into, and pray he was strong enough to weather the storm.

But standing here, with that raw, terrifying truth lodged in her throat, she realized something even worse.

She didn't know if she was strong enough to survive him.

The fear hit her harder than the pettiness with Lia ever could—the fear that she had finally found something too big, too consuming. That loving him meant handing over the only weapon anyone had ever been able to use against her. Herself.

Griffin stepped toward her, that storm-colored stare locked on her like he already knew what she was about to do. Like he felt the shift in her chest before she even said it.

"I just..." Her voice cracked, soft but shaking. "I need a second. Not to run—just to breathe. Just to feel this without drowning in it."

His jaw flexed, but he nodded. Didn't chase. Didn't demand. He just let her go with a look that told her he'd still be there when she was ready to come back.

So she did what she always did when things got too heavy, when the waves threatened to pull her under.

She ran.

Not far. Just far enough to catch her breath. Far enough to convince herself she wasn't unraveling at the seams.

She went to Aiden.

The brother who still hovered somewhere between forgiveness and fury. The one she gave three days to get his shit together. He'd sent a few half-assed texts, enough to show he was trying, but not enough to bridge the gap they'd blown wide open. Still, he was familiar. Safe. A reminder of who she was before Griffin turned her world on its head.

But even there, the spiral followed.

It always did.

It crept in quietly, like it wasn't planning to stay—just visiting long enough to poison her thoughts. She told herself it was nothing. That she was overthinking. But the questions didn't stop.

Would he have fought for me the way I fought for him? Would he have burned the world down if someone touched me?

She hated herself for wondering. Hated the way doubt slithered through her veins, tightening around her heart. Griffin had already proven himself in ways no one else ever had—taking hits, making sacrifices, standing by her when it would've been easier to walk away.

But fear didn't care.

Fear reminded her of every time she'd been left standing alone. Of every time she'd loved someone who didn't love her enough to stay.

And Griffin? God, Griffin—he was the one person she couldn't survive losing.

So, she started to pull away.

Not enough to raise alarms. Just enough to protect the parts of herself she wasn't sure she could trust him with yet. A hesitation here. A distance there. Small cracks in the armor they'd built together.

But Griffin noticed.

Of course he did.

She could see it in the way his eyes followed her like he was losing something he didn't know how to hold onto. In the way his jaw clenched when she didn't lean into his touch the way she used to. In the way his voice softened too much, as he was afraid if he pushed too hard, she'd shatter.

But he didn't call her out.

Not yet.

And that scared her more than anything.

Because if Griffin Hayes, the man who fought for everything, was giving her space to run... it meant he already knew she was halfway out the door.

And Wren wasn't sure if she wanted him to chase her—

Or if she was terrified that he wouldn't.

AIDEN WAS ALWAYS WATCHING. NOT THE WAY GRIFFIN DID—WITH HEAT and hunger and that storm-brewing stare—but quieter. Deeper. Like he was cataloging every breath she took, every one she didn't. He didn't give a damn about the space stretching between her and Griffin, not because it didn't matter, but because that wasn't what he was tracking. He was watching her. The way her laugh had dulled at the edges, the way she lingered in rooms just long enough to pretend she wasn't waiting for someone to follow.

She'd stayed longer than she said she would. Days stretched past the three she promised, bleeding into something that wasn't quite goodbye but sure as hell wasn't staying.

And Aiden, who knew her better than anyone ever had, better than she wished he did, finally said it.

"You gonna keep pretending you're fine," he asked, voice low as they stood in the kitchen, "or do you want to talk about how you haven't really slept since you got here?"

She didn't answer right away. Just stared at the mug in her hands like it might crack open and explain her heart for her.

"I'm not fine," she said eventually. "But I don't know what to do with that."

Aiden leaned against the counter, arms crossed, eyes locked on her with something softer than judgment. "You could start by not punishing him for being afraid the same way you are."

Her jaw clenched. "I'm not—"

"Yeah," he cut in gently, "you are."

And just like that, the dam cracked. Not enough to break, but enough to remind her it would if she didn't stop pretending.

He saw it all: every deflection, every stiff smile, every time she caught Griffin's gaze and had to look away because if she didn't, he'd know. He'd see the unraveling. He'd see that what terrified her more than loving Griffin... was that he might still love her back.

Would he fight for me like I fought for him?

Would he bleed for me?

Would he burn?

It was pathetic how easily fear could twist love into doubt. How fast old wounds could resurface and convince you that history would always repeat itself. She hated that the questions existed at all. Hated that no matter how many times Griffin had proven himself, there was still a part of her—a broken, jagged part—that whispered, *What if you're too much?* What if you love too hard, too fast, too recklessly—and he doesn't catch you when you fall?

So, she didn't ask him. Because if she asked, it meant she wasn't sure.

And if she wasn't sure, it meant she didn't trust him the way she swore she did.

Instead, she sat outside Aiden's place, fingers wrapped around a bottle she hadn't touched. Staring at the way the condensation slid down the glass, like it held all the answers, she was too scared to say out loud. It was easier to focus on something small. Something insignificant, rather than let herself feel the weight pressing against her ribs—the weight of loving someone so deeply it fucking hurt.

The door creaked open behind her. She didn't need to turn around. She felt him before she heard the heavy footsteps sink into the porch beside her.

Aiden didn't speak right away. He never did when it mattered. He knew silence was its own kind of scalpel, sharp enough to slice through walls if you let it linger long enough.

"Wren."

Her name was a sigh. A knowing. A callout she wasn't ready for.

She swallowed hard, fingers tightening around the bottle until her knuckles burned. "What!"

"You're doing that thing again."

Her throat constricted. She didn't need to ask. She knew exactly what thing he meant.

"What thing?"

Aiden let out a humorless laugh—short, bitter, cutting. "The thing where you pretend you're fine when every part of you is screaming that you're not."

Her grip faltered, the bottle clinking too hard against the wood as she set it down. "I am fine."

"Bullshit."

The word landed heavy between them, heavier than anything else he could've said. Because it wasn't an accusation, it was a truth she didn't want to face. The silence that followed stretched, thick enough to choke on.

Then softly, but firmly, the way only an older brother could manage, "Talk to me."

Her chest tightened, a sharp ache blooming beneath her sternum. She didn't want to talk. Didn't want to give breath to the thoughts that had been eating her alive for days. Because once she said it, once she let it out, she couldn't shove it back down. And God, she wasn't sure she was ready to admit just how scared she was.

But Aiden waited. And she was so damn tired.

So, the words fell out—fragile, wrecked, bleeding at the edges.

"I love him."

It wasn't a confession. It was a surrender. A truth that felt too big for her chest, tearing at the seams as it clawed its way out.

Aiden didn't flinch. Didn't offer comfort. Just sat there, like he'd been expecting it all along.

"No shit. You've told me."

A choked laugh burst from her lips, part amusement, part desperation. "Fuck off."

For a moment, the ghost of a smirk tugged at Aiden's mouth, but it didn't last. It never did when it came to this. When it came to her.

His voice dropped, quieter now, more careful. "So what's the problem?"

Her breath hitched, eyes burning as she stared at nothing. How the hell did she explain a fear that didn't make sense? How did she admit that loving Griffin felt like standing on a wire with no safety net—and knowing she'd still jump even if it snapped beneath her?

Her voice cracked when it finally came out, barely audible, but heavy enough to crush her. "I don't know if he loves me the same way."

Aiden's head whipped toward her, his expression darkening with something fierce and protective. "Wren—"

"No," she cut him off, the dam breaking, her voice splintering under the weight of everything she'd been holding in. "You don't get it. I don't love him in a way that makes sense. I don't love him like it's safe. I love him like I'm handing him the match and daring him to set me on fire." Her hands trembled as she raked them through her hair, her breath coming in sharp, uneven bursts. "I love like a fucking hurricane, Aiden. And if he doesn't love me like that, if he doesn't wreck for me, then what the fuck am I doing?"

The silence after that wasn't patient. It wasn't kind. It was suffocating.

And for the first time, she let herself feel the raw terror of it—the fear that she'd given Griffin every piece of herself. Only to find out he wasn't standing in the storm with her.

Aiden's gaze softened in a way that gutted her, because it was the same look he gave her when they were kids, and she scraped her knees but refused to cry. Like he knew she was breaking but also knew she'd rather die than admit it.

His voice was steady when it finally came, quiet but solid. "That man would burn down the fucking world for you."

Her throat closed. "You don't know that."

"I do," he said without hesitation. "Because I know you. And you wouldn't hand your heart to someone who didn't know what the fuck to do with it."

She wanted to believe that. God, she needed to believe that.

But belief was a fragile thing when doubt had already taken root.

Aiden wasn't done. His voice dropped lower, less sure of himself but more honest. "Look, I know I handled shit wrong with him. I know I didn't give him a chance." He let out a breathless, bitter laugh. "But even from a distance... I see it. Everyone sees it. Griffin Hayes hasn't just changed. He's *choosing* to."

Her heart stuttered.

"I was at a site yesterday. Heard his guys talking about how the boss doesn't stay late anymore. How he's different." Aiden looked at her then, really looked, and for once there was no fight in his eyes—only truth. "He's already fighting for you, Wren. Every damn day."

Her vision blurred, tears spilling over before she could stop them.

And then he said the words that shattered her.

"If you're the hurricane... he's the coast."

Her breath left her in a broken gasp.

"He's what's left standing when the storm passes," Aiden whispered. "When everything is blown away... the coast remains."

She couldn't speak. Couldn't breathe past the lump in her throat.

Aiden rubbed a hand over his face, his voice softer now, almost a plea. "Don't run from that, Wren. Don't ruin something that's already proven it's strong enough to handle you."

She let out a shaky breath, her heart aching so violently it felt like it might tear from her chest.

Because he was right.

She wasn't afraid that Griffin didn't love her.

She was afraid that he did—the same way she loved him. Reckless. Relentless. All-consuming.

And that kind of love? It didn't come without scars.
But maybe... Maybe scars weren't something to fear.
Maybe they were proof that you survived.
And for the first time in days, the world didn't feel like it was tilting under her feet.
It wasn't perfect.
But maybe, just maybe, it was progress.

31

WIND & RAINE

WREN DIDN'T LOVE in small doses.

She didn't know how.

Maybe it was written in her DNA, etched into her bones before she ever understood what love even was. Or maybe life had carved it into her the hard way, branding her with the kind of lessons that didn't fade. Either way, she wasn't built for halfway hearts or careful hands. She never learned how to ration out pieces of herself, never figured out how to give just enough to feel something without risking it all.

No—Wren Sinclair loved like she fought.

Reckless.

Brutal.

All-consuming.

She didn't offer love like it was a gift to be unwrapped delicately. She hurled it like a fucking grenade and dared someone to catch it before it exploded. There were no safety nets with her. No soft landings. If you got close enough to hold her heart, you better be ready to bleed for it.

And that's exactly why this—Griffin—was so fucking dangerous.

Because Wren didn't love lightly.

And this?

This wasn't light.

It was heavy. A weight she could feel pressing against her ribs, suffocating her in the best and worst ways. It wrapped around her like an anchor, pulling her under every time he looked at her like she was the only thing keeping him afloat. It wasn't a spark. It was a goddamn wildfire burning through every wall she thought would protect her.

It didn't hit her all at once. No, it was crueler than that. It crept in slow, like a tide rising at her feet. So subtle she didn't realize she was drowning until her lungs were already full of him. Until one day, she stood in the middle of the wreckage that used to be her carefully controlled heart—and knew.

She needed him.

And that scared her more than anything ever had.

Because Wren didn't need people. She made sure of that. She built her independence like armor, forged from the lessons that taught her love wasn't safe; it was a loaded gun you handed to someone else and prayed they didn't pull the trigger. She learned that young. Too young. And when she did? She swore she'd never be that girl again.

Seventeen. Too bold. Too much. Too in love with the idea that someone could stay. She believed in forever, only to realize some people say forever when they really mean until it's inconvenient. She gave him everything—her laughter, her trust, her heart—and when he left, he didn't just walk away. He left her standing in ruins she didn't know how to rebuild.

That's what love did. It didn't kill you clean.

It bled you slowly.

It haunted you. In every silence. In every empty bed. In every memory that used to taste like honey and now tastes like ash. It was waking up and remembering that someone once promised to stay and still left without looking back.

After that? Wren swore she'd never be that vulnerable again. She could fuck. She could flirt. She could let someone touch her skin—but never her soul. No one got close enough to matter.

Until Griffin Hayes barreled into her life and made her forget every goddamn rule she'd written in blood.

And now? She was standing in the eye of a storm she didn't see coming, realizing that she wasn't holding the reins anymore. That this wasn't just a fling or a reckless decision. It was love. Real. Raw. Reckless. The kind that could shatter her if she let it.

Because this wasn't just about wanting him.

It was about needing him in ways that made her chest ache. It was about the way her body moved before her mind did—throwing herself between him and danger. Like her heart had already decided he was worth dying for.

And that terrified her.

Wren had always fought for herself. She survived because she never let anyone else be the reason she stood or fell. But Griffin? He changed that. Without asking. Without trying. He became the exception.

She didn't hesitate to fight for him.

Not for a second.

Because he mattered.

And that was the scariest part of all. Because what if this ended like it always did? What if she gave him everything and he still left? What if he made her believe in safety just long enough to pull the rug out from under her? What if loving him wasn't enough to make him stay?

Because hurricanes didn't get to choose what they destroyed.

And for once, she wasn't the storm.

She was the fucking coast—waiting for impact, knowing that when it hit, nothing would be left standing.

She thought she was hiding it well. Thought the space she was creating between them was subtle. Barely noticeable.

But Griffin wasn't stupid.

Griffin saw her.

He saw the hesitation in her hands, the way her touch lingered like she was saying goodbye in pieces. He felt every kiss that tasted more like fear than desire. He heard the lies in the way she said she was fine.

And for three days, he let her pretend. Let her pull away; let her convince herself that she was protecting something by keeping him at arm's length.

Until he couldn't anymore.

When he found her in the kitchen, braced against the counter with her shoulders tense, head down like the tile had all the answers. He knew.

She wasn't slipping away.

She was already halfway gone.

Fuck. That.

He stepped in—close. Too close.

Close enough that she could feel the heat radiating off him, close enough that the air shifted and thickened, wrapping around her like a noose. She didn't turn at first. Not until the weight of him became impossible to ignore. And when she finally did, when her eyes flicked up to meet his, Griffin's chest caved in.

Because he knew that look.

Damn, he knew that look.

Wild.

Cornered.

Like a caged animal desperate to run but too scared to move.

It was the same fucking look she gave him that night—the night she let herself want him but was terrified of what wanting him meant. The night she stood on the edge of something real and couldn't decide whether to jump or retreat.

And now? She was staring at him like that again.

Like he was something dangerous.

Something she wanted but didn't believe she could survive.

Griffin's heart fucking dropped. His stomach twisted into a knot so tight it made him nauseous.

He was done.

Done watching her unravel in silence. Done letting her pretend like she wasn't pulling away inch by inch. Done letting fear dictate the story they were writing together.

"You're running." His voice cut through the tension like a blade—sharp, certain, and unforgiving.

It wasn't a question. It was a fact.

Wren's jaw tightened instantly. Defensive. Guarded. "I'm not—"

"Bullshit."

His voice snapped across the room. It wasn't loud, but it didn't fucking have to be. The weight behind it was enough to make her flinch, just the slightest jerk of her shoulders, like the truth stung worse than any accusation.

Her eyes darted away, searching for an escape that didn't exist.

But Griffin didn't let her have it.

Crowding her, he stepped in, cornering her not with force, but with presence. With everything he was. Everything she was trying to run from.

"You think I don't see it?" His voice dropped, rougher now, cracking under the strain of holding too much back. "You think I don't notice when you touch me like you're afraid of what it means? When you kiss me like you're memorizing me before you disappear?"

Her lips pressed into a thin line. Her silence screamed louder than words ever could.

"I see all of it, Wren," he ground out, chest heaving. "Every fucking time you pull away, every time you act like last week didn't happen. Like I didn't have you tangled in my sheets, moaning my name like I was the only thing tethering you to this world."

Her breathing hitched for just a second, but she still wouldn't look at him.

Wouldn't face him.

"I don't know what you want me to say," she whispered, voice brittle, like the wrong word would shatter her completely.

Griffin's hands twitched at his sides, the urge to grab her, to shake the truth out of her, damn near unbearable. "I want you to say the fucking truth, Wren. For once."

She shook her head, a sharp, desperate motion, like she could physically shake herself free of this moment. Like if she just denied it hard enough, it would all go away.

But Griffin wasn't going to let her disappear behind her walls this time.

He reached out, fingers wrapping around her wrist—not to hold her captive, but to anchor her. To remind her she was still here. Still his. His other hand cupped her jaw, tilting her face up, forcing her to see the man standing in front of her, the man fighting like hell to keep her from slipping through his fingers.

Her pulse thrashed under his touch—fast, panicked.

And that's when it hit him—

It wasn't him she was afraid of.

It was them.

It was everything they were becoming.

"I'm not afraid of you, Wren," he rasped, his voice fraying at the edges. "Not your fire. Not your fear. Not the way you love like it's a fucking war."

Her lips parted—like she wanted to deny it, like she needed to—but no words came.

Because they both knew he was right.

He could see it. The war behind her eyes. The battle between running and staying. Between fear and surrender. Between the part of her that had survived by building walls and the part of her that wanted him to tear them all down.

And for one fleeting second, he saw it.

She wanted to stay.

She was just terrified to admit it.

But then her gaze dropped again. Like looking at him was too much. Like facing what they were would make it too real.

And Griffin's heart snapped.

How the fuck could she still be pulling away when everything he was, everything he had, was standing right in front of her, begging her to stay?

His grip tightened, just enough to ground them both. His voice dropped into something darker, something dangerous.

"Look at me."

She didn't.

His jaw clenched, frustration and heartbreak colliding in his chest like a fucking explosion.

"Fucking look at me, Raine."

That did it. Her eyes flicked up, barely meeting his, but it was there. That hesitation. That goddamn hesitation that felt like a knife twisting in his gut.

He could see the fear. The doubt. The part of her that believed loving him meant losing herself.

And that's when his patience ran out.

His voice dropped to a growl. Low, wrecked, done.

"If you're so fucking scared of losing me, then why the hell are you pushing me away?"

Her breath hitched, her mouth opened—

But nothing came out.

Because there wasn't a good answer.

Because every excuse she could muster sounded hollow in her own head.

Griffin felt it—the final straw snapping inside him. His chest burned, his throat thick with words he didn't want to say but couldn't hold back anymore. His fingers trembled against her skin, holding on to the last thread of control he had left.

And then—

He let go.

The second his hand dropped from her face, Wren's entire body screamed for her to stop him. To reach out. To say something before it was too late.

But fear had her by the throat.

Paralyzed her.

Kept her frozen in place as the man who would've set the world on fire for her stepped back.

"I love you, Wren," Griffin said, his voice quiet but heavy, as if the words were breaking him open. "More than anything I've ever known."

A tear slid down his cheek, and that was when Wren felt her heart crack wide fucking open.

Because Griffin Hayes didn't cry.

Griffin Hayes never cried.

"I can't do this one foot in, one foot out shit," he continued, his voice splintering, like every word was a wound. "You need to figure out what the fuck you want. Are you still running? Or have you finally realized you're home?"

Her lips trembled, her throat closing around every desperate plea she couldn't voice.

Griffin's thumb traced her cheek one last time, a soft, lingering touch that felt like goodbye.

Like he was memorizing her before walking away.

And Wren?

She let him.

Because fear won.

Again.

He turned. Walked away.

The door slammed.

And when the silence swallowed her whole, when the weight of what she'd just lost crushed the breath from her lungs, her knees nearly buckled.

Because she hadn't just watched him leave.

She had pushed him out the door.

And Griffin?

He didn't look back.

By the time his truck roared to life, hot and bitter tears were already falling relentlessly down Wren's face.

Griffin wasn't driving away to clear his head.

No. He was driving straight to Aiden.

Because if Wren wouldn't give him answers—

He'd get them another way.

32

OLD TIES

GRIFFIN MET AIDEN AT MARSHSIDE, the scent of fried seafood and cold beer thick in the air. It mingled with the hum of conversation and the occasional burst of laughter from the bar. The place was crowded—it always was—but somehow, tonight, it felt different.

Maybe because this wasn't just two guys grabbing a drink. This was history sitting between them. The kind that didn't just disappear with a few beers and a plate of fried shrimp.

They found a booth near the back. Far enough from the bar to have some space, but still close enough to hear the dull roar of people talking, glasses clinking, and the occasional shout from someone who had one too many.

It started off awkward.

Aiden sat across from Griffin, fingers drumming against the table, jaw tight like he was still figuring out whether or not he even wanted to be here. Griffin knew the feeling. He'd spent months trying to convince himself he didn't miss this—that he didn't miss his best friend.

Turned out, that was bullshit.

The waitress came by, barely sparing Griffin a glance before her eyes landed on Aiden. "What can I get y'all?"

"Two beers," Aiden said, then flicked his gaze toward Griffin. "You still take your burgers damn near raw?"

Griffin smirked, leaning back in the booth. "Still got better taste than you."

Aiden rolled his eyes, but there was a flicker of something lighter in them now.

The waitress grinned. "Coming right up, boys."

The beers hit the table first, the dull thud of glass on wood sounding louder than it should've in the low hum of the bar. Aiden didn't speak right away, just lifted his glass, studying Griffin over the rim like he was still figuring out what to say. Still weighing years of friendship against weeks of silence and bad blood.

After a long sip, he set the glass down, fingers tapping against the condensation. His gaze didn't waver.

"You know…" Aiden's voice was rough, like the words were sticking in his throat. "I should've given you a fair shot."

Griffin's fingers curled tighter around his bottle, but he kept his expression neutral—like the weight of that admission didn't hit him square in the chest.

"Yeah?" he said, voice low, cautious.

Aiden nodded, rubbing a hand over his jaw, avoiding Griffin's eyes, like it made swallowing his pride a little easier. "I was pissed. And yeah, I had a right to be. But I didn't even let you explain. Didn't give you the chance to prove you weren't the same guy you used to be."

Griffin exhaled slowly, the tension easing just enough to get the words out. "I get it."

Aiden huffed, shaking his head like he couldn't believe how long it took to get here. "Yeah, well... Took me long enough."

Silence fell between them. Not the sharp, bitter silence that had hovered for weeks, but something else. Something heavier, but familiar. The kind of quiet that only existed between two people who'd known each other too long to fill it with bullshit. It was almost… comfortable. Almost.

Aiden's lips twitched into a small, knowing smirk. "Wren's stubborn as hell, you know that?"

Griffin let out a breathy chuckle, the corner of his mouth lifting. "No shit?"

For a moment, it felt easy again—like old times. The conversation picked up, the jabs came naturally, the space between them shrank with every sarcastic remark and shared memory. But it was only a matter of time before the universe decided to test just how far this reconciliation could stretch.

Griffin felt it before he saw it, the shift in energy, the way Aiden's smile deepened like he was watching a show he'd seen too many times before.

"Here we fucking go," Aiden muttered, tipping his beer back.

Griffin didn't have to turn to know what was coming. The click of heels, the confident sway, the too-sweet smile dripping with intent.

Tall. Dark hair. That look women got when they saw a challenge and were ready to win.

"Hey," she purred, leaning against the booth like she already owned the space—and him. "Haven't seen you around here before."

Griffin barely spared her a glance, his attention still on his beer. "I come here all the time."

Aiden nearly choked, coughing into his drink to hide his laughter.

But she didn't back down. Her eyes raked over Griffin, slow and deliberate, testing every inch like she was waiting for him to crack.

"Maybe I just wasn't looking in the right places."

Griffin sighed, finally setting his beer down and meeting her gaze head-on. Calm. Unbothered.

"Listen," he said, voice smooth but firm, "I appreciate the interest, but I'm not available."

Her smirk faltered for half a second, but she recovered quickly, too used to hearing yes to be rattled by a no. "That so?"

"That's so," Griffin confirmed, already glancing at Aiden. "But he is."

Aiden snorted, shaking his head. "Asshole."

The woman gave Aiden a once-over, unimpressed, then shrugged and disappeared back into the crowd.

Griffin lifted his beer, smirking. "That's one."

Aiden scoffed, rolling his eyes. "Oh, we're keeping count now?"

"Let's see how many more want to test me tonight."

And they did.

Fifteen minutes later, the second round arrived—this one blonde, cheeks flushed from a few too many drinks, smile too eager. She didn't wait for an invitation, just slid into the booth beside Griffin like she belonged there.

"You look like you need some company," she teased, fingers trailing along his arm.

Griffin didn't even blink. "I don't."

Aiden lost it, laughter spilling out before he could stop it.

The blonde pouted, leaning in like proximity would change his answer. "Come on, I don't bite."

Griffin offered a polite smile, already pulling away. "Glad to hear it. Still a no."

She huffed, pushing herself up and tossing Aiden a look like maybe he'd be the consolation prize.

"Your friend needs to loosen up."

Aiden leaned back, arms crossed, grin wide. "Nah. He's just taken."

Taken. That word hung in the air longer than either of them expected.

Griffin's gaze flicked to Aiden, something unreadable passing between them.

Aiden didn't elaborate. Just took another sip of his beer like he hadn't just acknowledged what neither of them had dared to before.

By the fourth woman, Aiden was done pretending he wasn't keeping score.

He tipped his beer toward Griffin, shaking his head. "Alright. I'll say it. You passed the tests."

Griffin arched a brow, a dry chuckle escaping. "You were testing me?"

Aiden shrugged, completely unapologetic. "Women were testing you. I was just observing."

Griffin scoffed, leaning back in his seat. "You think I'm that stupid?"

Aiden smirked, but there was something softer behind it now. "Nah. I think you're still the guy I trusted for years. Just had to remind myself."

Something loosened in Griffin's chest—a tightness he hadn't realized he'd been carrying since this whole mess started. This wasn't just beers at a bar. This was Aiden handing him a lifeline. Offering him a chance to be more than the past.

When the waitress dropped the check, Griffin reached for his wallet, but Aiden was faster, snatching it up with a look that dared him to argue.

"Don't be a hero," Griffin muttered, pulling out his card.

Aiden waved him off. "Consider it my apology for being a dick."

Griffin smirked, shaking his head. "It's gonna take more than one burger and a couple beers to make up for that."

Aiden laughed, clapping him on the shoulder. "Yeah, yeah. Let's get out of here before another one of your admirers shows up."

The air outside was cooler, the noise of the bar fading behind them as they walked toward the truck. For a moment, it was quiet—comfortable.

Then Aiden glanced over, his voice lighter but edged with curiosity. "Can I ask you something? And you shoot me straight?"

Griffin eyed him, wary but intrigued. "What's up?"

Aiden didn't hesitate. "Wren. How and why?"

Griffin let out a low chuckle, shaking his head as he opened the truck door. "That's a loaded question, man."

"I've got time," Aiden shrugged. "How did it start? How'd you know?"

Griffin leaned against the door, a small smirk tugging at his lips as the memories hit him. "We met here."

Aiden's brow shot up. "She told me."

Griffin laughed, the sound softer, almost disbelieving. "Yeah. She called me out on every move I made. Didn't let me get away with shit. We sat for hours, just... talking. No games."

As he spoke, Aiden watched the way Griffin's entire demeanor shifted —how the cocky edge softened into something real. Something permanent.

Griffin's voice dropped, almost like he was talking to himself. "She fought for me before I even realized I needed someone to."

And then it hit him.

His breath caught, his body going still as the weight of that truth sank in.

Aiden saw it. The exact moment realization knocked the air from Griffin's lungs.

"You know now, don't you?" Aiden's voice was quieter, almost proud.

Griffin exhaled hard, jaw tight. "She fought for us before we were even an us."

The determination that rolled off him after that was palpable. His shoulders squared, his fists clenched, and that smirk, the one that meant trouble, returned.

"She wants space? She can take the condo," he said. "But fuck if I'm not going down swinging now."

He turned to Aiden, grin widening. "And fuck your couch. I'm taking the guest bed. Might be two nights."

Aiden laughed, loud and full, clapping him on the back. "That's my boy."

And just like that, the night wasn't about tests anymore.

It was about Griffin Hayes realizing exactly what—and who—he was fighting for.

33

WAITING WEIGHT

GRIFFIN

THE TRUCK PULLED into the parking garage of Griffin's complex, the clock on the dashboard glowing 11:30 PM. The dim overhead lights flickered slightly, casting long, distorted shadows across the concrete. The place was empty, silent, except for the low hum of engines cooling and the occasional drip of a leaking pipe somewhere in the distance.

Too late for a conversation.

Too late for her to be awake.

Not that he expected to hear from her anyway.

Because she wasn't going to call.

Not tonight. Maybe not ever.

And that fucking destroyed him.

Griffin gripped the steering wheel too tight, his knuckles turning white as the frustration curled hot and sharp in his chest. He didn't even realize he was holding his breath until a long, ragged exhale escaped his lips. He forced himself to loosen his grip, but the tension in his shoulders refused to ease.

Nothing about this felt right.

Aiden sat in the passenger seat, his arms crossed, gaze steady. He wasn't pushing, wasn't saying much at all, but he didn't need to. He had already said everything that needed to be said.

Let her sit in it.

Griffin didn't know if this was the right move. If this was what would make her see. But fuck, what else was he supposed to do?

She needed space? Fine. She wanted time to think? Take all the fucking time in the world.

But he wasn't going to stand around waiting to be chosen. She either wanted him, or she didn't. And if she didn't? If this thing they had built meant less to her than it did to him, then he needed to know now. Because he couldn't do this back-and-forth shit.

Not anymore.

His jaw flexed, a sharp tick beneath his cheekbone as the silence in the truck thickened. "Give me five minutes," Griffin muttered, killing the engine and grabbing the keys. "It's late. I'll let her sleep."

Aiden nodded, barely looking at him. "Yeah, man. I'll be here."

Because Aiden saw it. The weight in his shoulders. The exhaustion bleeding through the cracks. The way this whole mess was wearing him the fuck down.

And hell, the guy was letting her stay at his place while he house-swapped—so he wouldn't wake her. After everything, Griffin still cared enough to make space for her.

He shoved the door open and stepped out, the night air biting sharp against his skin. He didn't pause. Didn't breathe. Just moved, fast and focused, toward the elevator, like if he walked quickly enough, he could outrun the ache clawing up his spine.

But the moment the metal doors slid closed around him? There was nothing but thinking. The hum of the elevator was loud, too fucking loud, pressing against his skull like a vise. Why the hell hasn't she called? It wasn't just about the fight anymore. It was about her silence.

She had every chance to reach out. One text. One word.

Something.

Was she still mad? Still convincing herself he was the problem?

Still twisting his love into something threatening, something dangerous?

He knew about her ex. Knew what that bastard did to her—how he turned tenderness into a trap, how he broke her trust until love felt like a setup for pain. Griffin had spent months proving he wasn't him, that she was safe, that she didn't have to flinch when someone got too close.

But was she standing in his silence now, letting those old ghosts whisper that this was the same? That he might break her, too?

His stomach twisted.

No.

He slammed the door shut on that thought.

She wasn't done.

She couldn't be.

Right?

The doors slid open. Griffin stepped into the hallway, his footsteps heavy in the stillness of the night. The silence was deafening. The air in the hallway was too still, too fucking quiet, the kind of silence that made his ears ring. He had walked down this hallway hundreds of times, but tonight, it felt different.

Like something was missing. Like something was already lost.

His keys jingled in his grip as he approached the door, the sound too loud, too sharp, cutting through the oppressive stillness.

For a split second, he hesitated. Just stood there, staring at the door. Because once he walked in, it would be real. The empty space. The proof that he wasn't staying. That she wasn't stopping him.

His throat tightened.

And then—

He unlocked the door.

And stepped inside.

WREN

Wren had told herself she needed space. That she needed time to think. That if she could just sit in it for a little while, let the silence settle, and let herself breathe, she'd finally figure out what the fuck she was supposed to do with all of this. But now that she had it?

It fucking sucked.

The bed was too big without him. The sheets still smelled like him, that mix of clean laundry and cologne that had somehow started to feel like home. But there was no weight beside her. No steady warmth. No Griffin. And she hated herself for needing it so bad.

She had tried to sleep. Tried to shut her brain off. Tried to pretend she was fine, that this wasn't wrecking her. But every time she closed her eyes—

All she saw was him walking away.

His face. That single fucking tear. The way his voice cracked when he told her he loved her, when he told her she needed to figure out what she wanted. She told herself he just needed to cool off. That he'd be back. That when she woke up, she'd find him asleep on the couch or, at the very least, in the kitchen, already making coffee.

When she heard the front door unlock, her breath caught in her throat.

She froze, every muscle in her body locking up as she heard the familiar soft creak of the door swinging open and the quiet shuffle of boots on hardwood.

Griffin.

Her chest constricted, her mind racing. He's here. He's here. For what? She stayed still. Forced her breathing to slow. Listened.

Every sound, every movement, every second of his presence filled the silence too much and not enough all at once.

The closet door slid open.

The soft clang of hangers shifting.

The dull thud of drawers opening, then closing.

She squeezed her eyes shut. Didn't move. Didn't dare move. Because she knew. She fucking knew.

He wasn't staying.

She heard every rustle of fabric. Every quiet movement. Every calculated, careful noise he made. He was packing a bag. He wasn't home. He was just here to grab what he needed.

Her chest ached, a deep, brutal kind of pain that settled in her ribs, twisting, spreading like an old wound ripped back open.

Then—

The bathroom. She heard the soft scrape of his toothbrush sliding out of the holder. The muted shuffle of the medicine cabinet opening. The familiar clink of his cologne bottle as it hit the counter.

Her throat burned. Her vision blurred. She gritted her teeth so hard her jaw ached, holding back the flood, refusing to break.

But every small noise was another crack in the dam she was desperately trying to keep from shattering.

She knew he was hurting. She could feel it. The weight in the air. The hesitation in his movements.

But the second she heard the door close, the second she heard the lock latch behind him—

She lost it all over again.

A sharp, aching sob clawed up her throat as she curled into herself, her hands fisting the sheets, her whole body trembling under the crushing weight of it.

He was gone. And she had no one to blame but herself.

For the first time in years—

She cried herself to sleep.

GRIFFIN

Griffin stood in the kitchen, fingers digging into the counter, his head bowed, shoulders tight, staring at the coffee maker like it had the fucking answers.

It didn't. Nothing did.

His chest felt too fucking tight. His breaths came slow, forced, like he was trying to keep himself from unraveling right there, in the middle of the kitchen that still smelled like her, still held the ghost of her laughter, still carried the weight of everything they hadn't said.

He knew her. Knew exactly how this would go. She'd wake up, head pounding, eyes swollen, throat raw from the tears she had refused to shed in front of him. She would walk into the kitchen. Go straight for the coffee.

Because Wren Sinclair wasn't a woman who let herself fall apart—not for anyone. Not even him.

She'd tell herself she was fine. She'd pour her coffee. And that's when she'd see it.

The note.

His pulse hammered in his ears as he stared down at the folded paper in his hands, the words already burned into his memory. His fingers tightened around the pen as he finished, pressing it against the counter for a long second, like he was willing himself to just fucking breathe.

Then, he saw it.

The smear. The single drop of ink blurred at the bottom of the page. No. Not ink. A tear.

His tear.

Griffin let out a breath, a sharp, shattered exhale, his jaw clenching so fucking hard it hurt. He ripped his gaze from the note, from the proof of his own fucking breaking point, and forced himself to move.

He set the pen down. He stepped back. Then, without another second, without letting himself hesitate—

He walked the fuck out.

WREN

Wren woke up feeling like she had been run the fuck over.

Her head throbbed, a deep, relentless pounding behind her eyes. Her throat burned, raw from every scream, every sob she had tried to choke down. Her body felt heavy, weighted by exhaustion. By regret. By the emptiness pressing in around her. For a second—just a second—she let herself believe it had been a bad dream. That she hadn't destroyed the best thing that had ever happened to her. That Griffin hadn't looked at her last night like he was watching the one person he loved most slip through his fingers.

But then—

The silence.

No footsteps in the hall. No soft rustling of sheets from the other side of the bed. No sound of coffee brewing in the kitchen. No Griffin.

Her stomach twisted, a slow, sickening knot forming deep in her gut. She pushed herself up, every limb aching. Her head swimming with the weight of too little sleep and too many regrets. She dragged herself out of bed, feet bare and unsteady, carrying her through the too-quiet condo.

And it wasn't for show. He left. It hit her like a fucking wrecking ball, the reality of it sinking in as she moved through the space.

Gone.

He was really gone.

Her fingers curled around the edge of the counter when she stepped into the kitchen, gripping it so tight her knuckles went white, as if she could somehow hold herself up, keep herself together. Her eyes scanned the space, desperate for something, anything, and then—

She saw it.

The note.

A small, folded piece of paper sitting next to the coffee maker, waiting for her. Her breath hitched, the air in the room suddenly too thick, pressing against her lungs as she reached for it. Her hands were shaking before she even read the first word.

And when she did?

Her world fucking shattered.

> *Wren,*
>
> *Giving you the space that you want or need or both, I don't fucking know. I'm not tiptoeing anymore. I'm not waiting around for you to decide if I am worth the risk, Wren. Either you fight for this—for me—for us…*
>
> *Or you let me go.*
>
> *—Griff*

Her chest caved in, a sharp, brutal ache spreading through her as she stared at the words.

That's when her eyes locked onto it. The tear stain on the page. Not hers.

His.

A fucking tear, smudging the ink, proof that this had hurt him. That writing this, leaving this, had broken him. And she was the reason. She did this.

She sucked in a sharp breath, but it didn't help.

Because she knew. Knew he had work in the morning. Knew he wouldn't be back tonight. Knew he had packed that bag because he wasn't coming home—not now, maybe not ever.

This wasn't him cooling off.

This was him giving her exactly what she asked for.

And suddenly, the air was too thick. Too fucking suffocating.

And she needed—

Aiden.

AIDEN'S INTERVENTION

Wren stormed through Aiden's front door, her heart hammering, mind so fucking chaotic that she couldn't even feel her feet hitting the floor. The rush of blood in her ears drowned out everything else—everything except the ache sitting heavy in her chest.

She couldn't breathe. She needed answers. She needed someone to tell her that she hadn't just fucked up the best thing that had ever happened to her.

But Aiden?

Aiden just stood there. Arms crossed. Waiting. Like he'd been expecting this exact moment. He spoke without even letting her ask, "Yes, Wren. He was here."

Her stomach plummeted, so fast and so hard that she nearly stumbled.

She opened her mouth, words caught in the back of her throat, but Aiden didn't give her the chance. "He stayed here last night. He showed up at my door—after I punched him, after I told him I never wanted to see him again. The man I forbade from being anywhere near my sister was asking for my help to keep her."

The words hit her like a wrecking ball, slamming through her chest, through her ribs, through the very fucking center of her. She froze, body locking up, hands curling into fists.

He didn't come here for him. He came for you.

The truth of it sliced through her, brutal and unrelenting, cutting through every single excuse she'd told herself.

Aiden's voice hardened, his jaw clenching as he took a step closer. "He's fighting like hell. Yeah, you fought and argued to protect him from Lia. But when the fuck are you going to fight for him?"

Her breath came shallow, fast, and uneven. Because she didn't have an answer. Because she had spent so much time trying to protect herself, trying to convince herself that this was the right thing. That pulling back, that creating space, that fucking running was the only way to keep herself from getting hurt. She hadn't even fucking realized she was the one doing the damage.

Aiden's voice cut through the air like a blade. "If you keep this shit up, Wren, you're going to lose him."

Her stomach twisted so hard she felt sick. She staggered back, head shaking, a weak, useless "I—" slipping past her lips.

Aiden didn't fucking let up. Didn't soften. Didn't let her hide. "I saw it last night. The way he talked about you, the pride in his voice when he told me how you met. The way he dismissed every single woman at Marshside like they didn't fucking exist. The way he stared at that condo when we came back—like walking away was killing him."

Wren sucked in a breath, but it felt like she was choking on it.

"And the worst part?" Aiden's voice dropped, quieter now. Sharpened. Cutting. Brutal. "The way he looked when it got quiet. That blank stare. That fucking emptiness."

Silence.

Wren couldn't breathe.

She couldn't fucking breathe.

Because it was real. It was so fucking real now, sitting in front of her, inescapable, unmovable, undeniable.

Griffin had walked out last night, but not because he wanted to. Because she had given him no other fucking choice.

Aiden just watched her. Waiting.

Letting it sink in. Letting her feel it.

And damn, she did.

She fucking did.

Her feet moved before her brain caught up.

She turned, heading straight for the guest room. She barely registered her own hands shaking as she gripped the doorknob and pushed it open—and the second she stepped inside—she lost her breath.

The bed.

One side of it barely disturbed. Like he had barely let himself rest there. Like he hadn't even let himself get comfortable. His scent still clinging to the pillow. And there on the nightstand—

His fucking clothes.

Her legs almost buckled.

She took one slow, hesitant step toward the bed, her throat burning, her vision blurring at the edges. She reached out, fingers trembling, brushing over the fabric he had left behind.

His hoodie. His fucking hoodie.

The one he always threw on after work, the one she had stolen too many times to count, the one that smelled like him, like home, like everything she had just thrown away. Her hands clenched around it, twisting in the fabric, pulling it against her chest like that would somehow bring him back.

Her breath came in ragged, uneven gasps.

She broke.

Completely.

Utterly.

Fucking.

Broke.

Because she felt it.

His absence. The weight of what she had done. The truth she had been too fucking scared to admit. This wasn't just about him leaving. This was about the fact that, for the first time—

She was absolutely terrified he wasn't coming back.

A soft knock on the doorframe pulled her from the spiral, and Aiden's voice followed, quieter now, but still edged in warning.

"I'm meeting him at Marshside for a late lunch."

Wren's head snapped up, eyes wide, heart slamming against her ribs.

"You've still got time, Wren. But not much."

34

WRECKAGE WADING

AIDEN SLID ONTO THE BARSTOOL, elbows resting on the counter. His fingers tapped out a restless rhythm against the worn wood. The bartender gave him a nod, already knowing their order—it was muscle memory by now. Two beers. One for him. One for the man currently sitting across the room looking like he'd forgotten what it meant to actually live.

Griffin Hayes.

The same guy who used to own every room he walked into. The guy who laughed too loud, flirted too easily, and carried the kind of confidence most men could only fake. But tonight?

Tonight, Griffin wasn't that man.

Aiden's gaze drifted to the booth—their booth. The place where all of this had started. Where Griffin met Wren and, without even realizing it, handed her every piece of himself.

Now, he sat there like a fucking ghost.

Leaning back, arms stretched across the top of the booth like he didn't have a single care in the world, but Aiden knew better. He saw the truth in the details most people would miss. The hollowness in Griffin's eyes—whatever light had been there was flickering out. The way his shoulders sagged when he thought no one was watching. The absent way his thumb traced patterns against his beer bottle—not out of boredom, but because it was the only thing keeping his hands from shaking.

He's fucking breaking.

And Aiden hated every second of it.

Because this wasn't who Griffin was supposed to be. He didn't resemble the man Wren fell for or the man Aiden called his best friend for years. Tired of waiting, tired of hoping, tired of fighting for someone who hadn't fought back, this was someone who'd been stripped down to nothing but exhaustion and heartache.

Aiden let out a slow breath, the weight of it pressing heavy in his chest.

He glanced over his shoulder, maybe out of habit, maybe because the air felt too still—too expectant.

And that's when he saw her.

The door swung open, and in walked every fucking nightmare wrapped in a familiar smile.

Lia.

Aiden's pulse spiked, his jaw locking so tight it felt like his teeth might crack. His entire body tensed, muscles coiling like he was ready for a fight. But he didn't move.

He just watched.

Because Lia wasn't here by accident.

No, she didn't scan the bar, she didn't hesitate or play coy like some wandering ex who just happened to stumble in.

She knew. She knew exactly where he'd be.

And with the precision of a predator, she made a direct fucking line for Griffin—like she still had the right to.

Aiden's stomach twisted, a sick churn of anger and dread clawing its way up his throat. He wanted to yell. To get up and put himself between them. But something kept him frozen. Maybe it was the shock, or maybe it was the brutal understanding that this wasn't his move to make.

This was Wren's.

So he stayed seated, watching with a knot in his chest as Lia slid into the booth across from Griffin like no time had passed, like she hadn't once shattered the man now sitting in front of her.

That smile—God, that fucking smile—curled on her lips, sweet and venomous. The same look she'd used to get whatever she wanted. And Griffin?

Griffin looked up, startled.

But he didn't push her away.

Not immediately.

And that's when Aiden felt it—that cold spike of panic. Because Griffin wasn't entertaining her. He wasn't interested. But he was too tired to shut it down.

Too fucking wrecked to care.

Aiden could see it in the way Griffin's eyes didn't really focus. The way his posture didn't tense like it should've. Like he didn't have the energy to fight off one more person tonight.

Fuck. No.

Aiden's hand flew to his pocket, pulling out his phone like it was a lifeline.

> Aiden: You need to get here. Now. Lia's here. She's sitting with Griffin.

He didn't even wait for a response. He couldn't. His eyes darted back to the booth, just in time to catch the moment.

Lia's hand, elegant and practiced, sliding across the table like it was second nature. Like claiming him was muscle memory. Her fingers curled around Griffin's forearm, nails lightly grazing his skin. Staking her fucking territory, as if she hadn't already burned that bridge to the ground.

Aiden's chest burned with fury.

Not again. Not this time.

He snapped a photo, the shutter sound far too loud in his ears. The image of Lia's hand on Griffin's arm seared into his phone—and into his head.

> Aiden: Check your phone. Now.

Seconds felt like hours before his phone buzzed in his hand.

> Wren: That bitch, I'll be there in 10.

Aiden let out a shaky exhale, his heart still pounding against his ribs.

He muttered under his breath, staring at the two of them—Griffin, hollow and fading. And Lia. Smiling like the devil in designer heels.

"Oh, this is gonna be a *fucking disaster.*"

Because Wren?

Wren was about to walk into hellfire.

And Aiden wasn't sure if anyone was making it out unscathed.

WREN

Her heart wasn't beating; it was pounding, a violent, chaotic rhythm that rattled through her chest like it was trying to escape. The tires screamed against the pavement as she flew down the road, but Wren didn't give a damn about speed limits. Didn't care about the blur of passing cars or the way her hands shook against the steering wheel.

All she could see was that picture.

Lia's perfectly manicured hand resting on Griffin's arm like she still owned him. Like she hadn't already shattered him once and wasn't about to try again.

Her stomach twisted, bile rising in her throat, but it wasn't just jealousy ripping through her, it was fear. Bone-deep, soul-crushing fear. Because this wasn't just any woman.

This was Lia.

The ghost Wren had been fighting since the moment Griffin whispered her name in his sleep. The woman who'd left scars on him that Wren had traced with careful fingers, trying to soothe what she couldn't erase.

And now, she was back.

Not Lia—her.

Wren.

She was the one who'd let that ghost back in. The one who hesitated. Who doubted. Who pushed him away instead of holding him tighter. Griffin was hurting. And it was her fault.

She let fear win. Let silence do the damage Lia never could. And now that hollow look in his eyes, the one that gutted her to her core, she put it there.

But not anymore.

She drew in a sharp and shaky breath as something inside her snapped into place. She was done running. Done letting fear write her story. This time, she wasn't choosing distance.

Not fucking today. Not after everything they'd survived.

Not after Wren had finally realized that losing him wasn't something she could come back from.

She was choosing him.

When Marshside appeared through the windshield, Wren didn't even think. She swerved into the lot, barely missing a parked truck, the tires skidding as she slammed it into park sideways. The engine was still humming when she flung the door open and stormed inside, door slamming behind her. The starting shot of a war she wasn't sure she could win.

The noise of the bar hit her—voices, laughter, glasses clinking—but it all blurred into nothing.

Because her eyes were already searching, wild and desperate, scanning every face. That's when her heart dropped to the floor.

Griffin was gone.

Her breath caught, sharp and painful, like someone had sucker-punched her straight in the chest. No. No, no, no. Where the fuck was he?

Her pulse roared in her ears, but then she saw them.

Aiden.

And Lia.

At the booth. Talking like they were old friends. Like her entire world wasn't currently collapsing in on itself.

Her body moved before her brain could process it. Every step fueled by adrenaline and the sickening dread pooling in her stomach. Aiden's eyes locked on hers first, relief flashing for half a second before it shifted to something far worse.

Resignation.

Like he already knew this was about to get ugly.

Lia turned, slow and deliberate, that venom-laced smile stretching across her face. She was thrilled to see Wren walking through that door.

"Well, if it isn't Wren Sinclair," she purred, every word dripping with condescension. "Took you long enough."

Wren's fists clenched so hard her nails bit into her palms, but she didn't flinch. She wouldn't give this bitch the satisfaction. "Where the fuck is he?"

Lia's eyes sparkled with cruel amusement. "Gone."

One word. That's all it took to rip Wren's heart clean out of her chest. Gone.

The room tilted, her breath catching somewhere between a gasp and a sob she refused to let out. But Lia—Lia thrived on the torment. She leaned against the booth back, casual and graceful, like she hadn't just detonated Wren's sanity.

"What did you say to him?" Wren snapped, stepping closer, her voice shaking with rage she could barely contain.

But Lia didn't so much as blink. That smug tilt of her head, that *I've already won* glint in her eye that made Wren's blood boil.

"Relax, sweetheart," Lia crooned, her tone mockingly sweet. "We just caught up. Old friends, you know how it is."

"Cut the shit, Lia." Wren's voice was sharper now. Her body practically vibrating with the urge to rip that fake smile off her face.

Aiden sat tense beside them, silent, watching the storm build, but even he knew better than to step between two women ready to draw blood.

Lia leaned in.

Close enough that Wren could smell the expensive perfume, could feel the chill of every word that followed.

"I'm not here for games, Wren," Lia whispered, her voice slicing through the air like a blade. "I'm here because my son deserves a father."

It didn't register.

Not at first.

The words floated there, heavy and incomprehensible, as Wren blinked—her heart stalling.

"What?" Her voice cracked, barely audible. "The fuck did you just say?"

Lia's smile widened. It was slow, predatory. Satisfied. "You heard me."

Wren's vision blurred, her stomach lurching like the floor had just been ripped out from under her.

No. No fucking way.

But Lia wasn't done. Oh no, she was savoring every second of Wren's unraveling. She reached out, fingers ghosting over Wren's arm in a touch so gentle it made Wren sick.

"You thought this was about jealousy?" Lia murmured, her nails dragging across Wren's skin like a taunt. "About getting under your skin?" She leaned in closer, her breath a whisper against Wren's ear. "This is about family. Griffin and I—we have unfinished business. And I'm not walking away this time."

Wren yanked her arm back like she'd been burned, her entire body trembling. Rage, fear, heartbreak all crashed together in a tidal wave that left her gasping for air.

Aiden finally stepped in, his voice low but sharp enough to cut through the tension. "Lia. That's enough."

But Lia just straightened, brushing invisible dust off her designer jacket. Completely confident in her obliteration of Wren's world.

"I'll be seeing you around, Wren," she said with a wink, before turning on her heel and striding out, heels clicking against the floor like victory bells.

Wren stood there.

Frozen.

The noise of the bar faded into nothing, the world narrowing down to the echo of Lia's, "My son deserves a father," repeating in her head like a death sentence.

Her throat tightened, her vision swimming with unshed tears she refused to let fall.

"Aiden…" Her voice was barely a whisper, broken and raw. "She's lying… Right?"

But Aiden didn't answer. Because he couldn't. Because neither of them knew the truth. And that was the moment Wren felt it—the true weight of what she was up against.

She wasn't just fighting for Griffin's heart anymore.

She was fighting against a past she couldn't rewrite. Against a ghost that wore a crown and carried his blood.

And for the first time, she wasn't sure if love was enough to win.

Aiden stepped in, his voice low but certain. "You're coming with me."

Wren blinked up at him. "What?"

"You're staying at my place tonight."

"But—"

"No arguments. Griffin doesn't need to come back to this. Not right now. Not like this."

She didn't have the strength to fight him on it. Not when her whole world was already in pieces.

Aiden pulled out his phone, thumbs moving across the screen.

> Aiden: Griff—she's with me. Safe.
>
> Do what you need to do, brother.

35

HOLLOWED

GRIFFIN HAD COME BACK to the condo.

Not because he wanted to. Not because it felt like home anymore. But because there was nowhere else to go.

The condo was too quiet.

Not the kind of quiet people romanticize—the peaceful kind where you can hear yourself think, where silence feels like a blanket.

No.

This was the kind of quiet that strangles you.

The kind that seeps into your bones and makes every breath feel like a burden you aren't sure you want to carry anymore.

The kind that reminds you—with every tick of the clock, every creak of the walls—that you are alone.

And worse?

That no one was coming to save you.

Griffin sat on the edge of the couch, elbows digging so deep into his knees it felt like he was trying to hold himself together by force. It felt like if he let go, even for a second, he'd fall apart in a way he couldn't recover from.

His fingers hung limp.

Empty.

Useless.

Because what was left to hold on to when everything that mattered had already slipped through them?

Red-rimmed, his hollow eyes locked onto the bottle on the coffee table.

That goddamn bottle.

It stared back at him like an old friend and a loaded gun all at once.

Half full of whiskey.

Half full of broken promises he wasn't sure he had the strength to keep anymore.

He hadn't touched it.

Not yet.

But fuck, he wanted to.

Not to blur it out. He didn't deserve that mercy.

Not to forget. Because forgetting meant those memories with her would fade too, and he couldn't lose those, not when they were all he had left.

No.

He wanted it because the burn might remind him that beneath all the numbness, beneath the shell of a man sitting in this dark, suffocating room —he was still alive.

But even that felt like wishful thinking.

The faint glow of his phone lit up the room.

Once.

Hope.

Twice.

Darkness.

No messages.

No missed calls.

No Wren.

The hope extinguished.

Each time that screen came to life, it carved him open a little deeper—because even when he told himself not to look, not to hope, that pathetic sliver of him still wished it would be her. Still begged for something he swore he was done begging for.

And when it wasn't?

The silence that followed was worse than any scream.

Worse than any fight.

Because at least anger meant someone cared enough to raise their voice.

This? This was abandonment dressed up as indifference.

Griffin's jaw clenched until it felt like it might shatter, his teeth grinding against the weight sitting heavy on his chest. That hollow ache wasn't just familiar now. It was permanent. A second heartbeat that throbbed with every reminder that he wasn't enough to make her stay.

It wasn't pain anymore. Pain would've been a relief.

This was nothing.

This was staring at the walls of a life he built for someone who didn't think twice about walking away.

This was the realization that he could scream at the top of his lungs and no one would hear him.

Because no one was listening.

Especially not her.

His gaze drifted to the hoodie slung over the armchair—the one she always stole like it was hers by right. The one that smelled like shampoo, and skin, and comfort. The one that used to mean she was here. That she was his.

Now? Now it felt like a fucking headstone. A marker for the version of him that died the second she decided he wasn't worth fighting for.

He swallowed hard, but it didn't push down the lump in his throat. It didn't steady the shaking in his hands or stop the flood of memories crashing through him. The tide was just too strong for him to swim against.

He dragged a trembling hand down his face, feeling the roughness of days-old stubble beneath his palm. Griffin Hayes used to own every room he walked into. Now he couldn't even own the reflection in the mirror.

Who the fuck was he without her?

Without them?

Because Griffin Hayes didn't wait for anyone. He didn't sit by the phone like some desperate asshole praying to be chosen.

But that's exactly what he'd become.

A man waiting for a woman who wasn't coming. A man who gave every piece of himself to someone who couldn't even give him a goddamn text.

At first, he'd blamed her.

For shutting him out.

For pulling away when he was still standing there with open hands, ready to carry all her fears if it meant she'd just let him in.

For making him believe that loving her—completely, recklessly—was a mistake.

But now?

Now, the blame wasn't so easy.

Because he stayed.

Even when every part of him screamed to walk away.

Even when it chipped pieces off his soul every time she looked at him like he was asking too much for simply wanting to be enough.

He stayed. Because, like a goddamn fool, he believed that love could fix it.

That she would wake up one day and see him standing there, bruised and bleeding, but still there.

He let out a sound—somewhere between a laugh and a sob—that echoed off the empty walls and slammed back into his chest like punishment.

"Stupid," he whispered, his voice so raw it barely sounded human. "So fucking stupid."

His hand twitched toward the bottle again.

Don't.

But why the hell not?

What was left to fight for when the only person he wanted to fight for had already surrendered?

His phone lit up one more time—bright against the dark.

And God help him. Hope still flickered in his chest.

That sick, twisted reflex he couldn't kill.

But it wasn't her. Of course, it wasn't her.

It was Aiden.

Checking in. Making sure his best friend hadn't completely drowned in the silence.

Griffin stared at the screen until it dimmed again, until the darkness swallowed him whole.

He reached out, powered the phone off, watching as the last light in the room died.

No more waiting. No more hoping. No more humiliating himself with the thought that she'd suddenly remember he existed. The silence that followed wasn't empty.

It was a grave.

His eyes burned, but he refused to cry. He'd already bled out every part of himself that mattered.

Now?

Now there was nothing left but a man sitting in the wreckage of a love story that never stood a chance.

And as he leaned back against the couch, staring at the ceiling like maybe it held answers the world refused to give him, Griffin realized the most brutal truth of all.

It wasn't that she didn't love him.

It was that love wasn't enough.

Not for her.

Not for this.

And that, more than anything, was what destroyed him.

Because he had nothing left to give.

And no one left to give it to.

AND JUST WHEN HE THOUGHT HE COULD DISAPPEAR—

Sink deeper into that merciless quiet where nothing could hurt anymore—

Where numbness was safer than hope—

A knock.

Soft.

Deliberate.

Like it wasn't just someone at his door, but fate itself coming to finish what it started.

Griffin didn't move.

At first, he thought he imagined it.

That his mind, already frayed and unraveling, was playing one last cruel trick before it finally gave out.

But then—

Another knock.

This one felt heavier. Like it carried weight he wasn't ready to hold.

His body protested every movement as he pushed himself off the couch, feet dragging like he was wading through concrete. His chest tightened with each step, dread coiling tighter with every breath.

He didn't ask who it was.

Because deep down, he already fucking knew.

When he opened the door, the cold air from the hallway hit him, but it wasn't the chill that made his heart drop.

It was her.

Lia.

Standing there like a ghost that refused to stay buried. Like she belonged in the ruins of his life.

No sweet smile.

No flirtatious tilt of her head.

Just those sharp, knowing eyes calculating every crack in his armor.

She didn't have to speak.

Griffin could already feel the noose tightening.

His throat burned as he forced out, "What the fuck do you want, Lia?"

His voice barely sounded like his own—hoarse from days of silence. From nights spent choking on words he never got to say to the one person he actually wanted at his door.

Lia's lips parted, her voice coming soft, too soft. The kind of softness that wasn't mercy. It was manipulation dressed up in vulnerability.

"If it wasn't important, I wouldn't be here."

And like always, she didn't wait for an invitation. She brushed past him, stepping into his condo like it was hers to claim. Like she hadn't already burned every bridge between them to ash.

Griffin didn't stop her.

Not because he wanted her there.

But because he didn't have the strength to fight a battle he'd already lost years ago.

He watched as she paced his living room—*his living room*—the same way she used to when she was bored. When she was restless and looking for a way to ruin him without ever raising her voice.

But tonight?

Tonight, she didn't need games.

Because she'd come armed with something far more lethal.

And when she finally stopped—when those ice-cold eyes locked onto his—she said it.

"I have a son."

Two seconds.

That's how long it took for his world to tilt sideways.

At first, the words didn't land. They hovered there, floating in the thick, suffocating air between them.

But when they hit?

It was a fucking detonation.

Griffin's breath caught, his chest seizing like someone had wrapped a fist around his lungs.

"What?" It was barely a whisper; more disbelief than sound. Like his brain couldn't process betrayal on top of exhaustion.

Lia's eyes shimmered with unshed tears—perfectly placed, perfectly timed. And Griffin hated that for half a second, they almost looked real.

"He's almost four."

Four. The number echoed through his skull—violent and merciless.

His knees nearly buckled.

Four years.

Four years of silence. Of wondering if she ever thought about what they almost had. Of trying to rebuild a life she shattered.

And now…

This.

"You're fucking kidding me…" His laugh came out broken, jagged, like it scraped his throat raw just to get past the lump lodged there. "You disappear for four goddamn years and show up with this?"

"I didn't know how to tell you," she shot back, voice trembling just enough to twist the knife deeper. "I didn't even know if he was yours."

Griffin stumbled backward, his hand raking through his hair as his pulse roared in his ears. The walls of the condo felt like they were closing in, each word shrinking the space around him until there was nowhere left to run.

"That's convenient," he bit out, but his voice cracked beneath the weight of it.

Lia's softness vanished—because it was never real to begin with.

"I didn't come here to fight."

"No?" His voice shot up, raw and bitter. "Then what the fuck did you come for, Lia? A reunion? Closure? Or just to remind me that no matter how far I get, you'll always be there to drag me back under?"

She stepped in, her gaze slicing through him like she knew exactly where every scar lived.

"I thought you'd want to know you might have a son."

"Might," Griffin spat, the word burning his tongue like poison. "You don't even know."

Silence dropped like a guillotine between them.

But Lia wasn't done. No. She'd barely started.

She took another step closer, her voice dropping to a whisper so venomous it could paralyze.

"You always said you'd be a better father than your own…" Her lips curved, not in kindness, but in victory. "Looks like fate's giving you that chance."

That was it.

The fatal blow.

His legs gave out, but he caught himself. Just barely, his palm slamming against the wall to keep from collapsing completely.

Because she knew.

She fucking knew.

Knew that every nightmare he had growing up was about becoming the man who left.

The man who forgot.

The man who didn't fight for his blood.

And now she was standing there, daring him to prove he wasn't that man.

But how do you fight a battle when every option makes you lose?

"I'm not him…" Softer this time, Griffin's voice cracked. Like saying it out loud was the only thing keeping him tethered to what was left of himself.

Lia's smile turned gentle—sickeningly sweet.

"Then don't walk away."

The room spun. His vision blurred—not from tears, but from the sheer force of everything crashing down at once.

He wasn't just drowning; he was sinking so fast he could already feel the pressure crushing his chest.

"Get out," he rasped, barely able to force the words past the storm in his throat.

Lia lingered. Watching. Memorizing the exact moment Griffin Hayes shattered beyond recognition.

And when she finally turned to leave, her heels clicking like a countdown to his destruction, he didn't breathe until the door clicked shut.

But by then, it was too late.

His body slid down the wall, every muscle giving out as his head dropped into his hands.

And that's when the dam broke.

No screams. No punches thrown. Just silent, soul-wrecking sobs that tore through him like they'd been waiting for years—like they'd been buried beneath every "I'm fine," every forced smile, every time he told himself he was stronger than the ghosts chasing him.

Because this wasn't just about Lia.

It wasn't even just about Wren.

It was about the brutal realization that no matter how hard he fought—

No matter how many promises he made—

He was still lost.

And as the tears kept falling, relentless and cruel, Griffin understood something that hollowed him out completely.

You don't have to die to stop existing.

Sometimes?

All it takes is love.

And betrayal.

And the weight of a past you never outran.

And Griffin Hayes?

He wasn't running anymore.

Because there was nowhere left to go.

36

FIRE TO ASH

WREN DIDN'T REMEMBER the drive back to Aiden's.

Didn't remember the turns, the lights, or the fact that her hands were shaking so violently she could barely grip the wheel.

All she knew was one second she was standing in the middle of Marshside, watching Lia walk away with that smug, victorious smile. And the next, she was sitting on Aiden's couch. Staring at nothing. Feeling like her entire world had been ripped out from under her.

The silence in the room was deafening.

Aiden had tried—God, he'd tried—to say something when they walked through the door. But one look at her, and he knew. There was nothing he could say to fix this. Nothing that could pull her out of the black hole swallowing her whole.

So now, he hovered somewhere in the background, giving her space. Watching her fall apart in slow motion.

Wren sat curled up in the corner of the couch, knees to her chest. Fingernails digging crescent moons into her skin as her mind replayed every single second of that conversation.

"My son deserves a father."

The words echoed—taunting her, wrapping around her throat like a noose she couldn't untangle.

She squeezed her eyes shut, but it didn't help. Because behind her lids, all she could see was Lia. Standing there with that fucking glint in her eye like she'd already won. Like Wren was nothing more than a temporary distraction in a story that had always belonged to someone else.

Her heart was racing, but it wasn't from fear anymore.

It was rage.

It was helplessness.

It was knowing that deep in her bones, she was fighting a battle she didn't know how to win.

How do you compete with a child?

How do you stand a chance against blood?

A broken sob clawed its way up her throat, but she bit it back, her teeth sinking into her lip so hard she tasted blood. She wouldn't cry. Not like this. Not because of her.

But no matter how hard she fought it, the cracks were spreading.

Her pride—the thing that had kept her from running to Griffin days ago—was gone. Shattered into pieces the moment she saw that photo. The moment Aiden's text confirmed her worst fear.

Lia wasn't just playing games.

She was playing for keeps.

Wren's vision blurred as her gaze flicked to her phone lying on the coffee table face down, taunting her. She hadn't touched it since they got back. Couldn't. Because every time she thought about calling Griffin… The same thought stopped her cold.

What if he doesn't answer?

What if Lia was already there—already inside his head, inside his home—rebuilding a life Wren had no place in?

Her chest tightened, that familiar ache settling deep, like something was rotting inside her ribcage. She wanted to scream. To throw something. To do anything other than sit here suffocating under the weight of her own what-ifs.

But all she could do was drown in them.

Her eyes darted to the clock. Almost midnight.

Where was he?

Was he sitting in that condo alone and wrecked? Or was he with her?

The thought gutted her so hard she physically doubled over, her fingers tangling in her hair as if she could rip the images out of her mind.

Aiden's low voice broke through the haze, cautious, like he was afraid she might shatter if he spoke too loud.

"Wren… You need to breathe."

She let out a sharp, bitter laugh, one that sounded more like a sob. "I don't know how to anymore."

Because how do you breathe when everything you love feels like it's slipping away—and there's nothing you can do to stop it?

Aiden sat across from her, elbows on his knees, eyes steady and full of that helpless kind of worry. The kind that said he'd carry the pain for her if he could but knew this was one she had to bleed through on her own.

"Lia's a liar," he said quietly, but even he didn't sound convinced.

Wren's head snapped up, her eyes wild and glassy. "Yeah? Then why does it feel like she's already won?"

Silence. Because they both knew the truth. Lia didn't have to win—not really.

All she had to do was plant the seed. Let guilt do the rest.

Wren pushed off the couch, pacing the living room like a caged animal, her arms wrapped around herself as if she could hold all the broken pieces together.

"I should've gone to him sooner…" she whispered, her voice cracking. "I should've—"

"Stop." Aiden's voice was firm now, standing up, cutting her off before she spiraled further. "You couldn't have known."

She shook her head violently, tears spilling over despite her best efforts. "But I did know, Aiden! Maybe not about the kid, but I knew she'd come back. I knew she'd wait until he was too fucking tired to fight her off. And I let it happen."

Her voice broke on the last word, shoulders trembling as she pressed a hand to her mouth, trying to silence the sob threatening to tear out of her.

Aiden crossed the room, gripping her shoulders, forcing her to meet his eyes.

"Then go to him. Now. Before she digs in deeper."

Wren swallowed hard, fear clawing at her throat.

But Aiden wasn't letting her back down.

"Whatever's happening up there, don't let her be the only voice he hears."

Those words snapped something inside her.

Because he was right.

Even if it destroyed her, even if Griffin pushed her away, she had to try. Because living with the regret of doing nothing? That would kill her faster than losing him.

Without another word, Wren grabbed her keys and wiped at her face with the back of her hand as she stormed toward the door.

Aiden called after her—something about calling him if she needed—but she barely heard it over the pounding in her ears.

By the time Wren reached Griffin's complex, she wasn't driving—she was surviving.

Her grip on the steering wheel was iron-tight, not from control but desperation. Fingers clenched, wrists trembling, her nails dug into her skin. The car felt too small, the air too thin, as if the whole world was shrinking around her.

She couldn't feel her hands. Couldn't feel anything but the crushing weight in her chest, every breath sharp and shallow, counting down to something she wasn't ready for.

She didn't remember the turns she took.

Didn't remember the highway. The lights. The endless stretch of asphalt that led her here.

All she knew was that her heart was clawing its way up her throat, and her stomach was a twisted wreck of fear, rage, and something worse—

Hope.

That stupid, reckless hope that maybe, hopefully, she wasn't too late.

Her vision blurred as she slammed the car into park, crooked and careless. She stumbled out, legs weak. Her body moving on instinct when her mind was nothing but static.

The pulse in her ears was deafening.

Every step toward the building felt like walking into a war she already knew she couldn't win. But she had to try. Because if she didn't—if she didn't at least fight—then what the fuck was left of her?

She pushed through the front doors, her fingers trembling as she hit the elevator button. Like it might save her from drowning in everything she'd been too scared to face.

The reflection that stared back at her in the steel doors wasn't Wren Sinclair. It was a woman unraveling. Mascara smudged, lips parted like she couldn't catch her breath, eyes wide with the kind of panic that only comes when you realize you've waited too long to fix what you broke.

The elevator dinged.

Just get upstairs. Just knock. Just tell him you're here.

The doors slid open.

And the universe, cruel as ever, tore the ground out from beneath her.

Lia.

Stepping off the elevator like she belonged to every nightmare Wren had ever had—and worse, like she knew it.

Her heels clicked with purpose. Her blonde hair flawless. Her perfume suffocating.

But it wasn't the way she looked that shattered Wren.

It was that smile.

That slow, knowing smirk. It wasn't just gloating.

It was final.

Their eyes locked. Wren's full of fire, barely holding back the flood, Lia's glittering with triumph.

For a heartbeat, the world stopped spinning.

"Oh," Lia cooed, her voice a dagger wrapped in silk. "You made it. Impressive... Though, a little late, don't you think?"

Wren's throat closed. Her chest caving in on itself.

Lia stepped forward, savoring every inch of Wren's unraveling like it was her favorite pastime.

"What's the drive from Aiden's?" she mused, pretending to think. "Twenty minutes? Thirty with traffic?" Her smile sharpened, vicious beneath the sweetness. "Must've felt longer with all that time to wonder if you'd still be welcome when you got here."

Wren didn't move. Couldn't. Because the words weren't what gutted her, it was the truth behind them. But Lia wasn't finished. No, she was just getting started.

She leaned in slightly, her voice dropping, intimate and cruel. "You should've seen him when I got there. God, Wren... He was wrecked. Sitting in the dark like he'd already given up."

Wren's vision swam, her heart slamming so hard it hurt.

"And then he saw me," Lia whispered, her lips curving like she'd already won the war Wren hadn't even gotten to fight. "Funny how history has a way of repeating itself, isn't it?"

Wren's hands clenched into fists, her nails biting into her skin so hard she thought she might bleed, but even pain couldn't anchor her.

Because Lia's words weren't just cutting. They were burying her.

Lia's gaze swept over her, taking in every crack, every fracture in Wren's armor.

"You really thought he'd be waiting," she said, her voice almost pitying. Almost. Then, like twisting the knife just to hear it snap, "Maybe next time," Lia purred, stepping past her, breath ghosting over Wren's ear, "don't hesitate when it comes to keeping what's yours."

Wren stood there frozen, every part of her splintering under the weight of it.

The scent of Lia's perfume lingered like smoke from a house already burned to the ground.

The elevator doors stayed open behind her, mocking her. Inviting her into a battle that had already been lost.

She didn't step forward. She couldn't.

Because what was the point of walking upstairs just to find proof that everything Lia said was true?

Her pride was gone.

Her fire was ash.

And as the doors slid closed, sealing her fate, Wren knew—this wasn't just defeat.

This was obliteration.

She turned on autopilot, her body moving without permission, without thought. As she stumbled back to her car. She didn't remember starting the engine.

Didn't remember the tears that blurred the road as she drove.

All she knew was that she had to get as far away from this place—from herself—as possible.

So she drove.

West.

Back to Winston-Salem.

Back to the version of herself that didn't know what it felt like to lose the only man who ever made her believe she was worth loving.

Back to her apartment.

And the entire way there?

She didn't scream.

She didn't cry.

She just shattered, piece by piece, until there was nothing left but a hollow ache where Wren Sinclair used to be.

Because sometimes, the worst kind of heartbreak isn't loud.

It's quiet.

It's the silence after you realize you were too late.

And no amount of sorry, or fighting, or wishing could ever turn back time.

37

HOLLOWED ECHOES

THE ISLAND FELT HEAVIER TODAY.

Like the air knew something he didn't.

Griffin couldn't explain it, but from the second he opened his eyes that morning, something was off. The kind of off that settled deep in your bones before your brain could catch up. The kind that made every breath feel just a little harder. Every step a little heavier.

He hadn't left his condo in days. Barely ate. Barely slept. Just existed in that suffocating in-between where time didn't feel real, and nothing fucking mattered.

But today, he'd forced himself out. Mostly because Aiden wouldn't stop blowing up his phone.

> Aiden: Answer me, Hayes.
>
> Aiden: I'm coming over if you don't respond.
>
> Aiden: You need to hear this from me.

That last message was still sitting there—unread but burned into his mind.

So here he was, walking streets that felt too familiar and too foreign all at once. People passed him, offering cautious glances, like they could sense the storm brewing beneath his skin. Like they'd heard whispers of what happened at Marshside. Like they already knew something he didn't.

Griffin kept his head down, his hands shoved deep into the pockets of his hoodie—the same one Wren always stole when she stayed over. The sleeves still smelled faintly like her shampoo, and it made his stomach fucking twist.

By the time he reached Aiden's place, he wasn't sure if he was ready for whatever this was.

But nothing could've prepared him.

The second he stepped onto the porch, the door flew open; Aiden stood there like he'd been pacing for hours, waiting for Griffin to finally show his face.

"Jesus Christ, man," Aiden muttered, raking a hand through his hair as he took in the mess standing in front of him. "You look like hell."

Griffin didn't respond. Didn't rise to the bait. He just stared, his eyes hollow, voice rough. "What do you want?"

Aiden's jaw clenched. He stepped aside, jerking his head toward the living room. "Get in here."

"Alright," Griffin rasped, his voice rough from days of silence. "What's so important?"

Aiden shut the door, leaning against it like he was bracing for impact.

For a moment, he didn't speak.

And that silence? That hesitation? It made Griffin's stomach fucking drop.

"Aiden…" Griffin's jaw clenched, his hands balling into fists at his sides. "Say it."

Aiden let out a breath, dragging a hand over his face like the weight of the next words might crush them both.

"She's gone."

The floor vanished beneath him.

Griffin blinked, his heart slamming against his ribs. "What do you mean, 'gone'?"

Aiden's eyes met his—steady, but filled with something Griffin didn't want to see.

"She left, man. Didn't even pack a bag, just… left."

The words didn't make sense. They bounced around his skull, refusing to stick. "No. She wouldn't—"

"She did," Aiden cut in, his voice low but firm. "She walked away. Left her shit here. Stopped the house search. No note. No goodbye. Just… Fucking gone."

Griffin stumbled back a step, like the air had been knocked out of him.

No. No fucking way. Wren was fire. Wren was fight. She didn't just disappear. Not without a word. Not without slamming a door or throwing one last punch.

But Aiden's expression told him everything he didn't want to believe.

"She didn't even—" Griffin's voice cracked, his throat closing around the words. "She didn't call?"

Aiden shook his head once. Slow. Final. Then his jaw clenched.

"I waited. Gave her space. Tried not to hover. But this?" He exhaled hard through his nose. "This isn't her. She's not just shutting you out, man, she's shutting down. And if you know anything about my sister, you know how fucking dangerous that is."

Griffin's chest caved in, his hands gripping the back of his neck like he could hold himself together if he just squeezed hard enough.

Why?

Why would she—

His mind raced through every moment, every argument, every second of silence that now screamed louder than any fight they'd ever had.

"She didn't—" His voice trailed off, too broken to finish.

"I thought you should know," Aiden said quietly, like he knew Griffin was seconds from shattering.

But Griffin didn't answer.

He couldn't.

Because all he could hear was the echo of that door slamming shut—without a goodbye, without a fuck you, without anything.

Just empty space where she used to be.

Without another word, Griffin turned and walked out, ignoring Aiden calling after him, ignoring the way his vision blurred as he stumbled back toward his condo.

By the time he locked the door behind him, his knees nearly gave out.

He stood there, his fingers still white-knuckled around the doorknob, knowing if he let go—that was surrendering completely. Like if he loosened his grip for even a second, he'd hit the floor and never fucking get back up.

She was gone.

Not just left for air gone.

Not needed space gone.

No.

Gone-gone.

And the worst part?

He didn't even know why.

No warning. No fight to anchor himself to. No blowout argument where he could tell himself *he said too much* or *didn't say enough*. No last look to haunt him in the dark.

Just silence.

A silence so thick it wrapped around his throat, coiling tighter with every shallow breath until he wasn't sure if he was breathing or just remembering how.

His eyes dragged across the dim light of his condo, where shadows stretched long and empty. And the place that once felt alive, once felt like theirs, now felt like a hollow fucking shell.

Because that's what it was.

A mausoleum.

A graveyard of memories that didn't know they were dead yet.

His gaze landed on them—those tiny pieces of her scattered like landmines, waiting to explode beneath his touch. The coffee mug sitting in the sink, still stained with the remnants of the morning she promised she just needed time to think—as if time was ever the fucking solution. The hoodie she always stole—the one he was wearing now. Her scent, still clinging to his skin, felt too heavy on his back. He pulled it off slowly, fingers curling in the fabric, like part of him wasn't ready to let it go.

He draped it back over the chair, waited for her to slip into it. Curl up next to him, and pretend she wasn't slipping away inch by inch.

But she wasn't coming back.

And then—

His eyes locked on the earrings.

Delicate. Familiar. The same ones he'd unclipped from her ears that night—*the* night—when she whispered that dangerous, beautiful promise.

I'm yours.

Griffin's chest caved in, a sharp, brutal ache clawing up his throat until he could barely swallow past it. His vision blurred, but he didn't dare blink. Didn't dare let those tears fall—not yet. Because if he did, it would be admitting this wasn't just some nightmare he could wake up from.

No—this was real.

It wasn't a room anymore.

It was a fucking tomb.

Every object a headstone. Every shadow a reminder that love doesn't echo—it haunts.

He forced himself forward, staggering like a man walking through the wreckage of a war he never signed up for. His fingers brushed the fabric of her hoodie—his hoodie—but it didn't feel soft like it used to. It felt like ashes. Like the last piece of a fire that had burned too hot, too fast, and now there was nothing left but ruin.

His breaths came harder, sharper, each one slicing through his lungs like glass. Moving didn't help. Pacing only turned the condo into a loop of torment.

The mug.

The hoodie.

The earrings.

The void.

No text.

No call.

Not even a fucking note.

Just a gaping absence where she used to be. Where they used to exist.

It wasn't anger that hit him.

It wasn't even betrayal.

It was something worse.

Emptiness.

A hollow so vast it made his bones ache. Like he could scream into it and never hear the echo.

She didn't just leave him—

She erased him.

Like he was nothing more than a story she regretted telling. A scar she couldn't wait to cover up.

His jaw clenched so tight his teeth hurt, but it didn't stop the sting behind his eyes or the way his heart felt like it was being gutted with every step he took.

He stayed.

Through everything.

Through her walls, her fears, her doubts.

He fucking stayed.

And still—

She walked.

His phone buzzed on the counter, a cruel, sharp vibration that cut through the suffocating quiet like a reminder that life didn't give a shit about heartbreak.

Aiden.

Of course.

Probably thinking he'd already lost his mind. Probably not far off.

Griffin grabbed the phone, staring at the steady, rhythmic flashing of Aiden's name on the screen like it was mocking the way his heart refused to stop beating when everything else had.

And then—

He snapped.

The phone flew from his hand before he could think, smashing against the wall, shattering into pieces that matched the ones splintering inside his chest.

But it didn't help.

It wasn't enough.

It would never be enough.

You can't throw a fist at grief. Can't outrun the ache that lives under your skin. Can't smash the memory of the woman who looked at you like you were it—until she didn't.

His legs buckled, and he slid down the wall, his hands tangling in his hair, pulling, gripping like he could rip the pain out by the roots. But all it did was make the shaking worse.

Because this wasn't heartbreak.

This was wreckage he might not crawl out of.

She didn't just leave the condo.

She left him.

And in the echo of that cold, sharp, and merciless truth, another voice slithered in. One he hadn't heard in weeks but had never truly forgotten.

Lia.

Her words poisoned the air, coiling around the open wounds Wren left behind.

"You always said you'd be a better father than your own."

His stomach twisted violently, bile rising in his throat as guilt sank its teeth in deep. Because what the fuck was he now? A man abandoned by the only person who ever saw past his armor? A man staring down the barrel of a life he didn't ask for—with a past he couldn't bury and a future that tasted like responsibility instead of hope?

A hollow laugh broke from his chest. Sharp. Bitter. The sound of a man who finally understood what it meant to lose everything.

He wasn't better.

Wasn't stronger.

Wasn't anything but alone.

The condo stayed dark, steeped in the same emptiness swallowing him whole.

Hours passed. Aiden knocked, his fist pounding on the door like maybe friendship could pull Griffin back from the edge.

But Griffin didn't move.

Didn't answer.

Because what the fuck was left to say when the woman you bled for leaves without a word? When the ghosts of your past come knocking with a kid who might carry your name? When the silence in your chest is louder than any scream you could let out?

What's left to fight for when the only thing keeping you together walks away—and you understand why?

Griffin buried his face in his hands, his body shaking from the quiet kind of grief that doesn't need to shout.

It just consumes.

And as the night stretched on, devouring the pieces she left behind, Griffin Hayes realized the one truth that shattered him more than Wren ever could.

It wasn't that she left.

It was that he would've left him too.

And that kind of truth?

That's not something you heal from.

That's something you learn to survive.

If you can.

38

ASHES OF ALMOST

THE HUM of the highway was the only thing keeping her from falling apart.

White lines bled together beneath her headlights, but Wren couldn't remember the last time she actually saw them. Her fingers were welded to the steering wheel, knuckles bone-white, nails carving half-moons into her palms like pain was the only proof she hadn't completely disappeared.

She hadn't thought.

It was late. Too fucking late for decisions, for logic, for bravery.

She didn't pack. Didn't tell Aiden. Didn't stop to breathe.

She just… reacted.

Because that's what Wren Sinclair did when the ground crumbled beneath her feet—she ran before it could swallow her whole.

Her chest ached like the cracking inside was permanent, knowing if she touched or acknowledged it, she'd shatter. Her pulse was a steady throb in her ears, loud enough to drown out the voice that kept screaming at her to turn around.

But there was no turning around.

Not after that look in Lia's eyes. Not after every insecurity she'd buried clawed its way back to the surface with one cruel, calculated smile.

"You really thought he'd still be waiting?"

God, it echoed.

Over and over—bouncing off every fragile piece of her that Griffin had tried so fucking hard to stitch back together.

And the worst part?

It wasn't new.

No, this wasn't just about Griffin.

This was history repeating like it always did. Her mind dragged her backward, whether she wanted it to or not, straight into the wreckage she thought she'd left behind in Winston-Salem. Straight to Josh.

Her ex-fiancé.

The man who promised forever with a ring and a lie tucked beneath his tongue.

She could still remember the way it felt. She remembered the slow, suffocating realization that she wasn't enough to keep his eyes from wandering. That no matter how hard she loved, no matter how fiercely she fought to hold things together, some people were always searching for more.

For someone else.

Late nights turned into empty beds, and excuses piled up like dirty laundry.

And Wren? She told herself she could fix it. That if she just held on tighter, he'd remember why he chose her in the first place.

But love wasn't a rope. It was a fuse.

And by the time she caught him with that girl from his office, the explosion had already happened.

She didn't scream. Didn't cry.

Not even a single punch was thrown.

She just left the ring on the counter, packed a bag, and never looked back.

Because that's what survival looked like when you'd been taught that staying only made the break worse.

And now—years later—different man, same fucking wound.

Only this time? There wasn't a ring to leave behind.

Just pieces of herself scattered across an island she no longer had the strength to stand on.

Her throat tightened, tears threatening, but she blinked them away with a force that made her vision blur. She was done crying for things she couldn't change.

Because what was she supposed to do?

March upstairs and ask Griffin if Lia had already made herself comfortable? If he was ready to play house with a kid who might share his last name? If he realized that Wren, just like before, was too scared to stand still long enough to be left?

No.

It was easier this way.

To let him believe she didn't care.

To let herself pretend she didn't, either.

Her phone vibrated again—angry this time, relentless—but she didn't flinch.

It wasn't him.

It wouldn't ever be him.

Not after she froze like a coward while his past walked out wearing victory like perfume.

Not after she, yet again, proved that when love got too heavy. Instead, Wren Sinclair dropped it before it could crush her.

Her chest cracked, a silent, aching fracture that felt too familiar.

She didn't leave because she didn't love him.

She left because somewhere deep down, she believed love was just a countdown to being replaced.

And this time?

Lia brought the fucking timer.

What if Lia was right?

What if there really was a child?

What if Griffin had a future that didn't have room for her anymore?

Those questions weren't whispers anymore; they were screams, echoing in every corner of her mind, relentless and cruel. The kind of thoughts that didn't give you space to breathe. The kind that wrapped around your throat and reminded you exactly why you'd never been the girl who got the happy ending.

How do you compete with blood?

How do you stand in front of the man you love and ask him to choose you? When somewhere out there is a kid who might have his smile? His laugh? His fucking eyes?

You don't.

You can't.

Her grip tightened on the steering wheel until her fingers went numb, but it didn't stop the shaking. Nothing could stop it, not when every mile marker was another reminder that she wasn't running toward anything.

She was running because it's all she knew how to do.

The Winston-Salem signs blurred through the windshield, and that's when her stomach gave out, twisting so violently she had to suck in a breath just to keep from pulling over and falling apart on the side of the highway.

Home.

God, what a fucking joke.

This place wasn't home. Not anymore. It was just where she ended up when life burned down around her. A crash site she kept crawling back to because it was familiar; because heartbreak always seemed easier when you could blame it on geography.

But standing still in pain?

Facing it?

That was something Wrenley Sinclair had never been good at.

Her phone lit up again, the glow slicing through the dark interior of the car like a spotlight on everything she didn't want to face.

Aiden.

Third missed call.

Another text.

> Aiden: Wren, call me back. Please. You can't just disappear like this.

Her thumb hovered over the screen, her pulse roaring in her ears.

But what was she supposed to say?

That she'd rather vanish than stand in front of Griffin and hear him confirm every fear Lia had ignited? That the second "My son deserves a father" left Lia's mouth, Wren had been right back in Josh's apartment—staring at a man who found something better, when she wasn't enough to keep his attention?

Because that's what this was really about, wasn't it?

Not just Lia.

Not just a kid.

But the gnawing, gut-deep belief that no matter how fiercely she loved, she'd always be second place to someone—or something—else.

Her chest cracked under the weight of it, a sharp, splintering pain that felt too familiar.

The what-ifs clawed at her like ghosts with unfinished business.

What if she'd fought sooner?

What if she hadn't let pride build walls between them?

What if Griffin wasn't alone right now but lying next to Lia, tangled in a future Wren never stood a chance against?

Her vision blurred, tears stinging, but they didn't fall.

Not yet.

By the time she pulled into the driveway of her old apartment, she was running on autopilot. The kind of numb that didn't come from exhaustion—but from giving up.

Unlock the door.

Step inside.

Pretend the walls didn't feel like they were caving in.

The place smelled stale—like dust and forgotten dreams—and the second she dropped her keys onto the counter, the sound echoed too loud. Too final.

She stood there, arms wrapped tight around herself, not for warmth, but to hold in the pieces threatening to spill out.

But who the hell was she kidding?

She'd already fallen apart. Quietly. Somewhere between that elevator and the highway.

The woman who once walked into Griffin's life with sharp comebacks and guarded smiles? The one who made him work to tear down her walls?

Gone.

What was left was hollow.

Ashes.

What was left was the version of herself she thought she'd buried after Josh—that insecure, terrified girl who didn't believe love could stay.

Her knees gave out before the first sob did.

She sank to the kitchen floor, curling into herself like she could make her body smaller than the pain ripping through it. Like if she just folded enough, maybe the ache wouldn't find her.

But it always did.

The hours bled together, shadows stretching across the walls as night turned into something uglier. Regret.

And that's when the truth, the one she didn't want to face, finally broke through.

She didn't leave because she was strong.

She left because, deep down, she believed she'd already lost.

Not just Griffin.

But the fight.

Because how do you stand next to a woman like Lia—beautiful, composed, holding a child—and not feel like you're a placeholder in someone else's story?

Her phone buzzed again somewhere in the dark, but she didn't move.

If it was Aiden, she had nothing to say.

If it was Griffin…

God, if it was Griffin, what would she even do?

Would she answer with the truth?

That she was scared shitless? That loving him felt like standing on a ledge, waiting for the wind to shove her over?

Or would she do what she always did? Hide behind silence because saying, *I'm not enough*, out loud made it too real.

The city outside began to wake. Light crept through the blinds, casting stripes across a woman who didn't recognize herself anymore.

And as Wren stared at nothing with her arms wrapped tight around shaking knees, one thought gutted her deeper than all the rest.

This wasn't just heartbreak.

This was proof that no matter how far you run, you can't outrun the version of yourself that's convinced you're destined to lose.

She closed her eyes, her lips parting around a breath that felt too heavy to hold.

Because maybe Lia didn't win.

Maybe Wren just handed her the victory the second she let fear drive her away.

And as that realization anchored itself deep in her chest, she knew—

If Griffin called now…
If he begged her to come back…
She didn't know if she'd believe she deserved to.
Because this wasn't just the end of them.
This was the end of believing she'd ever be someone worth staying for.

39

SILENT ECHOES

SOMEHOW, it's been a week.

A week since Wren left.

But days didn't exist anymore.

Not really.

There was no morning. No night. No markers of time except the dull ache in his chest and the suffocating weight that pressed down harder with every breath he didn't want to take. The sun could've risen and fallen a hundred times, and he wouldn't have known. Wouldn't have cared.

Because when the person who made you feel alive walks away—

You stop counting days.

You start counting the pieces.

The darkness wasn't just outside. It was inside. Stretching. Swallowing. Smothering. Hours didn't pass; they dragged him by the throat, choking the fight out of him, pulling him deeper into a version of himself he didn't recognize. And worse? One he couldn't fucking outrun.

Griffin Hayes, the man people used to know?

The man Wren loved?

He was dead.

What was left wasn't living.

It was survival in its cruelest form.

Breathing because biology demanded it.

Moving because gravity didn't offer a choice.

Existing because sometimes life doesn't kill you clean. It leaves you stranded in the wreckage, forced to feel every second of a heart still beating. When it should've stopped the moment she did.

He stood in front of the bathroom mirror, but he wasn't looking at himself.

He was searching for a reflection that didn't exist anymore. For proof that there was still something human beneath the hollow stare. The weight was dragging his shoulders down like he'd been carrying a coffin on his back.

But there was nothing.

Just dead eyes staring back.

Lifeless.

Soulless.

Not the eyes that used to flash with sharp wit and reckless charm. With that fire Wren said scared the hell out of her and turned her on all at once.

No—those eyes were gone.

Now, there was just this shell.

A shadow pretending skin was enough to keep him whole.

His fingers curled around the sink, knuckles whitening, veins bulging, the porcelain creaking under pressure that felt like it belonged somewhere else—like if he could just squeeze hard enough, he'd crush the ache instead of himself.

But nothing cracked.

Nothing gave.

Except him.

Pride? That was a joke now.

Pride doesn't crawl into bed with you when the silence starts screaming.

Pride doesn't drown out the echo of her laugh when it ricochets off walls she used to fill.

Pride doesn't hold you when the cold side of the bed is the only thing left loyal.

He barely recognized the man staring back.

Gaunt cheeks.

Stubble thick enough to blur the line between heartbreak and self-destruction.

Eyes hollowed out by the weight of things unsaid, undone, unfixed.

But it was the familiarity that gutted him.

Because those weren't just broken eyes.

They were his father's.

Not in color. Not in shape.

In defeat.

That same dead stare he swore he'd never wear—the one that haunted his childhood. The look of a man who lost everything worth fighting for and didn't bother fighting for himself after that.

You're no better than him.

The thought didn't whisper. It roared.

Tattooing itself across his mind like it had been waiting, just biding its time until Wren left and proved it right.

His vision blurred—not from tears. Tears would've meant he still had something left to give.

No, this was worse.

This was rage with nowhere to go.

Grief with no exit.

His fist flew before reason could catch up. Knuckles collided with glass, shattering the mirror, splintering his reflection until it looked exactly like he felt.

Broken.

Irreparable.

Blood seeped down his hand, bright and mocking against the pale porcelain. For a second, he watched it, detached—like it wasn't his.

Good.

At least something inside him still remembered how to bleed.

But pain wasn't enough to pull him out of this.

Nothing was.

He didn't bother cleaning the wound. Didn't bother wrapping it.

What was the point? Bandages were for healing. And Griffin Hayes… he wasn't fucking healing.

He staggered out of the bathroom, the sting in his hand fading into the background noise of misery that had become his constant companion. The condo reeked of stale liquor, sweat, and something worse—her absence.

The hoodie she left behind was still there, draped over the chair. A cruel reminder that she ever existed in this space. His space. Their space.

He hated it.

Hated that he couldn't throw it away.

Hated that he still reached for it at night, like a fucking addict, chasing a high that only smelled like her.

His new phone buzzed somewhere on the couch, but he didn't flinch.

Didn't need to look.

He knew it wasn't her.

It hadn't been her for seven days.

Seven fucking eternities.

Aiden.

Always Aiden.

Because his best friend still thought Griffin could be dragged out of this hellhole of his own making. Still believed a knock on the door or a text could fix a man who was already six feet under, just waiting for the dirt to hit.

Pick up the damn phone.

Stop doing this to yourself.

She's gone, but you're still here.

Griffin let out a bitter, breathless laugh, one that sounded more like a death rattle than amusement.

Still here?

No—the fuck he wasn't.

He'd disappeared the moment Wren stopped looking at him like he was worth staying for. The moment her silence screamed louder than every "I love you" she ever whispered.

He grabbed the nearest bottle—not for comfort.

Not even for numbness.

But because thinking was worse.

Because every time his mind wandered, it wandered straight to her.

To the way she used to trace patterns on his chest, like she was memorizing him.

To the way she bit her lip when she was about to say something reckless and beautiful.

To the way she made him believe, for a second, that maybe he wasn't destined to be just another Hayes fuckup.

But belief was dangerous.

Belief made you soft.

And soft men don't survive when hurricanes walk out without warning.

He tipped the bottle back, the burn barely registering.

Everyone leaves, right?

His mom.

His dad—emotionally long before physically.
Lia.
Now Wren.
Maybe it wasn't them.
Maybe it was him.
Maybe Griffin Hayes was just the kind of man people survived—not loved.
And that realization?
That was darker than the liquor.
Darker than the room.
Because once you accept that you're the storm that wrecks everything good—
You stop waiting for the sun.

His legs gave out before the thought could finish its descent, gravity yanking him down, like it was tired of pretending he had any strength left to fight it.

He didn't fall.

He surrendered.

Back against the wall, knees pulled to his chest, arms wrapped around himself, trying to hold the pieces together. Even though everything inside had already shattered beyond recognition.

His head tipped back, eyes dragging toward the ceiling like it held answers he didn't believe in anymore.

But all it offered were the cracks.

Thin, jagged lines spiderwebbing across plaster—silent proof that even the strongest things break when no one's paying attention. That decay doesn't announce itself. It creeps. Quiet. Patient. Until it owns you.

And fuck, wasn't that just poetic?

Because those fractures weren't just overhead.

They were carved into him.

Every split in the ceiling was a reflection of the fault lines running beneath his skin.

Every shadowed vein of plaster mirrored the weight pressing down on his ribs, threatening to cave in everything he'd pretended was solid.

No one tells you when you're breaking.

Not really.

You don't hear the snap.

You feel it. Slow and suffocating.

A quiet implosion masked by routine. By denial. By telling yourself you're fine while the foundation beneath you crumbles grain by fucking grain.

Griffin's stare blurred, but he didn't blink.

Didn't move.

Because moving meant feeling—and feeling was lethal now.

His throat burned, dry and raw, but no sound came.

There were no screams left.

No curses.

No desperate pleas to a God he stopped believing in the moment Wren's side of the bed went cold.

There was only silence.

The kind that didn't just fill the room; it invaded it.

Wrapped around his throat like a noose made of memories he couldn't outrun.

And then, like they'd been waiting for him to be weak enough, the questions came.

Uninvited.

Unforgiving.

The kind that didn't knock—they kicked the fucking door in.

What if the kid is yours?

What if your blood is already out there, waiting to hate you too?

What if you're not fighting fate—you're fulfilling it?

What if Wren saw the truth before you did? That loving you wasn't survival... It was suicide in slow motion?

His chest clenched so tight it felt like his ribs were splintering inward, like his body was trying to crush whatever scraps of a heart he had left before the world got another shot at it.

His head thudded against the wall, the hollow echo sounding too much like a countdown to something he didn't have the strength to stop.

Tears burned behind his eyes. But they didn't fall.

Couldn't.

He was past that now.

Even grief had its limits, and his had been bled dry days ago.

And then, barely a whisper, so fragile it almost didn't exist, the realization slipped past his lips.

"I don't know how to be without her."

It wasn't dramatic. It wasn't poetic. It was truth. The kind that left scars on your soul just for saying it out loud. Because this wasn't just heartbreak. This wasn't the shit songs that were written about or the kind of pain you drink away in a bar with your buddies slapping your back, telling you there's more fish in the sea. This was the kind of loss that hollowed you out from the inside.

The kind that didn't leave bruises—it left voids.

Permanent.

Unfillable.

Because when you give someone everything—

Every scar.

Every fear.

Every broken, jagged piece of who you are—

And they still walk away?

They don't just take your heart.

They take you.

And all that's left is aftermath.

Griffin didn't know how long he sat there, drowning in the silence.

Didn't care.

Time didn't exist when every second felt like a lifetime spent suffocating on what-ifs and could-have-beens.

Because hope?

Hope was the cruelest fucking liar of them all.

Hope told him Wren would stay.

Hope told him love was enough to outrun the past.

Hope told him he wasn't his father's son.

But here he was—

Sitting in the ruins of a life that looked exactly like the one he swore he'd never repeat.

Ashes, where trust used to be.

Smoke, where laughter once echoed.

Silence, where her voice should've been.

He let the darkness swallow him, but not in comfort.

No, this wasn't a blanket.

It was chains.

Cold. Heavy. Permanent.

Because fighting meant believing there was still something worth clawing toward.

And Griffin Hayes?

He didn't believe anymore.

He wasn't waiting for redemption.

He was waiting for the collapse.

Waiting for the ceiling to finally give out and bury him beneath the weight he'd been carrying alone.

Waiting for the ghosts to scream louder than his own thoughts.

Waiting for the moment when his body forgot how to breathe—and decided it didn't fucking matter.

The cruelest part?

No one would notice when he was gone.

Because Griffin didn't disappear all at once.

He'd been fading for years.

One heartbeat at a time.

And now?

Now he was just a shadow in a room full of memories that weren't his anymore.

40

ASHES REMAIN

THE WALLS of her apartment weren't just closing in anymore.

They were crushing her.

Every breath felt like a battle she wasn't strong enough to fight.

Every second stretched into hours, days. Into a hell she'd built with her own two hands.

Over a week.

Days of pretending she could outrun the wreckage. Lying to herself that silence was safer than facing what she'd done.

Days of waiting for her phone to light up with his name—knowing deep down it never would.

But tonight?

Tonight, it wasn't the silence that destroyed her.

It was the fact that Aiden, the one person who refused to give up on anyone, had finally stopped trying.

That's when she knew. Griffin wasn't just hurting.

He was gone.

Her fingers hovered over Aiden's name, her vision swimming with tears she didn't deserve to shed. The kind of tears that tasted like regret. And salt. Every unspoken word she should've screamed when she still had the chance.

You don't get to fall apart now, her mind hissed, cruel and relentless. *You already did that when you walked away.*

But her pride was gone.

Her walls were only dust from the broken drywall.

All that was left was a woman suffocating under the weight of her own cowardice as she hit call.

The phone rang.

Once.

Twice.

By the third ring, her hand was shaking so violently she nearly dropped it.

And then—

"About fucking time."

Aiden's voice wasn't just sharp; it was a blade slicing through whatever flimsy hope she'd been clinging to.

Wren's lips parted, but nothing came out except the pathetic rasp of a woman who didn't recognize herself anymore.

"I—"

"Don't," his voice cracked, and that was somehow worse than his anger. Because beneath it was exhaustion. Disappointment. A kind of heartbreak she didn't expect to hear from him.

Her knees buckled. She collapsed onto the bed like the truth was already sinking in.

But nothing could've prepared her for what came next.

"How is he?" The words were barely a whisper, like saying them too loud would shatter whatever was left of her spine.

The silence that followed wasn't empty.

It was deafening.

It was the sound of a man deciding whether or not she deserved to know.

"Aiden…" Her voice cracked, guilt clawing up her throat so violently she thought she might choke on it. "Please."

When he finally spoke, it wasn't anger that gutted her.

It was grief.

"He's gone, Wren."

Her heart didn't just break—it stopped.

"Not physically, but everything else? The Griffin who fought for you? The man who stood there, begging you to choose him while you ran in circles around your pride? He's fucking gone."

The sob that ripped from her chest wasn't human.

It was the sound of a woman realizing she hadn't just lost the love of her life—

She'd killed him.

Piece by piece.

Silence followed by fucking silence.

"He—" she gasped, pressing her hand against her mouth like that could hold it all in. But it was useless. The dam was already crumbling. "He doesn't..."

"He doesn't answer the door. Barely shows up to work." Aiden's voice cracked under the weight of every word. "He's drinking himself into oblivion, Wren. I don't even know if he wants to or if he can come back from this."

She curled into herself, the phone shaking against her ear as the violent and raw sobs took over, as if her body was trying to purge the guilt but couldn't.

Because this wasn't just a mistake.

This was unforgivable.

"So unless you're calling to tell me you're on your way back to fix this—" Aiden's voice dropped, colder than she'd ever heard it, "—don't fucking call me again. He is not the only one that you left, sis."

"Wait—" she choked, panic clawing through the grief. "Did he... Did he do it?"

Silence.

"Do what?" Aiden snapped, though she could hear it now—he wasn't just angry. He was hurt. Like even speaking to her was costing him something.

"The... The paternity test." Her voice was a ghost of itself. "I told you... He needed to know."

Another beat of silence.

Then, like a final nail in the coffin—

"Yeah. He did."

Her stomach flipped, bile rising as her mind spiraled through every worst-case scenario.

"And?"

"I don't know, Wren." Aiden's voice cracked wide open. "Because he won't fucking speak. He got the results. And after that? He wasn't Griffin anymore."

The phone slipped from her hand, landing on the bed as her world tilted violently.

She'd told herself it was helping.

That pushing him toward the truth was the right thing.

But now?

Now she saw it for what it was.

An excuse.

A way to justify running before he could break her heart—

So she broke his first.

Her body folded in on itself, sobs racking through her as she clutched at the sheets. Trying to anchor herself to a life that had already slipped through her fingers.

"I fucked up…" The words tore from her throat, raw and guttural.

"No shit," Aiden muttered, but there was no satisfaction in it. Just defeat.

Because even he knew, there was no fixing this.

Not when you've already lit the match and watched everything burn.

Wren's vision blurred, her chest caving under the weight of what she'd done—not just to Griffin, but to herself. To the version of her that believed she was capable of holding something that good without breaking it.

Silence settled, thick and unbearable.

"I love you," she whispered, the words barely audible, soaked in shame and sorrow.

"I know, I love you too, sis," Aiden said gently. Then nothing more.

She hung up before he could say anything else.

Because she couldn't breathe through it.

Couldn't be in it.

Not one second longer.

Because she didn't lose Griffin in that elevator. Didn't lose him when Lia whispered about a child.

She lost him the second she let fear drive the car—and pride keep her foot on the gas.

And now?

Now there was nothing left but ashes.

One brutal, unrelenting truth echoed through her mind as she lay there curled up on a bed that felt colder than any night she spent alone.

She hadn't been afraid of losing Griffin.

She'd been afraid of being loved by him.

Because love like that?

It demands everything.

And that's the one thing she never thought she could have.

The ceiling had nothing left to say.

Wren had stared at it for hours, watching cracks she never noticed before splinter across the white paint like veins of every bad decision she'd ever made.

It was poetic, in that cruel, cosmic way.

Because when you break everything you touch, even the walls start to show it.

Her body was numb, her mind anything but. Thoughts ricocheted in her skull like bullets—Griffin's face when she didn't show up. Aiden's voice laced with disappointment. Lia's smirk as the elevator doors slid shut behind her.

It was too much.

The weight. The silence. The suffocating reminder that she had no one to blame but herself.

So she did what cowards do when the walls get too close.

She ran. Again.

Only this time, it wasn't miles away.

It was a few blocks.

A shitty dive bar where broken people went to disappear.

No makeup. No fixing the tear-stained mess staring back at her in the mirror. She didn't care. Let them see her wrecked. Let them know she was the embodiment of regret in a worn-out hoodie and empty eyes.

The bartender didn't ask questions when she ordered whiskey straight.

Didn't offer a smile.

Didn't pretend to care.

Good.

She didn't deserve kindness.

The glass was cold in her hand, but she barely felt it. She just stared through it like maybe at the bottom she'd find who the fuck she used to be before she ruined everything.

But fate?

Fate wasn't done gutting her.

Because the universe has a sick sense of humor, and it loved watching Wren Sinclair bleed.

"Wren?"

Her heart didn't just drop—it fucking disintegrated.

That voice was a ghost she thought she buried years ago.

Too slowly, she turned her head, already knowing what fresh hell awaited her.

Josh.

The man who first taught her that love was just another word for eventual abandonment. The man who took vows meant for forever and traded them for attention between someone else's thighs.

And there he was, standing in front of her like fate had hand-delivered one final fuck you.

He looked worse for wear. Older. Guilt carved into the lines around his mouth. Eyes that used to hold charm now dulled by consequences.

"Didn't expect to see you here," he said, offering that same sheepish smile, the one he used to flash when he lied through his teeth.

Wren didn't blink.

Didn't breathe.

Because standing there, looking at him, she realized something far worse than anger.

She felt nothing.

"Yeah, well," she muttered, fingers tightening around her glass. "Neither did I."

Josh shifted on his feet, awkward in a way he never used to be, like life had finally taught him what it felt like to be the one left behind.

"Listen… I know I'm probably the last person you want to see. But—" he hesitated, dragging a hand through his hair like that would soften the blow. "I'm sorry. For everything. I was a fucking idiot."

Wren let out a hollow laugh, one that tasted like ash and old wounds.

"Yeah, Josh. You were."

He winced. Good.

Let him feel it.

Let him drown in the weight of apologies that came too late to matter.

But he didn't stop. Of course he didn't. Men like Josh never knew when to shut the hell up.

"I just… I heard you were back in town. Thought maybe…"

She cut him off with a look that could shatter glass.

"Thought maybe what?" Her voice was ice—steady, but dangerous.

"That I'd thank you for finally realizing you fucked up? That I've been sitting here for years waiting for closure?"

Josh's mouth opened—then shut.

Because what could he say?

There was no redemption arc for him.

"Save it," Wren snapped, her voice cracking at the edges. She wasn't because of him, but because the weight of everything else was already suffocating her. "I don't have space for your guilt, Josh. Not when I'm already choking on my own."

That hit harder than she expected.

For once, Josh didn't have a comeback.

Didn't flash that boyish grin that used to get him out of every mess he created.

His shoulders sagged, eyes dropping to the floor like maybe he finally understood what it felt like to stand in the wreckage of something he destroyed.

Silence stretched between them.

Heavy. Awkward. Final.

But then—

His voice cut through, softer this time. Almost… human.

"We're taking a break," he muttered, like it was a confession he hadn't planned on giving. "Me and… my fiancée."

Wren's stomach twisted, not out of jealousy, not even out of pity.

Just that bitter taste of, "Of course you are."

Because men like Josh never stayed where they were supposed to.

She swallowed the lump in her throat, arms crossing tighter over her chest like she could shield herself from caring.

"Shocking," she deadpanned, turning back toward her drink, ready to let this conversation rot where it belonged.

But Josh wasn't done.

"I don't know…" He hesitated, rubbing the back of his neck. The weight of his choices finally catching up. "Guess I'm just trying to figure things out."

Wren let out a bitter breath, her fingers tracing the rim of her glass.

"Yeah, well—some of us don't get the luxury of figuring shit out before it's too late."

The words slipped out sharper than she intended, but fuck it. Truth hurt.

Josh shifted again, clearly uncomfortable, but curiosity got the better of him.

"Someone else?" he asked quietly. "Is that why you're back in town looking like… this?"

Wren's jaw clenched.

She didn't owe him a goddamn thing.

But for some reason—maybe because she needed to say his name out loud, needed to remind herself he was real and not just some fever dream—she answered.

"Yeah. Griffin," she whispered, the name tasting like glass and memories she couldn't swallow down.

Josh's brows pulled together, confusion flickering across his face before something darker settled in.

"Griffin Hayes?"

Wren's head snapped up, her pulse slamming against her ribs.

"How the fuck do you know that name?"

Josh let out a dry, humorless laugh, one that made her skin crawl.

"My fiancée—" he said the word like it was already past tense, "—she talks about him all the time."

Wren's breath caught.

The room tilted.

"What?" Her voice was barely there, just a crack in the chaos roaring through her head.

Josh shrugged, oblivious to the way her entire world had just shifted on its axis.

"Yeah… Says he's some big name over on the coast. Owns a construction company or something. She mentioned working with him—said he's sharp. Focused. The kind of guy who actually knows what he wants."

Wren's heart fractured.

Because that was the Griffin she knew.

The Griffin she lost.

And now? Now his name was coming out of the mouth of the man who once broke her—and tied to a woman she'd never even met.

"Small world, huh?" Josh added, offering a weak smile like fate hadn't just sucker-punched her straight in the chest.

But Wren didn't smile.

She couldn't.

Because her mind was already spiraling.

Who was his fiancée?

When did she meet Griffin?

Why the fuck was she talking about him?

It was irrational. It was insane.

But heartbreak doesn't care about logic.

It only cares about the what-ifs that keep you awake at night.

"I hope you're okay, Wren. I really do," Josh said, his voice fading into background noise as he took a step back, giving her one last glance before turning away.

She didn't answer.

Couldn't.

Because in that moment, as the door closed behind him, Wren realized something far worse than running into her past—

She wasn't just haunted by the mistakes she made.

Now, she was haunted by the idea that Griffin's name—their story—was being spoken in rooms she'd never enter again.

By people who didn't know the way he kissed her like she was the only thing keeping him alive.

By women who didn't care that Wren had already left pieces of her soul in his hands.

And as she stood there—alone, shaking, her drink untouched—one brutal truth carved itself into her chest.

You can lose a man once when you leave him.

But the real torture?

Is knowing you might lose him again…

When someone else decides to pick up the pieces you shattered.

And Wren?

Wren wasn't sure if she could survive watching that happen.

Not twice.

Not when she was the one who handed him over without a fight.

41

SPARK REMAINS

THE ENVELOPE HAD BEEN SITTING on his counter for days.

Mocking him.

Every time Griffin walked past it, a pressure built behind his ribs—tight, suffocating. Like a few goddamn sheets of paper held the power to decide his worth, his future. His identity. It wasn't just a paternity test. It was a mirror. One he'd been too fucking scared to look into.

And for days, he let it sit.

Because part of him wasn't sure which answer would break him more.

If the kid was his—then he was tethered for life to a version of his past he had barely escaped. Bound to a woman who had once carved her name into his bones, only to vanish when he needed her most... And now had the audacity to crawl back and dress her destruction up as motherhood.

But if the kid wasn't his? Then what the hell had he been doing? Drowning in guilt that wasn't his to carry. Letting Lia's venom sink so deep that it began to sound like truth. Letting her rewrite the story of his life with ink that wasn't hers to hold.

And yet, today... Something shifted.

Maybe it was the sun finally cracking through the blinds. Maybe it was the way he'd looked in the mirror that morning—not like a man on the verge of shattering, but like someone who was sick of suffocating. Or maybe... Maybe he was just done letting other people decide how much of himself he got to keep.

His fingers hovered over the envelope.

Breathe steady. Jaw locked.

Then he tore it open.

A single motion. Sharp. Final.

Tearing through fear. Through shame. Through the lies Lia had wrapped around his throat like a noose.

His eyes scanned the results once. Then again.

Paternity Result: Excluded.

Not the father.

The page slipped from his fingers, landing softly on the counter.

But Griffin?

Griffin could finally fucking breathe.

A bitter laugh clawed out of his chest, raw and sharp like broken glass. He gripped the edge of the counter, shaking his head as something cracked inside him—not in pain, but in clarity. In freedom.

He wasn't his father.

He never had been.

And he wasn't about to become him. Not now, not ever. Not because Lia had a crisis, not because she wanted to manipulate him into a guilt-laced reunion, just because her own life was falling apart.

He didn't owe her a fucking thing.

The knock on his door came exactly as he expected.

She'd been showing up every day. Like ritual. Like persistence could overpower truth. Like maybe if she batted her lashes hard enough, he'd forget the years it took to rebuild himself after her.

But this time?

He didn't hesitate.

He yanked the door open like ripping off a bandage, and there she was.

Lia. Dressed in her curated perfection. Lip gloss. Designer heels. A look rehearsed to disarm, to charm, to confuse.

But she froze the moment she saw him.

Because this wasn't the Griffin who curled under her thumb.

This was a clear-eyed man standing tall, steady, dangerous in his stillness.

She blinked. "Griff—"

He held up the envelope. His mouth twitched. Not a smile. A warning.

"Save it," he said, voice low, slicing through the space between them. "We're done playing your game."

Her eyes dropped to the letter. For the first time since she came back, Griffin saw something real crack through her carefully constructed mask.

Panic.

"You don't have to—"

"I'm not the fucking father," he said, stepping forward, forcing her back with nothing but the weight of the truth. "So whatever fantasy you were spinning in that pretty little head of yours? It's over."

Her mouth opened, lips parting like she had a fresh batch of lies ready to pour out, but he cut her off again.

"Who is he?" Griffin's stare locked her in place. "The real father. The guy you cheated on me with."

She didn't answer right away. For once, she couldn't.

Her gaze dropped. Her shoulders slumped.

"Josh," she finally whispered.

The name hit like a sucker punch.

"Josh," Griffin repeated, cold and detached.

She crossed her arms like it might protect her from the blowback she deserved. "We... on a break. Trying to figure things out."

A humorless laugh ripped from his throat, sharp and brutal. "Jesus, Lia. You dragged me through hell just because your fiancé needed space?"

Her jaw clenched, the mask returning—fragile now. "I thought—"

"No," he snapped. "You didn't think. You never think. You wanted control. You wanted to see if you could still break me."

He stepped in, leaned close, close enough that she could feel every ounce of steel that had replaced the man she thought she left in pieces.

"But here's the thing, Lia..." he whispered, eyes blazing. "You can't break what's already been reforged."

She visibly flinched. Backed up a step.

He didn't chase her.

Didn't need to.

"Get the fuck out of my doorway," he said, straightening up. "And don't come back."

She hesitated, still clinging to the idea that maybe she had a hold on him.

But one last look at Griffin, and she knew.

She didn't.

Not anymore.

She turned and walked away.

He didn't watch her go.

He slammed the door and leaned against it, exhaling a breath that felt like it carried years of poison, regret, and grief out of his chest.

And for the first time in weeks?

He didn't feel like a prisoner in his own story.

He felt free.

Griffin Hayes wasn't someone's backup plan. He wasn't a lifeline for women who only knew how to love when it was convenient. And he sure as hell wasn't going to carry guilt that didn't belong to him.

He walked into the kitchen, picked the letter back up, folded it in half, and slid it into a drawer—not as something to hold onto, but as a reminder.

Of who he wasn't.

Of what he survived.

Of the man he refused to stop becoming.

Because this?

This was the moment the fire returned.

And from here on out, he wasn't burning for anyone else.

He was burning for himself.

THE NEXT FEW DAYS WEREN'T SOME MAGICAL FIX. THERE WERE NO LIFE-changing revelations. No dramatic soundtrack swelling in the background as Griffin pulled himself out of the wreckage he'd been drowning in. It wasn't a comeback story wrapped in perfection. It was slower. Messier. A fight that didn't come with a cheering crowd or a clear finish line.

But it was real.

It started with the razor. His hand felt too heavy as he dragged it across his jaw, scraping away weeks of neglect. He watched in the mirror as pieces of the man he used to be slowly reappeared beneath the rough edges and hollow eyes. It wasn't victory—it was survival. But when he set the razor down, he didn't look away. That alone felt like progress.

Then came the windows. One by one, he cracked them open. Letting salt air and sunlight cut through the stale darkness that had settled over his condo like a funeral shroud. The breeze stirred the dust, the light slicing across floors that hadn't seen daybreak in too long. It didn't erase the memories carved into these walls, but it reminded him that breathing wasn't just instinct. It was a choice.

His gaze landed on the hoodie—the one Wren always stole. The one that smelled like her laughter and promises—never kept. For days, it had been a weight he couldn't lift. But now, his fingers were steady as he picked it up. He didn't bury his face in it, didn't torture himself—but folded it. He finally let it be what it was: a memory. Something to tuck away, not a chain to keep him anchored to a version of himself that no longer existed.

When Aiden knocked that afternoon, Griffin didn't sit in silence, pretending he wasn't home. He opened the door. No words, no explanations—just a quiet acknowledgment that he wasn't dead inside. Not completely.

They ended up at Marshside, at their booth—the same one where everything began. The ghosts were still there, lingering in the corners of his mind. But when Aiden tossed out some half-assed joke about how Griffin looked less like death and more like a man who'd at least considered showering, something unexpected happened.

Griffin laughed.

It was rough. It was short. But it was real.

Aiden froze like he'd just witnessed a miracle, raising his beer in silent approval. Griffin shook his head, a faint smirk tugging at his lips before fading into something softer, something earned. The fire inside him hadn't died after all. It had just been waiting. For air, for light, for a reason.

By the end of the week, Griffin stood on the unfinished deck of the house he once dreamed of sharing with Wren. The siding materials still needed to be ordered. The dock was still incomplete, the fold-out chairs long gone, but he could still see her there. Feet kicked up, eyes challenging him under a sunset that used to mean forever.

It hit him like a punch straight to the ribs. But this time, he didn't turn away.

He let it hurt.

Because pain meant he was still alive—and Griffin Hayes didn't run from what hurt anymore.

His hand ran over the coarse wood of the railing, the splinters biting into his palm. Good. Let it sting. This wasn't a graveyard. This wasn't where his story ended.

This was proof.

Proof that even after being gutted—after Lia's lies, after Wren's silence—he could still stand. He could still build. Not for the past. Not for the version of love that left him bleeding. But for himself.

The sky bled gold and fire across the horizon, the salt air wrapping around him like a challenge.

And that's when he made the promise.

He wasn't finishing this house for memories. He wasn't holding onto shadows. He was finishing it because he still had a future, even if it wasn't the one he planned.

If Wren ever found her way back, she wouldn't find the broken man she left behind. She'd find him standing. Strong. Whole. Not waiting. Not begging. But alive on his own terms.

Because Lia didn't get to win.

His father's ghost didn't get to define him.

And love? Love wasn't supposed to be survival.

Griffin Hayes was still here—standing on the bones of everything that tried to bury him. And for the first time in a long damn time, he remembered exactly who the fuck he was.

Not a man destroyed.

But a man rebuilt.

One nail.

One board.

One breath at a time.

The world had tried to burn him down.

But Griffin wasn't ashes.

He was the spark that refused to die.

And now?

Now he was ready to set his own fire.

42

BOOTH CONFESSIONAL

MARSHSIDE WAS ALIVE THAT NIGHT, the kind of hum that seeped into your bones and made you forget for a second that the world ever hurt you. Laughter bounced off the walls, glasses clinked. The low thrum of conversation filled the spaces where silence used to sit too heavy.

Griffin leaned back in their usual booth, fingers wrapped loosely around a beer bottle, eyes scanning the room—not searching, not really. Just watching life happen around him while he kept his distance from it.

Six months.

Half a year since Wren left without a word.

Four months since Lia finally got the door slammed in her face and with it, every ghost she tried to drag back into his life.

Now? Now he was something else entirely. Not the man Wren met. Not the wreckage Lia left behind. Just... a version of himself stitched together by survival and sheer fucking stubbornness.

Aiden dropped into the seat across from him, that familiar shit-eating grin tugging at his lips as he slid two shots across the table. "Alright, Hayes. Enough brooding. Time to see if there's any charm left in that hollow chest of yours."

Griffin let out a dry laugh, the kind that didn't carry much weight anymore. "You're like a damn mosquito, you know that?"

"Yeah, but I'm the kind that keeps you alive." Aiden jerked his chin toward the bar, where a group of women were whispering and smiling, already eyeing them. "C'mon, man. It's been months. You gonna keep pretending your dick's in a retirement home forever?"

Griffin smirked, but it was more muscle memory than anything real. "Maybe I just raised my standards."

"Bullshit." Aiden leaned forward, elbows on the table, voice dropping. "Look, I'm not telling you to fall in love. God knows you barely survived that the first time. But talk to someone. Flirt. Prove to yourself that Wren didn't take everything when she left."

There was a pause. Aiden exhaled, gaze heavy but honest. "She's my sister, man. I'll always love her. But she fucked up. And if she can't fix it, if she doesn't try, then you don't owe her your misery."

For a second, Griffin thought about telling him to fuck off.

But then... Maybe he had a point.

So, with a sigh that felt heavier than it should, he stood. Rolled his shoulders back. Let that old swagger slip into place like a jacket he hadn't worn in years.

It was too easy.

The smiles came quick. The laughs even quicker. He knew the game—how to tilt his head just right, how to let his voice drop low enough to make them lean in. Twenty minutes of conversation, and he had them hooked. The charm wasn't gone.

It never was.

But when he walked back to the booth, Aiden was already smirking like he expected a phone number—or three.

"Nothing?" Aiden asked, dumbfounded.

Griffin dropped into his seat, grabbing the shot and tossing it back without a word.

"What's the point?" he muttered, wiping his mouth with the back of his hand.

Aiden's grin faded, replaced by something softer. Something dangerously close to concern. "Man, you really are a glutton for punishment."

Griffin didn't argue.

Aiden watched him for a beat, then reached for his beer. "You ever gonna talk about her?"

Griffin's jaw clenched, muscles twitching as he stared at the bottle in front of him. His fingers itched to throw it, smash it, feel something break that wasn't just him. But instead, he just sat there, his chest tight, head spinning, and waiting for peace that might never come.

His voice was low. Rough. Honest.

"What do you want me to say?"

Aiden stayed quiet. Let him spiral. Let him speak.

Griffin leaned forward, elbows on the table, head low. Like the weight of the truth was too much to carry upright anymore.

"That no matter how many smiles I see, none of them look like hers? That no one's laugh cuts through me the same way? That every voice sounds wrong until I hear the ghost of hers echoing in my head?"

He let out a breath—shaky, bitter, not quite a laugh. "You want me to admit that every woman I talk to is just noise? That I keep waiting for someone to shut me up the way she used to?"

He finally looked up, and there was nothing guarded in his face. Just exhaustion. And ache.

His knuckles tapped the bottle, restless.

"No one calls me on my shit like she did," he said, quieter now. "No one ever fucking dared. She could see through me in ways that scared the hell out of me."

Griffin closed his eyes for a moment, slipping into the memory and letting it take him.

"That I still hear her when I fall asleep? That I still check the damn passenger seat when I get in my truck, like some pathetic reflex?"

A pause.

"She was the only one who could compete in my games and not lose herself in the process."

His voice cracked then. Just slightly. Just enough.

"I started a letter," he added. "Got halfway through it and had to stop because every word felt like a goddamn funeral."

He dragged a hand down his face, exhaling hard as he slumped back against the booth. The truth wasn't just heavy. It was a fucking anchor in his chest, dragging everything down with it. And he was choking on it.

"I don't know how to stop loving her, man. And I'm not even sure I want to."

Aiden's expression shifted, less surprised now. More gutted. Because yeah, he'd asked.

But he hadn't expected that kind of answer.

SILENCE STRETCHED BETWEEN THEM, HEAVY BUT NOT UNCOMFORTABLE. The sort of silence you only get between two people who've seen each other at their worst and still show up anyway.

Aiden tapped his bottle against the table. "You ever figure out why she left?"

Griffin's jaw ticked, his shoulders curling in like the question alone bruised him. "No," he muttered, voice low. "And I probably never will."

Aiden's expression shifted, something like guilt flashing behind his eyes.

Griffin noticed. "What?"

Aiden hesitated, then leaned forward, elbows on the table. "There's something I never told you. About Wren."

Griffin's pulse kicked up, but he kept his face neutral. "Go on."

Aiden leaned forward, resting on his elbows. "You remember Josh?"

Griffin's head snapped up. "The ex?"

"Yeah." Aiden's eyes narrowed slightly. "She told me she ran into him a while back. Said he knew who you were."

Griffin blinked. "What? How the fuck does he know me??"

"She said he asked if you were Griffin Hayes. Which… felt weird at the time, but I didn't think anything of it."

Griffin's stomach twisted, breath catching somewhere between confusion and realization.

Josh. The same fucking name Lia had thrown at him the day she finally admitted the truth. Winston-Salem suddenly didn't feel like some distant echo anymore.

It felt like a map, leading him straight into the eye of every storm he hadn't seen coming.

Griffin sat back slowly, his mind racing, piecing together every red flag he'd ignored, every breadcrumb he'd let rot, because he was too wrapped up in self-destruction.

"Son of a bitch," he whispered, dragging a hand down his face.

Aiden raised an eyebrow. "You good, or… Are we about to commit a felony?"

Griffin huffed a laugh. "Depends on your definition of felony."

Aiden smirked. "If it ends in bail money and you telling me I was right all along, I'm in."

Griffin shook his head, that old edge creeping back in but different now. Sharper. Clearer. "Josh isn't just Wren's ex. He's Lia's fiancé."

Aiden's mouth fell open. "No fucking way."

"Oh, it gets better," Griffin muttered, voice dripping with that kind of clarity that only comes when rock bottom starts to crack open. "They're 'on a break.' Trying to 'figure things out.'" He made air quotes with a roll of his eyes.

Aiden blinked. "So let me get this straight… Wren's ex is Lia's fiancé, and somehow that manipulative trainwreck managed to wrap you into their dysfunctional engagement spiral?"

Griffin raised his beer. "Cheers to being everyone's emotional support punching bag."

Aiden laughed, but it was edged with disbelief. "That's some soap opera shit, man."

"No kidding. Just waiting for someone to tell me I've got a twin I never met and a secret inheritance."

Shoulders loose, hearts a little lighter, but not unbruised, they sat in that.

After a minute, Aiden's voice softened. "You still love her, don't you?"

Griffin didn't answer right away.

He didn't have to.

He stared down at his beer, then lifted his gaze slowly. "She deserves a love that is bound by the tide."

Aiden's expression shifted—gone was the teasing, replaced with something real. "Then what the hell are you still doing here?"

Griffin looked out across the bar. It wasn't crowded, but it buzzed with the kind of background noise that used to distract him. Now, it just made him feel farther from everything that mattered.

Aiden was quiet for a beat, then leaned in. "That letter you were talking about writing. Go write it."

Griffin looked at him.

"I'm serious," Aiden said. "Write it. Finish it. Mail it. Burn it. I don't give a fuck. Just get it out. You've carried this long enough. And for what it's worth…" He paused, shaking his head like he couldn't believe what he was about to say. "I'm rooting for you two. Always have been."

Griffin didn't speak. Just nodded.

But something cracked open inside him. Not in a bad way. Not like before.

It was quiet. Steady.

Like something was coming back to life.

That night, when he got home, Griffin didn't head straight to the fridge or the couch or the silence.

He went to his desk.

Pulled open the drawer.

And stared at the half-finished letter he hadn't touched in months.

The ink was still dark. The paper still smooth.

But the man holding the pen?

He wasn't the same one who wrote those first few lines.

Griffin sat down.

Took a breath.

And started writing again.

This time, not from a place of desperation.

Not from a place of hope.

But from truth.

Because the spark that used to be his and Wren's?

It still burned—quietly, stubbornly.

And maybe it wasn't about reigniting it.

Maybe it was just about finally learning how to carry the fire without burning himself alive.

43

TWISTED FATE

AIDEN

AIDEN WASN'T the sentimental type.

He didn't buy into fate, soulmates, or any of that Hallmark bullshit people clung to when life kicked them in the teeth.

But after six months of watching Griffin barely survive Wren's absence?

Yeah... even he had to admit—something bigger was pulling the strings.

And if those two idiots were too damn blind to see it, well, someone had to be the one to shove fate's hand.

So, he did what any good brother—by blood or bond—would do.

He stirred the damn pot.

And tonight? It started with a simple text.

> Aiden: Pick up your damn phone, Wren. I'm done carrying this tragic love story on my back. My shoulders hurt.

When Wren finally called, her voice sounded like it had been chewed up and spit out by every bad decision she'd made.

"Hey..." The single word was barely audible. Fragile. Like the word itself might crack in half if she breathed too hard.

Aiden smirked, leaning against his counter, beer in hand, already bracing for the storm he was about to unleash. "Well, look who remembers how to dial. Thought I'd have to send a search party—or a damn priest."

"Cut the crap, Aiden. Why'd you text me?" Wren was defensive, sharp.

Classic Wren—throwing up walls before he could finish digging the foundation.

It was one of the reasons she and Griffin worked; they didn't do surface-level. They were war zones and truce lines, always pushing, always pulling. Gasoline and a match, waiting to see who'd light it first.

Aiden let the silence sit, just long enough to make her squirm on the other end before he threw the first punch.

"Figured you'd wanna know your boy Hayes is still out here making the rest of us look bad."

The pause was deafening.

Then soft and unsure, "What do you mean?"

He heard it.

That crack in her voice.

That flicker of hope she probably hated herself for feeling.

Aiden's lips curved—half a smirk, half something sadder. "Here comes that tough, brotherly love. Wren, I mean, he's still soft as hell over you."

He let that land but didn't give her time to recover.

"We went out the other night," he continued, his tone lighter than the weight of his words. "I pushed him into turning on that infamous Griffin Hayes charm everyone can't seem to get enough of."

There was a beat.

"And?" Wren's voice was tighter now, like she wasn't sure if she wanted the answer or if it might tear her apart.

Aiden let out a low chuckle, shaking his head at the memory. "Well, once I convinced him? The bastard was better than ever. Shoulders dropped, neck rolled like he was stepping back into a ring. And then there it was—that old shit-eating grin, the kind that used to piss guys off and make women forget how to breathe."

He could practically hear Wren's heart pounding through the phone.

When she finally spoke, her voice was barely holding together. "Did he… Did he actually flirt?"

"Oh, he flirted," Aiden said, amusement lacing his words, but underneath it, something heavier. "But you wanna know what he said when he sat back down?"

Silence.

Because yeah, she wanted to know.

Even if it killed her.

Aiden's voice dropped, serious now. No jokes. No buffer.

"He said, 'What do you want me to say?'" Aiden repeated, letting each word cut through the static. "'That no matter how many smiles I see, none of them look like hers? That no one's laugh cuts through me the same way? That every voice sounds wrong until I hear the ghost of hers echoing in my head?'"

Wren's breath hitched—sharp and broken.

Aiden heard it and twisted the knife, because sometimes the truth had to bleed.

"He let out this laugh, if you could even call it that. Said, 'You want me to admit that every woman I talk to is just noise? That I keep waiting for someone to shut me up the way she used to?'"

Aiden swallowed hard, the memory of Griffin sitting across from him looking like a man stripped bare still fresh in his mind.

"He tapped that bottle like it was the only thing keeping him grounded," Aiden continued, softer now. "'No one calls me on my shit like she did,' he said. 'No one ever fucking dared. She could see through me in ways that scared the hell out of me.'"

Wren didn't say a word, but Aiden could feel the sob she was holding back.

Could feel it because Griffin had worn that same silence.

"And then he said... 'I still hear her when I fall asleep. I still check the damn passenger seat when I get in my truck, like some pathetic reflex.'"

Aiden's chest tightened, but he pushed through because she needed to hear every damn word.

"'She was the only one who could compete in my games and not lose herself in the process.'" His voice cracked, just like Griffin's had. "'I started a letter. Got halfway through it and had to stop because every word felt like a goddamn funeral.'"

Aiden let out a shaky breath, dragging a hand through his hair. "He leaned back like it physically hurt to sit with that truth. And then he said, 'I don't know how to stop loving her. And I'm not even sure I want to.'"

The line went dead quiet.

Not because she'd hung up.

But because Wren Sinclair was too busy breaking on the other end—silently, completely.

And Aiden?

He just closed his eyes and whispered, "Yeah… That's what you left behind."

The sharp inhale on the other end of the line?

Yeah, Aiden heard that. Loud and fucking clear.

It was the sound of a woman realizing that the walls she built weren't keeping the pain out—

They were locking it in.

"He told me the other night…" Aiden's voice dropped, the usual sarcasm stripped away, nothing left but weight. The kind of weight that knew exactly where to land. "…he hopes you're happy."

Silence.

Not the kind where you're searching for words.

The kind where breathing becomes a goddamn chore.

"And coming from Griffin?" Aiden pushed, his tone sharper now, not to be cruel, but because some truths needed to cut deep. "That's basically Shakespeare, Wren. You broke the man who doesn't break."

Still nothing.

No defense. No denial.

Just the hollow sound of someone realizing they'd shattered something priceless with their own two hands.

Aiden could feel it bleeding through the phone—the guilt, the regret, the suffocating ache of knowing you can't rewind time when it matters most.

But he wasn't done. Not yet.

"Oh—and that letter?" His voice shifted, too casual, like he was tossing her a live grenade just to see if she'd catch it or let it blow her to pieces. "Yeah… he finished it."

The breath on the other end wasn't steady. It was broken. Shaky and hollow, the kind of sound that didn't just fill the silence… It haunted it. It was the sound of someone coming apart but trying like hell not to.

"When…" Her voice fractured on impact, barely making it through the line. "…when did he send it?"

Aiden let his head fall back against the cabinet, staring up at the ceiling like it might offer him a damn script for how to navigate this mess. Because, if he was honest, this hurt more than he expected.

"Two days ago." Those three words landed like a final nail in a coffin neither of them wanted to admit was built by Wren's own hands.

The silence that followed wasn't empty, it was suffocation in its purest form. The kind of quiet that wraps around your throat and forces you to sit with every mistake, every 'what if' you never thought would matter until it was too late.

If guilt had a sound, this was it.

Track one on the playlist titled: *You Fucked Up The Best Thing You Ever Had.*

Aiden dragged a hand through his hair, all the usual bravado bleeding out of him, leaving nothing but raw exhaustion behind. "Look, I give you shit because it's easy. And yeah, you've earned most of it."

A broken laugh cracked through the line, sharp and bitter, soaked in self-loathing.

"Yeah," Wren rasped. "I know."

He closed his eyes for a second before letting the next words slip out— softer, quieter, like he wasn't used to hearing himself lean into hope.

"But for what it's worth, I've always been rooting for you two. Even when you made me wanna bang my head through a wall. I wasn't on board at first, but Griff is not the man I once knew. He's better."

There was a pause, heavy enough to crush them both if they weren't careful.

"You've got a funny way of showing it," she muttered, no venom left. Just a woman too damn tired of bleeding out alone.

Aiden smirked, but it didn't touch his eyes. "Hey, someone's gotta keep you idiots from choking on your own pride."

Another beat of silence, this one softer. Sadder. The kind that lingers long after the conversation ends.

"Besides…" His voice dropped, landing like a quiet truth neither of them could deny. "If this were easy, it wouldn't be your story."

Wren didn't argue.

She couldn't.

Because they both knew exactly what Griffin and Wren were.

They weren't some fairytale wrapped in pretty bows and perfect endings.

They were fire and ash. Bruises and battle scars.

And Aiden?

He was just the poor bastard standing in the smoke, making sure neither of them burned alone.

WREN

Fate wasn't done kicking her while she was down.

"By the way..." Aiden's voice shifted—too casual, too timed. The kind of tone people used right before they dropped a bomb they knew you'd never crawl out from under. "...Griffin figured out who Lia's kid belongs to."

Wren's stomach twisted so violently she thought she might be sick. Her grip on the phone tightened, knuckles white.

"Who?" The word barely made it past her lips, more a breath than a question.

Aiden didn't flinch.

"Josh."

It wasn't a name.

It was a wrecking ball.

Josh.

Her past.

Griffin's betrayal.

Both of their worst fears wrapped in one cruel punchline from the universe.

Sharp and unrelenting, she didn't need time to process it—the ache hit instantly. Because of course it was Josh. Of course the man who once promised her forever was tangled up in the same web that nearly destroyed Griffin.

Fate didn't just have a twisted sense of humor, it was fucking merciless.

Aiden kept talking because he was Aiden, and silence wasn't his style. "Seems like those two deserve each other. Guess some people never change."

Wren sank deeper into the couch, her pulse roaring in her ears, drowning out everything but the sound of every bad decision she'd ever made, clawing its way to the surface.

She could almost see it—Josh and Lia, two liars bound together by the messes they made. The same faces that haunted both her and Griffin in different ways now tied together like fate wasn't just playing games… It was writing tragedy in permanent ink.

Aiden's voice softened then, just enough to let her know he wasn't completely heartless.

"Look, Wren…" He exhaled, like even he felt the weight of what he was about to say. "I told you before, fate's got a fucked-up sense of humor. But maybe… Maybe it's just been forging you two by fire."

Her throat tightened so hard she thought it might collapse in on itself. She didn't trust her voice. Not when every word felt like it would shatter on impact.

So she stayed quiet.

Let the burn settle deep in her chest where no one could see it.

But after a moment—because she was still Wren Sinclair, and no matter how broken she felt, she needed to know—she forced the question out.

"How is he?"

Aiden didn't answer right away.

She could hear the faint smile in his silence, the kind that knew more than he was saying.

"He finished the house," he said finally, voice low but laced with something almost proud.

Her chest caved in.

The house.

Not just any house. *The house.* The one built from dreams and dockside promises. The one Griffin talked about like it wasn't just wood and nails, but a future he could finally put his name on.

Their future.

Her breath caught, the ache settling somewhere between her ribs, sharp and cruel.

"Do you—" she swallowed hard, hating how fragile she sounded, "—do you have a picture?"

Aiden's grin deepened. She didn't need to see it. She knew that smirk, knew the way it wrapped around his words when he was about to hit her with some unfiltered truth.

"He's having a get-together tomorrow afternoon. I'm heading over there in the morning to help him get everything ready." A pause. "I'll send it then."

Before she could respond, before she could beg him not to, the call ended.

And Wren was left staring at her phone like it held the weight of every 'what if' she'd tried to bury.

Because fate wasn't done.

Not yet.

44

RIPTIDE

THE NEXT MORNING, Wren sat on the edge of her couch, elbows on her knees, hands tangled in her hair, staring at the front door like it was a loaded gun pointed straight at her.

Any minute now.

Aiden had promised he'd send a picture of Griffin's house today.

The house. The one that wasn't supposed to exist without them in it. The one Griffin described in late-night whispers. Simple, elegant, nothing flashy. Tin roof, wide porch, a dock where forever didn't feel so fucking scary.

And now?

Now it was finished.

Without her.

Her stomach twisted at the thought, a sharp ache blooming behind her ribs. She wasn't ready to see it. Hell, she wasn't even ready to think about it. But fate didn't give a damn about readiness, it just kept showing up, uninvited and unapologetic.

A knock at the door snapped her out of the spiral.

Her heart lunged before her body did, feet moving fast like some desperate part of her thought this was it—that Aiden had gone rogue and overnighted her past in a goddamn frame.

But when she yanked open the door, breath shallow and pulse racing, it wasn't fate waiting for her.

It was a delivery guy, holding a box she barely remembered ordering.

"Morning," he muttered, handing it over along with a stack of mail that looked heavier than usual.

"Thanks," she managed, her voice a rasp of nerves and disappointment.

Kicking the door shut behind her, Wren set the box on the counter and thumbed through the mail—anything to keep her mind from shattering under the weight of what was coming.

Electric bill. Some magazine she never subscribed to.

A perfume sample that smelled too much like the version of herself she pretended to be.

Then her hands stopped moving.

Her breath caught.

There it was.

His handwriting.

Slanted. Sharp. Unmistakably Griffin.

The envelope felt heavier than the rest. Like it knew exactly what it carried. Like it could feel the way her chest hollowed out just staring at it.

She should've waited.

Should've set it down, walked away, given herself time to build whatever walls she had left.

But how do you brace for words written by the man who once held every broken, beautiful, reckless piece of you—and loved you anyway?

You don't.

So, with fingers that wouldn't stop shaking, and a heart that already knew it wasn't ready—

Wren tore it open.

Wren,

I never planned to write this. Hell, I swore I wouldn't. I thought if I stayed quiet long enough, the ache would settle—that eventually, the ghost of you would loosen its grip on my ribs and let me breathe again.
But silence never saved me.
And pretending? You and I both know I was never any good at that—not with you.

So here I am.
Bleeding through ink, because words are the only thing I have left that still feel like mine. And even now, they're shaking. I've started this letter more times than I can count— burned it in my head before it ever touched paper. Because how the fuck do you explain what it feels like to lose something you were never convinced you deserved in the first place?
You don't. You can't.
You just pour every broken piece onto the page and hope to God it's enough to quiet the storm for a while.

I never wanted love.
Not the kind that strips a man bare and leaves him standing in the ruins of everything he thought made him strong.
I wanted control. Predictability. The comfort of walls built high enough that no one could see how hollow it was inside.
And then you happened—you looked at me once, Wren. Once.
And those walls that took everything I had to build, didn't stand a fucking chance.
You didn't ask permission. You didn't knock.
You just walked in—like you'd lived there your whole life. And suddenly, I wasn't a man surviving anymore.
I was a man feeling. Every terrifying, beautiful, all-consuming thing I swore I'd never let touch me again.

You wrecked me.
But not like a storm you run from. You wrecked me like the ocean wrecks the shore. Again. And again. Until it forgets what it looked like before the waves claimed it.
And I let you.
God, I let you.
Because drowning in you was the only time I ever felt alive.

AARON MCLEAN

You want the truth?
Here it is—

I didn't fall in love with you.
I sank into it.
No life jacket. No shore in sight.
Just you—and every current I didn't bother fighting because part of me always knew…
If I was going to go under, it was always meant to be you dragging me down.
When you left—you didn't just walk away. You let the tide pull you out and never looked back to see if I was still reaching.
And I was.
God, Wren—I am still fucking reaching.
Even now, when I know better. I've spent months gasping for air in rooms that feel too big without you. Trying to rebuild a man who only existed because you made him believe he could be more than his past.

I finished the house.
Not because it felt right. Not because I wanted to.
I finished it because I needed to prove to myself that I could still stand. Even if every board creaked with the memory of you barefoot in the bare, unfinished kitchen, humming that stupid off-key song, while you stole my hoodie like you owned every piece of me.
And that's the part that guts me, Wren.
Not the silence. Not the empty bed or the dock that still whispers your name when the wind shifts.
It's the little things.
The ones no one else would understand.
Like how I still sleep on the left side—because that's where you'd curl into me at 2AM when your guard finally dropped.
How I still reach under the table—instinctively looking for your leg, like I'm telling you without words that I've got you—even when you're not there.
Or how that song—your song—still hits like a fucking freight train every time I hear it, because I can't separate the melody from the way you laughed when you caught me humming it days later.
It's pathetic, isn't it?
This… Remembering.

But loving you was never about the grand gestures.

It was the quiet moments.
The ones only we knew existed.
And those?
Those are the ones that haunt me the most.

This letter isn't a rope I'm throwing across the distance.
I'm not asking you to come back—I'm not that naïve.
I'm writing this because if I don't, I'll drown in the words I never said.
I loved you, Wren Sinclair.
Not the way people write about in stories with happy endings—
But the way the tide loves the shore. Violent. Unforgiving. Relentless. Pulling away just to come crashing back harder—because staying gone was never in its nature.
And if you're wondering... Yeah, I'm still crashing.
Even if I've learned how to do it quietly.

Some loves don't fade.
They erode you. Slow. Constant. Inevitable.
You don't move on from that. You build on top of it. Knowing the foundation cracks will always be filled with your name...

So here's my truth—
I'm not waiting at the shoreline anymore.
I've learned how to swim without looking over my shoulder.
But if fate ever decides to pull you back in, you'll find me standing. Scarred. Salt-soaked. But alive.
And every piece of me that still remembers how it felt to be yours?
That part will never stop reaching.
Because some men are made of stone.
But me?

I was meant to be yours.
I was always meant to be bound by the tide.

—*Griffin*

Wren's hands trembled as her eyes traced every word Griffin had poured onto that page—every raw, unfiltered piece of him that she didn't deserve, but God, she craved. Each sentence was a blade, carving through the walls she'd tried so hard to rebuild since she left. By the time she reached the end, her vision was a blur of tears she didn't remember letting fall.

She wasn't just broken.

She was stripped bare. Every defense torn down, every piece of her laid open by a man who still loved her in the ruins—after the silence, the running, the way she left him drowning—gasping for air in the aftermath.

Her chest ached so violently it felt like her ribs might crack under the weight of it all. Because this wasn't just a letter.

It was Griffin handing her his heart one last time—without expectation, without strings—just to remind her that some loves didn't fade. They stayed. Like scars. Like saltwater in your lungs. Like the tide pulling at your ankles, daring you to fight what was inevitable.

She clutched the letter to her chest, as if holding it tighter could stop the spiral in her head. But nothing could prepare her for what came next.

Her phone buzzed on the cushion beside her.

> Aiden: Incoming Photos.

Her stomach dropped. She wasn't ready, not after this. Not after Griffin's words had already torn her apart from the inside out.

But her thumb moved before her brain could stop it.

The first photo opened, and her heart shattered all over again.

It was simple. Just a wooden sign at the start of a gravel road.

Tide Bound Lane.

She gasped, her hand flying to her mouth as fresh tears burned down her cheeks. Her legs gave out beneath her, and she sank to the floor, staring at the name like it was a confession carved in wood.

He named the road after them.

After the pull that never stopped. After the promise they never said out loud but always felt—the tide always returns.

Her fingers hovered over the next image, chest heaving like every breath was a battle she was losing.

When the second photo filled the screen, it nearly stopped her heart.

The house.

Her dream house.

Every detail—down to the stormy gray siding, the black roof, the golden weathered oak accents—was exactly as she'd described it that day on the dock. The stone columns, the porch swing, the lanterns lining the dock that stretched out like a memory made real.

It wasn't just a house.

It was home.

Their home.

The one she never thought she deserved. The one she abandoned before it was ever built.

The phone slipped from her hand, landing beside her as she crumbled under the weight of it all. Because after all this time, after every reason she gave him to hate her, after every mile of silence, he still chose her.

He didn't just build a future for himself.

He built theirs.

Every board, every nail, every inch of that house was a testament to a man who loved her long after she stopped believing she was worth loving.

And now?

Now she was sitting on the floor of an apartment that felt more like a prison than a home, clutching a letter soaked in tears and staring at proof that Griffin Hayes never let go.

Her heart wasn't just breaking.

It was begging. For forgiveness, for a second chance, for a way back to the man who built her dreams even when she wasn't there to share them.

But the cruelest part?

He didn't ask her to come back.

He didn't beg.

He didn't chase.

He stood tall in that letter—in that house—and showed her exactly what real love looked like.

Not loud.

Not desperate.

Just steady. Like the tide.

Always pulling. Always waiting. Always bound.

And Wren?

For the first time in her life, she didn't know if she could survive the weight of being loved like that.

Because Griffin didn't just build a house.

He built a reminder that no matter how far she ran, he was always going to be the place she came back to.

Even if she didn't deserve it.

Even if it was too late.

Her phone buzzed again, but she couldn't bring herself to look. Because fate had already done its job. Every piece of her—every heartbeat, every breath—was still tied to a dock hundreds of miles away.

Bound by tide.

She let out a shaky breath, pressing her palms to her eyes like she could somehow rub away the image of that house burned into her mind. But it was useless.

Just like pretending she could move on.

Because how do you move on from a man who built your dreams when you weren't even around to remind him of them?

How do you breathe knowing someone loved you so completely, so relentlessly, that even your absence didn't make him stop?

The truth was—

You don't.

You just drown in it.

Her phone buzzed again, vibrating against the hardwood like it was taunting her. Demanding she face the weight of everything she'd tried to bury.

With a trembling hand, she reached for it because ignoring it wouldn't change reality. And God knows she was done running from the truth.

Aiden's name lit up the screen, followed by a message that nearly knocked the air from her lungs.

> Aiden: Figured you'd want to see the dock at sunset. Looks like it's waiting for something... Or someone.

Attached was a photo.

Her thumb hovered over it, chest tight, fear and longing warring inside her. But she opened it anyway. Because she had to.

And when the image filled her screen, her heart completely collapsed.

The dock stretched out over the water, bathed in gold and amber light. The lanterns flickered like beacons—like they were calling her home. At the end of the dock sat two chairs. Black. Simple.

Waiting.

Just like she described.

Just like he remembered.

She let out a broken sob, clutching the phone to her chest like it could hold her together when everything else was falling apart.

This wasn't just a dock.

It wasn't just a house.

It was Griffin—

Loving her in silence.

Loving her without conditions.

Loving her without knowing if she'd ever come back.

And that's when it hit her.

The letter wasn't a goodbye.

It was a map.

A way home.

A reminder that no matter how far she drifted, there was still a place where her heart belonged. Where he was.

Her hands shook as she typed out a reply, but she stopped halfway through.

What was she supposed to say?

That she finally understood?

That the walls she'd built weren't armor—they were chains?

She swallowed hard, wiping at her cheeks as she stood on unsteady legs.

No.

This wasn't something you text back. This wasn't something you explained over a phone call.

Some things—the real things—you show up for.

Her gaze flicked back to the letter, now resting on the coffee table like it was daring her to stop being afraid.

She took a deep breath. Because fate might've done its job, but Wren Sinclair was finally ready to do hers.

And this time?

She wasn't running away.

She finished typing out the message and hit send.

Four simple words carried the weight of everything she'd never said.

45

BOUND BY TIDE

AIDEN'S PHONE buzzed in his pocket, barely catching his attention over the hum of conversation and the crackle of the fire pit out back. The get-together at Griffin's place was still going strong—friends, coworkers, and a few familiar faces from Marshside were all laughing, drinking, completely unaware that the man hosting was only just learning how to breathe again.

He fished his phone out, expecting some meaningless notification. But when her name lit up the screen, his smile faded.

> Wren: I am coming home.

Aiden's heart stopped for half a second before it kicked back with a vengeance. His eyes dropped to the time.

5:17 PM.

"Shit," he muttered, running a hand down his face as the weight of that text hit him square in the chest.

Four hours.

It was a four-hour drive from Winston-Salem to the island.

Quick and sharp, he did the math in his head.

That meant tonight.

She was really doing it.

After all this time, after months of silence and heartbreak, Wren Sinclair was finally pulling her head out of her ass—and straight into Griffin's world again.

A slow grin spread across Aiden's face. Not cocky, not teasing.

Proud. Proud that his sister was finally going to get the man of her dreams. The one she was meant to be with. Who just happened to be his best friend.

Because he knew what this meant.

Fate wasn't just nudging anymore.

It was shoving.

His gaze drifted across the yard, locking onto Griffin standing at the edge of the dock, beer in hand, watching the sun start its slow descent like it was just another evening.

He had no idea.

Not yet.

Aiden tucked his phone back into his pocket, heart still racing. He didn't say a word. Didn't call out. Because some moments? You don't ruin them with warnings.

You let fate do what it was always meant to do.

And tonight, fate was about to rewrite everything.

FOUR HOURS LATER

The last of the laughter had faded. The soft hum of conversation was gone, replaced by the kind of silence that didn't suffocate but settled. Heavy. Familiar.

Aiden watched from the porch, leaning against the railing, eyes locked on the man standing at the edge of the dock.

Griffin.

Lantern light flickered against the dark. Casting shadows over the rough lines of his face, the ones life carved deeper these past six months. His hands were shoved in his pockets, shoulders tense, gaze fixed on the endless stretch of water, like it held answers he'd stopped asking for.

Aiden could hear the faint creak of the dock beneath Griffin's boots as the wind rolled in off the sound, tugging at the edges of a conversation neither of them had started yet.

"You ever regret building it out here?" Aiden called out softly, his voice carried by the breeze.

Griffin didn't turn.

Didn't move.

His eyes stayed on the horizon, where the last sliver of sun bled into the water.

"Nah," Griffin finally said, voice low. Steady. "It's the only place that feels honest."

Aiden's throat tightened at that, because he knew exactly what Griffin meant. Out here, there were no walls to hide behind. No distractions. Just the sound of the tide and the ghosts you brought with you.

"You did good, Hayes," Aiden said after a moment, his tone lighter—trying to cut through the weight hanging between them. "This place… It's more than I ever thought you'd build."

Griffin let out a breath that wasn't quite a laugh. More like a release. "Yeah. Just wish it didn't feel so fucking empty sometimes."

Aiden's hand stilled on the bottle, fingers going rigid. His heart was already racing, knowing what was coming. Knowing *who* was about to shatter that emptiness.

His eyes flicked toward the driveway, his pulse kicking harder when he saw it.

Headlights.

Soft at first, just a glow through the trees.

Then brighter.

Closer.

The car crawled up Tide Bound Lane, gravel crunching beneath the tires like the universe was holding its breath.

Aiden pushed off the railing, standing straighter, his chest tightening with every second.

Griffin didn't notice yet.

Too lost in his thoughts.

Too used to expecting nothing.

The engine cut off.

Silence fell again—sharp and expectant.

Aiden's gaze locked on the figure stepping out of the car, her outline illuminated by the faint glow of the lanterns lining the dock.

Wren.

She stood there, frozen—scared that if she moved too fast, the whole moment would shatter. Her arms wrapped around herself, hair tousled from the long drive, eyes fixed on the man who hadn't seen her yet.

Aiden swallowed hard, his throat thick with something he'd never admit to.

This was it.

The kind of moment people wrote books about—the kind where fate didn't just knock, it kicked the fucking door in.

He took a slow step forward, his boots echoing against the wood as he approached Griffin—who still hadn't turned around. Still watching the tide like it was the only thing that ever came back to him.

Aiden stood behind him for a beat, the weight of six months pressing down on his shoulders.

Then softly, but with all the meaning in the world, he reached out, tapped Griffin on the shoulder, and said—

"Go get her, Hayes."

Griffin stiffened.

Confusion flickered across his face as he glanced back at Aiden. But the moment his eyes shifted past him, toward the start of the dock...

The world stopped.

His breath punched out of his lungs like he'd been hit.

Because there she was.

Wren.

Standing at the edge of everything they'd lost—and everything they could still be.

The lantern light caught the shimmer of unshed tears in her eyes; her lips parted like she was stuck between apology and hope. The wind tugged at her hair, but she didn't move.

She just stood there—waiting.

Griffin's heart thundered in his chest, his feet refusing to move at first—like his body didn't believe what his eyes were seeing.

Six months.

Six fucking months of silence, of pain, of trying to convince himself that this moment would never come.

And now?

Now she was here.

Not in his memories. Not in his dreams.

Here.

Aiden took a step back, a quiet grin pulling at his lips as he watched Griffin come undone in the best way possible.

"Go," he murmured again, softer this time. "Before she thinks you forgot how."

Griffin didn't need to hear anything else.

His feet finally moved, slow at first, like every step was shaking off the weight he'd been carrying for far too long. The dock creaked beneath him, the distance between them shrinking with every heartbeat.

Wren's breath hitched as he approached, she saw the storm behind his eyes that hadn't settled since the day she left.

Neither of them spoke.

Because what the hell do you say when the tide finally brings you back to shore?

When Griffin stopped in front of her, just a breath away, he searched her face like it held every answer to every sleepless night.

And Wren?

She looked at him like she'd been drowning every day since she let him go.

The silence between them wasn't empty.

It was everything.

It was six months of pain, of longing, of words unsaid. And love that never died.

Griffin's jaw clenched, his hands twitching at his sides like he was holding back from reaching for her—like touching her would prove this wasn't real.

But Wren moved first.

Tentatively, she lifted a shaking hand and placed it flat against his chest, right over his heart.

It was racing.

So was hers.

Her lips parted, but the words caught in her throat.

Stormy and unsteady, Griffin's eyes burned into hers. Like he was standing in the wreckage of every hope he swore he'd buried.

But Wren didn't flinch.

Didn't look away.

Her hand trembled against his chest, feeling the wild rhythm of a heart that still beat for her—after everything.

Tears blurred her vision, but her voice—God, her voice—was steady when it finally broke the silence.

"We both deserve love… Bound by tide."

Something flickered in Griffin's eyes. Quick. Raw. Like the words had sliced clean through him, deeper than any goodbye ever had.

His throat worked around something too big, too raw to swallow.

Because she wasn't just standing there.

She was giving him everything he thought he'd never hear again.

Not an apology.

Not an excuse.

But a promise.

His hands—those calloused, steady hands that had built walls, houses, futures—lifted slowly, like he was afraid she'd vanish if he moved too fast.

His fingers brushed her jaw, tilting her face up to his, thumb catching the tear slipping down her cheek.

For a beat, he just stared at her.

Taking her in.

Memorizing the moment he never thought he'd get.

His voice was wrecked when he finally spoke. It came out low and reverent, like confession and surrender all in one breath.

"I was always yours, Wren."

Her lips quivered, another tear falling—but this time, it wasn't just grief.

It was relief.

It was coming home.

Griffin's forehead dropped to hers, eyes closing as he exhaled the weight he'd been carrying for far too long.

They stood like that—two people stitched together by every scar, every storm, every fucking tide that tried to pull them apart.

And when his lips finally met hers, it wasn't desperate.

It wasn't rushed.

It was everything.

Soft.

Certain.

The kind of kiss that didn't ask for permission. Because it already knew it belonged.

Behind them, Aiden stood at the porch, arms crossed, a grin pulling at his mouth as he watched the two idiots finally find their way back.

He shook his head, muttering under his breath with a pride he'd never admit out loud.

"About damn time."

The lanterns flickered around them, the dock swaying gently beneath their feet as the tide rolled in—like even the ocean knew this was where they were always meant to be.

Bound by pull.

Bound by pain.

Bound by tide.

And as Griffin cupped Wren's face like she was the only thing keeping him grounded, she whispered against his lips, broken but sure.

"I'm not running anymore."

Griffin smiled—small, raw, but real.

"Good." His thumb traced her cheek, his voice dropping to something only she could hear. "Because I was ready to chase you."

She let out a shaky laugh, the sound cracking under the weight of everything they'd survived.

But they weren't surviving anymore.

They were living.

Together.

And as the sun disappeared beneath the horizon, as Aiden turned back into the house with one last proud glance over his shoulder, Wren and Griffin stood at the edge of the dock—no longer drifting.

No longer drowning.

Just holding on.

Because love like theirs didn't fade.

It didn't settle.

It pulled.

Again and again.

And this time—they let it.

EPILOGUE

I told you the story.

I warned you that this love wouldn't float peacefully on the surface—it would drag you under, into depths so dark you'd forget what sunlight felt like. It would plunge you deeper than your lungs ever imagined, forcing you to gasp in pain. And prayer. Into a raw, chaotic truth so visceral you'd wonder if you'd ever breathe normally again.

I meant it—all of it. Every bruising warning. Every scarred ounce of wreckage. Every brutal, honest word.
Because love like this? It isn't made of candlelight and promises whispered through rose petals. It's shards of glass and midnight confessions. It's trembling silences and words that spill from your mouth like blood from wounds you didn't even know existed. It's a fire that burns you so deeply it leaves scars in places you swore were untouchable.

This love was never meant to be safe.
It was always meant to gut you.
To claw its way into your chest with merciless fingers. Tearing violently through every carefully stitched facade you built around your battered heart. Until every lie lay shattered at your feet. It was meant to rip you open, vein by vein, memory by excruciating memory—making you bleed out every hidden version of yourself you'd buried to survive. To burn you to ash and agony. And then, mercifully, painstakingly, stitch something real from the wreckage. Not cleaner. Not simpler. Just truer.

It would drag you screaming into the darkest corners of your soul, confronting every secret shame, every selfish fear. Every unhealed ache

you tried desperately to hide— then, in that devastating moment of brutal honesty, you would choose love.
Not despite the damage—but because of it.
Because someone sees every broken piece of you and stays.
Because their touch doesn't flinch—it steadies in your flames.

> Maybe for the first time, you're not striving to be whole to be loved.
> You're just seen.
> Just wanted.

But what I didn't say back then, what I couldn't dare admit—maybe because I hadn't yet felt its truth or because the pain hadn't taught me how—is that sometimes, the tide that drowns you, the current that shatters your heart and soul…
It's the same one that carries you home.

It's been three years since I stood on this dock. Hollowed by grief. Haunted by guilt, choking on the absence of a woman whose laughter had once been my entire compass.
Three years since Aiden's hand rested steady on my shoulder, gripping tight, like he knew before I did that turning around meant my entire fucking world was about to shatter again.
And it did.
Because when I turned, there she was.
Wren Sinclair.
Messy. Beautiful. Terrified. Eyes wide, shimmering with all the words she couldn't voice, trembling like she expected me to run.
But she was there. Still there.
Her feet remembering every desperate step back to me.

She didn't come back with grand gestures or rehearsed apologies.
Didn't try to erase the past or pretend we weren't covered in the wreckage we'd made of each other.
She just looked at me—eyes shaking, heart wide open—and gave me eight quiet words that undid every fragile thread holding me together:

"We both deserve love that's bound by tide."

AARON MCLEAN

And something deep in my fractured soul shifted. Not toward perfection, not toward painless ease, but toward possibility.
We didn't pretend away our brokenness. Didn't reach for fairy tales.
We chose brutal truth. Bloodied and broken in the wreckage we'd made, looked each other in the eyes and said… This. This is our start.
Didn't go back to who we used to be.
We built something new—something stripped of illusion, grounded in honesty.

Something built from fire, baptized by storms.
Something that wouldn't crumble beneath the waves.
Something built not to outrun the surge, but to survive it.
To stand in the waves together and know… This time, we wouldn't drown.

Now?
Now, every morning I wake beside the woman who once ran from me, who once looked me dead in the eyes with love and walked away anyway. And every damn morning, when my eyes find her—messy hair, warm skin, breathing slow and peaceful—I whisper a thank you to every cruel twist of fate that brought her home.

That house she used to describe like a fragile dream?
It's ours.
It smells like salt, coffee, and something new. Peace. Real peace, the kind you bleed for.
It smells like hope.
The faint, quiet scent of possibility.

The spare room that mocked our fear?
It's a nursery now, soon to hold the echo of dreams we thought we'd lost forever.
Sometimes, I find her there, hand softly cradling the curve of her belly—a future neither of us dared imagine.
Her eyes soft. Her body glowing in the low light. Her heart still all fire.

And I swear to God—

Every damn time,
I fall in love all over again.

Aiden still storms in like he owns the place, arms wide, mouth loud.
Making himself at home in the way only people who saw you at your worst know how to.
Still calls me soft every chance he gets, like the fact that I love her out loud is something to be ashamed of.
Still raids my fridge without asking, feet on the counter, beer in hand, smirk on his face like I should be grateful he graced us with his chaos.
Still acts like showing up is the greatest gift he's ever given me.
And the truth?
It is.

Because every time his boots hit this dock, every time his reckless grin lights up the air, there's an unspoken truth between us—
We fucking made it.

We didn't just survive the storm. We let it rip us apart. It washed away the lies, the fear, and the old versions of ourselves. Until what was left was something unbreakable.
And then we had the audacity to build something beautiful from the bones.
But here's the part no one ever warns you about survival—
It's not clean.
It's not pretty.
It's not some cinematic rise from the ashes where the pain disappears, and everything is perfect.

Survival is crawling out of the wreckage with blood on your hands and bruises on your heart.
It's raw. It's violent.
It's choosing love again and again—especially when it hurts.
Even when it's hard.
Especially when it's hard.

I once thought strength meant silence.

That surviving was guarding your softness behind barbed wire.
But real strength?
It's handing someone your shattered heart and whispering,
"Here. Take it. Even if it burns. I'll rise from the ashes."

Because love?
Real love isn't a fucking lullaby. It isn't tender glances and easy mornings —not all the time.
It's a war cry.
It's clawing through the dark. Choosing someone even when the past still echoes louder than you want to admit. Even when staying feels like the bravest and most terrifying thing you'll ever do. It's standing in the ashes of every version of yourself you used to be, looking them in the eye and saying, "If you're going to wreck me, then fucking do it. But I'm not walking away."

And that's where love lives.

Not in perfection.
Not in fairy tales or flawless chapters.
But in persistence.
In the mess. The aftermath. In shattered pieces you hold out to someone and hope they don't drop them. The nights when you lie awake asking yourself if staying is still the right choice.
If rebuilding is still worth it.
If they are still worth it.
And then deciding, every damn time, that they are.

So if you're reading this—wrecked and raw, terrified of the tide—if you're wondering if this kind of love is worth the heartbreak it'll cost you...
It is.
Let it break you. Ruin you.
Let it tear through every wall you built and drag you under, screaming. Bust through every wall until all that's left is truth.

Because one day, when you surface, gasping and broken, but alive and see

them standing there drenched by the same storm, refusing to let go—you'll understand.
You weren't meant to float.
You were always meant to rise.

I didn't survive Wren Sinclair because I was strong—I survived because I let her in.
Because love like ours wasn't built for calm seas. It was always a hurricane.
Wild. Relentless. Tearing through our lives without mercy.
In the wreckage, twisted and breathless, we found each other again.
Bound not by calm, but by chaos.

And now?
Now I sit here—on this dock, in this moment, with her beside me—not waiting. Not drowning.
I'm breathing again.

Her laughter dances in the wind, her hand finds mine. And the tide whispers around our ankles, gentle now, as if it knows our story.
Two people.
Wrecked.
Rebuilt.
Reckless enough to love each other after the storm.

So I'll leave you with this final piece—
If you ever get the chance to love someone like that...
The kind of love that doesn't whisper safety but screams truth—
That drags you out past every line you swore you'd never cross—
Past the fear. Past the wreckage. Past the pieces of you. You were certain no one could ever stay for...
Don't hesitate.
Don't play it safe.
Don't wait for calm waters.
Jump.

Let the tide take you.
Let it wreck you.

AARON MCLEAN

Because sometimes the wreckage…
Is exactly where you finally feel like home.

Because yeah, it'll hurt.
It'll cut deep.
It'll strip you bare in ways you didn't know you could bleed.
But it'll also show you what it means to live.
To feel everything.
To fall, to break, to scream. And still crawl toward something that looks like hope.

And if you're lucky—
Lucky enough to find the person who doesn't just survive the wreckage with you…
But becomes your anchor inside it?
You don't let go. You don't run. You hold on with every cracked, trembling part of yourself.
And fight like hell.
Then you thank every storm that tried to ruin you.

Because that's where the real stories begin.
Not at the surface.
Not in the light.
But in the depths.
In the dark.
In the moments when love isn't easy—but it's real.

Because true love?
It was never built for shallow water.
It was meant to drown you and then bring you back gasping, breathless, undone—with their name on your lips.

So yeah—
We're still here.
Still reckless with our hearts.
Salt-stained from everything we've survived.

Still stubborn enough to choose each other, even when it would've been easier to walk away.
Tangled in something wild and untamed.
Still bound by tide.

And God—
I wouldn't have it any other way.

—Griffin & Wren Hayes

BOUND BY TIDE

AARON MCLEAN